A **GEEK GIRL'S**
GUIDE TO **MURDER**

Previously published Worldwide Mystery titles by
JULIE ANNE LINDSEY

MURDER BY THE SEASIDE
MURDER IN REAL TIME

A GEEK GIRL'S GUIDE TO MURDER

JULIE ANNE LINDSEY

W❂RLDWIDE.®

TORONTO • NEW YORK • LONDON
AMSTERDAM • PARIS • SYDNEY • HAMBURG
STOCKHOLM • ATHENS • TOKYO • MILAN
MADRID • WARSAW • BUDAPEST • AUCKLAND

Recycling programs
for this product may
not exist in your area.

A Geek Girl's Guide to Murder

A Worldwide Mystery/February 2017

First published by Carina Press

ISBN-13: 978-0-373-28397-2

Copyright © 2015 by Julie Anne Lindsey

Printed in U.S.A.

A **GEEK GIRL'S** GUIDE TO **MURDER**

ONE

"GOOD MORNING, BERNIE." I swiped my badge at the guard gate outside Horseshoe Falls, my home away from home, and forced a tight smile. Normally, arriving at work was my favorite part of the day. I also preferred to sleep until six, but my day had started at five when an unprecedented email from the boss rocketed me out of bed. Apparently this was a day for change.

I could count the number of 5:00 a.m. emails from my manager on one finger. I didn't need any fingers to count the number of problems with my computer system. Receiving the former with accusation of the latter had me on edge and out for reconnaissance. Add a mandatory staff meeting to the cryptic predawn message, and the day was ruined before it started. Preparing for an ambush was harder than it sounded.

Bernie emerged from behind the candy-cane-striped lever with a smile. Her park ranger-esque uniform worked seamlessly with the recorded bird songs piping through hidden speakers along the ivy-covered walls. "Hi, Mia. Did you read my blog today?"

Bernie was at least twice my age, with a round face and kind eyes. Her parents had named her Bernice after a Hawaiian princess, and she kept a blog, *Aloha from Ohio*, about growing up on the Big Island. My grandmother could barely work her VCR.

"Of course." Bernie's blog served as the unofficial

Horseshoe Falls rumor mill and who's-who resident guide, complete with vintage photos and anecdotes from the Aloha State. What wasn't to love? Today's scandal was a new head of security, which seemed irrelevant to me or my system. "I loved the post. Quite intriguing. Have you heard anything about a problem with my network?"

She shook her head. "No. How is that even possible?"

"Right?" I relaxed against the cool leather of my seat. "Randall called a staff meeting this morning. He said something about a system problem. I hoped you might've heard something so I could prepare a defense or fix the glitch before the meeting."

Bernie rocked back on her orthopedic track shoes and shook her head slowly. "No. I've got nothing. There's some hostility with residents about staffers not honoring appointments, but I don't pay much attention to that. I say, make another appointment or go somewhere else. There's a great big world out there." She widened her arms and smiled at the gates to the outside.

"Okay. Thanks." I tapped my thumbs along the curve of my steering wheel. "Hey, I'll check out the new guy this morning and give you the scoop."

A mischievous smile stretched over her face. "If you say so."

"Mmm-kay." Whatever that meant. Reading between the lines wasn't my strongest social skill. Neither was being objective or making small talk, which probably explained my love of technology and nearly-thirty-and-still-single status. Computers never cared if I was five minutes late to dinner or asked why I wasn't dating.

I waved goodbye and accelerated to the posted speed limit of twenty-five, careful to steer clear of road-crossing ducks and frolicking squirrels. My MINI Cooper motored along the quaint cobblestone roads toward its parking space outside the clubhouse, practically on autopilot, but stopped a few feet short. I shoved black cat-eye sunglasses onto my head and took another look. I wasn't imagining it. An obnoxious oversize blue pickup filled my space and spilled across the yellow lines on either side. Giant black mirrors protruded from the truck's cab and reached for the cars in neighboring spaces. A line of spotlights stood sentinel across the cab's roof. The metal beast had too many tires, dual rears and a bed large enough to park my MINI inside, which I had half a mind to do.

I craned my neck, looking for an explanation. That was my spot.

The phone in my handbag buzzed to life. Marcella's face appeared on the screen.

I shifted into Park behind the blue monstrosity and kneaded my forehead with one hand. "Hello?"

Marcella's words whipped through the receiver. "Where are you? Randall's on a rampage."

I eyeballed the truck and surveyed my parking options. "I'm in the lot. Someone took my space and the lot's full."

She sighed. "That's because he called a mandatory staff-wide meeting this morning, *gorda*."

Apparently the other employees had the same idea about arriving early. I shifted into Reverse and drove around the building. "I'll have to park across the street. Give me five minutes."

As Public Relations Manager, Marcella kept the residents of Horseshoe Falls happy and the employees in line, mostly with love and baked goods. She called me fat girl, an odd term of endearment I was earning this year. I had a new double-digit dress size to prove it.

I parallel parked outside the Sweet Retreat ice cream parlor and jogged past a couple on horseback as I made my way to the clubhouse. Horseshoe Falls was an elite gated community designed for nature lovers. Its peculiar futuristic-frontier-living mash-up led to people riding horses to the nearest recycle bin. I crossed the clubhouse parking lot, glaring at the mammoth truck parked in my space.

Marcella opened the front door and motioned for me to hurry. I tiptoe-ran on new heels, clutching my cross-body laptop bag and praying my glasses stayed on my nose.

She clucked her tongue. "You shouldn't run in those heels. If they were mine, I'd display them on a pedestal and polish them with Cupid's tears."

"Yeah, well. You could use my tears. I think my toes are bleeding."

Marcella's wide eyes dropped to my shoes again. She pressed a palm to her chest and muttered something in Spanish, punctuating the lament with the sign of the cross.

I had a feeling the prayer was more for my shoes than my toes.

"The conference room is filling fast. Let's get seats before we have to stand."

"Already? What's going on? If this is about my system, why's everyone so eager to be here?" Computer issues bored staffers. They never cared about software updates or my efforts to reduce redundancy, save them time and streamline their processes. My system was a burden they endured. A kink in their flow.

Marcella smoothed her hair and heaved a sigh. "The founder called. Residents are in an uproar and the pressure is on Randall to fix things."

"An uproar about what?" Was she intentionally being cryptic or was I completely dense? "What is happening?"

She pressed a stout finger to crimson lips and pointed to the rapidly filling conference room. So much for having time to prepare.

The voice of Randall Gershwin, clubhouse manager, boomed from inside. "I'm going to get started. I need everyone at their stations on time, so I'm going to move quickly through this thing. Take a seat. Come on in." A bead of sweat rolled over his temple.

I followed Marcella on silent feet to a pair of empty seats in the back of the room. Bodies in various Horseshoe Falls uniforms filled the space. Salon workers, golf and tennis pros, restaurant and spa staff. Warren, my only IT subordinate, sat up front with a tablet, ready to take notes. Warren wasn't the keenest staffer, but he had skills and typed ninety words a minute. I'd learned to ignore his blatant thrift-store look and luminous white-and-silver tennis shoes. Fashion wasn't for everyone.

Randall paced the far wall, hands clasped behind him, chin high. His khaki pants sagged from recent weight loss, something I envied but lacked proper motivation to achieve. Unfortunately, his trimmer look hadn't come with any perks like a shave or haircut. "Thank you all for coming. I'll make this quick so we can get out there and serve the fine residents of Horseshoe Falls. IT has agreed to take notes and get copies in every hand. If you miss something, you'll get a copy in your email later today. If you don't, look for Warren."

Warren lifted his hand in an awkward wave.

Randall scanned the room, stopping when he spotted Marcella and me. "As most of you know, the community's had some unprecedented troubles lately. In addition to two residential break-ins, there's an ongoing snafu with our community email and appointment system."

I glanced at Marcella.

She nodded.

I lifted my hand. "Did you say there's a snafu? How long has this been going on? Why am I just hearing about it?"

Creases lined Randall's forehead. "Apparently this has been happening for upwards of two weeks, though residents have only recently gone to the founder with complaints. If it makes you feel any better, I hadn't heard of it before last night either. I received a courtesy call from the founder and he wasn't feeling very courteous during his explanation." He patted a handkerchief over his brow. "If clubhouse staffers had come to me sooner, we might not be in this mess today, but they didn't and here we are."

A groan rolled through the crowd. Whispers climbed the walls and stood the hair on my arms at attention.

Randall continued pacing. "When you have a problem with a resident, you come to Marcella or myself. Always. No exceptions. It's our job to smooth these things over. Confrontation is never an acceptable response. Neither is pretending it didn't happen or telling residents they can't have what they want."

I raised my fingers. "I'm sorry. What exactly is going on? You said it's an email problem?"

Warren looked over his shoulder and shook his head. It seemed this was the first he'd heard of it, too.

Randall slumped. "I don't know what's going on with our network, but people are coming to the clubhouse expecting appointments they never made—at least as far as we can tell—but they insist they scheduled online after receiving a clubhouse email."

Warren cleared his throat and adjusted his glasses. "We haven't sent any emails about an online scheduling option."

Tension zinged through the room. People shifted in their seats. The word *mob* popped into mind.

A woman dressed in the day spa uniform stood and addressed me. "How is that possible? We're accepting fake coupons and honoring specials customers seem to have made up. I'm losing money. I lease my massage table here and I'm working for free to avoid losing clients."

Randall clapped his hands, returning the attention to himself. "Yes, and you aren't alone. Employees are frustrated. Residents are irritated. The board of directors has threatened to replace us all if we don't get our act together fast. In the meanwhile I need all workers to start documenting these things. Keep detailed lists of resident names when they come with these problems. Record the types of specials you're honoring. Ask when they received the emails and get any other details you can without upsetting them further."

He looked long and hard at Warren and then me. "I need our IT staff to find out what's happening and get it fixed. Yesterday."

Yikes. I hopped to my feet. No flaw in my system would put anyone out of work. I'd make sure of that. "I'll look into it right away."

I bowed to Marcella and headed to my office, by way of the concierge desk. Why did I bow to Marcella? Group settings brought out the weird in me. I slipped out of my shoes and chose an extra-large cup from the disposable selection.

My toes curled and stretched in the island of plush carpet around the concierge desk. Not bleeding as I'd expected, but in desperate need of a wiggle. Thanks to my morning jog in four-inch couture heels, all ten of my little piggies were crooked and numb. I circled my ankles one at a time to circulate blood flow and filled my cup with liquid enthusiasm.

The decibel level rose behind me as golfers returned from early morning tee times or arrived for clubhouse services. The building was laid out like a compass. North was the front door and main parking lot. South was the exit for outdoor amenities and activities—tennis courts, group exercise, a pool and a café. Other compass points stopped at clubhouse services: pet groomer, hair salon, restaurant, conference center and a hall leading to employee offices. Natural light twinkled around me, illuminating dust motes in the air. Floor-to-ceiling glass walls showcased local flora and fauna, giving inside people like me the illusion of outdoor living.

Scents of buttery hotcakes and syrup wafted through the Derby Steakhouse door. I breathed through my mouth to avoid unbearable carbohydrate temptation. One more whiff of pancakes and I might order a dozen hot doughnuts for second breakfasts.

I dashed my coffee with cinnamon and grabbed a little wooden stir paddle. Bernie's blog was right. There was trouble at the clubhouse. I pressed the cup to my lips and inhaled tendrils of bitter steam. My eyes slid shut while I counted to ten and organized my thoughts. What exactly were residents receiving in email? Whatever it was, it hadn't come from me and I doubted it came from the clubhouse system. Could they be lying? How many complaints were there?

A long shadow overtook me.

My lids popped open, and I jumped to attention,

stuffing swollen feet back into their luxurious torture devices.

The shadow had a stiff-looking man in his midthirties at the end of it. "Mia Connors?" His voice was deep with a hint of Southern charm.

Hmm. White dress shirt. Shiny shoes. "Are you a cop or a salesman?" I squinted through foggy glasses and set my coffee aside. "I met with our software rep last week, and we're all up-to-date on licensing, so I guess cop." Cops wore uniforms and carried twenty extra pounds but, for some inexplicable reason, most men liked being mistaken for one. He was definitely new to Horseshoe Falls. Resident? Guest?

He frowned. "I look like a cop?"

I wasn't expecting the frown. I gave him another long look. The light bulb flickered on in my scrambled brain. "Oh." I dug into my handbag, searching for my business cards. "Are you looking for some technical assistance?" I stage-winked. Detailed internet research was my specialty. If the information existed, I could find, compile and deliver it with great discretion. For a reasonable fee.

"Technical assistance?"

"Sure. Online. I can clean up anything you need or get details on anything you want."

He tented his brows.

I backpedaled. "Research is a passion of mine."

He shifted foot to foot and stretched a hand in my direction. "Before you say anything else and this conversation takes a whole new turn, I need to introduce myself. I'm Jake Archer. I'm the new Horseshoe Falls Head of Security."

"You're not wearing a uniform." I gave him another once-over. "Why are you in a suit?"

"It's my first day. I'd hoped to make an impression. Disappointed?"

Disgusted with my lack of insight. Of course he was the new guy. Bernie described him on her blog. Handsome. Sullen. "I thought you'd be more brooding."

He slouched forward and looked at me with narrow eyes. Like I wasn't making any sense. Which I wasn't.

I pinched my lips between my teeth. "I mean, someone said you were brooding. Not me." I flailed mentally. "Not brooding." Swarms of staffers rushed past us. The meeting was over.

A nervous laugh bubbled up, and I tamped it down. "I meant serious. You're very serious. Probably in cop mode. Security mode? I'm sure you're not at all brooding. I've got to go." Ugh. I turned away, stuffing napkins and sugar packets into my bag for later. I'd finish mixing my coffee behind the safety of my office door.

He followed me down the narrow hall toward the line of employee offices, easily matching his pace to mine. "Anything you want to tell me?"

"I sometimes help people erase things they don't want online. I also help them with research. I thought you were approaching me for my help."

"Anything else?"

"Nope."

"Why'd you assume I was a cop?"

"Or a salesman." I slowed my pace, relieved to reach my office door. "It was just a guess. You know, like when you go to a restaurant or a party and someone catches your attention, so you make up what you think they're saying, what they do for a living and why they're there. Then you get closer to see if you're right."

Jake blinked. "No."

Of course not. Normal people didn't do that kind of

thing. Socially awkward girls with insane imaginations did. "Well, anyway. This is my office." I turned my back to the door, hoping he wouldn't follow me inside. "I've got work to do if I want to get the system's problems worked out before we're all fired, and I'm having a rough day anyway so…"

He didn't make a move to leave.

My heart stammered. Why was he grilling me like this? I couldn't take confrontation. I babbled. I behaved stupidly. I filled quiet moments with my personal brand of crazy.

Two seconds later, I caved. "First, some jack—someone took my parking space, and now I have to fix whatever has happened to the email system or lose my job." I exhaled deeply. "You should go."

His scrutinizing blue eyes pierced me to the door. "Why do I make you nervous?"

I tugged at the neckline of my dress to circulate the suffocating air and chomped on the inside of both cheeks. *You're too close. Asking a whole heck of a lot of questions and way too close.* My fingers curled at my side. I shut my eyes and cried out to the Universe, *Help!*

"Nothing else you want to tell me?"

I rolled the back of my head against the office door. "Uh-uh."

"Mia." My name reverberated off the polished foyer floor. I smiled at the sound.

My best friend, Nate, and his buddy Baxter moved confidently down the carpeted hall toward me, smiling widely and puffing for air. Jake stepped aside, rigid as a statue. Nate kissed my cheek and opened my office door. "Your lot is crammed. We had to park at the falls and run. We're on our way to work and carpooled so we could show you something. Come on." He grabbed my bag and tugged me with him through the doorway. Baxter followed.

Nate had become my best friend the day I moved into his apartment building. Baxter was a New Year's Eve mistake I diligently tried to forget.

I concentrated on Nate, refusing to look at Jake, who'd entered the lair uninvited. "What are you guys up to?"

Nate collapsed into my desk chair and spun. "Baxter has something for you."

Baxter gave me a creepy wink.

"Stop it. What do you really want?"

Jake took a slow nosy lap through the room. His critical expression irked me. I'd spent months designing and outfitting the IT office with the best of everything from equipment to furnishings. I'd agonized over the placement of every item for maximum efficiency and even consulted my sister, Bree, the psychology nut, before choosing a new wall color, quicksilver. She'd delivered staplers, penholders and tape dispensers in buttercup yellow as strategic accent pieces. Apparently quicksilver lowered stress, but we needed the yellow to keep us awake. As if I could sleep in an office this amazing. Our workstations were streamlined, feng shui accurate and accompanied with ergonomic comfy chairs.

Jake returned from his tour with a grunt.

Nate's sharp green eyes twinkled. His gaze lingered on the oversize grump at my side.

I waved a palm in his direction. "This is Jake. He's new. What's going on?"

Nate nodded. He scanned the room and stopped on Warren, who was trying to look invisible at his desk several feet away.

I smiled. "He's fine, too. Tell me what's going on."

Energy buzzed through the room. Whatever they'd made a special trip at eight o'clock to tell me had to be big. "Tell me. Tell me. Tell me."

Jake cleared his throat. "Do you normally invite civilians into your office, Miss Connors? Am I wrong in understanding this room is the singular IT hub for all of Horseshoe Falls?" He rolled the sleeves of his dress shirt up to his elbows and crossed thick muscled arms over a broad chest. His grim expression dared me to let the guests remain in a room he'd declared off-limits.

Challenge accepted.

Baxter fidgeted with a string on his cuff, twisting it between his thumb and first finger until it broke. His peach dress shirt and yellow tie illuminated the unnatural flush of his olive skin. He moved a determined gaze to me. Ignoring Jake's not-so-subtle hint that his presence in the IT office was inappropriate, Baxter moved into my personal space. His usual confidence wavered, but he didn't stop. He lowered his mouth to my ear.

I leaned away. "Knock it off."

He shot a meaningful look at Nate, then Jake. His fingers curled over mine, and I yanked free.

"What are you doing?"

His insistent nature was almost charming over pizza and drinks on the weekend, but at work, in front of everyone, I was shocked and appalled. It wasn't like him to be so public.

Baxter wrinkled his face. His expression morphed from worry to determination. He settled a warm hand on my shoulder. "I just need five minutes. Alone."

My heart raced at his nearness, and a traitorous shiver rolled down my spine.

Jake stalked forward. "Seriously. What is going on in here?"

Embarrassment burned my cheeks. Had everyone seen me shiver? A quick look confirmed they had. Nate, Jake and Warren stared at Baxter and me.

I rose onto my tiptoes and forced authority into my voice. "This isn't the time or place to be alone. Please step back or else."

He stepped away, hands fisted.

Jake moved to the door and pressed wide palms over trim hips. "I'm going to have to ask your guests to leave. This is a restricted area. You can meet with your friends outside this room and on your time."

Nate wrinkled his nose. "Sure. Yeah. Okay." He stood and exchanged a look with Baxter. Their height differences were almost comical. Baxter and I were eye-to-eye when I wore the right heels. Nate towered over everyone in the room. That was true in any room.

Whatever they wanted to tell me, they were both clearly disappointed to have lost the chance. Nate pressed on. "See you at home?"

"Yeah." At least at home we could split a pizza and talk about it as long as we wanted. Whatever *it* was.

Baxter's expression was just short of a kicked puppy's.

"You coming, man?" Nate moved to Jake's side and shot him a sidelong glance.

Baxter looked repentant as he passed. "Sorry. That didn't go down like I planned. Look me up later, okay?"

I entered the space between my desk and Warren's, matching Jake's bossy stance. "Sure. Are you okay?"

Baxter dipped his chin and disappeared through the doorway.

Jake escorted them outside. He lifted a palm to stop me from joining them.

I slid onto my seat. "What's his problem?"

Warren shrugged.

I sent Nate and Baxter a quick text. Sorry about the new guy. Pizza tonight?

They both responded immediately. Pizza tonight.

Warren swiveled in his seat. "Where should we begin with the email things?"

"Why don't you perform a system scan to check for changes since the last backup? We want to rule out the possibility someone invaded the system. I'll see what I can do to soothe irritated residents and take a look at the server log."

I composed a heartfelt email for the Horseshoe Falls community on behalf of the clubhouse staff. I apologized gratuitously for the confusion over coupons, discount codes and links sent to them for the purpose of scheduling appointments from home. Putting the blame on myself wasn't fun, but there was no reason to alarm residents into thinking someone contacted them with malicious intent. Paranoia was contagious.

I hit Send and moved to Warren's desk. "Anything since the last backup?"

"Nope. Nothing's changed here. I went back three weeks. You want me to go further?"

I tapped my nails on his stapler. "Yeah. If there's something to find, let's find it."

I fell back into my seat and pulled up the email server log. It didn't take long to confirm what I suspected. "No emails were sent from this system with the subject or content Randall described. I'm going to tighten things up anyway."

I ran a complete diagnostic of the system before finishing my coffee. Everything looked solid. I updated the firewalls and changed all my access codes anyway. Someone had accessed email addresses for multiple

Horseshoe Falls residents. They didn't necessarily get them from my system, but if someone had been in my system before, they wouldn't find their way back.

Time evaporated as I combed the system, locking it down by extreme measures.

Baxter sent a text at seven to confirm our plans for pizza.

I responded affirmatively, with a pizza emoji and a quick message. Working late. Lost track of time. Be there soon. Time to find out what those goofballs came to work to show me.

I STOPPED BY Nate's apartment on my way home. He didn't answer, which worried me. He hadn't returned any of my calls or texts since I confirmed with Baxter. Not even the smiley face emoticon with glasses and a ponytail got a response. I pounded a little louder on Nate's door, and the door beside his popped open.

Argh. I speed-walked toward the elevator.

"Mia of Camelot." Nate's neighbor, Carl, whistled like a catcaller on holiday. His snotty high-pitched voice stood my arm hairs at attention.

"Carl." I punched the elevator button and tapped my foot.

"Looking for your pal?"

"Have you seen him?"

"Nope. Didn't see his car outside either."

The blessed elevator doors slid open. "Let him know I'm looking for him if you do."

He puffed his chest and struck a pose in the doorway of his apartment. "Anything for you, my queen."

I jumped onboard and pressed the down button until

the doors closed. All the apartments in our building were one or two bedrooms, yet somehow at least six hipsters lived in the apartment beside Nate's. Carl was the boldest and most ironic, which was a compliment to any decent hipster. The others mostly snarked and slunk around being under-enthused about everything they came into contact with. Carl's attitude toward me improved after he attended last year's Renaissance Faire "ironically" and ran into me working Grandma's Queen Guinevere booth, intentionally.

I tried Baxter's number while waiting to hear from Nate.

Nothing.

Nate wasn't home. He wasn't online. He wasn't taking calls.

By nine I was punchy. Baxter hadn't responded either. I'd relived their visit to my office a thousand times. Nate said they had news. Baxter tried to get me alone. Maybe that hadn't been a line. Maybe he needed to tell me something in private. What kind of secret could those two have for me?

I grabbed my keys and took a ride. Ten minutes later I pulled up at Nate's favorite coffee shop. No Nate. I twirled the key ring around my finger, forcing a bad feeling from my gut. Nate was a big boy. A big Irish boy with happy eyes and a righteous left hook. Maybe he was at the pub? I'd drive past Baxter's building and look for their cars. The pub wasn't far from his place. They might've stopped for a few drinks and lost track of time. That scenario wasn't like them, but neither was standing me up.

My tummy growled. When I found them, they owed me an explanation with my pizza.

I grabbed my vibrating phone from my pocket as I headed for my car. "Nate?"

The vibration continued until I realized it wasn't an incoming call. I'd programmed my cell to alert me and the local police if the clubhouse alarm went off. I angled behind the wheel of my MINI and sailed down Perry Drive to Horseshoe Falls. The alarm never went off. What kind of day was this?

The phone rang for real as I slid my badge through the guard gate reader.

"Hello?"

"Mia Connors? This is local police dispatch. We have notice of a silent alarm at 10012 Horseshoe Falls Drive."

I jammed my ID into my pocket and sped the short distance to the clubhouse, thankful the town was dark and quiet. "Yes. I'm here now. I'm parking. I'll go inside and shut it off in the next three minutes."

"Yes, ma'am. Give us a call if you need us."

I disconnected and jogged across sprinkler-wet grass, tugging open doors until I reached the alarm panel. I entered the security code and waited for the blinking red light to settle into a steady green. Area Secured.

Moonlight streamed through wide glass walls. A sinking feeling settled over me. What if the area wasn't secured? I took a lap through the building. All the doors were locked. No signs of an intruder. Probably a flock of birds or a deer hit the window.

One more stop and I'd hit the pub in search of the guys.

I pressed the levered handle on my office door, and it creaked open without effort. "Warren?" I poked my head inside. Another thought occurred. "Jake?"

Security lighting cast an eerie glow over the room already filled with blinking lights and endless monitors set to blue home screens. The silhouette of a man seated in my chair stopped my breath and sent my frantic heart into overdrive.

I slapped my palm against the light switch. Overhead lights snapped on, illuminating the intruder at my desk.

The scream that followed was mine.

My hands wiggled helplessly in the air, wanting to help, knowing he was dead. I dashed to his side and pressed two trembling fingers against his neck, praying for a pulse. His skin was cold and pale. His face was streaked with blood and speckled in glass. No pulse. I whimpered. Fumbling for my cell phone, I nicked the wheels of my desk chair with one foot, and Baxter faceplanted onto my keyboard.

TWO

AN HOUR LATER, a dozen people swarmed my office. Jake mingled with the uniforms, whispering things in confidence. I chewed my shredded fingernails and wondered how he liked ten people rummaging around my office when he was so rude to the two I'd invited, one of which was suddenly, inexplicably dead.

I collapsed in the corner farthest from Baxter and the bustle of the investigation surrounding him. Nate still wasn't answering calls, texts or emails. A tear slid over my cheek, and I swiped it away. I could have a proper breakdown at home. This wasn't the time.

My scrambled brain raced with questions. What if Nate was dead too? Maybe that was the reason he wasn't answering his phone. If he wasn't dead, I needed to find him and tell him about Baxter. He shouldn't hear of his best friend's death on the news.

I caught another hot tear on the pad of my thumb and pressed the heels of my hands against my eyes. We were supposed to have pizza tonight and laugh about Jake's overzealous interpretation of his head-of-security duties. Baxter was going to share his secret intrigue and I was going to buy a round of our favorite drinks while we talked about it. Images of the three of us making silly toasts around a pub table dissolved into tears. Gone. Like Baxter.

I reopened my lids with resolve. I'd do something to

honor Baxter. He shouldn't be gone. I'd sit down with Nate and we'd come up with a way.

Jake wound through knots and clusters of people, grimacing as usual, wholly focused on me. "You want to tell me what happened here?"

I scoffed. As if I knew anything. As if he hadn't already spoken to every man in the room. "Why don't you ask an officer? They wrote my story down. I've told it ten times tonight."

Jake squatted beside me. "Make it eleven."

I narrowed my eyes and kneaded my hands, suddenly desperate to be anywhere else. "No."

"No?"

"Yeah. No. I'm not here to entertain you. One of my friends died tonight and another's missing, so find someone else to play cop with."

Jake pulled his chin back. "I'm not playing cop."

"Pft."

He stood and assumed the cranky pose. Arms crossed, eyes blazing. "You threatened the guy a few hours ago. What exactly did you mean by 'step back or else'?"

I stared.

"You sure you don't want to tell that story one more time?"

I shot to my feet and nearly fell over. My legs wobbled like soggy noodles. I pressed one hand to the wall for casual support. "Hey!" I lifted a finger between us. "You're the one who insisted Nate and Baxter leave. You stood around like a caveman, grunting and glaring. You're the one who had a problem with him, not me. Maybe you should answer a few questions. Where were you at nine-thirty tonight?"

He hacked a throaty noise into the air. "Last I heard,

looks don't kill, and I don't recall threatening the man. That was you."

I growled and stamped one rubbery foot, hoping to wake it. "I didn't hurt him, and you know it." My voice edged higher.

The murmur of voices and flash of crime-scene cameras drew me back to Earth. I counted silently to ten.

"Do I?"

I crossed my arms like him. If this was some sort of contest, I could be just as difficult as he could.

"Mia."

My teeth chattered.

Jake dropped his arms to his sides. "Was anything taken?"

"No."

"Did you check?"

"Of course I checked. The *actual* police officers covered all this before you got here. They asked me to look for anything missing, damaged or otherwise tampered with. Everything is perfect. Nothing was touched. They dusted my keyboard for prints and found nothing. Only mine. Happy?"

"Not particularly."

A pair of uniformed officers watched us from across the room.

I turned my back on them. Being the center of attention was for the birds and my sister. I preferred a deserted island to a fishbowl any day. "I haven't figured out who triggered the silent alarm, but I shut it off when I got here."

Jake raised an eyebrow. "Don't you think Baxter triggered the alarm?"

"Well, he didn't kill himself. Someone smashed his nose with a tablet and then cracked him over the head with something heavy. Maybe the killer was already here when Baxter came."

"How do you know it was a tablet?" He rocked back on his heels, looking pleased.

"What?"

"You said someone hit Baxter with a tablet. That's very specific. Also, how do you know the tablet wasn't used for the injury on the back of his head? How do you know the broken nose came first?"

"I recognize the splinters of glass all over his shirt and the floor. I've replaced enough tablet screens to know the glass when I see it. Ever drop a smartphone, Mr. Security? Touchscreens shatter into a million tiny fragments, some so small you'll find them in the carpet with your bare feet, months later, regardless of how hard you looked or how many times you swept. Also, it doesn't make sense to hit him in the face after knocking him dead, so they must have hit his face first, but hitting his face busted the screen, so it wouldn't have made much of a weapon after that. Heck, a tablet couldn't kill anyone, even if it wasn't broken. Have you seen a tablet lately? They're like this thick and this big." I mimed the estimated sizes with my fingertips and palms. "Is there a reason you challenged my assessment? Something more you want to say?"

Jake didn't look impressed. "Any idea why your friend was here after hours?"

"No. Of course not."

He squared his shoulders. "I heard you make plans to hook up later."

I glared. "Are you accusing me of something?"

Two EMTs loaded Baxter into a black coroner bag and onto a gurney. The eerie echo of lacing zipper teeth went on forever, curling ice into the pit of my stomach.

My breath hitched as they rolled him through the doorway and out of my life. The officers followed, along with the medical examiner. Oxygen filled the room in their absence. A lone man dusting for prints kept up the investigation.

I rubbed cold palms over chilled arms and turned in a circle, desperate to leave, unable to move. "It's freezing in here."

Jake touched his hand to the small of my back before dropping it and stepping away. "You're probably suffering from a bit of shock. It's nice outside. The fresh air will help. Let me walk you to your car."

I tried to nod, but my stiff neck jerked back and forth like a human bobblehead doll. I let Jake guide me away from the terrible scene.

The night was clear but dark. Silent police cruisers flanked the ambulance and other official vehicles, none of which used their emergency lights. Only the ghosts of headlights and taillights guided the strangers as they made their way out of the lot.

I moved in a daze to my MINI and unlocked the door.

Jake snorted.

Adrenaline surged in my veins for no good reason. "Something wrong?"

He shook his head, a look of disbelief on his face. "Are you positive you didn't invite Baxter here? Maybe he got a little too hands-on, if you know what I mean? Perhaps you acted in self-defense?"

Exhaustion tugged my mind and limbs. "Beating someone over the head isn't self-defense. Besides, if I want someone to leave me alone, they do." Having a cop for a father and six years of college dating experience assured that much. I'd completed dozens of campus self-defense workshops by graduation. If I wanted a man to back off, I could make him.

Jake Archer included.

I gave him a long appraising look. He was lean, almost to the point of lanky. Big feet, long appendages. He was probably slower than he thought and, with his high center of gravity, I was pretty certain I could put him on his back before he knew what happened.

"Yeah, I bet." His cheeky grin contradicted the words.

"What's that supposed to mean? You think I'm defenseless because I wear heels and work in IT?"

"Oh, I don't know. Maybe it's your short skirts, bite-sized pink car and glasses."

My head whipped back. "Excuse me? My skirts are not short, and I like pink. Stella's easy to maneuver, cost-effective and easy on the environment. The glasses are a medical necessity, thanks to bad genes and probably too much time at a computer screen. Anyway, which is it? Either you think I'm capable of murdering a man twice my size or you think I'm a dainty princess. If you want to solve this crime, you'll need to narrow your theories a bit."

That earned me a chuckle. He opened my car door for me. "Not if I believe both."

I slid onto the cool leather seat and slammed the door before powering down my window like a boss. We weren't done arguing, after all. Who knew what ridiculous thing he'd say next? I kept my chin high, but the stupid seat belt took three tries to latch. So much for a dramatic exit.

He patted the car roof. "Be here bright and early so I don't have to come looking for you. Murderers some-

times try to make a hasty getaway. I watch television."
He tapped his temple to mock me.

I reversed out of the space. Pretending he didn't mind
my you-aren't-a-real-cop digs didn't work on me. It
shone in his eyes. He was on a mission, just like me. I
wanted to find my best friend, but what was Jake up to?
Maybe he was the one who sabotaged my computer system, sending those bogus emails to residents. His sudden appearance was beyond strange. Until he appeared,
I had no idea Mark, the previous security head, had any
intention of leaving. According to Bernie's blog, no one
did. Corporate espionage situations saturated the news.
Maybe Jake worked for a rival upscale community feeling the pressure to steal our older, wealthier residents
by making our setup seem unprofessional.

The MINI bounced over a row of speed bumps, and
I caught sight of Jake walking across the empty parking lot. He shot me a weird salute before climbing into
the giant blue truck I hated.

Why hadn't I seen that coming?

My NEIGHBORHOOD WAS silent as I drifted to the curb outside the renovated bank building where I lived. Nate's
car wasn't on the street.

My decision to move downtown was a choice my
family hated. They'd belonged to middle class America
for far too long. I preferred hundred-year-old city buildings to the squat ranch homes of suburbia. My building
had character and charm. Living downtown was being
part of history. Living in the suburbs was being in a
time warp. I wasn't ready for a time warp.

I dropped my keys into the blown glass dish inside

my door and locked up behind me. I poured cold coffee into a mug and shoved it into the microwave. I hadn't predicted much correctly today, but I had no doubt it would be a long night. I redressed in sweat pants, a T-shirt and slippers before the microwave dinged.

I curled up on the couch with hot coffee and balanced my laptop on my thighs. Unopened email made me nuts. I scanned the content of an email from Grandma's company, knowing it was perfect. I'd spent an entire weekend choosing each word for the newsletter. This automated mailing had a special bonus. One free invitation to the Renaissance Faire as Grandma's guest.

My attention, meanwhile, bounced erratically. It was well after midnight, but I needed to talk. Bree had a baby, so it was anyone's guess whether or not they were asleep or awake at any point in the day. I sent a quick text about the Faire to see if she responded.

My phone rang three minutes later. Mom's face appeared on the screen.

"Hello?"

"This is Bree. We're at Mom and Dad's playing canasta. You want to come over?"

"No." I double-checked the clock. "Don't you have to work in the morning?"

She laughed. "I'm working from home tomorrow." The words were drawn out. "Tom's asleep on the couch."

I stretched my legs and wiggled my fuzzy slippers. "Are you drinking?"

"Yep." She let the *p* pop into the receiver.

I set my glasses on the coffee table and rubbed my aching eyes. I'd tell her about Baxter tomorrow, when she was sober. "The Renaissance Faire starts tomorrow night. Are you going?"

"We're all going. Everyone's going." She paused. "Why? Aren't you?"

"I'm going. I just…" saw a friend dead and needed to talk. "I hoped you'd all be there. I miss seeing everyone." A lump formed in my throat. I'd almost forgotten I promised myself an ugly crying jag.

Bree sighed. "You see us constantly. What's wrong?" Her lazy slur vanished.

Oh no. Big-sister mode had been initiated, and I'd already decided not to talk about Baxter tonight. This meant only one thing. A fight.

"You know I can hear when something's wrong with you. I can feel it." She exaggerated the word *feel* into multiple syllables. "Don't say you don't want to talk about it. If you didn't want to talk, you wouldn't have texted."

"Jeez, you're annoying. Nothing's wrong." I picked at swollen cuticles I'd chewed raw at the clubhouse. Where the hell was Nate? Why was Baxter dead? Why was he in my office after hours? What did they want to tell me?

"Fine. Don't tell me. I already know anyway. For once I wanted to hear your problems from you instead of from someone else, but I shouldn't expect miracles. Tell me one thing, Mia. Why don't you ever tell me things? What's the point in having a twin if we live two separate lives?"

Our well-worn twin argument thickened the air and my tongue. The words piled behind clenched teeth, begging me to answer her tired question for the ten thousandth time. *Because we are two separate people.*

If I took that path, I'd incite her ire, per my usual, and face an inevitable makeup the next time I saw her, which was tomorrow, and Bree was a hugger. I nearly bit my tongue in half stanching the words. I counted to ten and settled for "You're a crabby drunk."

The phone clattered. Mom's voice rang through the line. "Honey, are you okay? I hoped you'd call sooner. I was giving you space until breakfast, then I was storming the castle to comfort you."

I sniffled and laughed at Mom's *Princess Bride* reference. She made them often, but rarely correctly. "What do you know?"

"I heard about Baxter from Bunny Majors. She called when she saw the ambulance and police cars at Horseshoe Falls. She and Charles were scouting for owls. They thought Mark might've had a heart attack. He's not in the greatest shape, you know, but, then again, the clubhouse isn't usually open at night. When the police spotted Bunny and Charles watching, they questioned them. Randall was there. He'd told her what had happened. The officers asked if she knew Baxter, which she did, of course, through you." Mom pulled in a new breath and finished with a bang. "She told them how the two of you argued so often and what good friends you were."

My head fell into my waiting palm. "That's an oxymoron. We were good friends but why would she say we fought all the time? No wonder Jake thinks I killed Baxter."

"Who's Jake?"

Apparently Bunny didn't know everything. "The new head of security."

"What about Mark?"

"He's gone. No one knows why he left. I'll ask around." The stress of the day crushed my chest. My head pounded. My limbs were too heavy. I didn't need coffee, I needed rest. "Mom, I've got to go. Make up with Bree for me, okay? I'll talk to you tomorrow."

"All right, sweetie. If you need anything, just call. Your father and I are always here for you."

I disconnected and tipped over on my couch. Images of Baxter's face cluttered my mind. The way he laughed when I teased him about his eternally sunny disposition, or how he pursed his lips when we argued, as if he wanted to say something mean but never would. I'd never had many friends, but I'd had him and he was true.

I wrapped my arms around my middle and squeezed. "Where are you, Nate? Baxter is gone and I can't lose you, too." A shuddered breath rocked through me. "Please be okay."

THREE

My PHONE BUZZED to life, literally. "Flight of the Bumblebee" was Bree's assigned ringtone. Bree was the bee. Big sisters were like that as far as I could tell, especially ones who reminded you for nearly thirty years they were two-and-a-half minutes older, wiser and more mature. I slapped the screen blindly until her voice burst through the speaker.

"Mia?"

I moaned, too tired to form words.

"I'm sorry about last night. It wasn't nice of me to set you up and then get mad when you did exactly what I expected. How are you feeling today? Gwen's at daycare and Tom's at the university. I can come over and bring you coffee or meet you for lunch."

I swung suddenly anxious legs over the couch's edge. *Coffee.* "I need to go. I want to find Nate, and he always goes to The Beanery on his way to work." I sloughed off the blankets and dashed into my room. I yanked open my closet door. "Maybe on the lunch offer. I'll call you later."

Bree sighed. "No, you won't, but thanks for saying so. Hey. Don't forget you're coming over this week for dinner. We're celebrating the new grant Tom and I secured."

I flipped through the closet, in search of my longest skirt. "Wouldn't miss it."

NATE WASN'T AT The Beanery, and Jake's monstrous truck of stupidity was parked in my space again. There were plenty of open parking spaces today, which could only mean one thing. He wanted to tick me off.

Done. Success. He could mark it off on his list of victories because it wouldn't happen again.

I stopped at the concierge desk and poured myself some coffee.

"Mia?" Lacy Foster sidled up to the desk and leaned her narrow hip against it. "Can I talk to you?"

"Sure. What's up?"

Lacy was about ten years older than me. She was a trophy wife for fifteen years until her dripping-with-money husband died of old age and left her everything. It was a tough job, being a trophy wife. The old ones didn't all last as long as Hefner and then you woke up forty and single. Finding a replacement for Mr. Moneybags was a lot harder when the competition was half your age. I felt genuinely bad for Lacy. She was exquisite, kind and had been raised in poverty. She worked hard for the Mrs. Moneybags status and seemed to have truly loved Mr. Foster. Now she was reaping the rewards and repercussions of trophy-wife-ism simultaneously. In other words, she was rich but lonely.

"I'm going on an important date this weekend." She slid a business card across the counter to me. "I wish I knew how to find out if he had any skeletons in his closet. Pending lawsuits, recent love children, arrests, fetishes I can't accommodate."

I smiled, unsure if she was getting at what I thought she was, especially after my misread on Jake yesterday. "If only, right?"

Her oversculpted brows furrowed. "Oh. Wait." She flattened a second business card over the first. This card was black, front and back. Not a stitch of font or color, save one little picture in the corner. A small almond blossom embossed into the card signified a promise. Mine to the holder and the holder's to me. I would keep their trust, and they would keep mine. Someone had told Lacy my secret.

I covered both cards with my palm and slipped them into my bag. "I'll have a packet prepared for you this afternoon."

Her smile widened and wilted into a pleased cat-that-ate-the-canary look. "That's fast. Thank you. What will I owe you?"

"Let's see how I do and you can decide." I'd learned that people were far more generous than expected, and assigning a price led to underpayment most of the time. Plus, in my business, there was plenty of pressure to keep me happy, so I wouldn't blab. Which I wouldn't. I believed in what I did.

Lacy sauntered away as Jake approached with a handsome but overly cliché-looking detective wielding a pocket-sized notebook and pen. "Miss Connors, do you have a moment?" the detective asked. His badge hung around his neck on a beaded silver chain.

"Sure."

Jake watched Lacy until she disappeared through the front door. Maybe she didn't have to look too far for a new man. Of course, head of security lacked the prestige of vice president of National Bank, the man's title on the business card she'd handed me.

The detective poised his pen and widened his stance. "Where were you when the silent alarm went off last night?"

"Outside The Beanery on Wales Avenue."

"Is there anyone who can verify that?"

I shot Jake an unfriendly look. Had he told the detective I threatened Baxter? "Or else" could mean anything. Between Baxter and me, it meant I'd give him trouble in one of our online games or spike his coffee with an energy shot, nothing more.

The men waited for my answer with matching humorless expressions.

"The alarm notification came to my phone. You can check the call log and verify with my GPS."

He worked his shoulders as if they ached or were bunched from tension. Hazard of the job, I supposed. "Tech-savvy people tend to turn their GPS off."

"I don't. If I'm ever abducted, I want to be found. Plus, it comes in handy whenever I'm accused of murder."

Jake rubbed a hand over his lips, hiding a smile. I didn't know his face did that trick.

Detective Pen Poser didn't laugh. "Is it true you threatened the victim earlier that day?"

There it was. I glowered at Jake and his smile fell.

The detective pressed on. "Warren Smith stated he heard you threaten to break the victim's face."

My head fell back. I counted to ten. Warren was the kind of guy who ran when someone else screamed. Of course he'd rat on me. "I didn't mean it and I didn't threaten to break his face yesterday. That was an argument we had last week. I had that kind of relationship with Baxter. Please call him Baxter, not The Victim."

"He is the victim."

I curled my fingers at my sides. "Yeah, well, he was a lot of other things too."

The detective considered me a moment. "What kind of relationship did you and Baxter have? Precisely."

"That feels a little nosy," I hedged.

He waited.

He was better at the stare down than Jake.

"Fine. We were friends. I met him through my best friend, Nate, Nathan Green. Nate was here with Baxter yesterday morning." My gaze slid to Jake. Hadn't he relayed all this? Hadn't I covered this eleven times already?

"Friends? Warren got the impression you and the— Baxter—were more than friends."

I pulled in a long breath. Humiliation scorched my cheeks. Jake saw it too, from the expression on his face. Impish smile, raised brows. Jerk. "Baxter and I had a night. One night. A long time ago."

"And you weren't dating him now?"

"No. He pursued me afterward, but it didn't go anywhere. We settled into a routine of him trying too hard and me shutting him down. It was our thing." A lump wedged in my throat. I had been too hard on Baxter. What if he'd been serious in his efforts? What if my rejections had hurt him? My heart sank. I was a colossal, clueless meanie.

The detective tapped his pen against the little notebook. "Seeing anyone else right now?"

"No." My back stiffened. "What's that got to do with anything?"

He shrugged. "Jealous boyfriends are unpredictable. If Baxter came on to you regularly, it might've ruffled feathers." He smirked. "Plus, I'm nosy."

Jake and the detective moved away from me and performed an elaborate handshake, followed by a weird one-armed guy hug. Bizarre versions of one another.

Instinct tickled my scalp. I followed them. "What did you say your name was?"

The detective lifted his shield. "Detective Dan Archer."

Four matching blue eyes seared my brain. Their identical cocky expressions popped my mouth open. "Brothers?"

Dan's smirk split into a wide toothy smile.

Argh. I spun on my heels and headed back to the concierge desk for my cooling coffee.

Randall appeared out of nowhere. "There you are. Why isn't the appointment system fixed yet? I've got rampaging octogenarians demanding hair appointments, and the salon doesn't open for an hour. I'm giving free golf lessons to hordes of men claiming to have tee times with the pros. For the record, 'free' means I'm paying for those lessons because there's no way the pros are doing anything pro bono, and it's not their asses on the line over this scheduling snafu. That's all me, and I'm not going down alone. You said you'd fix this yesterday."

I hiked my laptop bag higher on one shoulder and topped off my coffee. "I lost a friend last night, Randall. I'm looking into the problem. I'll get answers to you as soon as I have them." My voice wavered. "Can you remember the names of some of the people lodging complaints? I'd like to know when they made the appointments, and get a look at the email they received. I locked the system down tight before I went home yesterday, but for the record, those emails weren't sent from our system."

He blanched. "Oh, no. Are you saying we have a hacker? This is serious. You have to fix this." He turned a business card over and listed several names. He handed the card to me with softer eyes. "I'm truly sorry about your friend, but this is bad."

"It's not a hacker. I checked after the meeting yesterday. No one was in my system, but I'll find out what happened and keep you posted. Thanks for the list."

I turned the corner and stopped short at my office. A thin line of crime-scene tape crossed the door. I turned in a small circle, uncertain. Wasn't I allowed inside? My heart sank with memories of the night before. *Of course not.*

I texted Warren. He'd headed this way while I poured coffee.

A few seconds later, a quiet whistle broke the silence. I whipped around. Warren leaned across the threshold of an office down the hall. "We moved."

Huh. I gave the crime-scene tape one last look and went to meet Warren. "What's going on? How long are we kicked out of our office? Why didn't anyone tell me? I just talked to Randall, Jake and a detective."

Warren stepped aside to let me pass. "I don't know. Detective Archer let me get some things from our office and bring them here. He said if we need anything else in there, we should ask Jake."

I guffawed. The cops had collected my key the night before. "Don't I get to take a look? Is it locked? What if I want something from my desk?"

He shrugged. "Jake took the key after Randall locked up."

Of course he did.

I scanned the makeshift IT hub. Most of our essentials were lined up on a small conference table against the back wall. Two desks in the center of the room were pushed together like the ones in television police stations. I took the empty seat. My Loki bobblehead nodded his welcome. I poked him. "Thanks for salvaging this."

He slid into his seat and tapped the mouse. "I couldn't take much and they logged everything I touched. Even Loki. We'll have to connect with our laptops today, but I have newer towers at home I can bring tomorrow if you want."

I shook my head. "That's really generous of you, but I'll take care of it. I'm sure they'll release our desk computers soon." I slunk into my new chair and huffed. Facing Warren eight hours a day couldn't last. "Can we move our desks apart later? This is weird."

"Definitely. I'll take care of that at lunch."

"Deal." I fidgeted in my new digs. Change wasn't my favorite and too many things had changed too quickly these past twenty-four hours. I smoothed my skirt and examined the drab beige walls.

Warren sat idly at his desk, tapping on the mouse, probably playing solitaire. He looked up suddenly. "I told them about you. When you threatened the guy."

"I know."

"Sorry."

"It's okay. It was the truth."

He nodded. "Cops make me nervous." He heaved a sigh and went back to his work.

Restless energy flooded through me. Our new office was a tiny conference room. It didn't fit. It looked wrong and smelled wrong. I wiggled in my new seat, trying to get comfortable. I missed my old chair. But I couldn't use that chair again. Baxter's ghost was probably sitting there, still trying to tell me whatever secret he'd come to share.

I tapped Randall's business card with my fingernail. A quick search of the resident database brought up numbers for the names on the back of the card. I dialed.

"Hello, Mrs. Fisker? This is Mia Connors calling

from the clubhouse. You were here this morning for an appointment?"

She huffed into the receiver. "And turned away in my hairpins and bonnet. Yes."

"I'm truly sorry about that, Mrs. Fisker. I'm working on the system now and wonder if you can tell me when you received the email to set the appointment."

"Two weeks ago. When I came home from my last appointment, there was an email. I assumed my visit triggered the contact. It's a brilliant concept, setting appointments without having to call or stop in. Too bad it doesn't work. When will it be fixed?"

Never, since my system didn't auto-email residents.

"We're working on it. Until then, please disregard any correspondence you receive from the clubhouse with regards to scheduling and don't click any links in email from us. I'll make an official announcement when the system is fixed."

"All right."

"Would you mind forwarding the appointment email to me? I'd like to have a look. It could help me get things straightened out."

"I deleted it."

I smiled into the receiver. "Nothing's ever really gone…"

"I took your class a few years ago. Do you remember? Your grandmother gathered us at Derby and we had tea. You showed us how to stay safe online. I learned to delete and empty my trash."

My forehead hit the desk. Grandma begged me to give that little class to her friends and neighbors after someone's husband was bamboozled by a con artist.

"Do you remember?"

"Yep." I lifted my face. "I remember."

She continued proudly. "I delete my browser history, too, and I don't post photos, check in anywhere or stay online more than necessary. I know all about those online criminals and I don't want to be targeted, tracked or otherwise spied on."

I pictured Mrs. Fisker with an aluminum foil hat and reached for my cell phone, ready to tell Nate or Baxter about her. A weight settled on my chest as reality rushed back. "If you happen to receive another email like the last, will you please let me know?"

"Certainly."

I disconnected and crossed her name off Randall's list. The other conversations went the same way. Nothing recent and no one kept the email for me to examine. Apparently the rules of online safety had spread in this community and morphed into near paranoia. Everyone loved the concept of online scheduling, however.

Warren stopped pretending not to listen and stared as I ended the final call. "What did they say?"

"Everyone said they received their scheduling emails in the last two to three weeks. Same with the coupon emails. I left a message for the only resident on the list who didn't answer."

He nodded. "Nothing last night."

"No. The system's airtight. The scheduling emails aren't coming from here. They never were."

I slid the card into my desk drawer. "I'm going to send another email. We should remind everyone about the problem and caution them about clubhouse email offering coupons or offering to set appointments."

I set up my laptop and cracked my knuckles. My fingers hovered over the keyboard. I needed the right words, strong enough to persuade them to listen, but vague enough not to induce a panic.

An hour later, I'd finally settled on the right words and hit Send.

My phone buzzed with a text and I accidentally knocked it off my desk rushing to get a hold of it. Every new text sent a rocket of hope through me. I swooped it off the floor and swiped the screen to life. Was it Nate? No. Bree had sent a picture of her baby trying on hats at the mall. I relaxed against the back of my chair and forced away images of Baxter's face from my mind.

A jolt of possibility jerked me into motion. Maybe Nate had tried to contact me through REIGN, our favorite online role-playing game. Maybe he'd avoided contacting me directly for a reason. He could be on the run. The killer might be after him. Nate could be a witness to Baxter's murder. My imagination threw together endless scenarios as I pulled up the login screen and accessed my kingdom. REIGN would be a brilliant way to trade messages. He, Baxter and I played every day and often into the night. Our kingdoms were allied. I had three messages in the forum. One commoner requested refuge in my castle in exchange for a leather pouch of pixie dust. The second message came from my seers and warned of spies in the midst. The last message announced the success of my archenemy, Punisher, in poisoning my apple orchard. No message from Nate. No activity on his account.

"Dammit." I clenched my teeth.

Warren looked worried.

"Sorry. Not you. It's this game. Never mind." I exhaled and left a message for Nate, then set a trap for the dirty punk who poisoned my apples. "Poison my land again and my people will stone you to death with all these foul fruits." I spoke the words as I typed.

Warren leaned away from me.

I needed a plan to annihilate my nemesis before he or she stole all the fun I had playing REIGN. I sent messages to other kingdoms by falcons. Maybe a few strong adversaries could fortify my kingdom. I loathed Punisher the minute I saw his dumb screen name. REIGN is a medieval kingdom game. Punisher is a Marvel Comics character. Get your fandoms straight, man.

I logged off.

Next task: Research for Lacy Foster. Who is Wilbur Donahue?

I opened a set of saved websites and printed everything I found on Wilbur from a copy of his driver's license to his credit reports, mortgage papers and college transcripts. Half an hour later, I knew more about Wilbur than he did. For example, I wasn't the only one checking up on him. Someone else had pulled all his recent records and left a cyber-footprint behind. Interestingly, Wilbur had lived in Horseshoe Falls during the same time period I'd once lived here with Grandma. I didn't remember him, but I guessed Lacy had met him then, too, while her late husband was alive.

My tummy growled. I'd forgotten breakfast in the rush to catch Nate at The Beanery. I printed and hole-punched the last set of papers on Wilbur Donahue and secured them into a discreet black folder.

I shook my empty coffee cup. "I'm going to get fresh coffee and a bagel from Derby. Do you need anything?"

He shook his head.

"I'll be a few minutes. I need to see one of the residents while I'm out. Can you look into purchasing versus building an auto-email system for follow-up appointments at the clubhouse? Everyone liked that. Too bad it was bogus." And I hadn't thought of it. "We should put a cost analysis together once we figure this mess out."

He nodded. "Got it."

"Thanks." I shuffled toward the door and dropped my empty cup in the trash. Lacy's requested information was tucked safely in the folder under my arm. "Be back in a few."

Jake was leaning against the wall outside my new office door.

I clutched the buttons on my blouse and sucked air. "What are you doing?" I speed-walked away from him, no longer wanting breakfast. I wanted to escape.

He followed me down the hall and out the front door. "Checking up on you. How do you like your temporary office? Do you have everything you need?"

I blinked against the sun. "It's fine." I wasn't sure I'd ever be ready to sit at my old desk again. The ability to deal with traumas wasn't in my mental toolkit. Denial and I, on the other hand, were intimately familiar. "You know, your new title is head of security not head of stalking Mia. There's a whole community out there for your creeping pleasure." My tummy growled, and my heels snapped against the cobblestone walk.

He exhaled loudly, as if *I* exhausted *him*. "Where are we going?"

"*I* have something to do. I have no idea what *you* are doing."

I climbed into a staff golf cart parked outside the maintenance door and set Lacy's folder on the seat beside me.

Jake climbed inside and opened the folder.

"Stop it." I whipped the folder free of his fingers and slapped it against his shoulder. "That's not yours."

"Does this have anything to do with the leggy blonde

who slipped you something shady this morning at the coffee counter?"

"Get out."

"No."

"You're impossible." I started the cart and pointed it down Freedom Drive toward Lacy's house. "This is none of your business, and that leggy blonde has a name. Lacy Foster. *Lacy* is a person, not an object to be ogled. Also, the concierge desk is not called a coffee counter."

"I wasn't ogling her, and you avoided the part where she passed you something suspicious. Was it cash? Drugs?"

I jerked the wheel around a pile of road apples some horse left behind. "You think Lacy deals drugs? Wait. Was I the one selling the drugs or her?"

"You tell me." He stretched and bent his legs, seeking comfort uselessly in the small vehicle.

"What are you wearing?"

He tugged the collar of his crisp white T-shirt and stroked the khaki material over his thighs. "Clothes."

"Where's your uniform? Mark wore a red blazer with a nametag."

"You're obsessed with uniforms. What do you think Freud would say about that?"

I turned my eyes to the road. "Don't analyze me." His words toiled in my mind. Was he suggesting I had a thing for men in uniform? Implying I wanted an authority figure in my life? Whatever. What did Freud know? He'd studied his patients. They were already cuckoo. Was Jake insinuating I belonged in psychiatric care? I leered at his smug face. "You want to know what I think? I think I don't like you."

"Right."

My foot eased off the pedal. "I mean it. I try to like everyone, but the more time I spend with you, the more this feels right, you know?"

The left side of his mouth curved up.

"I'm not kidding."

"That's too bad because Detective Archer thinks I should keep a close eye on you. You're the prime suspect right now."

I jammed the gas and his head bobbed forward. I jammed the brakes and watched it again. "You mean your brother, Detective Archer? Funny. Let me think. Who do I know who would cast me as the number one suspect? Hmm." I tapped my chin for dramatic effect. "Did someone who looks exactly like you come to mind for you too?"

His smile grew. "My brother's a good detective. You can trust him to follow the facts, not my advice."

I gunned the cart, and Jake braced a hand on the dash. He sounded too much like Bree. She spent so much time announcing I never listened to her that I eventually stopped listening to her intentionally.

This wasn't about me. This was all him. "Is that why you try so hard to figure everything out? Are you trying to impress your big brother?"

"Younger brother."

I whistled. "Ouch."

"No. Not ouch. I'm proud of my family. We come from a long line of cops and military. We make your world safer."

"Thanks."

"You have a problem with our military?"

"What? No. I didn't say that. What is wrong with you? Are you deliberately trying to tick me off or does my face irritate you so much you can't help yourself?"

He turned away instead of answering my question. "Whatever."

Jake spun back around, twisting in his seat and resting one arm across the seatback behind me. "Why were you late this morning?"

"I was looking for Nate."

"Did you find him?"

"No. I haven't been able to reach him since you threw him and Baxter out yesterday. He wasn't home or at The Beanery, a coffee shop down the street from our building. He hasn't been online or answered any of my texts. I don't know if he knows about Baxter or if he's in danger." My grip on the steering wheel turned white.

"You live with him?"

"No. He lives in an apartment upstairs from mine."

"Good to know." Jake looked relieved for some convoluted reason. I refused to guess. He'd twist my words anyway.

"That we don't live together?"

"No, that you were looking for him and not trying to cover something up or help him skip town."

"Right. Because Nate's a suspect too. He killed his best friend and left him in my chair. Why would he do that?"

His serious eyes twinkled in the sunlight. "That's what I plan to find out."

I secured my game face. Maybe this wasn't a game to him. Maybe he did want to solve this crime and not just irk me to death. "Get in line."

FOUR

I PULLED THE cart into Lacy's driveway and gave Jake a threatening look. "I'll be right back. You wait here."

"I don't get you."

I climbed out, tucked the black folder under one arm and scrunched my nose so awkwardly I had to adjust my glasses.

"You're like a hostile Brainy Barbie. You seem like a nice lady, but you go around threatening people's lives, mostly mine today, and I get confused."

"Sorry about your luck." I strode up to Lacy's door and rang the bell. The golf cart was close enough to hit with a rock. I was tempted. "Women can be both cute and fierce, you know. Try joining the millennium. Take notes or something. Oh, and don't ever call me Barbie again."

The door sucked open, and a woman wearing a pale blue dress and white orthopedic sneakers greeted me. "Yes?"

"I'm here to see Mrs. Foster."

The woman shook her head. "Mrs. Foster isn't having visitors."

I smiled. "I understand. Would you please see that she gets this for me? She'll know who it's from."

The woman eyeballed the folder. "What is this?" She put her hands behind her back.

"Mrs. Foster asked me to do a little research for her. She wants this folder." I pushed it forward.

The woman shook her head. Negative.

"It's not a summons or anything. I swear. Look." I pointed to the cart in the driveway. "I'm Mia Connors. I work at the clubhouse."

Her face cracked into a giant grin. "You're Mia Connors? Mary's granddaughter?"

"That's right."

Her arms sprang forward, and she pulled me into a hug. "Your grandmother saved my daughter's wedding. Her products are magic." She whispered the final word. "You're an angel."

Behind me, someone snorted. I refused to look.

"I'm glad you're happy with the results. These papers are for Mrs. Foster. She asked for them earlier."

This time the woman took the folder and clutched it to her chest. "I'll bring them to her now. She's in the garden getting some sun."

"Thanks. Tell her I said I approve." I bounced back to the cart like my personal brand of superhero. Wilbur Donahue was a nice old widower with twenty solid years left in him. Grown kids. Good health. Summer house in Nice. He and Lacy could be quite happy together.

Jake squinted against the sun. "What was that about?"

"She knows my grandmother." I started the cart, enjoying the rush of delivering good news.

"Why did she call you an angel?"

I shrugged, reversed out of the drive and stopped abruptly. A lady wearing a mink stole and tweed dress slacks, despite the summer heat, waved me down with one arm. A set of leashes in her other hand restrained a pack of miniature dogs.

"What the…" Jake leaned toward me as the woman and her tiny pack of canines approached on his side.

"You." She leaned over for a better look at me. "You're in charge of scheduling?"

"Well…I run the computer systems here." I adjusted my posture to hide behind Jake's wide shoulders.

"I've scheduled hair appointments for my babies twice this week only to show up and learn the appointments weren't real. That's not acceptable. I pay obscene dues to the homeowners' association so my fur babies are assured royal treatment."

Jake choked.

The woman turned cold eyes on him.

I worried for his safety. "Mrs. Freemont, right?"

Her focus drifted back to me. "That's right."

"My grandmother is a member of your book club. Her name is Mary Connors. My sister and I occasionally came to your house when we were younger."

Mrs. Freemont worked her jaw. Jet black hair fell against her cheeks and forehead, emphasizing an uncanny pallor. Sharp brown eyes scrutinized mine. "I remember you. You're the one who argued about the stories with my group."

My cheeks burned. "I was an opinionated kid."

Jake puffed air.

I tried to give his side a quick warning pinch but failed. His skin fit snugly over a frame of unyielding concrete. I'd think about that later.

"Mrs. Freemont, I'm on my way back to the clubhouse now. We're aware of the scheduling issues. I promise I'm looking into it, and I'll see what I can do to get your appointment reset as soon as possible."

She straightened with a snap. "See that you do."

"Yes, ma'am." A shiver rocked my body. She always reminded me more of an avenging specter than a retired judge. Bree and I called her Vampira and told scary stories about how the eyes of her paintings followed us through her home. The only fun thing about book club with Grandma was provoking Mrs. Freemont in hopes she'd show her true form, float around breaking things and prove our theory. Never happened, though, and I'd made her pretty mad.

Jake straightened on the seat as we motored back down Freedom Drive. "I guess not everyone thinks you're an angel."

"I'm not an angel. I'm like everyone else. I use my manners, avoid confrontation and mind my own business. I screw things up, too. I've literally lost my best friend, and I have no idea who sent those bogus emails or why. Worse: the residents liked the scheduling option. Some random nut knew my residents better than I do. I'm looking into making online scheduling available as soon as possible. Warren and I can make that happen pretty easily, I think."

Jake watched me without speaking.

"I'm also bunnytrailing. I do that." A lot.

I concentrated on my driving before I said something he'd deem incriminating or I'd deem humiliating.

Fresh-cut grass peppered the air. Maintenance crews were out in full force, mowing, pruning and mulching everything in sight. Emerald-green grass glistened between flower beds bursting with the colors of summer. Kites cluttered the sky near Horseshoe Lake, and puffy white clouds sailed across the sky behind them.

Jake's rough voice yanked me back to our cart of hostility. "You didn't answer my question."

"You didn't ask anything."

"What's your story? If you aren't up to something sketchy, how do you explain the three-hundred-dollar shoes and the four-hundred-dollar bag you stuff your two-thousand-dollar laptop into? You don't make enough at the clubhouse for those things."

The cart zipped into its designated space outside Maintenance and rocked to a sudden stop.

I pried frustrated fingers off the steering wheel. "I don't have to answer those questions."

"Why not?"

"Because they're rude. You never ask a woman about her shoes. Compliment them, maybe, but you don't point out what they cost." I swiveled away, landing my adorable shoes on the sleek concrete slab. "Where are you from anyway, Mars?"

He jumped out and rounded the back bumper, meeting me in two more long strides. "I'm from Ohio, just like you. Are you sure you aren't doing anything illegal? What was in the folder you gave Lacy Foster?"

"I can't tell you, so stop asking, and no, I don't do anything illegal." The wind picked up, and I pressed both palms against my skirt, which wasn't short. "How do you know what I make working at the clubhouse? IT jobs pay well."

He smirked. "Not well enough to keep you in Jimmy Choos."

A smile tugged my lips. "You drive a dirty farm truck and wear work boots. What do you know about Jimmy Choos?"

"Enough. So, do you have a sugar daddy living in Horseshoe Falls?"

I started walking. "Nope. Never poop where you eat."

He kept pace. "Rich boyfriend? Run an escort service?"

I guffawed. "I won't dignify that with an answer. Do you have any idea how sexist and…rude…every one of those assumptions are? I think you just set modern societal progression back a hundred years."

I yanked open the glass door and jumped inside. Shockingly, he didn't follow.

Warren startled when I opened our temporary office door. He'd moved our desks side by side and separated them the way we had them in our old office. A wad of orange and blue cables poked free from his grip. "The cords are a mess, but I got the desks moved."

The wave of frustration Jake had delivered fell away. "Thanks. This is great." I went straight for my desk and collapsed onto the uncomfortable chair. "I got another complaint while I was out. People responded really well to the bogus emails. We need to get that feature going for real. And soon."

He gave up on the cables and slicked long black bangs across his forehead. "I bookmarked some sites and compiled some figures. We can probably build what we need in house."

"Thanks for looking into that." I rubbed the bridge of my nose beneath my glasses. As important as work was to me, I'd rather uncover the truth about what happened to Baxter and why Nate vanished than deal with a bizarre email scheme. Restless energy set me on my feet with nowhere to go.

Warren lowered his voice. "How are you doing?"

Terrible. "Staying busy." I looked at the closed door. "Did you hear anything about why Mark left?"

Warren shook his head.

I cracked open the door and peered into the empty

hallway. "Me either. I'm going to go ask Randall about Mark."

I got in line at the Welcome Desk and checked my text messages. Bree sent three. Ren Faire tonight. Don't forget. Don't be late.

Be there at five. Tell me you got this message.

Ren Faire tonight!

Mom left a voice mail, *"How are you, sweetheart? I know you're hurting. We love you. Let's talk."*

Randall rapped his knuckles on the desk. "You're up, Mia. Tell me you fixed the system."

The line in front of me had vanished. "Sorry." I crossed six feet of empty space to Randall. "The system is fine. Something else is going on. Don't worry. I have a plan to find out."

He dropped his forehead onto the cool granite desktop. "I have no idea what that means. I hope it means there won't be any more emails promising things they shouldn't. You're killing me."

"That's what it means."

He lifted his face. "You don't know how much I hope you're right. Anything else?"

"I came to see what you know about Mark. Is he okay? Why'd he leave? Will he be back?"

"Ah. The second most popular question of the day." Randall tugged heavy caterpillar eyebrow hair between his thumb and first finger. "It's murky. Mark took some family leave time. He has twelve weeks off. He didn't say why. What's wrong? You don't like the new guy?"

"Not particularly."

"Huh." He scanned the area. "He seems pretty good. Very thorough."

"Tell me about it. He's been following me, trying to catch me doing something illegal."

Randall's eyebrows hit his hairline. "Like what?"

"Anything." My phone rang, and I answered without looking at caller ID. "Hello?"

Bree huffed into the receiver. "Finally. Where are you? You didn't return any of my messages."

"I just got them. I don't know why you get so worked up. I've never missed the Ren Faire, and I'm usually not very late."

"Good. Are you home? I'll come pick you up on my way. Is four okay?"

I checked my watch and cringed. "I'm at Horseshoe Falls."

"Oh. Okay, that's good. You're riding with Grandma?"

I slunk away from the Welcome Desk with an apologetic wave to Randall. Guilt slowed my pace, but I powered on. Randall was counting on me to fix the email problem. My family was counting on me to be at the Faire tonight.

Nate wasn't on REIGN, but he might be at the Faire. We could talk there, away from prying eyes. I hustled down the hall to my office.

"Bree? I'm working, but I'll be there at five. See you tonight." I hung up, hoping my enthusiastic tone bought some time before she called back. Just in case, I told my phone to send her calls to voice mail.

I BABY-STEPPED CLOSER to the green velvet gown hanging on my door and stuck both arms under the skirt. When my fingertips reached the gown's armholes, I flopped twenty pounds of material over my head and let the hanger clatter onto the hardwood floor. I shimmied until the gown settled onto my curves, accentuating a bounty of good genes in the Connors family pool.

The best part of playing Queen Guinevere was the pair of delicate golden flats. As much as I loved designer heels, there was something magical about wandering flat-footed through the forest. I smiled at my reflection and started on the makeup.

An hour later, I'd curled endless brown locks into perfect medieval spirals and was officially late. I grabbed Queen Guinevere's elaborate golden crown and stuffed it into my bag. The crown never fit inside the MINI. Not on my head anyway.

Bree's texts started fresh at five sharp. Late or not, I couldn't leave without checking Nate's apartment one more time. I grabbed his dusty key from the dish at my door and pushed the up button for the elevator. Nate had given me a key to his place in case he locked himself out or needed me to take in his mail. He made me swear never to use it. A promise I'd upheld until he disappeared.

I slid the key into Nate's lock and turned the knob with bated breath. An attack of nerves coiled my tummy. Who knew what I might find behind this door? I swallowed hard, talking myself into the invasion. What was the worst thing that could happen? I'd rather find him in a compromising position than not find him. Of course, if he was inside and unharmed, he might get a good thumping from me.

I flipped on the lights and crept through the apartment. No Nate. A cereal bowl and coffee mug sat unwashed in his sink. His bed was unmade. Dresser drawers were ajar. Boxing gloves, high tops and wrist tape lay on the floor outside his closet. The giant black gym bag he carried them in was gone. Not a good sign.

His spare laptop was open on the nightstand. I swiped my finger across the mouse pad and the screen flickered to life. The official website for Ohio Comic Con glowed in the darkened room. Not exactly the case-cracking clue I hoped for.

The alarm on my phone dinged, and I nearly fell into the wall. I was beyond late. I crossed Nate's apartment to the door on hurried feet. There was still a chance he'd show up at the Faire. I slipped back into the hall and locked Nate's door behind me.

Carl and a woman in Harry Potter glasses stared. Their matching mechanic shirts had names embroidered over the pockets—Rick and Amy. Carl's shirt hung open. He wore a vintage Atari T-shirt underneath. His messy black hair poked free from the base of a giant beanie. Hipsters were the bane of my existence.

I grabbed the bulk of my skirt in both fists and scrambled to the elevator before it left our floor.

To his credit, Carl didn't say a word. As the elevator doors closed, he performed an elaborate bow. Their laughter followed me to the first floor.

Hipsters.

Twenty minutes later, I was with my people. Hundreds of others dressed in variations of medieval attire filled the parking lot at Camelot. A giant wooden sign with a red arrow pointed the way to the Enchanted Forest. In the off-season, the Enchanted Forest doubled as a popular apple orchard and picnic area. I parked the MINI near the road, where it was least likely to get stuck in the soft field, and unloaded my portable peasant cart from the back. A few quick assembly moves and I was in business. I filled the cart with my things and pulled it toward the trees.

A soldier approached with his cap pressed to his

chest. "Milady." He bowed. "Allow me to assist you with your burden."

I nodded magnanimously, and the man took my cart. He followed me down the well-trodden path toward the evening marketplace, which officially opened for business in thirty minutes. Families lined up for a chance to have their picture taken in the stocks. Men wielding mugs of ale and giant turkey drumsticks roared with laughter as a jester worked two silly-faced marionettes. The music in the forest lightened my step. A hundred yards later we arrived at Guinevere's Golden Beauty, Grandma's booth, located outside the jousting arena.

The booth looked amazing. Bree arrived hours before every event and transformed the standard lackluster space into something magical. She'd outdone herself this time. Twinkle lights lined the counter and colorful roofline where rich green and blue fabric hung over the edges in flag-like points. Eight-foot poles stood at every corner bearing full-color vertical logo banners with intricate gold detail. Baskets decorated the display surface, brimming with product samples in tiny organza drawstring bags tied with twine and a business card.

Some vendors went for a shabby chic look at their booths. Bree went for stun-them-into-stopping. And it worked every time.

Grandma and Grandpa had made a modest living selling organic lotions, holistic remedies and all-natural skin treatments before organic, holistic and all natural were *en vogue*. Bree and I grew up attending Renaissance Faires, like Mom had before us. Kids at school thought the concept was weird, but I loved it. Medieval costume play was a family tradition. When Grandpa died, Grandma went into a funk. She stopped going to the Faires. She said it wasn't the same without him.

One night I heard Mom tell Dad Grandma would lose their tiny house on Middle Street if she didn't get back to work soon, so I decided to help.

I set up the Guinevere's Golden Beauty website and accepted orders on a global scale. Every day after school, I visited Grandma and told her my friends and their moms had placed orders. I helped her make and package the products on her dining room table. When the website was featured in *Ren Faire Magazine*, sales skyrocketed, and I had to confess what I'd done. For some reason, Grandma didn't believe I landed twelve hundred eye cream orders at the skating rink.

When she saw the site, she thought it was a sign from Grandpa that he wanted her to continue building the brand they'd created together. That was how I became a sixteen-year-old Chief Information Officer and the face of Guinevere's Golden Beauty. Grandma sold the house on Middle Street and moved into Horseshoe Falls my junior year in high school. I lived with her for a while after graduation as the company adjusted to its growing pains.

I nodded my approval to the soldier commanding my cart.

He parked my supply cart beside Grandma's booth and bowed dramatically. "May I get you anything else, Queen Guinevere?"

"That will be all."

He walked away with a jaunt to his step.

Before I had a chance to turn around, Mom attacked me with love. "Oh, my stars! I thought you were hurt or worse."

"I'm fine." I extricated my limbs from her death grip and smiled. "The booth looks amazing. Sorry I'm late."

Grandma's voice scratched the air. Her long white

braid hung over one shoulder to her waist. "Don't mention it. We've got another fifteen minutes before the evening marketplace opens. I don't know why everyone makes such a fuss about helping me set up. I've done this for longer than most of you have been alive. I don't need help."

"Hi, Grandma." I smiled at her grumpy face. She loved this as much as I did. Costumes. Family. Make-believe.

The overall transformation of an otherwise ordinary orchard to Camelot, kingdom of Lancelot, was remarkable. The regulars went to great lengths to shut out the ordinary world and submerge visitors into another realm. The fruits of their efforts stole my breath. The setting made the costumes natural, fitting and enchanting. I smiled against Mom's shoulder. Inside Camelot, all was well. As daylight turned to dusk, the scene became magical.

Mom stiffened. Her hand stilled on my back. "Here come those blasted tree faeries again."

I snickered. Mom hated the faeries. Every Ren Faire had a group of women in minimal clothing, occasionally plastic leaves and painted skin. They wore headpieces made of flowers and danced around in big lithe steps. In the orchard they were tree faeries. I loved their pretty costumes.

They moved like ballerinas through the trees. Four faeries sashayed to my side, lifting tendrils of my hair and whispering to one another. Two were blue and two were green. All were doused in body shimmer. They held hands and circled me, skipping for the queen. "Oh, you look marvelous, your majesty! Marvelous," they chanted, "beautiful, enchanting. So much prettier in this. Your disguise as a harlot didn't suit. No. No. The harlot didn't suit."

Mom butted in, separating their joined hands. "All right, that's enough. That's my daughter you're talking about. Scram."

The faeries skittered away, casting ugly looks at Mom.

"Faeries," she harrumphed.

"Never mind them. Give me a hand." Grandma, the one who didn't need help, called us to adjust twinkle lights on flags and banners with my younger face on them. The coy expression and soft lighting made me look like the real deal, a true Renaissance beauty. The banners stretched over Grandma's display and anchored the posts on either side.

A strand of white lights dropped through the tree-tops, closely followed by a string of curses.

I cupped my hands around my mouth and spoke into the thick leafy branches. "Hi, Daddy."

"Hello, darlin'."

Nope. Grandma didn't need any help. Just a light-ing man, a face for the company, some sales reps and help with her banners and flags. She had everything else under control.

I fed the lost lights back up Dad's ladder and helped Mom adjust the banners. Grandma stacked her prod-ucts on enormous tree stumps and a makeshift set of natural display tables.

Trumpets screamed through hidden speakers. The jovial boom of a man's voice announced, "Jousting will begin in five minutes. Bring ye banners and ye kin for the battle of the century. Don't forget: roast chicken, drumsticks and ribs meals are available at the Peddler's

Marketplace outside the arena for twelve dollars. Commemorative shirts are available at the castle gates."

Another blast of trumpets and madrigal music replaced the announcer's voice.

Mom clapped her hands. "Look alive. When the joust ends, the crowd will be worked up and primed to buy."

Grandma tossed an empty product box out of her booth and adjusted her Visa and MasterCard Accepted sign. "It's a crying shame. These things get more commercialized every year."

I tossed the discarded box into my cart and scanned the area for someone to take it away. "What did the faeries mean about me dressing like a harlot?"

Mom helped Dad down the ladder and brushed him off.

Dad kissed my head. "Bree's dressed as a harlot, and Tom's a pirate."

"A pirate?"

Mom nodded. "Yes. It's all part of their study on human sexuality. She's selling the goods, and he's stealing enough booty to buy him a little."

"Mom!"

She wrinkled her nose and looked at Dad. "That's what she said, isn't it?"

My parents were dressed as gypsies. They used the Ren Faire as a free pass to drink more than necessary and relive their youth. For a retired cop and second-grade teacher, that meant two bonus goblets of rum punch and some public necking. I hated the canoodling when I was younger, but lately I'd found it kind of sweet.

Dad heaved a sigh. Apparently he wasn't as impressed with Bree and Tom's role-playing, even in the name of research. "Have you heard from Nate?"

"No." Another wave of anxiety flooded through me. "It's like he vanished. I can't reach him online or by phone. I tried his apartment, and it looked like it always does. A little messy, nothing notable. His gym bag was emptied. The bag was gone, but maybe he put it in the laundry."

Dad rubbed his chin. "Could he be on the run?"

My tummy somersaulted. "I don't know. I thought the same thing and I hate it." I scanned the area. "I'd hoped to find him here. If he needed to see me, this would be the perfect place."

"Your mother and I have been here since the gates opened. I haven't caught sight of him yet, but I'll keep an eye out, maybe do a few extra laps through the forest."

I patted Dad's arm. "Thanks. I think he might be in real trouble. He and Baxter had something to tell me. They practically ran down the hall to get to me at the clubhouse, and then our new head of security threw them out. I never got to hear what they wanted to say. That night, the alarm went off. You know the rest."

"Did you find his laptop? Maybe you could do your thing and find out where he went, who he talked to last, something like that."

"His laptop." I was so incredibly dense. Why hadn't I looked through his laptop? I'd checked the last page he visited but left the computer behind. If his place was on fire, he'd run into the street wearing nothing but a sheet if it meant he could save his laptop. If Dad was right, Nate wouldn't have left his laptop behind for no reason, not even his spare. If he was on the run and needed help, he would've left a clue there intentionally.

"Great idea. I'll go straight there after the Faire."

Tom appeared behind Dad, swinging a giant curved

sword. "Ahoy! I have plundered my fair share of treasure and am headed to the whorehouse!"

Dad's eye's drooped shut. "Mia, whoever marries into this family is fundamentally insane."

I patted his back. "Daddy's right, Tom. It's called a brothel."

Tom's sword flicked upward and smacked a low-hanging limb. "Ho there, yonder harlot."

Bree stormed to my side, boobs bouncing. The fifteen pounds she'd kept after pregnancy tested the stitching of her costume. "There you are."

"Here I am." I moved one palm in a circle between us. "And there you are, a whole-heck-of-a-lot of you. Aren't you cold?"

Tom grabbed her by the waist and hauled her to his side. "I claim thee as my wench." He lowered his voice to a whisper. "Is anyone looking?"

Dad went back to the lights, shaking his head.

"I can't stop staring at your boobs," I admitted.

Bree beamed. "Good. We don't want to skew the study into traditional male/female perspectives." She arched her back. "Do you want to touch them?"

"Ew. No. I'm your sister, and they look exactly like mine."

"Mine are bigger."

"So's your ass."

Grandma laughed. "Come now, girls. Guinevere, bring your wench and pirate friends."

We moved in a horizontal line toward Grandma, with Bree at the center.

Tom spoke over Bree's head. "Are you ever attracted to women? For example, if they weren't your sister's breasts. What then?"

I groaned. "I like men."

He frowned. "Always?"

"Pretty much."

Tom made a face. "When you said you couldn't stop looking at her breasts…"

"They're my identical boobs, and they're on display. It's unnerving." I motioned to the plunging neckline of my gown. "This is as low as I go." I lifted a finger toward Bree's top. "That is sinful."

Bree laughed. "A working girl's got to show off the goods if she wants men to pay for a sample."

Dad groaned, abandoned his post and headed toward the Peddler's Marketplace. "I need more rum." And a place he couldn't see or hear his harlot daughter, apparently.

A chuckle spread through my family.

Mom covered her lips with one hand and looked at Bree and Tom. "You two realize this sex study will probably give him another ulcer."

"Yeah," I added, "or a stroke."

A peddler pushing a cart full of pint-sized wooden barrels passed us and stopped at Tom's side. "Greetings, fair countryman. Can I interest ye in a keg of ale?"

Grandma whistled. "Got any rum punch in those barrels?"

"Why, yes. I have four, milady."

Grandma held a fistful of cash overhead. "Sold!"

Bree grabbed my arm and squeezed. "I'm so excited you're coming to dinner the day after tomorrow. We're celebrating the human sexuality grant, and I'm planning a themed dinner."

Oh, boy. I accepted my pint-sized barrel of rum punch with a curtsy. "Wouldn't miss it."

REALITY HIT HARD as I parked outside my building. Still no sign of Nate's car on the street, not that I'd expected to see it anymore. My hopes that he'd pop up with a decent explanation dwindled by the hour. Nate had officially been missing for twenty-four hours. After I nabbed his spare laptop for a closer look, I planned to call the police and file a report.

The elevator ride to Nate's floor was excruciating. Had it always taken so long to climb three floors? Anticipation collected in my chest and strangled me. When the doors finally opened, I hiked my skirt up and hustled to Nate's door.

The door stood open several inches. After a consult with my better judgment, I kicked the door open and screamed, "He-yah!"

Nothing.

I flipped on the lights and gasped at the scene around me. Cushions were overturned. Cupboards emptied.

I ran to the bedroom. No more laptop. "Oh, no." My heart sank.

Now I had two reasons to call the police.

Detective Archer arrived first. Jake came with him.

"You say you let yourself in?" the detective asked.

"After work, yes. I have a spare key for emergencies."

He raised a questioning brow. "And you came back a second time. For what reason?"

"I came to see if he'd made it home yet." I followed the lie with a true statement to keep karma at bay. "I've been checking on him constantly since he left my office yesterday morning."

"And he hasn't attempted to contact you?"

"No."

"And the place didn't look like this after work today?"

"No. Someone did this while I was away."

He gave me a tender look. "You were lucky. Clearly you came close to sharing space with whoever did this. Better you weren't here when the intruder came to tear the place up."

My stomach dropped.

"Can I file a missing person's report? It's been more than twenty-four hours."

He nodded. "Already done. For future reference, you aren't required to wait twenty-four hours to file the report, though our response time is determined on a case-by-case basis."

That was brand new information. Wait. "Did you say there's already a report filed?"

"Absolutely. I want to find your friend as much as you do. I need to bring him in for questioning."

Nerve-slicked hands curved over my hips. Indignation burned in my gut. "If Nate's on the run, he's probably in danger."

Detective Archer matched my stance. "If he's on the run, he's probably guilty." He walked away.

I didn't miss him.

Jake leaned against Nate's kitchen counter with an amused expression. "Dan is assigned to this case. He's a homicide detective, so you'll be seeing a lot of him."

"I assumed."

"We were together when he got the call tonight. I recognized the address, so I tagged along."

I slumped against the wall.

"Dan's good at his job. He'll find your friend and collar the killer. Don't worry about it."

Dan picked his way through the debris with a look of determination I appreciated.

I lifted my gaze to Jake's. "What do you mean, you recognized the address?"

"From your personnel file."

"What?" My teeth snapped shut. Was he kidding?

He turned his palms to face me. "Hey, it's just personnel stuff. Nothing interesting or personal."

"Right. Nothing personal. Just my address, phone number, social security number and résumé."

He blinked. "Those aren't the kind of things I want to know."

I crossed my arms in a fit of pique, and my constricted bosom heaved. Heat rose up my neck as I realized why he and Dan looked so mightily entertained at a crime scene. I lifted my chin. "What do you mean? What do you want to know?"

"For starters? How about why you're dressed like that?"

I gathered my skirt and headed for the door before the humiliation burning in my neck and face caught fire. "Goodbye. I'll be back to clean up after you leave."

Jake chuckled. "Really? What sort of costume will you wear for that?"

I tapped my foot outside the elevator. "Shut up."

The silver doors parted, and Carl stepped out with his buddies, Quake and Ben. Quake wore a fedora and pencil tie with a tuxedo T-shirt and baggy black slacks. Ben wore white polyester circa *Saturday Night Fever*.

"What's up?" Quake asked.

I climbed inside the elevator and pressed the close button.

Carl clapped Quake on the shoulder. "She lost her friend, dude."

"Bummer."

The three of them sucked on sodas and stared until the doors shut.

Men.

FIVE

I PULLED INTO the clubhouse parking lot an hour early, thanks to the triple-shot iced espresso I'd chosen in lieu of breakfast. As anticipated, my bladder was full and my parking space was empty. Today would be a good day. I shifted into Park and patted the steering wheel. "Nice work, Stella, but Mama's got to go." I grabbed my bag and waddled full speed to the ladies' room.

I emerged five minutes later to Jake's bored expression. He was leaning against the hallway wall, looking nothing like a wallflower.

"Jeez!" I straightened my knee-length pencil skirt and adjusted my blouse, angry that his snide comment on my skirt length resulted in me trying on seven skirts before work.

I dug up my inner blasé. "You know that's creepy, right? Lurking outside the ladies' room? I'm a social mess and I know that much."

He frowned. "Are you a social mess because you're single or because you like to dress in period costumes?"

I pointed a finger at his infuriating two-day stubble. What was I saying?

"Are you going to use that finger for something or put it away?"

"I'm thinking. Oh, yeah. I was dressed as Queen Guinevere of Camelot because I am Queen Guinevere of Camelot. Ask anyone at the Renaissance Faire.

They'll tell you. I like dressing up and so does my family. It's fun, so take your judgy little look and stow it."

"Your whole family, huh?"

I sighed. "Yes. All of us. We're a completely codependent bunch of nuts." My mind raced back to the point I'd had in mind earlier. I shook my finger. "I'm single because I choose to be, by the way. Single is a choice, not a disability, and dating is an unnerving, exhausting, occasionally crude ritual I'm thankful to be finished with."

He smiled. "Is that so?"

My cheeks heated under his stare. "Yes. That's so. As it turns out, brains and brawn don't spend nearly enough time together."

"Ah." He levered his lean frame off the wall and stuffed long, tan fingers into his pockets. "Brawn is something you look for?"

"Brains too."

"Huh. You shared some private time with the vic, and I don't mean to speak ill, but…" He tilted a palm left and right, implying he thought Baxter was only so-so. Nice of him to have an opinion on someone he'd seen for less than five minutes.

"His name is Baxter, and I don't want to talk about that. Baxter and I were a mistake." I made my way along polished stone floors to the carpeted hallway where our offices hid.

"Would you say you make a lot of those mistakes?"

Nice try. "Turn up your hearing aid, buddy. I said I'm not talking about it."

His step stuttered. "How old do you think I am?"

"I don't know, forty?" I doubted he was a day over thirty-five, but irritating him was a nice turn of play.

"I'm thirty-three."

I feigned indifference.

His cocky disposition recovered smoothly from my jibe. "Fine. You don't want to talk about Baxter. What would you like to talk about?"

"I see you haven't managed to dig up a uniform. What's the problem? Couldn't find one to fit your ego?"

"That's a very funny joke," he deadpanned. "Anything else on your mind?"

I stopped and lifted a distrusting eyebrow. "What do you mean?"

He shrugged. "You always look like you want to say something, but you never do. I thought I'd just ask."

I bit my lip. It was hard enough not to babble in his presence. An open invitation to spill my guts on any topic of my choosing was like tossing a tennis ball to a terrier. I'd never stop if I got started. Praise the Lord, my new office door came into view. "This is where I get off." My cheeks scorched, and I cast my gaze away. "I have to work on the system. Busy, busy, busy." I slid inside the office and leaned against the closed door.

Warren stood at his desk, removing his laptop bag from his shoulder. "Morning."

"Hi, Warren."

He sank into his seat. "Any more mysterious emails?"

"Nope." I tugged my lip between my thumb and first finger. "I was up last night thinking about it. What could be the purpose for fake scheduling? Phishing, right?" I released my lip and gave Warren a long look. He'd have access to resident emails and the specs for our logo. "Any chance you sent the email to Horseshoe Falls residents? Maybe you were looking to make an impression. Drum up clubhouse business. Build rapport between our department and the community. Anything like that? If you had an idea and ran with it, but something went haywire and you didn't want to tell me before…now's a great time to clue me in. Nothing wrong with a little initiative." I forced a smile. I'd kill him with my bare hands if he'd caused this hellacious mess and hadn't fessed up yet.

"No."

I heaved a sigh. "I didn't figure." I flopped into the unforgiving chair. "I don't get it. Someone caused this mess, but why? It's like the Salem witch trials, and we're the ones on trial."

Warren cleared his throat. "Funny you should say that. Have you checked your company email this morning?"

I eyeballed my laptop. "No. What now?"

"Witch hunting."

I booted up my laptop and opened my email with trepidation. At this point, anything was possible. The Horseshoe Falls founder and his army of suits were meeting at Derby inside the clubhouse for lunch. I could only guess what they wanted.

"I need more coffee and a lot of answers before they get here. What should I say if they corner me? I can't explain what happened. It's nonsensical. It's…inconceivable."

Warren tapped his fingers on his desk. "I bet they're coming to fire us. They'll probably do anything to make a point."

"What point?"

"That they can." The tight set of his jaw told me he was as happy about the boss coming as I was.

Warren and I might not have long meaningful conversations, but we had camaraderie.

"Right." I'd lost one friend and misplaced another, but it was time I figured this out before others started losing their jobs. "Do we have an exact date on when the last round of bogus emails went out?"

Warren twitched. "Last week, I think." His inflections said he had no idea. "Why? What are you thinking?"

"I don't know yet. At least we know the system is locked down. If an unauthorized hack touches my network, I'll be able to find them. I warned the residents to contact me if they get any correspondence from the clubhouse with links and not to click them until further notice. Now, I have to hope they read my email."

I worked steadily until noon, keeping my mind as busy as possible until I could get a look at the email in question. Thirty minutes later, I grabbed an information packet I'd compiled for a regular of mine and made plans to meet him in the lobby. He always had something for me to look into. Sometimes it was the scoop on a man his daughter dated. Sometimes it was a comparative analysis of new car models. Whatever he wanted to know, I turned the information over with pleasure.

"I'll be back." I tucked a completed summary of the best retirement communities in Italy under one arm and left Warren to his work.

I turned the corner, scanning for my client in the pro shop and found something better. Quinn Masters, Operating Manager of the Doggy Diva Day Spa, was scooting a canine cupcake display outside the doggy salon's door.

I zipped to his side and struck a pose. "How do I look?"

He did a stage sigh. "You look like the cover of a magazine. How do you do it? One day your hair is hanging long and luxurious, accentuating the gifts God gave you, the next day it's twisted into a chignon so elegant it could stop hearts."

I curtsied. "Oh, you."

Quinn's green eyes twinkled over frameless glasses perched at the end of his nose. "Honey, I'm not kidding. Somewhere out there, ballerinas are killing themselves because they don't have that chignon."

"I love you."

He tapped his gelled bleach-blond spikes with careful fingers. "I surrender. What do you need?"

I pursed my lips. "I ran into Mrs. Freemont yesterday."

He pretended to stab himself in the eye then shoot himself in the head. "She's been here three times this month, loaded down with dogs, demanding I honor appointments she never made." His chin flipped up. "Doggy Diva is the number one day spa in this city, nay, the state. She can't waltz in here expecting me to honor her bogus malarkey."

"But..."

"She didn't have an appointment. She still doesn't."

I put my giant brown eyes to use and sidled up to Quinn. My resting expression was a little like deer-caught-in-headlights, but I'd learned to adjust the look to variations of puppy-dog eyes and the ever-useful "Who? Me?"

Quinn didn't protest, so I slipped an arm around his narrow waist. "Here's the thing. There's something wrong with my system, and residents think they made appointments, but the appointments don't register at the clubhouse."

He groaned.

"It wasn't her fault. She really thought she had appointments. I don't know what's happening, but I'm looking into it. I promised her I'd see what I could do about getting her fur babies a nice shampoo and blow-out."

He rolled his eyes up to the ceiling. "When?"

I bounced on my toes a little, jostling him. "She's meeting her book club at Derby in forty minutes. Imagine how happy she'd be to bring the dogs with her and pick them up after book club, with pretty pink bows and freshly polished toenails."

He groaned. "I do love to paint their little nails."

I nodded.

"And those teacup Pomeranians are like baby bunnies." He cupped his hands as if he cradled one inside.

"It's true."

Quinn's head fell back. "Oh, okay, you win. Give me an hour to move some things around."

I hugged him. "Forty minutes. Thank you so much. I totally owe you."

"Yeah, you do." He tapped my nose with one finger and strode away like the runway model he was meant to be.

Next stop, the beauty shop. The clubhouse manager had made a point of saying the hair stylists were honoring fake coupons. I needed a look at one of those coupons.

"Excuse me." The thick British accent I loved snuck up behind me and turned me in a new direction.

I held the folder out to him. "I was just looking for you."

"Did you have any trouble?"

"Not at all, and I'm always glad to help. Hopefully, I've given you plenty to think about and enough information to make a proper decision. If you need anything else, you know how to find me." I tapped the black business card with one gold glimmer nail.

Mr. Greaves dropped the folder into his satchel. "You're quite amazing. I'd bet there's nothing you can't find." His sharp black suit and salt-and-pepper hair gave him the distinguished look I admired. His blatant flattery and sexy accent didn't hurt either.

I didn't want to think about the things I couldn't find. Like a six-foot Irishman. "You'd be surprised."

Frustration burned my belly as I waved goodbye. I could unearth the intricate details of retirement communities in Rome, but I couldn't find my human best friend living upstairs. Carl asked about Nate's car. I hadn't even thought about Baxter's. How did he get here that night?

I slunk toward the beauty salon and rang the bell on the front counter. I'd call my skills flimsy at best, maybe even a hoax.

What did I do, really? Use a search engine? Who didn't? And I let people pay me? Low. Very low.

The herd of questions that had ruined my sleep stampeded through my mind. Where could Nate be? Assuming he was safe, which was the only assumption I'd allow, where would he hide? Until this week I'd have guessed he'd hide out at my place, but he definitely wasn't there. Why hadn't he contacted me to let me know he was safe? The toughest question still was who knew where I worked and where Nate lived? More assumptions. It only made sense that whoever killed Baxter had also ransacked Nate's place.

I tapped the bell again.

Juanita Jenkins hummed her way to the counter in no particular hurry. "Settle down. I heard you." She looked me over and apparently picked up on my funk. "Well, who peed on your pancakes?"

I tried to look less loser-like. "Hi, Juanita. I'm looking into the email glitch. Some residents are getting false coupons, and the system's making appointments that don't register. I understand you were given one of the bogus coupons for services. Did you keep one of them? I'd love to have a look."

She dropped two in front of me with three-inch hot pink talons.

"May I keep them?"

"They aren't doing me a lick of good." She stuck a jumbo nail into her platinum-blond hair and pulled out a pencil. "May I make you an appointment while you're here? Maybe I can do something with that hair? Give it a little lift?"

My head shook out a big no before my lips could form words. "No. Thank you." I stepped backward into the clubhouse atrium and exhaled when she turned away.

I turned the papers over in my fingertips. The little coupons were professional looking. They matched our website's color and font scheme perfectly. Weird. Who'd go to such lengths for a discount haircut from the clubhouse salon? There was an idea. Could the whole scheme be the work of a resident hoping to save a little cash? Worse: What if the coupons were legit and someone hired a consultant for marketing without telling me? Maybe my job was on the line way before I realized.

I pressed a palm to my tummy and headed for the closest chair.

Jake sauntered past with a woman at his side. She looked upset, dotting a handkerchief under each eye.

They must've known one another. Zing! I moved my fingers to rub my temple instead of my tummy.

The woman shook his hand and accepted a business card from him. They didn't know each other. Apparently, he made strangers cry. The woman disappeared through the double glass doors, and Jake turned back. He seemed shocked to find me in a lobby chair.

I did a small wave.

He moved to the couch across from me and leaned against the arm. "Now who's stalking who?"

"I'm resting. This isn't a good morning."

"You've had a lot of those."

"Mostly since you arrived."

He chuckled. "Touché. Did you recognize the woman I was speaking to?"

"Should I?"

"It seems you told me the truth about your relationship with Baxter. That was his girlfriend, Jillian Nader, and she said they'd been dating exclusively for a month."

"That was Jillian?"

He nodded. "Something to add?"

"No. Not a thing. She's cute." Blond hair, blue eyes, freckled cheeks. If she was twenty-five, I was a hundred. "Young." That suited Baxter. Which was to say he had a Y chromosome.

"Not especially. Her driver's license said twenty-nine, so she's about your age. I guess she just has good genes."

I nodded appreciatively until the insult sunk in. "Hey." I pushed to my feet. "Rude."

"Relax. This is good news. Unless you were the mistress, I can see now you weren't involved with the vic— Baxter. You're looking less guilty every day."

I shot him a crazy face. "Excuse me. I didn't know I was a suspect."

"Well, I'm not sure how that information eluded you. You seem smart enough, and I tell you you're a suspect every time I see you."

"Do not."

I shut my eyes and counted down from ten. Was I really going to have a playground "Did too /Did not" argument at my age? It was reckless and irresponsible to let him ruffle my feathers.

"Why were you talking with Baxter's girlfriend? Why would she come here?" I lifted my eyebrows. What was he up to? I stepped closer to him. "Head of clubhouse security doesn't investigate murder. Did your brother put you up to it? Why didn't he talk to her himself? Why'd she agree to come here?"

Jake blinked. "I'm sorry, was that one long question? Your words slur together at that speed."

"I do not slur." My over-enunciation prompted an infuriating grin on his face. I narrowed my eyes, ready for battle.

A doggy yodel and chorus of yippers broke my concentration. Outside Doggy Diva Day Spa, Quinn greeted Mrs. Freemont with over-the-top zeal. She didn't look impressed.

I dragged my stare back to Jake. "I thought you were joking about me as a suspect." At least I'd hoped he never considered it seriously.

Not to mention the elephant again, but it didn't matter what Jake said anyway. He wasn't a cop. Also, I couldn't take anything he said seriously. Every word he spoke seemed designed to frustrate me.

Jake nodded toward Mrs. Freemont. "She looks pleased. You have anything to do with that?"

"Maybe." I walked over to meet Mrs. Freemont outside Doggy Diva. Jake followed. So much for getting a little distance.

"Hi, Mrs. Freemont. I'm so glad your appointment worked out this morning."

She made a sour face. "Quinn told me this was your doing. I suppose I owe you a thank-you."

"It's no problem."

She sidestepped me. "Very well."

I chased her across the atrium. "Mrs. Freemont?"

She was fast without her dogs.

Calling after her earned me a cold stare.

"Sorry to bother you again. I was wondering if you could tell me whether or not you received any coupons like these." I held the coupons from the beauty salon between my fingertips.

She scoffed. "As if I'd let those Dolly Parton look-alikes touch my hair. Do I look like someone interested in a wig to you? How about a beehive? And who in their right mind would print a coupon? It's demeaning."

I'd take that as a no on the hair salon coupons. "Have you ever received an email offer for Doggy Diva?"

Recognition dawned in her eyes. "Actually, yes. The email said I could schedule the fur babies' appointments by clicking on the link, which I did. If I show you, will you go away so I can enjoy my book club without any arguing?"

"Of course."

"It's here in my BlackBerry." She sorted through her phone for several minutes before presenting it to me.

I forwarded the email to myself so I could stare at it later. "Thank you. That helps very much."

She left.

Jeez.

Jake chuckled. "Get your case solved, detective?"

"I'm working on it." I looked around the atrium for anyone out of place, overdressed or staring. Corporate espionage seemed more likely by the minute. After finding Baxter in my chair, I couldn't shake the feeling of being watched. I gave him my most pointed stare. "Can we go somewhere alone? There's something I want to show you."

He laughed again. "Lead the way, my golden beauty."

That's what I get for telling him about my role in Camelot. It wasn't hard to find out why I was there.

I gave him the stink eye. "Congratulations, you can use the internet. You must be so impressed with yourself."

"Well, that will depend heavily on what you're about to show me."

SIX

I BYPASSED MY office for privacy and entered Jake's instead. Mark had used the office for years until his sudden vacation. The room was exactly as Mark left it, save Jake's battered brown satchel on the desk. Wherever Mark was, hopefully he was safe and well. His absence weighted the pile of things I couldn't understand this week.

I organized my mounting thoughts and questions while opening Mrs. Freemont's email on my phone. I read it quickly to myself before clicking the link. The link had stopped working.

Jake arrived on my heels and stared. "Why'd you bring me to my office?"

"I came here so we'd have privacy."

He leaned against the doorway. "What are you up to?"

"I forwarded Mrs. Freemont's bogus scheduling email to myself for a better look." I handed my phone to Jake. "The link's broken now, but the email looks legitimate, and I don't know what that means. I'm worried the founder might have hired a consultant and set up these promotions without telling me. Maybe he planned to try a new email promotion campaign. If the consultants mucked it up, the emails could've gone out prematurely. Hopefully, I'm wrong about that." I chewed the tender skin around one finger. "Can I use your laptop?"

He motioned for me to take the chair behind his desk.

I logged into my email. "If the founder hired someone to work in the system without telling me, it can only mean one thing. He's firing me. Warren says the founder's coming in for lunch at Derby. He never does that. This is a bad thing."

Jake tapped my screen and set the phone on the desk beside his laptop. "I forwarded that to myself. Anything else on your mind?"

I sucked air. "Oh no."

"What?" He leaned over my shoulder, peering at the screen before us.

"Look. See that?" My fingers dashed over the keys, opening new windows. "If you pull the IP address from the email header, you can see where it originated. I don't think this has anything to do with the founder. Maybe, but…" I looked over my shoulder at him and scrunched my face.

"What are you saying?"

"I don't know. Something's hairy. This email was relayed off an anonymous server."

Jake pushed off the chair and leaned against the desk. "And that means?"

"Whoever did this knew what they were doing. They went through a lot of trouble to cover their tracks. I'm not sure the founder and some consultants would go to those lengths. Why bother? Plus, someone capable of this doesn't strike me as the kind to accidentally let a test email go out."

"Okay, then. Any other theories?"

"Just more questions. Always more questions. I find a lead and instead of getting answers, I get more confused."

He laughed softly. "Well, most investigators run

down their share of dead ends before something pans out, and if they were honest, they'd shock you with the number of cases that go unsolved."

I needed aspirin. "Great."

"Something else you want to tell me?"

"Sure." I spun the chair until I faced him. "I didn't go back after the Faire to check on Nate. I'd given up hope he'd magically reappear. I went back to take his spare laptop. He clearly packed a bag but left the laptop, so it had to hold a clue for me. I say 'me' and not 'the police' because Nate came to see me that day, and not because I think your brother is too daft to figure things out. Not that he's daft at all. I don't know why I keep saying 'daft.'" I pressed the heel of one hand to my forehead. "I was there for the laptop." I lifted my palms to the sky. "Happy?"

Jake opened the minifridge beside Mark's desk and handed me a cold bottle of water.

"Thanks." I sipped. The cool water settled my chaotic mind. Was investigation as bleak a career as he described? Maybe that's why he didn't follow his family footpath. I liked solving puzzles, not cutting the pieces into pieces until the whole thing was impossible. I couldn't live like this. It was the most defeating two days of my life.

I set the bottle aside and twisted the cap in place. "I don't know what I was saying."

"You were confessing intent to steal your friend's laptop."

"Oh. Right. I planned to keep it until we found him. He left it for me. I'm positive. When I got there the second time, the place had been tossed, so I called the police. Do you know if anyone has checked Baxter's apartment?"

"I assume. Jillian said she went by and told the land-lord what had happened. Baxter's parents are flying in from Ecuador to handle his estate. Why are you smiling?"

"Baxter's neighbors feed the cat. If they heard he was gone, they'd have gone inside to take the cat. They have a key."

Jake leaned forward. "Are you suggesting we ask his neighbors to let us inside? Do they even know you?"

I bit my lip. "Not really, but it's worth a try, right? If his computer's still there, I can find out why he wanted to talk to me that day and maybe solve his murder."

"And if the computer's not there?"

"Then we visit Jillian."

Jake took his phone out of his pocket and ran his thumb over the screen.

"What are you doing?"

"Letting everyone know I'll be out in the commu-nity this afternoon, not in the office. If they need me, they should text me."

"You're such a liar." I poked his ribs.

He grinned. "It's not a total lie. We'll be in the com-munity. Not *this* community."

I nodded, relieved.

"Mia?"

"Yeah?"

"Anything else you want to confess?"

"You make me nervous."

"Back at ya."

WE TOOK JAKE'S wooly mammoth-sized truck and did our fair share to ruin the ailing ozone. He refused to let me drive us in Stella (because he's a chauvinist), despite the fact I knew how to get to Baxter's. When I offered him the keys, he snorted. Whatever that meant. With no way around entering the beast, I did my best to climb into the cab without looking stupid. I was thankful for my clingy pencil skirt. My usual swing skirts would've given the unfortunate bystanders a look at my Spanx. I felt like a child sitting in Dad's recliner. The interior smelled of wet earth, spearmint and cologne.

I had no idea what to say, so I pretended to text and respond to imaginary emails.

The drive to Akron was brief but informational. I learned, for example, that Jake had a lead foot, no regard for posted speed limits or regular oil changes and he liked country music. The oil change sticker clinging to his windshield curled up on the edges and appeared to have a date from three years ago. A row of CDs with men in tight jeans and cowboy hats lined the visors overhead. Parking stubs from a farmers' market caught my eye.

"I didn't peg you for a farmer." The truck, definitely, but Jake? "When do you have the time?"

Surprise turned to understanding as his gaze moved from my face to the papers on his dashboard. "You don't miss much."

"I lost my best friend."

"We'll find him." Jake drove the truck half onto the curb outside Baxter's building and climbed out. "Baxter lived here?" He frowned at the pink stucco building.

"Pretty, right?"

"Adorable."

"Are you going to leave your truck like that?"

He looked over his shoulder. "Yeah. It's a narrow street. I don't want anyone to come by and hit her."

I never had to park Stella on the sidewalk for her protection, but I doubted he wanted to hear that.

Baxter's neighbors were reluctant to believe my story about leaving a treasured heirloom earring the last time I slept over, but eventually they let us in after Jake took them aside and said who-knows-what. It didn't hurt that Baxter's neighbors were both women and Jake was easy on the eyes. Not as easy on the ears, but no one was perfect. He slid the spare key into Baxter's lock and pushed open the door with a smug expression. Men.

Everything looked normal to me. Cereal bowl and coffee mug in the sink. Messy bed. A video game controller on the coffee table.

No signs of an intruder. No laptop.

Jake breezed through the rooms and back to the front door. "No one's home. Let's visit Jillian."

According to the DMV database, which I did not hack into with ease, Jillian lived two blocks away on Canal Street. This time, Jake settled the blue beast in her driveway before he rang the bell.

Her door swept open, and I let out a long whistle. An honest-to-goodness underwear model leaned against the doorframe, one arm slung overhead, one hand resting on the waistband of his basketball shorts. He was the Tuff Stuff guy. I ogled his larger-than-life torso every morning when I turned off I-77 North on my way to work. On the Tuff Stuff billboard, he braced a baseball bat on one shoulder and sported black boxer briefs. Their slogan was one for the ages. "Tuff Stuff Underwear: Made for men who play hard." Hubba hubba.

Jake elbowed his way around me. "Is Jillian Nader home?"

The model cocked his head back. "Honey? Company."

Jake shot me a disgusted look and walked inside while I gathered my marbles.

I shuffled behind him, planning ways to tell Bree about this and contemplating a quick phone pic while he wasn't looking.

Did he call Jillian honey?

Jillian was curled under a cream cashmere blanket in the living room. She repositioned herself on the couch and smiled at Jake. "What brings you by, Detective Archer?"

I snorted. Everyone looked my way. Oops.

I turned my rapt attention to the nude oil painting over Jillian's mantle. It wasn't her sexy model friend, but the piece was gorgeous. She had good taste. Her home was well furnished and I loved her hair. I wondered idly what she did for a living and a white lab coat caught my eye. The coat was flattened under a giant baseball jersey, which I assumed was the model's. The navy emblem on the lab coat sleeve was from the company where Baxter worked.

Jake spoke in a steady, authoritative tone I hadn't heard before. "We were in the neighborhood. I thought I'd see if you were doing any better."

The sexy man sat beside Jillian and nuzzled her head with one cheek.

Jake looked at me. The weird strangling sound must've been mine.

I cleared my throat. "Do you have any idea what Baxter and Nate were up to in the days before he…" I couldn't bring myself to say it. "Nate's missing now and, after what happened to Baxter, we need to find him. He could be in danger."

Jillian sniffled. "I don't know. They were working on something for their idiot friend, Mia, I think."

Jake choked back a laugh.

I narrowed my eyes on Jillian. "What do you mean?"

She adjusted the blanket to cover both shoulders. "Who knows? They're such adorable dorks, you know? I think they're both secretly in love with her. I've never met her, but the guys called her Queen." She smirked. "They literally called her Queen. Can you believe it?"

"Nope."

"I guess they wanted to stop some online bully from messing with her in this weird role-playing game, so they tag-teamed him and ended up with some incriminating pretend-evidence or something."

"Aw." They'd worried about me.

Jillian squinted. "What did you say your name was?"

"Uh, well," my brain scrambled for a name. Any name. Elmo. Ronald Reagan. Ronald McDonald. *A woman's name!* "Excuse me. I'm so sorry to be rude." Jackie O. Madonna. "I should have introduced myself."

Jake waited while I mentally flailed. I squinted at him until something cracked in my head.

"I'm Guineve…" My tongue knotted inside my mouth. "Gwen A…Gwen Avon." Mental head-slapping. *Dumb. Dumb. Dork.*

"I'm Jillian. I guess you know that. This is Smoke."

Jake's forehead wrinkled. "Smoke?"

She beamed. "It's his stage name. He's a model."

Jake nodded. "Of course. Well, Mr. Smoke, what is your relationship with Miss Nader?"

Smoke cupped his hand over Jillian's knee. "Jilly Bean is my main thing. My forever girl. My one and only. Ya know?"

I made a mental note to tally up another loss to brawn over brains. "How long has Jillian been your forever girl?"

He shrugged. "Couple weeks."

Jillian's eyes doubled in size. She'd told Jake she was exclusive with Baxter for a month.

I clucked my tongue and waved a dismissive hand. None of that mattered now. "Any chance Baxter or Nate left a laptop over here?"

She shook her head and gripped Smoke's muscled forearm. "I think I need to lie down. Would you show them out?"

He raised one nicely sculpted eyebrow. "I'll meet you upstairs."

Oh boy.

Outside, I wondered, "I don't suppose those two have an open relationship."

"Why? Are you interested?"

"I mean, did she tell Smoke about her and Baxter?"

Jake climbed behind the wheel of his truck and blew out a long breath. "I think she told Smoke that Baxter was just a friend and vice versa." He chuckled darkly.

"Aw. Poor Smoke. All that muscle and not a single clue. Hey." I twisted on the seat to face him. "What was the laugh for? Are you one of those Neanderthals who think men and women can't be friends without wanting sex from each other?"

"Yep."

I groaned. "I think you're trying to provoke me." I turned away and buckled up. "Let's focus, please. You called me a suspect when you thought I was involved with Baxter. Is Jillian a suspect now? What about Smoke? Jealous boyfriend rage? Maybe he knew more about the two of them than he let on and snuffed out the competition. Your brother said jealous boyfriends are unpredictable."

Jake reversed out of the driveway and headed back

toward Horseshoe Falls. "Doubt it. Smoke wouldn't have to kill Baxter. Something tells me that guy could say the word and Baxter would have cut out. Besides, why would the two of them be at the clubhouse?"

I wanted to argue, but he was probably right. How attached could Baxter have been to a girl he only dated for a month? Especially when he hit on me over pizza last weekend? Baxter wasn't the jealous type or the kind of guy who fought over a woman. "Jillian had the same lab coat as Baxter. That explains how they met and she and I never did." I examined the side of Jake's face. "You really don't think men and women can be friends? Nothing more."

He peeked at me. "Not really."

"You're wrong. Look at Nate and me. Surely you have female friends. You and I get along fine."

Jake slowed at a stoplight and turned curious eyes on me. "Jillian thought Baxter and Nate were in love with you."

"That's nonsense. I'd know if that was the case."

"Really? You strike me as the kind of girl who only sees what she can accept."

I turned my face away.

We moved on as the light turned green. "What was she saying back there? You have an online bully?"

I rolled my head against the backrest of his bench seat. "There's this guy playing REIGN online. He poisoned my orchard. Before that, he stole my sheep and burned down my brothel. I hate him."

Jake laughed. A big belly laugh.

"Hey, don't judge. That brothel made a lot of money and provided jobs." I looked away. Good grief. What was I saying? Did I sound like a pimp? I shoved that thought aside. "The guy's a jerk and, thanks to him, I've got soldiers doing farming and my castle's under siege. I sent word to allies in surrounding kingdoms, but the falcons haven't returned yet."

"Sure." Jake nodded. "Can I ask you something?" He glanced at me, seemingly oblivious to my gaming rant. "What's going on with the secret black folders and hush-hush exchanges you make?"

"I told you, I research. That's all I'm saying. It's nothing illegal. I try to help people, and confidentiality is paramount."

"Are you selling corporate secrets? Hacking bank accounts or transferring funds to people who shouldn't get them?"

"Of course not. I use my powers for good." I crossed my legs and looked out my window. "What do you think of me?" I scrutinized his expression, unsure I wanted an answer. "Besides being a murderer, I mean. Do I look like a cyber-criminal, too?"

"White collar criminals never look like criminals. You want to know the truth?"

"People who ask that question are ridiculous."

"I think you're hiding something, and I want to know what it is. You're clearly too smart and completely over-qualified to run the technology department at Horseshoe Falls. Half the residents can't use a smartphone. The other half hate technology, which is why they moved to the little Stepford community in the first place. Horseshoe Falls is all about nature and frontier days living. Why are you there?"

"Don't knock Horseshoe Falls. We have Wi-Fi. Residents can work from home or from the golf course. I make their days better by allowing them to commune with nature while still getting their jobs done. It's peaceful."

"What'd you do, memorize the brochure or write it?" I bit my tongue.

"I checked your personnel file. You make half my salary, and you went to three Ivy League schools. You have to owe more on education than I'll make in a lifetime." His eyes dropped to the diamond tennis bracelet Grandma gave me when sales topped a million dollars my senior year. "You can't be for real. I want to know what's under the façade."

Sheer force of adrenaline curled my toes. If I had the power of teleportation or indestructibility, I'd have jumped from the moving vehicle. He had a sharp eye and some valid points, but they all ended with me being a criminal. A murderer. A thief. A hack for hire.

"I'm not a façade and stop looking in my personnel folder." I dug my fingernails into both palms. "What do you mean I make half as much as you? Head of security makes less than forty thousand a year. I'll have you know I don't make half that. Your records are mistaken."

He focused on the road, unspeaking.

"Wait a minute. Are *you* lying about something? Did you slip up, and I caught you?"

He increased speed, which had dwindled as we argued.

A sense of pride rippled through me. "You have a secret, and I intend to unearth it."

He ignored me and swiped his badge at the guard gate. Bernie nearly keeled over when she spotted me in the passenger seat. I did a little finger wave.

Jake pulled the truck around back and cut the engine. "Do you know everything about the Horseshoe Falls network?"

Okay. Change of subject, then. "Yes. Well, except

where the bogus emails came from, but I'm working on that."

"I have a few questions I think you can help me answer, but I need an assurance of confidentiality."

I watched his face for some sign he was teasing me again. "Go on."

"I'm looking into the recent break-ins. Can you tell me why the security cameras at some residences cut out during the specific time the homes were broken into?"

Randall had mentioned the break-ins at the staff meeting, but I hadn't given them much thought. The notion seemed more fiction than reality. That sort of thing didn't happen here. Then again, I was waist-deep in things that weren't supposed to happen here. "How many were broken into? I'd heard two. Were there more?"

His solemn expression worried me. "No. Just two homes, but the cameras cut out both times and the alarms didn't sound."

"They probably don't set their alarms."

He wrinkled his forehead. "Why not? Why have alarms and not use them? That's careless and, well, dumb."

I motioned to the mini Garden of Eden around us. "Gated community, so..."

He dropped his forehead to the steering wheel. "Everyone here is rich, and the walls are supposed to keep intruders away."

"Yeah, the walls and you. There's a head of security for a reason."

He tilted his face to look at me. "Not helping."

I popped the passenger door open. "Sorry. I want to take a look at the camera and alarm settings. Can you text me a list of specific addresses you'd like reviewed?

I'll see what Warren knows about the timers and if he's heard of any hiccups. Could be related to the problematic emails; could be something else completely."

"Don't say anything to Warren. I need as few people in the inner circle as possible. This way if information on what we're up to is leaked, we'll know it had to be one of us."

I smiled. "I'm in the trust circle? Who else?"

"My brother, Dan."

I swung my feet through the open doorframe. "We sound like the makings of a limerick or a dirty joke. A detective, a security guy and a geek walk into a bar."

"Why do you do that? You're not a geek."

I slid onto the concrete and shut his door. "I am a geek. Haven't you heard? Geek is the new chic." I pulled the pins from my chignon before my brain exploded, and shook wavy brown locks down my back.

Jake jogged to my side and touched his fingers to the small of my back, steering me toward the building.

I rejected the electric sizzle buzzing against the base of my spine. Maybe my butt fell asleep during the ride.

"I know it's not likely, but if the founder hired consultants to create those discounts and scheduling emails, and they sent them before they were ready, they could've caused other problems while they were at it. Anything's possible and consultants are buffoons. Consultants could bring the whole global internet down accidentally, given proper admin rights. I need to ask Randall and the founder about that. I'll feel better if I can mark that possibility, however remote, off my theory list."

Jake pulled the glass clubhouse door open and held it for me. "I'll talk to the founder. You talk with Randall."

I paused to look at Jake as he cleared the threshold.

He tented his brows. "Something else?"

I blew out a frustrated breath. "I'm not a gold digger. I work here because I like the job and I like computers. Yes, I could run this place in my sleep, normally, but I like it here. I like the people, so this is the perfect job. When I said I was a geek, I was serious. I like social media and graphic novels. I obsess over shows, movies and books. I like board games, and I enjoy dressing as Queen Guinevere for the Renaissance Faire. I can't help it. I like things other people think are dorky."

"Like tiny pink cars."

"Yes." I grinned, hyperaware of every staff member and resident in the oversized atrium pointing curious faces our way.

"That is dorky."

I turned away from onlookers and lowered my voice. "There's also my obsession with vintage clothes and online role-playing games like REIGN. I like medieval times and science fiction, and I'm not just the face of Guinevere's Golden Beauty. I own part of the company and act as the CIO. I have since high school when I set up the website that launched my grandmother's company into the public eye."

He stopped smiling.

"So, I'm not a criminal. I'm not a gold digger. I don't need any more money than I already have. Understand?"

Silence.

"Jake?" I dared a look around the room to see who was watching. Predictably, everyone.

He blinked twice and walked away with a wave. "Got it."

The atrium bustled anew with activity. Jake vanished down the employee hallway.

What just happened?

SEVEN

I WORKED DILIGENTLY through the afternoon, hoping to locate the origin of the mysterious emails despite the sender's attempts to cover the trail. Busy as I was, my mind never wandered far from my friends. What had Baxter and Nate learned about my online nemesis, Punisher? Why hadn't I pushed for details from Jillian? Probably she didn't have details. She didn't seem very tech savvy, and she called my friends dorks.

After hours of searching, I hadn't found any answers, but I did update every aspect of the system, down to the minutiae. I examined the email I'd forwarded myself from Mrs. Freemont's phone. The links were broken, but nothing deleted is ever truly gone. I dug up a cached copy of the page residents landed on after clicking the link. The page was impressive, matching my clubhouse emails in every manner, right down to the font. I tried scheduling an appointment, but none of the buttons seemed to work.

Who would go through so much trouble? Corporate espionage came to mind again, but the knot in my tummy insisted there was something more.

I forced the creases off my forehead as mental exhaustion crept over me.

Warren stretched his arms overhead, and I jumped. "Wow. I forgot you were in here."

He smiled and went back to whatever he was working on. "Sorry."

"No problem. I guess I was more focused than I realized." I turned my seat to face his. "The founder and the board have had Randall in their lunch meeting for more than two hours. How do you think it's going?"

He turned his monitor to face me. The founder's face appeared in grainy shades of gray. Warren had been watching them on Derby security cameras. "Randall left them twenty minutes ago."

"Oh!" I jumped up. "Excellent. I need to talk to him."

Would he have gone to his office? I dithered in the hallway, unsure which direction to go. No. As long as the founder was at the clubhouse, Randall would want to be seen working. I turned on my toes and dashed toward the lobby.

Bingo! Randall was squatting beside the concierge desk, picking up fallen sugar packets.

I crouched beside him and helped. "Hey, how was the meeting?"

He stood with an easy smile. "Good. I think I bought us some time. He knows you can figure this computer thing out and Marcella and I can smooth the issues over with the residents until you do."

I straightened to my feet. Air whooshed from my lungs. "That's amazing."

"You're welcome." He looked me over. "Any chance your family might want to build a home here? Your folks would love the community."

"You don't give up." I laughed. "You know them. Horseshoe Falls isn't their style. Plus, they'd never accept any money from me, and they can't afford it here on their pensions."

"Fine, but I won't stop asking. Your family is perfect for Horseshoe Falls. They just don't know it."

"True. Hey, do you think it's possible the founder hired someone to send those emails? What if he was working with a consulting firm to drum up more money for clubhouse services and the consultants somehow sent the emails? Maybe this was a marketing thing gone bad."

"No. I don't think so. He didn't give an indication of anything like that. His main concern seems to be the security breaches. Our community has plenty of competition without being labeled as a crime mecca."

"What about corporate espionage?"

His jaw dropped. "What are you saying?"

I waved a hand between us. "I'm just exploring all the options. You mentioned the break-ins during the meeting the other day. Can you tell me more about that?"

"It's the weirdest thing."

"The security cameras missed the intruder."

Randall leaned against the desk. "How'd you know?"

"Lucky guess." Intuition pinched my ribs. "I think this is all related. Someone's doing more than sending emails to residents. They're using them for crime. What else can you tell me? Anything at all. How much was stolen during the break-ins?"

He puffed out his cheeks. "That's the thing. Nothing was taken. Not a darn thing."

My mouth opened and shut. Who would go through the trouble of hacking a system to cut the cameras so they could break in and leave empty-handed? "That doesn't make any sense. Did the alarms scare them away before they had a chance to take anything? What about barking dogs?"

He shook his head. Negative. He nudged me with his elbow. "How's Bree? Still married to the wealthy brainiac?"

Randall's clear blue eyes twinkled when he said Bree's name. The spark between them was ten years old and sadly, one-sided. "Yep. Three years now. Their daughter's one already."

He gripped his chest in faux agony, though some of the pain was probably real. "She's the one that got away. Don't make my mistakes, Mia. When you find a keeper, hold on to him, or someone wiser will snatch him up and leave you heartbroken."

My cheeks burned. Awkward conversations were my kryptonite.

"Ah, come on." I nudged him back. "She's one fish in an ocean of fish, or something like that. Besides, if you ask me, Bree isn't much of a looker."

His eyes widened and he gave a tiny chuckle. "Yeah, you Connors girls are real hard on the eyes. Ask anyone."

Jake crossed the hall in the distance, phone pressed to his ear.

Randall leaned closer. "What do you think of the new security head? I see him with you a lot. Is he looking into the email thing? Has he said anything about what he thinks happened here that night?"

"I don't know what he's up to. His brother is the detective on the case."

"Detective Archer seemed okay. He asked a lot of questions about my hours and everyone on staff. What do you think that was about? Kind of a wide net."

I scoffed. "Sounds like they've got nothing to go on and they're turning over rocks. Who else did they talk to?"

"Everyone. Ask Juanita." He motioned to the salon where Juanita was pushing a broom over shiny marble floors.

She perked up, stowed the broom and jogged to us on platform wedges. Her neon-pink hot pants and off-the-shoulder top screamed Attention Hound. Her clothes didn't lie. "What's going on? What's the scoop?"

The only one in Horseshoe Falls with bigger stories than Bernie was Juanita.

Randall leaned in her direction with a conspiratorial look in his eye. "I was just telling Mia about the way Detective Archer interviewed everyone after Baxter's death. She thinks that means they don't have any good leads. What do you think?"

Juanita mulled it over. "I don't know. I heard they suspected Mia."

I turned a palm up. "See."

She scanned the area. "Then again, you can't believe everything you hear, and as a hairdresser, I hear plenty."

Randall drew back. "Like what?"

I leaned in.

"Everything." She straightened her blouse, looking a bit guilty. "If you ask me, looking for dirt under every throw rug is bad for business. Things were going along just fine until now. Who knows what they'll find, digging like they are. Nothing good will come from it."

I bit my tongue.

Randall sucked air. "What do you mean?"

She ran the pad of one finger over glossy red lips. "Who knows? This many people working in one place? There's bound to be scandal somewhere. Rule breakers. Hookups. Petty thefts. We'll know soon enough, I suppose. Do either of you know if the new guy's single? Wonder if he's into older women?"

Randall raked both palms across his head. "He's the enemy, Juanita. Focus."

She snapped her gum and smiled. "Maybe. Maybe not, but if he lasts until Christmas, I bet I can get him under the mistletoe."

I pulled my phone from my pocket. "Oh, look, a text for me. I'd better take care of this." I darted back to my desk with a million new questions, not the least of which was why Randall thought Jake was the enemy. Did Randall have something to hide?

I plopped into my desk chair and spun to face Warren. I rubbed the rough brown chair arms. "Looks like we've got a hacker. I found a cached version of the landing page sent out in emails. It replicates my work. Right down to the font. Randall confirmed the founder hasn't hired any consultants. If that's true, then someone is up to no good. I can't understand the point of sending a fake email for scheduling appointments at the clubhouse, though. All they had to enter was their name and address. Worst phishing scheme ever, right? If the community was targeted, the email creator already knows where they live. Do you think someone just wanted to get the owners out of the house so they could be robbed?" That seemed possible. Except no one took anything, which kind of ruined my theory the break-ins were about theft. "It's all very strange, don't you think?"

Warren shrugged, stood and pulled keys from his pocket. "I'm lost. Hackers. Faux coupons. Break-ins where nothing's taken. It's like we're facing a band of random criminals doing random crimes to send us on wild-goose chases or mock us or..." He rubbed puffy eyes with one hand and dangled his keys in the other. "Maybe it's residents' kids playing games? I have no idea. I need to give my mom a ride home from work. Her car's in the shop."

"Take as long as you need."

"If I take more than an hour, I'll make it up during lunch tomorrow."

"Okay." I dialed Jake's extension, mind racing. Were all these things random? Did none of it amount to anything?

"Archer."

"Hey. I need the addresses. This is Mia. The addresses of the homes with the break-ins, I mean. I want to see if there's a pattern. Same street? Were the owners friends? Oh!" I snapped my fingers. "Were the houses broken into while the owners were at the clubhouse trying to get their fake appointments? Maybe the scheduling thing was meant as a guide for the crook to know when the owners would be away from home."

"Who is this?'

"Mia Connors." I stopped short. Didn't I say that? Maybe he didn't recognize my name. "Short. Brunette. You think I'm a criminal."

He sighed. "It was a joke. Obviously I know who you are."

I smiled against the phone. "Could I be right about the scheduling?"

"No. It's a smart theory, but I already looked into that. None of the break-ins happened at a time when the owner came in for a service. One guy said he flagged all club correspondence as spam. He never even saw the emails, and he said coupons were beneath him. If he wanted a service, he'd decide for himself and pay the going rate."

"Wait. Did everyone get the same emails? Scheduling and coupons? Maybe he never got them. Is he sure they went to his spam folder? How often does he empty his spam?"

"I don't know. Why?"

"The hacker might have been targeting homeowners. He screwed up on that guy, but maybe not on the others."

"What do you mean?"

I slapped the desk beside my keyboard. "That guy hated coupons. Why send coupons to a guy who'd never dream of using one? People who are new to money clip coupons. People born with money or who have a new but endless supply of money do not clip coupons. You're terrible at this job, Jake Archer. I need to know which residents got which emails. Hang on. I'm coming to you."

"Meet me out back. Let's grab a coffee and talk somewhere outside the clubhouse."

"'Kay. Let me stop at Stella first. I've got to grab my sunglasses."

I dashed outside on a fresh rush of adrenaline. I needed to contact the clubhouse department heads and ask for a list of residents who complained about scheduling issues or brought in coupons. Why hadn't Randall gotten a complete list to me by now? He seemed desperate for answers, but I asked for a list during the meeting when I learned about the emails and coupons. *Coupons.* What self-respecting country club offered coupons? They cheapened the impact of gated community living.

Sunlight blinded me as I rushed across the half-empty lot toward Stella. She looked comfy in her special parking space, carefully chosen for the ample shade of a large neighboring oak, while maintaining a safe distance from dripping sap, dropping nuts and pooping tree birds.

I plucked the fabric of my blouse away from my skin. The humidity was disgusting. Luckily, I'd had the forethought to leave my windows down.

I popped open the driver's door and stumbled backward. Confusion weighted my mind. I blinked to clear the image, but when I reopened my eyes, it was still there. A shiny silver butcher's knife was crammed into the leather headrest. Someone had dragged the blade down the backrest to approximately belly button height before lodging it up top. I swallowed back bile. My mouth was as dry as the desert, and my tongue filled every inch of space behind my teeth.

I freed my phone with fumbling fingers and dialed Jake.

Black grease letters scrawled over my camel interior demanded STOP.

Jake picked up. "I'm at the truck. What's taking so long? Let's go."

My chin tipped back. My mouth fell open. "Stella!"

EIGHT

THE CIRCUS ARRIVED ten minutes later. Word of the vandalism spread through Horseshoe Falls at an impressive speed. Small knots of residents drifted near the clubhouse parking lot under the guise of dog walking and bird watching when, in fact, no one had been anywhere around when I needed a witness. The clubhouse wasn't a popular hangout this time of day. Unsurprisingly, the cameras covering the lot were down. Whoever had taken them out at resident homes had the same MO. I could only assume his crudely carved message meant for me to *stop* looking into that. The plan backfired horribly. I'd already chewed off half my nail polish, reworking the conundrum.

Jake knocked on the passenger side window for the third time in as many minutes. It became harder to ignore him with each knock. "Come on. Get out of there before you mess up the crime scene."

I glared and turned away. I needed a quiet place to figure this out and my car had seemed the fastest, most obvious choice until Jake started knocking. I'd chosen the passenger seat so I wouldn't disturb the crime scene.

What was I missing?

"Come on, Mia. Dan's here. Get out."

A gas-guzzling four-by-four angled into the lot and parked behind Stella. Custom lights flashed inside the oversized silver grille. What was it with Archer men? Did they hate the ozone?

Jake met Dan outside the truck. Both brothers wedged hands over hips, sneaking looks in my direction and appearing like loose replicas of one another, save the drastic personality differences. I powered down the passenger window. A breeze swept inside, relieving the oppressive greenhouse effect and filling the small space with the sweet fragrance of lilacs. I hadn't dared to open the window with Jake outside complaining about the crime scene.

Dan pushed dark glasses onto his forehead and circled the car. "Get out. You're ruining the crime scene."

Jeez. Maybe they were more alike than I thought.

I motioned to the destroyed leather seat beside me when Dan cornered the hood in my direction. "That is the crime scene."

I wasn't leaving Stella again. She'd been good to me. Never broke down. Never had squeaky brakes or flat tires. I loved her and her bumper-to-bumper maintenance agreement.

Large fingers curled over the window frame at my side. Dan's face poked inside. "The car is the crime scene. If whoever ruined your seat sat there to do it, you've destroyed our chances of finding any clues."

I made a crazy face. "Why would a vandal sit inside the car?"

Dan swiped his sunglasses off and rubbed his forehead. "Oh, I don't know. Maybe it would look less conspicuous if the car was closed up than if someone with a butcher knife and black grease left the driver's door hanging open while they leaned inside and carved up your seat."

Huh.

I opened the door and knocked into him. "Fine."

Jake raised his hands overhead and swore. "How many times did I say that?"

I shut the door too roughly behind me and cringed. "You never said that."

"I did." He ground his teeth. "I told you the exact same thing a hundred times, and you refused to get out. He says it once and out you come. Ridiculous."

I shut my eyes and turned my face away. Jake swore, and Dan chuckled.

My eyes popped open. "This is not funny."

Dan shook his head. "No, ma'am." He opened the driver's door and squatted for a closer look at the damage.

Jake moved behind him. "Cameras were off less than five minutes. The system did an auto shutdown and reboot. No one saw anything. I've got a list of everyone with permissions to the security room, but the door wasn't locked when I went in."

Dan snapped on a pair of blue plastic gloves. "What about the knife?"

"It's a match for Derby's flatware. Grease looks like shoe polish from the lobby's shoe shine. I bagged an unopened can and a swab sample from Mia's seat."

I inched closer to the men, attention locked on Jake. "You did all that? When?"

Dan stood. His gaze swept between us. A cocky grin changed his detective face.

Jake narrowed his eyes. "I had plenty of time while you barricaded yourself inside the crime scene."

"And the swab from my seat?"

He smirked. "I think you were cursing, fanning the air and trying not to cry."

"Oh."

Jake took notice of Dan's inexplicable amusement, and the brothers exchanged a long look.

"What?" I tapped my foot and rolled my shoulders back, trying to look bigger and less like a victim. "What's that look about? Don't say 'It's nothing.'"

Dan released a full smile. "I'll let you handle this." He clamped a hand over Jake's shoulder and crossed the lot to the clubhouse.

Jake let out a long breath. "This isn't a random act of vandalism. The person who did this left a message for you."

The word etched on my seat was burned into my mind. "Stop."

He nodded. "Whoever did this has a beef with you. They know your car. They could know your address. Considering your link to whatever is happening with the computer system and this week's murder victim, it's reasonable to conclude you're in danger. You should talk to your parents. Lake Cable is a nice, quiet community. Stay with them until we know who did this."

I dropped my hands to my sides in shock. "Do you know how many strokes my parents would have if I told them a murderer might be after me? That was a silly question. You can't know, so I'll tell you. Lots. They would have lots of consecutive strokes if they thought anything worse than a telemarketer bothered me. I'm fine at my apartment. I have locks, chains and a security system approved by an overprotective, ex-cop father. I can defend myself between parking on the street and entering the building."

He looked skeptical.

"What? I dated in college."

Jake's tan hand snapped out and grabbed my wrist. He hauled me closer to him than I'd have ever dared.

Scents of cologne and cinnamon gum strangled my thoughts. Rough fingers locked around the delicate skin at the underside of my wrist.

"Hey." My protest and escape attempts were equally feeble.

"Get free."

"What?" I raised my eyes to his and squinted against the sun. I suppressed the urge to tug my collar and adjusted my glasses instead. "Why?" Duh. Why? Because he grabbed me. Because he taunted me. *Dared me.*

"Get free or I'm dragging you off someplace dark where I can take my time." The menace in his voice told me this was a test. The storm in his eyes made me enjoy the challenge.

I inhaled. Counted to three and stamped my heel into his instep. With my free hand, I smacked the side of his neck, connecting with his carotid artery thrumming beneath the skin.

Jake's knees buckled, and he released me.

Onlookers took a few steps away, giving us a wide berth and whispering loudly, apparently having forgotten their guise of not rubbernecking.

I clamped ice-cold fingers around my wrist, where he'd held me. "Did I pass?"

He shook his head like a wet dog and blinked. "Yep."

That carotid artery move was one of my favorites.

Something he'd said jumped to the front of my thoughts. "How do you know my folks live in Lake Cable?"

Sunlight glinted off the flecks of green and gold in his careful blue eyes. I'd knocked him sideways, but he didn't seem upset. He looked almost…impressed. A bubble of pride filled my chest.

He dropped his gaze to my wrist. "You okay?"

"Yeah. You're stalling. How do you know where my folks live?"

"You're not the only one who can use the internet." He seemed to recover from his lighter mood. The corners of his mouth turned down. "At least let me drive you home and sweep the place before you lock up for the night."

"What about Stella?"

"Stella's a crime scene." He forced the final two words between clenched teeth.

Dan reappeared, notebook in hand. "You two get things sorted out?" From the look on his face, I assumed he'd been there longer than I realized.

"I'm driving her home." Jake looked at me. "Get your stuff. You can work from your place, right?"

My hip popped on principle. "Excuse me? Get my stuff?"

Jake rubbed his face. "I'll get your stuff. Happy?"

"Not really."

Jake skulked away.

Dan opened his truck door and paused before climbing inside. "Do you have dinner plans?"

"Um." My mouth opened, but my brain blanked. Was he asking me out? Was that inappropriate considering our relationship, detective and victim/murder suspect? Was I still a suspect? Was his question a trap meant to coax information from me regarding Nate's whereabouts? Well, the joke was on him because I had no clue where Nate was hiding. Though I couldn't shake the nagging sensation I should, or I did and hadn't realized it yet.

His eyes were kind and sincere but curious. Jake's eyes reminded me of the sea during a storm. Jake wasn't curious. He was intense, determined. A force of nature. My brain skittered past the troublesome thoughts. Maybe I had been closed up inside my car too long. I'd fried my brain.

Dan's friendly blue eyes prompted me for an answer. *Did I have dinner plans?*

"Uh. No. No plans. I mean, except that I should probably go home and lock myself inside until morning."

He scanned the area and frowned at my car. "Or, you could come out to our grandparents' farm for a barbecue. Spend a few hours away from whatever's going on in Horseshoe Falls." He flashed hopeful blues back to me. "Our baby brother got engaged last month, and Grandma's throwing a party to celebrate. Half the town will be there."

My brain picked up the word "town" among the deluge of others it couldn't process. "Stone Creek?" Did he say something about an engagement?

"That's right. Do you know it?"

I smiled. "I've heard of it." I wasn't a half-bad detective either.

"Ready?" Jake appeared across the lot with the strap of my laptop bag grappled in one big fist. He stopped short. "What's the matter?"

Dan smiled a charming, easy smile. "I'm trying to convince Mia to join us for dinner at the farm tonight. I thought she could use a break from this week, and I know everyone would love to meet her. You weren't planning to miss Eric's engagement party, were you?"

Jake's eyes widened a moment before settling back into his easy frown. "She doesn't want to hang out on a farm."

"Why not?" Dan and I answered in unison.

I hadn't wanted to go a minute before, but if Jake

was uninviting me, maybe I wanted to go. What was wrong with me?

Jake looked at his brother with contempt. "She just doesn't."

"Maybe I already said yes."

Dan tented his eyebrows. "Yeah?"

"Yeah."

Jake glared at me in challenge. "IT girls and CIOs of million-dollar companies don't spend time in Stone Creek."

Dan smiled. "You figured that out, huh?" He winked. "She's got a graduate degree, her own place, a car, a job and half a company. Actually, she's the face of the company, too. Bet you didn't know that."

"I knew that."

Too many social cues were flying over my head and under my radar. I used to be smart. "I'm sorry." I waved an open palm to Dan. "Are you coming on to me?"

His faced opened into a gorgeous youthful smile.

Nerves forced my lips into motion. "I'm not suggesting you are. I'm just trying to figure out what's happening, and body language and eye contact, and all those things most people get a bead on, kind of elude me, so if you could just state your intentions, that would be amazing."

He turned his smiling face to Jake, who looked like I'd hit him with my MINI. "Seven okay?"

Jake answered. "We'll be there."

Dan slid behind the wheel of his truck and pulled it around the side of the building, freeing the cars on either side of Stella from their spaces, should the owners return.

Jake walked to his giant blue beast and opened the passenger door. He tossed my laptop bag onto the seat.

"Watch it!" I hurried to his side. "Your brother didn't answer me. Was he asking me out or not, because I can't handle ambiguity."

Jake motioned me inside. "Do you want him to ask you out?"

What was wrong with these guys? Did they ever give a straight response?

"Do you?" he pressed.

My tummy tightened and my mouth dried. "No."

"Why not? Too good for my brother?"

"No. No! Jeez. It's nothing like that."

Red marks lined his neck.

"Sorry I whacked you earlier."

His lips twitched. "Can I drive you to the farm or do you want Dan to pick you up?"

"You can drive me." The words tumbled over themselves, too breathy and soft. I blinked my eyes free of his stare.

Jake shut the door and paused several beats before rounding the tailgate to the driver's side. He climbed in, gunned the engine to life and looked at my legs. "You own any blue jeans?"

"Yes."

"Boots?"

"Riding boots."

He nodded. "You ride?"

"Yeah, you?"

He turned his face to mine. A full-teeth smile illuminated his face. "Yep."

A horn honked behind us as Dan's truck pulled onto the road. I clutched the dash to keep from jumping out the window.

Jake shifted into gear. "You like animals?"

A tow truck rumbled into the lot as we rolled out. I waved goodbye to Stella. "I like animals."

"Domestic or livestock?"

"I like all animals."

He navigated free of the guard gate and headed for the highway to my apartment. We hit the on-ramp at seven miles over the posted speed limit. "Fishing?"

"I'm not any good. Patience isn't one of my stronger personality traits." I rolled my window down. The wind ripped through my hair. I dared a look in Jake's direction. "I don't want Dan to ask me out."

Jake shifted into fifth gear and turned away. His cheek lifted in a lazy smile as we cruised toward my apartment.

WE PULLED UP to my building fifteen minutes later. I called Marcella and Randall from my bedroom as I dug for clean jeans and a cute shirt that looked as if I didn't toil over choosing it. My riding boots still had clumps of mud from the last time I visited the Horseshoe Falls stables. I loved riding with the owner, Jennifer. Jennifer was a tiny blonde with a pixie cut and a personality that could command armies. When I needed a boost of inner strength, I spent time with her. Probably why I never had the heart to properly clean my boots after we rode. Tangible evidence I had a cool friend.

Marcella promised to explain to Warren about the vandalism and ask him to be careful. With one IT staffer away for the day, he might take the brunt next. Marcella cut our call short so she could ease the scuttlebutt. Apparently being a victim of vandalism made me a target for gossip. Residents were concerned I was "in trouble with the law" and how that might reflect on the community. She sounded a little too enthusiastic when she turned the phrase. Randall didn't care about gossip. He insisted I find out who sent the emails and why. He didn't care if I did it from home or Tahiti, as long as he managed to keep his job. I reminded him to get me the list of affected residents.

"Ready?" I emerged from the hallway into the living room, where I'd left Jake.

He turned on his heels and appraised me. I'd picked butt-hugging jeans. I'd held my breath to zip them. My simple silk tank top hung loose from my shoulders and fluttered over my hips, hiding what the stubborn zipper on my jeans revealed. I'd gained seven pounds since I bought this pair. The leather jacket in my arms matched the mud on my boots.

He turned his back on me. "Yep."

"Everything okay?"

"Dan called. They did a sweep of your car and came up empty. Whoever did the damage was in and out. They didn't linger, and they didn't leave prints inside. No prints on the knife either."

I nodded. "They knew the cameras were down. They had a time limit."

"What are all these?" He pointed to a crystal candy dish Bree gave me as an apartment warming gift. I'd filled the dish with candy twice, only to eat the candy and hate myself. Now I used it decoratively, instead of as a trough.

"Thumb drives."

He turned to face me. "What's on them?"

"Nothing. They're novelties. I picked up a few in college. People noticed and started buying me new ones. Then my family tried to outdo one another with more unique finds." I waved him off. My family took more than words to explain. Alcohol helped. "It's a whole thing we do." *Compete. Argue.*

"You have a bowl like this in your office at work. Anything on those?"

"Nope. They're just for fun."

He gave me another unsettling look and moved toward the door. "Anything else you need to do before we go? If we get there early, Nana will put us to work."

My lips cocked to the side. "Nana?"

A blush rose up his neck into stubble-covered cheeks. "Come on. If you're going to tease me, I'll let Nana put you to work."

I swung the door open, and Jake held it as I passed. "I think it's sweet you call her Nana. What do you call your grandpa?"

He chuckled and wiped his mouth roughly. "Papa."

I laughed, locking the door behind us. Without forethought, I slid my arm through the crook in Jake's and headed for the elevator.

Panic climbed my chest. This wasn't someone I knew well enough to touch without permission. People had personal boundaries. My cheeks flamed with nerves. I needed to drop his arm. If I moved too fast, I'd be obvious. If I took too long, I'd look crazy.

We slowed at the shiny silver doors, and I loosened my fingers from his biceps. If I pressed the elevator button with my clearly possessed right hand, I could shove it in my pocket afterward and pretend I hadn't attached myself to him like a spider monkey.

Jake's arm pressed against his side, trapping my hand

between the warmth of his torso and taut muscle of his arm, before I could disengage.

Frozen under his touch, I watched as he pushed the elevator button.

NINE

THE DRIVE TO Stone Creek was beautiful. We arrived early and, as promised, Nana put me to work. The men and women separated without complaint or instruction. It was an odd scene. I scrubbed picnic tables, and Nana covered them with red-and-white-checked linen tablecloths. The tables were set in rows. Eric's fiancée, Parker, arranged mason jars full of sunflowers in a line down the center of the tables. Giant citronella candles created centerpieces, or they would have if the parade of picnic tables had discernable centers. The resulting aesthetic endeared me to the little farm.

Parker and Nana stopped working almost simultaneously. They looked over my head, locked arms and strode into the house, smiling.

"Didn't I tell you?" Jake lumbered into view, resting on the picnic bench as I finished wiping down the last table.

A dozen men and children filled the side yard, tossing horseshoes and, if the sound of robust laughter and size of their arm motions were any clue, telling tales. Bright summer sunlight warmed my skin. As a child of the suburbs and former resident of Horseshoe Falls, it occurred to me I might have a skewed idea of what it meant to live in the country. The air smelled different on the Archer farm, not like carefully tended flower gardens and fresh-cut grass but like earth and oxygen.

I dropped into the space beside him. "Do the men and women always split up like this?"

"Yeah. Age-old country traditions. The women tend to the meal, set up and clean up, though I suspect they spend the time talking about the men." He waited as if I might confirm his suspicion.

"They didn't say much to me."

"Did they badger you with questions?"

"Not really, but I get nervous and ramble. You think I scared them off?"

"Nah, they're giving you space. Don't worry about offending them. They're tougher than they look. Archer women have to be to put up with Archer men."

Squealing children ran in circles around a red wagon set between horseshoe stakes. A man in overalls waved his hat and chased after them.

Jake chuckled. "If you ask me, the women have the better chores on days like this. Those kids are wild."

So the men weren't shirking duties in some country-accepted show of chauvinism. "You watch the kids? Keep them out of the kitchen?"

He smiled as the man in overalls loaded the rug rats into a wagon and towed them away. "Those are some dirty, sneaky, ornery kids."

"Archer kids." I caught on to the rhythm of this new place and idly imagined what my kids would act like. Probably neurotic.

He turned to look at me, but I didn't dare catch his gaze. I focused on the men lining up their next throw and trailed the path of flying metal over the lawn. A satisfying chink preceded some sort of victory dance on the thrower's side.

Jake's stare drew heat across my cheeks.

"What?" I tipped my chin his way without looking.

"If you don't use the thumb drives, then where do you keep your files? Do you back them up somewhere?"

"Of course. I use the cloud."

Saving on the cloud meant I never had to worry about losing my data, and I could get to it from anywhere with Wi-Fi, even if I didn't have my laptop. Best yet, if my laptop died a horrid death, the files were safe somewhere else.

I opened a window on my phone and held it between us, flicking through the list of files. "See?"

"Gotcha."

A message popped up from my online game.

"What's that?" Jake's long finger touched the screen and opened the message.

I pulled the phone from his reach. "Rude." Curiosity pulled my eyes to the screen. "It's an update from REIGN, the online game I play. Looks like I have a new knight in my kingdom." A knight was a stroke of luck. Getting strong players to join my kingdom wasn't easy since I refused to give them things for joining. Honor was what I offered. People didn't play for honor anymore. They wanted privileges or special treatment or kingdom coins.

Jake leaned closer. "A knight's good, right?"

"Yes." My smile grew. "I captured my nemesis's spies. Ha!" I pounded my feet against the earth. "Eat that, Punisher." I pumped a fist in the air.

He snickered. "Your nemesis is named Punisher. Punisher's a supervillain."

My eyes widened. "Right!"

"Dumb. Do you have any idea what information your friends might've gotten on that guy?"

"No, I looked into him once, but his profile is basic,

and I couldn't get a thread on who he is outside the game."

"Could someone find you outside the game?"

He posed a good and terrifying question. If someone had enough skills to hack my system and thwart my searches, anything was possible.

A line of dust drew my attention toward Nana's bumpy gravel drive. A four-wheeler tore over the dips, tossing dirt and stone into the air. A line of open-top jeeps and trucks followed.

Jake stood, arching his back and grimacing. "Party time."

The yard quickly filled with neighbors, family and friends of the Archers. Endless platters and bowls of homemade food traveled along the picnic tables, hand to hand. Eric and Parker were adorable in matching plaid shirts and cowboy boots. He wore jeans, and she wore a denim skirt. They belonged on the cover of a country album or maybe the local tourist guidebook. Jake didn't spend much time with me, but he never moved far away either. Dan kept a careful eye on both of us. So much so, I couldn't help wonder who was under investigation, Jake or me.

After shortcakes and apple pie, Dan moved to my side, blocking my view of the enormous evening bonfire. "You doing all right?"

I inhaled sweet country air and nodded. "Yep." Except for the crowd of family and friends watching me with intense curiosity. For some inexplicable reason, no one questioned my unprecedented appearance outright. Instead, they stared. I shifted on the picnic bench, turning my back to the table and crossing booted feet beneath the seat.

Night swallowed the last remnants of evening light,

releasing fireflies into the inky sky and reducing the temperature a dozen degrees. A handful of kids ran through the blackened field with sparklers blazing.

Dan grunted, sipping what looked like sweet tea from a mason jar. "You look uncomfortable."

"I don't know anyone."

He scanned the crowd. "They're nice folks."

"I'm sure they are, but do you think it's strange no one's said more than hello to me?"

"I'm sure they're all talking about you, if that makes you feel better."

I frowned. "I have no idea how to start a conversation with someone I don't know. I should probably introduce myself, but outside of professional settings, I'm genetically incapable." All night I'd considered asking friendly faces how they liked life in Stone Creek or how they knew the Archers or the happy couple, but my tongue swelled, my throat tightened and my stomach threatened to expel the ten pounds of dinner I'd eaten. "I'm technically your guest. Why didn't you introduce me?" That was basic etiquette wasn't it? Maybe this wasn't my problem.

"From where they're standing, you're Jake's date, not mine."

I snorted, immediately pressing a palm over my nose. "Why am I really here?"

"Protection."

Intuition buzzed up the back of my neck. "You didn't look at me when you answered. Is that because you're lying? When Jake takes me home, I'm reading up on signs of dishonesty." What a frustrating waste of time. "I don't understand why people don't just say what they mean."

I followed Dan's gaze to Jake, who was standing several feet away. An adorable blonde flipped long barrel curls over one shoulder and touched his arm. He stared over her head at Dan and me.

Dan cleared his throat and gave me his full attention. "Truth?"

"Obviously."

He smiled. "You're here because I'm not convinced you know as little as you say. You're too clever. Originally, I thought you had it in for Baxter and I'd uncover some twisted reason for your attack on him. After the incident with your car, I think you're in danger, probably by whoever hurt your friend and possibly from the guy you're trying to find."

"You think Nate threatened me?" I rolled my eyes until they hurt.

"I invited you here tonight so I could keep an eye on you without missing my brother's engagement party."

My cheeks burned. I'd accused Dan of asking me out on a date. He just needed to accomplish two things at once and watching me was one of them. The feeling of rejection curled over me, piercing my sides and flattening my lungs. Why did I care if Dan wanted me around? I didn't. It wasn't like we were friends. We'd only met a few times and only because of Baxter's death. The word broke in my brain. He was dead. Dan was investigating his murder. I retrieved my drink from the table and sipped gingerly to settle my stomach.

Jake squatted in the grass before me. "You okay?"

I sniffled. "Why does everyone ask me that?"

He offered me a hand. "You're shaking."

"Oh." I set my drink aside and tucked breeze-tussled hair behind both ears, wishing the ground would open up and swallow me. No one would remember the awkward, shaking girl if something of geological significance was involved. "It's been a terrible week, and I'm ready to go home. If that's okay." Hopefully they weren't planning to make me stay forever. Could cops get away with kidnapping?

"What are you thinking about?" Jake's slow voice drew my attention.

I lifted my eyes to his, hoping to see if he truly cared or if Dan had put him up to interrogating me through a false friendship scenario. That seemed like a solid tactic. Good cop/bad cop. One made me feel safe then stole all my secrets.

If I was honest, there was a flicker of hope when Dan asked me to the party. The idea someone unrelated to me wanted to get to know me was nice. I hadn't made a new friend since Nate, and that was years ago. My tummy coiled. Where was he? Was he hurt? Scared? Dan's offer was a ruse and a mean one. "I'm thinking things are never what they seem and that sucks."

Jake kneaded the back of his neck. "Yep."

"Just yep?" No words of wisdom? Bree would've tried to fix the problem for me. Nate would've made excuses for Dan. Nate saw the best in everyone.

Jake unfolded his tall body until his knees came into view. "Come on. I'll drive you home."

I nodded and pushed off the picnic bench.

Jake said his goodbyes to half the guests, hugging necks and shaking hands as he moved, keeping me within arm's reach as if I might run off into the darkness.

He helped me into the cab of his truck and swung himself behind the wheel.

I marveled. "Why didn't the dome light come on?" *Is that some sort of stealthy, creeper move?* "Don't say it burned out."

The truck was far too new for something so trivial, plus Jake struck me as someone who'd pop a new bulb in without thought. He was probably the kind of guy who could make a shelter from tree sap and pinecones. I touched the dome light and begged for a reasonable, non-serial-killer reason to have disabled the bulb.

"You okay?" He shifted into Drive and turfed through his nana's yard, avoiding the lines of vehicles behind us.

I pressed my body against the door. "I'm distrusting and experience mild paranoia when I'm in potentially dangerous situations."

He turned to me, but his face was hidden in shadow. "You think you're in danger? Now? From me?" He barked a laugh.

"You mean alone in a moving vehicle with a man twice my size?"

"What happened to the fierce little tiger who throttled me outside the clubhouse?"

She wasn't blinded by darkness and alone in a strange, eerily rural town. I bit my lip.

"Bugs."

"What?"

He tapped the dome light. "I go night fishing, and the light attracts bugs. Every time I come back to change the radio station or grab a beer, a thousand damn mosquitos and moths climb in behind me. I loosened the bulb so I can open the door in peace."

I tipped my chin toward the open window as we turned onto the highway. Warm summer wind beat against my skin and fluttered my hair against my chest. *Bugs.* I nodded and smiled into the night. "How long will you be at Horseshoe Falls?"

"Depends."

"On what?"

"On how much time your other guy has off. I'm only filling in, remember?"

I turned to face him, wishing for telepathy. Something in his voice told me his answer cost him. But what and why? I spun the words uselessly in my head.

I rolled the window up and pointed a vent at my face. The cab quieted. "I'm going to find Nate and prove he's innocent."

He chuckled. "Oh, yeah?"

"Yeah." I nodded, hoping to beef up my confidence. "He has to come home. He's my only friend, and I just realized how much I need him." My voice cracked and I mentally groaned.

Jake freed a handkerchief from his hip pocket and dropped it in my lap. "Keep it."

I twisted the soft material around my fingers, hoping I wouldn't need it.

He peeked at me this time, turning quickly back to the road. "Well, you've been through a lot. You lost one guy you cared about and misplaced another."

I nodded. "I'm going to figure out what happened to Baxter, too. I owe him that."

The truck swerved. I braced my palms to the dash as we zoomed onto the shoulder and stopped in a haste. "What happened?" I turned in my seat, searching the dark road for a person or puppy or something.

Jake released his seat belt and turned to face me, cocking a knee onto the bench seat between us. "Listen to me, Mia. Leave the murder investigation to Dan. That's his job, and he's good at it. If you want to look for your friend, go right ahead. I think that's a grand idea, and I hope you find him alive. I mean that, but someone's clearly got it out for you, and we don't know it's not the killer."

I unbuckled and matched his body language. I read about that move online. If you want to make a good impression, or in my case, sway someone to your side, you mimic their movements.

"I think I can do this. I don't mean get myself into the killer's clutches and hope Dan finds me before I'm killed. I mean, I really think I can do this. Back at the party, I sorted the facts I have from the facts I need, and I realized something."

Jake rubbed his face with both hands, turned forward and rebuckled.

I followed suit.

He pulled onto the road, and I accepted that as a go-ahead for my story. "Crime investigation isn't very different from REIGN or my research assignments. I'll use what I know to find leads and use those leads to learn more. Eventually, I'll be back to the time of death and know who was in the office with Baxter." I smacked my palms together, and Jake groaned.

He didn't press me about my intended course of action. We rode in silence to my building, where he pulled half onto the curb.

He met me on the sidewalk.

I squinted at his face, backlit by a streetlamp. "What are you doing?"

"I'm walking you to your door."

I strode ahead, digging for my key. "Why? This wasn't a date."

He held the building door while I located the key at the bottom of my bag. I stumbled inside. "Stupid hall light."

Jake caught me by the elbow and released me the moment I regained footing.

"I trip over the dumb jamb every time I come home after dark. I'd have installed a new overhead bulb by now if I could reach it. The landlord says he has bigger problems and there's security lighting, but…"

No one else complained and one frustrated tenant in a building of two dozen happy tenants didn't worry him much.

Jake motioned me ahead. I pressed the elevator button and turned to wait, wondering how literal he'd meant "walk you to your door." He stared at the dark ceiling.

The elevator doors opened, and he climbed inside behind me.

"So, you're walking me to my door-door?"

He dipped his chin in a stiff nod. "I told you I'd like to take a look around. Just in case."

"In case someone's there to hurt me or in case I'm hiding something?"

"Both."

I mulled that over. "Fair enough." I wasn't hiding anything, and I really didn't want to end up like Stella.

I unlocked the apartment door and kicked off my boots. Jake circled the kitchen and living room before heading for the hallway with my bedroom and bath. He stopped outside my bedroom door, and I swallowed a brick of wild anticipation. He cupped steady fingers around the faux glass knob and glanced my way. "Mia?"

I nodded, speechless, mid-stroke.

"I know Nate means a lot to you, but he's not your only friend." His gaze bounced to the floor and back. "Or, he doesn't have to be." Jake disappeared into my room.

I flopped onto the couch for a girl moment. It was the most vulnerable I'd ever seen him. Dan didn't want to be my friend, but Jake did. Wasn't that what I really wanted anyway? Wasn't Jake the one whose conversations I replayed at night while trying to fall asleep? He wanted to be my friend, too.

After a thorough check of my apartment, Jake was back in grumpy cat mode. He watched as I set the security alarm before leaving as promised. Now I knew "take a look around" wasn't guy code for sex.

I flipped the dead bolt, unsure how I felt about the revelation, and went to make coffee.

My bell rang.

I turned on my heels and reopened the door. "Forget something?" I leaned headfirst across the threshold. Where was he?

"You're supposed to check the peephole before opening the door." Jake's angry voice thundered over my head.

I screamed, clutched my chest and marched in place. "Oh my goodness, are you trying to kill me? Why would you scare me after telling me I might be in danger?"

He glared. "Always check the peephole. I know you know that."

"I checked."

His expression darkened. "No, you didn't."

I squared my shoulders, sticking to the story. "Yes, I did. I saw it was you, so I opened the door."

His face turned a creepy shade of red. "No, you didn't. I pressed my back to the wall so you couldn't see me, and you still opened the door."

Panic flooded through me. I suddenly understood all those children headed for the principal's office. Embarrassed and afraid. Ashamed and nauseous. "Fine.

I didn't look. Are you happy?" I clamped both hands over my mouth and shook my head before I said anything else or threw up.

He narrowed his eyes and pointed to my open door.

I closed the door and locked up without a goodbye. I watched him board the elevator through my peephole. My place was at the end of the hall, so the peephole gave me a clear view of anyone coming or going on my floor. When the doors shut behind him, I hustled across the room to see if he left the building. I didn't trust him not to ring the bell again.

He stepped onto the sidewalk and looked up toward my window. I ducked, sliding on a stack of recent *Marie Claires* and landing on my can. My heart hammered painfully. I peeped over the windowsill's ledge, thankful for the streetlight illuminating him. Jake climbed into his truck and made a call.

My phone dinged, and I smiled. Was he calling me? I slid my thumb across the screen, bringing the cell to life.

Not Jake.

I had a new email from Nate!

I opened it, overcome with hope and joy. "Comic Con at six."

I sent an immediate response. He wouldn't stay online long if he was hiding. "Got it. Be safe."

I'd see Nate again in two days.

TEN

I SQUINTED AT bright morning sun reflecting off the glass door to my building. I pushed a hand in the air, attempting to shade my eyes while moving slowly onto the sidewalk. When my eyesight adjusted, a big black truck at the end of my block came into view. Dan Archer pressed a newspaper to the steering wheel, turning pages under a glazed stare.

I speed-walked to the window and rapped my knuckles against the glass. "Knock knock, Detective Archer."

He jerked his chin high and lifted a travel mug in cheers. I tapped again, and he powered the window down. "Morning, Miss Connors."

"What are you doing?"

He sipped from the mug and cringed. "Waiting on you."

"Mmm-hmm. Been here all night?"

"Yep."

I tapped my foot in indecision. Should I tell him about Nate's email? Dan was following me and if he knew I met with Nate secretly, he'd accuse me of withholding evidence. "Well, at least let me buy you a cup of hot coffee. Whatever you have in the mug must be awful by now."

"It is." He smacked his lips. "And I accept."

My phone rang. I lifted a finger and tucked the phone against my ear. "Hang on. This is my mom."

Dan chuckled. "Following you isn't a half-bad gig. You're buying me coffee, and I get to go to Comic Con."

I guffawed, lowering the phone before saying hello. "How do you know that? Did you bug my apartment or are you tapping my emails. Oh." I pressed my lips tight, forcing back swears my mom might overhear. "Jake did it, didn't he?" Heat raced over my cheeks. *Oh, let me come inside and make sure you're safe.* Let me inside to spy on you was more like it.

"Hello?" Mom's voice cranked through the phone's speaker. "Mia? Is that you?" She dropped her tone to a whisper and complained to someone in the background. "I meant to call Mia, but I don't know. Is this her number?"

Dad's voice boomed into my ear. "Yeah, that's her number."

"Mom." I closed my eyes against Dan's faux-innocent face and focused on my mom. "Yes. It's me, Mia. Sorry about that. This is a bad time. I'm on my way to work. Can I call you back when I get there?"

She huffed in the overdramatic manner saved just for me. "Your father and I want to bring you one of our cars until yours is fixed."

My eyes popped open. I scanned the street. "Stella." *Is a crime scene.*

Dan chuckled again, obviously overhearing both sides of my conversation and enjoying my reaction.

My enthusiasm for the day took a turn south. "No. That's okay. Don't come all the way into the city to drop off a car. I'll be fine."

"Well, at least let us rent you a car. Your father's free today. He can drop it off. Oh! He can be your driver." Mom's giddy voice emphasized how much she loved the terrible idea.

"No. No. Nope." My lips formed a tight seal as my brain scurried for a reasonable excuse. I had nothing.

Dan motioned to his truck. As if riding to work with him was an option.

I glared. "I already have a ride, but thank you."

Dan smiled.

I'd call a cab as soon as we hung up.

"Who?"

"What?" I blinked. "Who what?"

Mom huffed again. "*Who* is your ride?"

Definitely not the police detective currently stalking me and bent on arresting me for murder. Not anyone Mom and Dad knew either, or I'd be caught in my lie.

I needed a name. Any name. A fake name. "Jake Archer." *What is wrong with me?* Not him!

Dan's brow hitched. He smiled smugly, as if he knew something I didn't, and I loathed him for it. I covered the phone with one palm and shook my head violently. "Go away. I'll buy you coffee another time." I had bigger problems than him. My parents were after me.

"Who's that?" Mom asked. "Who are you talking to?"

"No one."

"Was that Jake Archer? The one you said is driving you to work?"

Dad's voice overtook Mom's. "Who the hell is Jake Archer?"

I pressed a sweat-slicked palm over my forehead. "He's the new head of security at work. He's just a friend." Who'd possibly bugged my apartment, under the guise of protecting me, while in league with his nosy brother.

Dad groaned on the other end of the line. "You can't

get in a car with someone you just met. You know better than that. I'm coming to get you."

I willed my voice to find a nice place between firm and rude. "No. Thank you. I appreciate the offer. I do, but I already have a ride."

"At least let me drive you home tonight. You can tell me more about this Archer."

I kicked loose gravel with the point of my shoe. "Really. Don't drive out here. I'm fine. Jake can bring me home. He'll already be at the clubhouse. It makes sense for him. Not for you."

Dad made an ugly noise. "This is a terrible idea. You cannot tell that man where you live. For goodness' sake, Mia. You're the smart one. Have you at least run a background check on him?"

Once a cop. Always a cop.

My chest constricted and I floundered for words under his clear disappointment. "It's okay. He's a nice guy from a nice family." Excitement raced through me. That was right. And true! The words bubbled free, relieved from further lying. "I was at his grandparents' farm last night for his brother's engagement party."

"Are you telling me you're dating this man?" Dad's voice rose an octave. Secrets weren't something my family handled well.

My mom squealed in the background.

"Uh." I puffed the material of my dress away from my chest, attempting to circulate the stifling air. "Not officially, but I can assure you he isn't dangerous, and I know for a fact I can take him out if he tries anything inappropriate. So, you see? I'm fine, and I'll talk to you soon, but I'd better get to work. Bye-bye." I pushed the phone into my bag and imagined screaming into the air "I'm not thirteen! I'm thirty!" but that seemed like it might negate my argument.

Dad never treated Bree like that, as if she'd break. Then again, Bree was an official grown-up with a husband to protect her and a family to legitimize her full-fledged adult standing.

Plants died in my care.

I stomped back into my apartment and ordered a bug detector online so Dan would see, assuming he'd bugged my computer. If my apartment was bugged, it wouldn't be in twenty-four hours. I rounded up my unmentionables and stuffed them into drawers just in case. Back in my living room, I grabbed my laptop and locked the home system down tight enough NASA couldn't hack in.

Ten minutes later, I climbed into the backseat of a green car with a Yellow Cab sign and glared at Dan pulling away from the curb behind me.

Buildings blurred past my window, growing sporadic as we moved from the city to the highway and headed for Horseshoe Falls. I wiggled against the warm vinyl seat, missing Baxter and worrying for Nate. Carpoolers in the lane beside me laughed and chatted, passing donuts over seats and reminding me how alone I was. What had my friends gotten themselves into and what did it have to do with me?

I rolled my head against the headrest and steepled my fingers. If I couldn't solve Nate's mystery, maybe I could make sense of the strange happenings at work. The emails were connected to the break-ins. Coincidences didn't happen. But how were they connected? And what about the cameras? There had to be an inside man. Someone had rebooted our cameras before every break-in and before violating Stella. That person knew how to take down individual cameras and how long the reboot lasted. Security guards had access to cameras. I could start by talking to them and anyone else who knew how to push a power button. I fisted both hands.

Who was I kidding? The clubhouse wasn't a high security facility. I found kids in the employee break room eating Marcella's birthday cake last year and a duck in our server room at Easter.

The cab pulled up beside Bernie at the guard gate, but several feet from the ID scan.

I waved my arm out the back window, key card in hand. She swiped it for me and passed it back through the window. "I was sorry to hear about Stella."

"Thanks."

I paid the cabbie and headed for the clubhouse door. My phone buzzed. A message to the staff from Marcella. Staff meeting in Conference Room One. Now.

I made a pit stop at my desk and headed for the morning meeting. The room filled slowly, like my coffeepot. Employees arrived in drops at first, a few in pairs, others on their own. By eight, the room spilled its excess into the hallway.

Marcella waved at the crowd as Randall pulled the door shut, forcing everyone inside. He nodded for her to begin.

I sucked in my gut and squeezed through the masses, popping free from the too-tight crowd and bumping into Marcella. "Sorry. Hi. Sorry."

She eyeballed me. "Mia? Everything okay? I'm ready to start the meeting."

I cleared my throat. "I just need a quick second before you begin."

Marcella nodded, clearly confused and probably wondering about my sanity. I avoided the spotlight. Religiously. I ducked out during my office birthday party before they could sing "Happy Birthday," and I'd faked sick when she introduced the new employees during my first week on the job.

"Hi." I swiped the back of one hand over my forehead. The last time I'd intentionally stood in front of so many people was for a grade. My tummy churned out a horrendous noise. I imagined falling face-first into a row of agitated employees pulled abruptly from their morning coffee for their second mandatory staff meeting in a week. "I'm Mia."

"What do you want?" A man's voice carried over the crowd.

My spine stiffened. I used my Queen Guinevere voice. "Who here can reboot a computer?"

Every hand went up.

I nodded. "Who can tell me how long the process takes?"

Dozens of voices called out variations of the same correct answer. Not long. A few minutes.

True.

"Which of you has access to the camera room?"

They frowned. In near unison the answer came. "All of us. Everyone. Employees."

Right. Anyone with a badge could get into the employee wing or camera room. Plus, those children and that one duck. "Just checking. If you've dealt with a resident complaint about scheduling or bogus coupons, will you please email me their names? I'm working to right the error and names would be helpful." I curtsied to the crowd and slid away from Marcella. "Thank you."

Randall was dragging his feet about providing the list. If employees helped, I could at least look at the recipients for a connection as names became available.

I slunk through the crowd, leaving Marcella behind. I could only imagine the look on her face as she called her meeting to order.

Jake clapped slow and silent as I passed his seat and leaned against the wall behind him.

I lifted my chin and stared at Marcella.

He tipped his chair in my direction and whispered, "Nice sleuthing. That was top-notch detective work."

"Shut up."

"I'm not kidding. All you need is a magnifying glass and a tail. We can call you Pink Panther. Next time I'll take notes."

I shook my head. Moron. The Pink Panther solved his cases. Just like I would.

The remainder of the meeting moved quickly. Marcella gave an incredibly motivational pep talk and promised a thank-you dinner for staffers when things were finally resolved and settled. She appreciated everyone's continued patience and professionalism in the face of hostile residents and updated us on the situation. Fortunately, there were no new complaints and the whole mess seemed to have blown over as quickly as it had blown in. In conclusion, we celebrated with trays of Marcella's flan and sopapillas.

The golf and tennis pros left without desserts, everyone else filled a to-go plate and mingled. I piled sweets onto a napkin and headed for the door. Jake cornered me before I could escape. "Dan told me about this morning."

I hated Dan. "It's no big deal. He caught me off guard and so did my mom's call. I'd completely forgotten Stella was gone."

His blank expression made it impossible to gauge his thoughts, testing the promises of my antiperspirant. "I can give you a ride home if you need one. Just stop by my office when you're ready to leave."

I glanced around the semi-crowded room. Several employees were staring openly. The others angled themselves in our direction as they snacked and pretended not to listen.

"Excuse me." My dad appeared at the door. "Is Mia Connors in here?" He scanned the room and stopped on Jake and me.

"Hi." I wiggled free from my position between Jake and the wall. "You feel like flan or sopapillas?" I motioned Dad to the table covered in sweets.

"Nah. I'm just checking to see you got to work safely."

I kissed his cheek and squeezed his hand. "Yep. All good. What's on the agenda today?"

He turned his attention to Jake, following on my heels. "I don't believe we've met."

I pulled Dad toward the door. "Not hungry? How about a walk? I hear it's a beautiful day outside."

Dad anchored himself in place just beyond the threshold.

Jake extended his hand. "I'm Jake Archer, Horseshoe Falls' new head of security. You're Mia's father?"

The men shook hands and scrutinized one another.

My gut leaped into my mouth. I grabbed Dad's sleeve. "Dad, this is Jake. Jake, Dad." I wedged myself between them and forced a smile at Dad. "Maybe I can buy you a coffee at Derby?"

He leaned around me and pulled the grenade pin. "Jake Archer? You're the man dating my daughter?"

Jake's mouth fell open.

Onlookers burst into whispers.

I prayed for another sinkhole.

ELEVEN

JAKE LED DAD and me to the garden beside the tennis courts. When he finally stopped walking, I explained myself at full speed. Frustration clipped my hurried words. The sentences fell over one another, and my disposition soured further with every word. I wouldn't have had to lie or explain myself if Dan hadn't staked out my apartment.

My hands cut through the air with the final recap of events. "I was trying not to worry you about the detective lurking outside my apartment. I used Jake's name as a cover because you know everyone else I know. I don't want you worrying about me." I squeezed Dad's hand and leaned against his side. He'd retired early from the Cleveland police department after a heart attack. Raising twin daughters for twenty-some years and fighting crime for thirty would do that to a person. "I'm sorry I lied."

He patted my back. "It's all right. I only came by to make sure you were safe and that you had a car. You didn't give us the chance to tell you on the phone. I'm meeting the fellows here this morning." A proud grin split his face. "So, you aren't dating?"

"No." Jake and I answered in unison, though he could've sounded a little less thrilled about it.

I leaned away from Dad. "You don't have to worry about me. I'm a grown woman with a desk job and a sensible car. I have savings and a security alarm. Plus, I can defend myself. Boring. Sensible. Safe."

Jake cleared his throat. "That's true. The part about defending herself."

Dad narrowed his eyes. "How do you know?"

Jake blanched.

I smiled. Nice to see his cocky grin and grouchy face put away for a change. "See? Nothing to worry about. Can I buy you a coffee?"

He kissed my head and released me. "Nah. I'm going fishing with some golf buddies. They'll be here soon if they aren't already. You can join us for breakfast if you'd like."

"Wow. Breakfast and fishing?"

"Yes. Breakfast at Derby then an afternoon on the lake. Days like these remind me why I retired." Dad took a few steps and stopped. He turned slowly to face me. "Just to clarify. You're not dating this man?"

"I'm not dating anyone." I drew a cross over my heart.

"Were you really at his grandparents' farm last night?"

Heat crept over my cheeks. Jake would probably think I bragged about it or something equally obnoxious. "Yes."

Dad swung his gaze between Jake and me, stopping on Jake. "How long have you been a security guard?"

"Not long."

"How old are you?"

"Thirty-three."

Dad arched a brow. "You like your family?"

"Yes, sir."

"Did you go to college?"

Jake gave me a sidelong glance and responded with

one firm nod. "Yes, sir." He clutched his hands behind his back like the Secret Servicemen in movies, minus the black suit and ear thing.

Dad lifted his chin. "Were you military?"

Another nod. "Ten years."

What the hell was happening here? A strange zing of tension buzzed between them.

Dad matched Jake's stance. "Army?"

"Yes, sir. You?"

Dad smiled. "Intelligence."

Jake's face lit up. "Rangers."

"Well." Dad seemed satisfied. "I'd better go look for my buddies. Keep an eye on Mia for me?"

"Yes, sir."

"Any particular reason you aren't dating her?"

"Dad!" I jumped to action, shoving his shoulder toward the clubhouse. "He's joking," I called over one shoulder to Jake.

"She scares me, sir."

Dad lifted a thumbs-up over his head as I pushed him through the clubhouse door. "He seems like a nice guy."

"Stop that. What's wrong with you? One minute you don't want me dating. The next minute you're trying to pawn me off on a man you just met." One of my favorite things about Dad was his disinterest in my love life. He'd never questioned my decisions to date or dump anyone.

Dad's friends filled every seat of the clubhouse lounge area. They stood when we got close. Dad smiled. "What? I'm a curious man. You know that. It runs in the family."

I puffed air into my bangs.

Dad furrowed his brow. "Have I missed something?"

"He said he's afraid of me."

"He respects you."

"Right. Well, you'd better get going."

He dropped a set of car keys into my palm. "You can keep my car until yours is repaired. Dinner at Bree's tonight."

Gross. "Great. Bring booze."

"I always do." Dad and his buddies shook hands violently and clapped one another on the back before disappearing into a cloud of Old Spice.

Jake sauntered to my side. "Your dad seems like a nice guy."

"He is." My phone rang, and I yanked it from my pocket.

Mom's face graced the screen.

"Hello?" I used the distraction as a polite exit and headed for my office.

"Mia? Is your dad with you?" Mom asked.

"I just left him with his buddies."

Warren tipped his chin when I opened our office door, and went back to whatever he'd been doing.

Mom clucked her tongue. "He'd better not be late tonight. He doesn't love Bree's research, but he has to support her in it. That's what family does. He remembered to leave you his keys, I hope."

"Yep." I fell into my new desk chair and spun in a circle, inhaling the smooth leather smell. "I'm driving the Crown Victoria tonight." Dad's car was twice the size of Stella and at least twenty years older. Mom and Dad bought it used the year Bree and I started middle school. Dad threatened to give it to us to share when we got our licenses. We dodged that bullet by getting jobs and buying deathtrap clunkers. Little ones. Mom wanted Dad to trade it in for something new, but he refused. Bree said the Crown Vic probably reminded him of his cop days, riding around in giant cars, feeling authoritative and virile. With Bree, everything came back to that last part. She thought sex ran the world. She literally said so once at Christmas.

"Did you hear me?" Mom snapped.

"What?"

"Are you daydreaming or ignoring me? Never mind. Don't tell me. Just promise you'll be at Bree's tonight and don't be late. You know how she gets when you're late. I don't want to hear it."

I opened my email and sorted through the things that needed my attention and sent the rest to Warren. "I'll be there. I told her I would."

"You can't be late. This research grant is very important to her. She planned the whole party around her project and even baked a theme cake."

Warren's computer dinged. Incoming mail. From me. I avoided eye contact. The workload this week had doubled any other. I'd be lucky if he didn't quit.

"I've got to go, Mom. If I don't get my work done, I'll be late tonight."

Mom squeaked a goodbye and let me off the phone.

Hours bled together as I responded to clubhouse email and triple-checked every inch of my now perfectly operating system. No new names arrived in my email. Apparently staffers weren't motivated to drudge up a problem they perceived as over.

I twirled a pen between my fingertips. Why hadn't I nailed the person behind this yet? Maybe I wasn't young and in tune anymore. What if my skills were failing? Maybe turning thirty would ruin me.

The clock on my computer warned me about the time. It was after two and I had a dinner party with a prompt arrival policy in a few hours.

I spun to face Warren. "I'm leaving early. I sent you some things to handle, and I'm going to deal with the rest from home. If you need me, text." I grabbed my bag and headed for the lobby. "See you tomorrow."

I made a pit stop at Randall's office. I knocked on his open door. "Hey. I'm going home to work on the system problems. Warren has everything under control."

Randall frowned. "You sure he can handle things by himself? You've got a real disaster going on."

"He can hold it together here. We haven't had any complaints in days. The emails stopped being sent. The links on the page are broken. I think whatever happened is done. I'll look into it more from home, but don't underestimate Warren. I may be the one you see running around, but he's smart. I trust him." Worry bit into me. If we didn't come up with a satisfying explanation to give the founder soon, Warren might lose his job with the rest of us.

Randall walked around his desk with a bottle of water in one outstretched hand. "If you say so. Are you okay? You look a little piqued."

"I don't like questions without answers." Every time I said it aloud, a chunk of my soul withered. How could I *not* know by now? "I'm certain the email was a phishing scam. I'm just not sure to what end."

"Fishing?"

"Phishing. It's when some hack puts up a fake site that looks and feels like a legitimate site users know and trust. The hackers send emails enticing users to click links and go to their sites, then they collect sensitive information from users who use the site, believing it's the site they know and trust." I reworked the explanation in my mind. "Did I explain that right? It feels jumbled."

"Someone set up a lookalike site and lured our residents there, hoping they'd input sensitive information?"

"Yes."

Randall flopped back into his chair. "Don't you think someone with the talents to pull this off could've gained the information on their own?"

There was the wall I hit every time I worked through the problem.

Randall rolled his chair back to center, and the edges of a blanket and pillow came into view. Both were stuffed inside his credenza, holding its door partially open. I cast my gaze around the room. Food wrappers and takeout cartons filled his trash can. A toothbrush stood among his pens in the caddy on his desk. "How many hours are you working these days?"

He chuckled. "No more than everyone else."

Strange. "Okay. Well, call if you need me. I'm scheduled for forced merriment and sex cake in six hours."

He tented his eyebrows.

"Never mind." Why didn't things sound that ridiculous *before* I said them? I waved on my way out the door.

"Mia?"

I turned on my heels, half afraid of the question he'd pose following my talk of sex cake.

Randall leaned in and whispered, "If this thing blows up, maybe you could start some kind of hacker-equivalent to a PI firm. You know. Online investigations or something."

I shook my head. "I'm not a hacker. I just grew up online. Besides, I can't even find whoever sent these emails."

"You will."

I smiled. "Thank you."

"Right after your sex cake."

It had better be delicious.

TWELVE

As SUSPECTED, I got a lot more done at home than at the office. By four, my inbox was clean, but I still had no leads on the bogus emails' origins. At least there weren't any new ones sent this week. I closed my work screen and double-checked the time. I had an hour before Bree expected me. The commute from my place to hers was half that, so I logged into REIGN to check on those falcon messengers.

The screen loaded with a red warning sign in the corner of my kingdom. More bad news. I hovered my mouse over the warning. What happened now? The sky fell? Everyone died of dysentery? I clicked the button.

Loss: Messenger falcons slain by archers.

"What?" I yelled. "Who would do that?" I sat on the couch and pulled my feet up with me, balancing a laptop on the couch's wide arm. "Punisher!" I'd hoped to avoid him until he found someone else to pick on, but this was unforgivable. What kind of person killed another kingdom's messenger birds? I slid my fingertips beneath my glasses and rubbed tired eyes. "Jerk." No more Mrs. Turn-the-other-cheek. This was war.

I rang the Town Hall bell and waited to see who was online in my kingdom. I needed an attack plan for destroying Punisher, and that meant brainstorming with my compatriots. A few names popped into the chat box. I scrolled through the list. I recognized most, but it seemed my new knight had brought friends. Excellent. I wrung my hands like a cartoon villain and smiled at the screen. Time for Punisher to get…punished.

AN HOUR LATER, "Flight of the Bumblebee" rang through my phone, and I sucked air. Bree! I vaulted from my chair and lined up excuses as I dove headfirst into the elevator, laptop bag in one hand and car keys in the other. *Trouble at work. Traffic. I lost Dad's car keys. Climbed a small tree to save a kitten.* "Shoot." The doors closed behind me and I pushed the first floor button ten times, waiting for hyperdrive to kick in. Were elevators all as slow as mine? I pushed again but continued descending at the pace of a stoned octogenarian. When the shiny silver doors parted at the lobby, Carl and a girl in Hello Kitty glasses climbed onboard. Carl bowed theatrically, until I thought he'd collapse.

I saluted and made a run for Dad's car.

Five o'clock traffic crammed the highway. My phone buzzed every few minutes. I hit the ignore option with various excuses suggested by the software as I crept down the fast lane. I'm in class. I'm in jail. I'm driving. The last one was true, if I could call sitting motionless in bumper-to-bumper traffic driving, but Bree probably wouldn't believe it. On the outskirts of her neighborhood, I hit the liquor store for a bottle of red wine. She couldn't be mad if I brought wine, right? And if she was…I still had wine. The good stuff, too. Twenty bucks a bottle.

I minded the speed limits on her street. Mostly because the Neighborhood Watch signs and fluorescent yellow plastic men holding orange "Children at Play" flags freaked me out. I imagined being cuffed over the hood of my car for doing twenty-seven in a twenty-five while angry mothers beat me for endangering their children. Who was the Neighborhood Watch anyway? Residents? Rental cops? Could they carry guns? Taser me? Organized civilians scared the bejesus out of me. Those sorts of groups were always formed by power-hungry commoners with angry hearts, except Friends of the Library. I stood behind those ladies.

I coasted into Bree's drive and parked behind Mom's car. Mom met me on the little cobblestone walkway. Gwen toddled through the grass, pulling dandelions and dumping them by dimpled-fistfuls into her fairy garden. I kissed my niece on the head. "Looks like your mommy made the faeries a house just like yours."

Gwen drooled onto her shirt and stuffed a ceramic toadstool in her mouth.

"Ah, ah, ah." Mom swooped in and liberated the toadstool, returning it to the little replica stone house covered in dandelions.

Bree and Tom lived in a bigger version of the faeries' house, but it was the smallest people-home on their street. The smallest home in the most expensive neighborhood they could afford. Within a year of their purchase, they'd put their psychologist brains together and turned the little fixer-upper into a centerpiece. Their cottage now resembled a storybook home, complete with a dwarf rose garden, flower-laden trellis and wooden swing dangling from the historic oak tree. They'd swapped the old brick walk for manufactured cobblestone and hung flower boxes from the front windowsills. Robust planters and a red rocking chair added flair and charm to the welcoming stoop. A length of white picket fence lined the walkway. The whole thing was extremely adorable. My apartment would be infuriated if it saw the effort Bree made on her place. I still had unopened moving boxes in my closet.

"Sorry I'm late." I clutched the wine to my chest. "I brought a peace offering."

Mom rolled her eyes. "Well, you're going to need that." She scooped Gwen off the grass and led me inside.

"There you are!" Grandma grabbed my cheeks between her palms and squeezed. "Bree was just wondering where you were."

"I have wine."

Grandma winked. "Bree's had a little, too."

I exhaled deep and long. "Thank goodness."

Grandma handed me a blue-and-cream quilted bag. "I have another virus. The thing's slower than dialup. Every page is loading and loading and loading…" She circled a wrist in the space between us. "My notebook's a mess."

I accepted the bag. "I'll take a look."

Tom wiped his hands on a dishtowel and motioned me in. His mouth was full.

Fifties music played through hidden speakers in the kitchen. The display of appetizers was phenomenal. Tiny plates with half-eaten food lined the counter near the sink where Tom worked. "We're just sitting down for dinner. Grab a couple appetizers and go on in. I'm finishing up here and then we'll get started. Everyone's in the dining room."

"Thanks." I stuffed grandma's laptop bag next to mine and set them aside. I held onto the wine.

Tom turned back to the dishes, humming pleasantly.

Why couldn't everyone be so content and happy? Like his wife, for example.

In the dining room, Bree glared at me over the rim of her glass. She swigged her wine and cocked her head. "Hello, Mia. Have any trouble finding the place?"

"I brought wine."

"Awesome." Her tone implied otherwise.

I took the seat between Dad and Grandma, my biggest fans. Mom settled Gwen into her high chair as Tom arrived with the salad.

The table was decked out with our great-grandmother's china, passed down from Potter woman to Potter woman on her wedding day. One day Bree would hand it over to Gwen.

Bree stood at the head of the table and smiled at her husband. "Thank you all for coming tonight to celebrate with Tom and me." She motioned him to her side and took his hand. "As you know, we applied for this grant nearly two years ago, and while we enjoyed studying the impacts of stress and sugar substitutes on fertility, this was our dream project, and it's finally here." She bounced on her toes. "Sexuality is a global standard that has fascinated us since we met in grad school. It flattens the world and connects all people. This is our chance to understand the most basic human drive, aside from food and shelter."

She shook her head, presumably realizing sexuality wasn't the hinge pin she thought it to be.

Tom tipped his head left and right. "And water."

"Death," Grandma added. "Sleep and general safety."

Bree huffed. "Humans were designed to be sexual creatures, and that is true regardless of culture or ethnicity, age or gender. We're honored to have the university's blessing and financial backing to delve into

exactly what sexuality is and how it changes our lives."
She glanced at me but saved her comment.

Tom poured a glass of wine and raised it to Bree.
"To exploring sexuality."

She beamed. "To sexuality."

Dad downed his drink.

"Cheers," the rest of us called.

Tom came to my side. "I'm so sorry. I didn't realize
you needed a drink. Let me open that bottle for you."
He motioned to my lap, where I was still cradling the
peace offering.

I passed him the wine. "None for me. I'm driving."
And I wasn't much of a drinker. One more difference
between my family and me. I preferred to get my calo-
ries via cake.

He set the bottle on the table. "I bought a nice selection, but we'll keep this close in case we run low
on red."

"Deal."

When my dinner plate was empty for the second
time, Dad passed a basket of rolls my way. "Any leads
on your case?"

I sucked down some ice water and swallowed. "No,
but I locked down the system and there haven't been
any more problems."

He nodded, chewing slowly. "How about Nate? Any
word from him."

"Yes. He'll be at Comic Con tomorrow night." Unfortunately, so would Dan. "Dad? Do cops need war-
rants or something to bug an apartment or hack into
your computer?"

He set his roll aside. "Why?"

"Just wondering. I'm curious how investigations

work and what they're doing on their end." Not total lies.

"I guess it depends on the circumstances. It's been a while since I was on the force, and I wasn't a detective. I'm sure Detective Archer's following the laws, otherwise the evidence collected won't be admissible in court."

Bree cleared the table one-handed, wineglass in the other. "Thanks for coming, Sis."

I smiled. "I wouldn't have missed it."

Tom helped her manage the load of empty dishes.

A moment later, she called through the doorway. "And now, for the *pièce de résistance*." Bree reappeared carrying a large tray with a flesh-colored cake. She set it in the center of the table.

Mom gasped. Dad's mouth fell open and his cheeks turned red.

I roared with laughter.

"Do you love it?" Bree's slight drawl showed the wine was doing its trick.

Tom entered the room with a fresh pile of plates, his attention fixed on the unfortunate cake. He nearly tripped over his wife.

She scanned the room. "What's wrong? I told you I was making a themed cake. The icing didn't go perfectly, but I'm not a professional."

I uncovered my face and peeked again at the dessert. Another outburst overtook me. Tears rolled over each cheek.

Thin black lines of icing fanned out from the middle of the peachy oval cake. In the center, a smaller oval with a little circle was drawn in an odd shade of rouge.

"Is that a vulva?" Tom was clearly impressed by his wife's artistic ability.

I, on the other hand, understood the problem, which made me laugh harder. Bree's creative talents ended at home design. Whatever happened to the icing, I wasn't sure, but that was part of the hilarity. "It's not a vulva. It's an eye." I gave a loud, painful snort. "It's an eye." I gripped my aching side and snapped a picture with my phone. This was one for the scrapbooks. Bree's face was perfect. I snapped a picture of her, too.

Mom and Grandma burst into laughter while the men wrinkled their noses.

Bree slapped the table. "She's winking! The white icing got all smudged up, but it's a wink. You see that, right?" She pointed to the vulva. "These are lashes. This is the lid, mostly shut, and her little pupil. She's winking. It's an international show of flirtation."

The ferocity in Bree's tone, coupled with the way she said *pupil*, set me over the edge. I ran for the bathroom to settle down.

Is that a vulva?

I pressed my back to the wall and clutched my chest. My family was insane, and I loved them so much.

Two hours later, I entered the elevator at my apartment with the unopened bottle of red wine and Grandma's laptop. She'd probably downloaded something she shouldn't have and gotten another virus. I warned her about the ads on Renaissance dating sites, but she couldn't resist a man in a kilt.

My key slid easily into the lock and the door swung open before I turned the knob. Had I not locked the door? I'd left quickly, but surely I'd locked my door. Hadn't I? I peeked inside. Clutching my phone and keys in one hand, I set the bottle of wine on the table beneath my light switch. My heart rate doubled. I flipped on the lights. Everything was overturned, emptied or otherwise destroyed. On the wall over my table, large red letters spelled, *You were warned.*

Panic seized me.

I stumbled backward, away from the crime scene, praying the burglar wasn't inside, that he wouldn't chase me if he was. I ran past the elevator to the stairs, putting my fear to work. I speed-dialed Dan Archer and bolted outside. I locked myself inside the Crown Vic until he pulled up five minutes later.

Dan jogged past me on his way to the building.

"Hey!" I waved my arms and dashed along behind him.

Dan swore. "Where did you come from?"

I pointed to the Crown Vic.

He exhaled. "You're okay? Unharmed."

"Yes."

"Have you seen anyone leave the building since you called me?"

"No."

He opened the door and stepped aside. I slipped in and pushed the elevator button.

"Dan, wait up." Jake called from a distance.

I froze at the familiar voice and forced my attention to the shiny silver doors before me.

He stopped inches away from his brother. "Is she hurt? Did she see anyone? Were there any unusual cars outside when she got home? Have you talked to the neighbors?" He huddled closer, talking as if I wasn't there.

A gray sedan angled against the curb outside.

Jake nodded at the window. "Are those your guys?"

"Yep."

The elevator opened. "Are you going to get in or should I wait for you upstairs?" I looked into the empty elevator. I didn't particularly want to go up alone. "Guys?"

The Archers turned to me with furrowed brows and boarded the elevator.

Dan took point when we reached my floor, striding into my apartment as if he had no worries a killer might lurk within.

I followed him in and grabbed the discarded wine as I passed.

Jake entered on my heels. He left the door open and lingered near my side. He moved methodically through the kitchen, fingering my things and ogling my photos. "Who's this?"

He wedged a snapshot between two long fingers.

"Tom."

"Tom?"

"MacAngus."

He squinted at me. "What kind of a name is Mac-Angus?"

"Scottish."

He snapped the photo back onto my refrigerator with a *Star Wars* magnet. "Have you known Tom long?"

"Since college."

"What does Tom do?"

Why did he keep saying *Tom*? "He studies human sexuality."

"I bet."

I glared. "What are you doing here?"

His meanie expression wavered. "What do you mean?"

"I mean, you're not a cop. You're the temporary head

of security at my office. I called Dan about the break-in."

A pair of men in navy windbreakers waltzed through my door, speaking in low tones and acronyms. One knelt at the doorknob and went to work dusting the frame and knob for prints. The other posed a high-end camera to one eye and photographed the threat wall.

Dan sauntered down the hallway with his little notebook flipped open. "I called him. Where were you tonight?"

"I was at my sister's for dinner. Where were you? Aren't you supposed to be following me? Why would you call your brother? This isn't any of his business."

Dan glanced at Jake. "I took the night off. You weren't here, and I had a date. Plus, between you and me, I don't think you're guilty."

"Right." I grabbed a couch cushion and pulled the furniture back together.

Dan followed me through the living room. "Who knew you'd be out tonight?"

I righted the folders and books on my coffee table. "Randall from work. My family, who were all at Bree's with me, and your brother."

Dan curled his lip in a strange half smile. "Anything unusual happen while you were at your sister's?"

I folded an afghan over the back of my tidied couch and dropped onto the cushions. "We ate a vanilla winking vulva cake, but I can't say that was unusual. My sister's a culinary nightmare."

Dan's little pen hovered over his notebook. "See anyone following you or an unfamiliar car outside the building when you got home? Anything at all that you found strange while you were away?"

"No."

"Have you taken a look around? Anything missing?"

"The only things I keep here with any value are electronic." I motioned to my flat screen and shelving unit with game systems, games, movies, phone dock and speakers. "Everything else is basic household stuff or apparel."

Jake stared at the defaced wall. "Someone broke in to leave that message. This mess was for fun. A little icing on your threat cake."

I dragged the quilted bag onto my legs and pulled Grandma's computer from the cushioned pocket. A tremor rocked my hands. I'd finish cleaning when the Archers left. Until then, I'd stay busy with things I understood. "Thank goodness I took my laptop with me."

Dan snapped back to life. "Why'd you do that? Do you always take your computer to dinner?"

I gave Dan a crazy face. "I never leave without my laptop. This bag is like my purse. Everything I could ever need is in here. My phone. My wallet. My laptop. My tablet."

Dan eyeballed Grandma's laptop. "Is that your computer?"

"No. Mine's in the bag."

"Who does that one belong to?"

I booted up Grandma's laptop and ran an antivirus program. "This is my grandma's spare. She prefers her desktop with the twenty-one-inch monitor, but she's a reader, so she keeps this one with her when she goes out." The little line indicating the antivirus software's performance inched across the screen. My mind reeled, working double time to put together a set of revelations. I jumped to my feet and lifted a finger in the air. Two viruses were identified. "Grandma had a virus."

Dan and Jake closed in on me.

Jake lifted his palms in a calming gesture. I'd seen Dad use it to break up fights at the ballpark. "And that makes you angry?" He nodded in mock understanding.

I turned my back on him. *Loon.* Maybe Dan would understand. "Grandma gets viruses that slow things down all the time. She can't resist men in kilts. When the pages take too long to load, she asks me to scrub for malware."

Dan stared over my head, presumably at Jake. "And that makes you angry?"

I stomped one foot. "I'm not angry." Geez. "The emails at work weren't spam. They were viruses."

Dan scribbled in his notebook. "Keep talking."

I opened my laptop and brought up the cached page. "This is the page residents landed on after clicking the link in the scheduling email. I think whoever wrote the emails wanted their recipients to click the link. I'd bet my original Lasso of Truth all emails from this sender, coupons, scheduling, whatever, were all designed for the same purpose."

"To give residents' computers a virus?"

I nodded. "Residents installed spyware and never had a clue. They clicked on the link and were sent to another page. When they entered their names and addresses, they were prompted to download the coupons or scheduling software and boom. They accepted and installed the spyware instead." I raised my hands overhead in a V for victory and collapsed back onto the couch. "Infected. From there, the hacker had access to their computers. The hackers weren't phishing for names and addresses, they were getting an invitation, via download, to spy."

Dan crouched before me. "What kind of spyware?"

"I don't know. None of the buttons on the page work anymore."

"How can we find out?"

Did a police detective ask me how to proceed with his investigation? My fingers itched to call and brag to Dad. The thought of telling Mom about the break-in stanched my enthusiasm. I put on my professional face. "Can you ask the people who complained about the emails to bring me their computer? Warren and I can look for programs and files shared by all the computers that opened the emails. If we find the files, I can figure out what it did when they clicked."

Dan tapped his notebook against one palm. "I can ask them, but I can't make anyone hand over their computer. People don't like to part with their electronics, and no one wants a cop nosing through their files. They have things they don't want seen. If I ask, some will lie about opening the emails or which computer they used to open the links. Most people have more than one computer, so it'd be hard to know if we collected all the corrupted machines."

"Why don't people save their shame to the cloud?" I leaned forward. "Maybe we don't need them all. Wait a minute. Can't you commandeer them?"

He stood and arched his back in a lazy stretch. "I'll see what I can do."

An hour later, Dan moved to my door. "You've got my card. If you find anything missing, make a list. Let me know if you need anything else and set this alarm next time you leave. They don't work when they're not set."

"Ha. Ha."

The camera and print duo met Dan at the door and

murmured something that caused him to nod. They left him for the elevator.

Dan tucked his little notebook into his back pocket. "We'll let you know if we get a hit on any prints or a bead on the message." He pointed his pen at the wall before slipping it into his pocket. "You heading out, Jake?"

Jake was stacking fallen cookbooks on the shelf over my sink. He lifted his chin in response to his brother. "I thought I'd stick around and help clean up. This is a pretty discouraging mess, and she'll need someone tall to erase the love note on the wall."

I shivered. *You were warned.*

Dan turned his cop face on me. "Is that okay with you?"

I glanced at Jake and swallowed a pang of something I didn't like. My traitorous head nodded. "Yeah. It's okay with me."

THIRTEEN

I CLOSED THE door and headed for the kitchen. "I'm going to open this wine."

Jake froze.

I grabbed my favorite coffee mug and smiled. "I'm not coming on to you. I'm not trying to get you drunk. I have no ulterior motive for opening this bottle. Unless you count escapism. When I think of someone sneaking in here and destroying the place…" I shivered. "I need a drink."

Jake squinted. "Completely understandable."

I uncorked the wine and poured a mug full. I couldn't reach the proper wineglasses I kept for when Mom and Bree visited. I didn't have the energy to bother with appearances. "The glasses are on top of the refrigerator. If you want, you can help yourself." I lowered my lips to the nearly overflowing mug and sipped until I could lift it without spilling.

Wine and frustration warmed my tummy. "I have to scrub a threat off my wall and clean up the mess a killer made when he broke in here while I was away today."

Jake unscrewed the spout of a plastic sippy cup Bree left for Gwen and filled the little tumbler with wine. "I'll clean the wall. You deal with your personal things."

I sucked another mouthful of red wine between trembling lips. "Why are you helping me? Are you pretending to clean but really you're bugging my apartment?"

Jake finished his tumbler and set it on the counter with a smack. "What kind of person do you think I am?"

"The lying, manipulative sort, apparently."

He refilled the little pink cup. "I won't resent that in light of your pathological trust issues."

Touché. I scanned the messy room. "Do you think Baxter's killer is the one who did this? When I said a killer was here, you didn't argue."

Jake's frown deepened. "What are your thoughts on coincidences?"

"What are yours? You asked me what kind of person you are. Dan staked out my apartment last night, and this morning he knew I'm meeting Nate at Comic Con tomorrow night. How could he know that? Is it a coincidence you were here the night before?" I set my cup aside and formed little air quotes with my fingers. "'Checking to make sure my apartment was safe.' Is that when you bugged me?"

"What?" His crazy face almost made me smile. Almost. "Have you lost your mind?"

"Yes. As a matter of fact, I think, maybe, yes. I consider the possibility every night. These sorts of things don't happen to me. I'm a good girl." I waved a hand in the direction of my threat wall. "This is not who I am."

Jake's expression softened. "I didn't bug you. Dan knew about Comic Con because I told him. When the investigation began, I asked around the clubhouse about you. Everyone agreed you're into gaming, Renaissance Faires and Comic Con. You told me about REIGN and your participation in the Renaissance Faire, but you didn't mention the comic convention, so Dan checked. You purchased tickets with your credit card. Nate did the same thing. Since the convention is tomorrow and

Nate's in the wind, it seemed like a good place to keep an eye out. Dan plans to be there just in case."

"Oh."

He smirked. "Yeah. Oh."

"So you didn't bug my apartment?"

He shook his head slowly, as if I were a little slow. "Anything else you want to ask?"

I chewed my bottom lip. "I want to know what the email recipients had in common. What was the point of the emails? If I'm right about the virus, what then? What does the virus do? Why those particular recipients? What about the break-ins? Were those homes targeted or was the whole community targeted. What's the common denominator?" I took another long drink and processed my questions. There had to be a bottom line.

Jake refilled his cup and matched my stance, leaning on his elbows beside me. "Everyone in Horseshoe Falls is loaded. Does that count?"

"Maybe." I turned cowardly eyes away as I weighed my next question. "Why'd you get weird when I told you I was rich?"

He shifted away from me and walked to the table. "I don't know what you mean."

"Liar." I followed him, fueled by sudden wine-induced bravery. "You blew me off the minute I confessed."

He barked a humorless laugh. "Confessed? You must feel guilty about it to choose that word."

"Don't analyze me, cowboy. I said *confess* because the minute people hear I have money they react more bizarrely than they already do toward me. It's just money."

"Until you don't have any."

I stared. What could I say to that? I had more money than I needed or wanted, and Jake apparently didn't have any. Maybe. I needed to rehash this conversation with Bree. Sometimes people said what they meant. In my experience, that was the exception, not the rule.

Jake blew out a long breath. "I didn't mean to act weird. I'm sorry if it came off as rude. Why'd you taunt me about my role as temporary head of security?"

"I didn't."

He guffawed. "You did. You said I was jealous of my little brother's career, and you made endless jibes at my lack of motivation, then teased me for aspiring to be a real cop, which I never said I did. Come to think of it, you've been mean in general."

He was right. I had been mean. "Fine. I didn't intend to be mean to you either. Sometimes I say things without thinking and when I'm cornered, I lash out. I'm not great with people."

"I don't believe that. I've seen you with people all week. You love people."

I sighed. "Well, they don't all love me. I have a bad habit of saying the wrong things and misreading social clues. People are hard."

Jake laughed and nodded. "That they are."

I moved to the couch. "I don't like problems I can't solve."

He followed me with our cups and the mostly empty bottle of wine. "Then you'd hate being a detective."

I propped my feet on the coffee table. "Probably. I need closure and victory." I dropped my head back to stare at the ceiling. "In my perception, life's like a big puzzle. There are no coincidences, just cause and effect or intent and action. Emotions mess that up, but more or less, I'm right. There's a pattern, a rhythm to life and to people. I'm always looking for it, but I never really see it the way I expect to. Those aren't the right words to explain it." I rolled my head to face Jake, hoping I'd made at least a little sense.

His eyes were shut, his lips parted. A little pink tumbler leaned against his massive palm.

"I'm a stimulating conversationalist too. Did I mention that?" I collected Gwen's cup and set it on the table. "Looks like I'm cleaning the threat wall alone."

SIX HOURS LATER, Jake woke with a start. "I fell asleep."

I pressed a palm to my caffeine-boosted heart. "Yes. And you just gave me a heart attack."

He stood, wiping sleep from his eyes and looking like a kid caught with one hand in the cookie jar. "I didn't mean to do that. I don't drink, and I haven't slept well in…years. I'd better go. I'm going to go."

I swiveled in my desk chair to face him. "It's no big deal. I wasn't thrilled about being alone last night. It was nice knowing if the burglar came back, I wouldn't be."

Jake stared at the threat wall. "You cleaned it? I meant to do that. It wasn't a line to justify staying here."

I shrugged. "Like I said, it was nice knowing I wasn't alone. Besides, it came off easy. Face paint from my cosplay trunk."

"Cosplay trunk?" He moved to the window and peeled back the curtain.

"I dress up as favorite comic book heroes or television characters. It's a big deal at the conventions, and it's fun."

He dropped the curtain and stuffed his hands into his pockets, managing to look guiltier. "Did you sleep?"

I went to the window. "No. I couldn't, so I made coffee and did some reconnaissance for the investigation."

I peered between the curtain panels. Dan's truck sat behind Jake's across the street. "I created a spreadsheet of everyone living at Horseshoe Falls. Names, addresses and places of business. After that, I pulled random information, everything I could, looking for commonalities. What they owe on their homes, the banks they used for the mortgages, where they went to college, credit scores. Basic stuff. Are you upset because your brother is outside and knows you stayed here last night?"

He snarled. "Aren't you?"

I made a show of checking my watch. "Nope. It says here this isn't 1955 anymore, and I'm a grown-ass woman."

"Your watch says all that?"

I laughed. "Ow." Apparently staying up all night was harder at my age with or without the assistance of stress, adrenaline and coffee. "I have a headache. I'm going to bed."

He headed for the door. "I'll let everyone at the clubhouse know what happened here and that you won't be in."

I unlocked the dead bolt and pulled the door open for him. "I can do that myself. Again—" I waved hands over my body. "All grown up."

He coughed into his fist and hustled out the door.

"Hey," I called after him.

He looked back with one eyebrow cocked high.

"Why didn't you go to detective school like the rest of your family?"

He frowned and climbed into the elevator.

"Fine." I relocked the doorknob and dead bolt. I added the chain before setting the alarm. "Don't tell me your secrets, Jake Archer. It's not like I can't find them myself." I yawned into my palm and sent a line of texts to work, family and my rental insurance agent. The coffee had officially given out.

My head pounded me awake. It felt like five minutes later. The clock said noon. Apparently, time flew when I was mentally and physically exhausted. My head wasn't pounding. The door was. I'd slept almost seven hours.

I shuffled to the door with one eye open. "Stop. I'm coming." I unlatched the chain and looked through the peephole. A line of hipsters trailed from my door to the elevator. "What do you want?" I leaned my forehead against the door. "I'm sleeping."

"We brought food." Carl's voice crawled through the thin walls and under the door. "Mashed potatoes and gravy, meatloaf, baby carrots and chocolate lava cake. It's all organic and gluten free, but there's sugar in the cake."

I opened the door, suspicious.

Rich, buttery aromas greeted me. "That smells amazing."

Ben, Quake and Carl motored past me, carrying small Crock-Pots and casserole dishes. Three women followed.

I stood, dumbfounded, holding the door. "What's happening?"

Carl gathered his crowd beside my kitchen counter. They put things in the fridge, covered platters on the counter and generally followed his lead. "We heard about what happened here last night. I know Nate's gone, and we were feeling kind of bad for you. I mean, it's got to be hard being a single weird chick and to then lose your only friend. Someone robbed your place." He shook his head. "We've got so much, we thought we should give a little something to someone who needs it, you know? The hot foods are in slow cookers. The guys plugged them in so you can eat whenever you feel like it. We're clean eaters, so we take food pretty seriously."

"Thanks?" I forced a pleasant expression. Sleep addled my mind, and food talk got my tummy worked up. Did the lead hipster just call me a weird chick?

"We watch Nate's apartment for you. No one's come or gone. If you want us to split up and hit the streets we can. We know everyone."

"That's okay. I'm okay. Thank you for the food. I think I'm going to go back to bed."

A WNBA-sized woman, with dreadlocks and striped knee socks, folded her hands in prayer pose and tipped her head toward me. "Peace and love be with you."

I was officially awake. "Okay. That's enough. I'm fine. Thank you for the food." I opened my arms in a corralling motion and herded them to the door. "I appreciate your time and your food. I'll get these plates and slow cookers back to you tomorrow, but you *really, really* shouldn't have."

The line stopped short of a pileup outside my door, making teddy bear eyes at me. "If you need anything…"

I waved and shut the door. "Thanks again," I called through the wall. I was being pitied by hipsters. I couldn't process that without coffee and maybe a piece of cake.

I stared at the counter filled with food in vintage containers. *They* thought *I* was weird. Good grief.

"Flight of the Bumblebee" poured through my bedroom door. I ran for my nightstand to grab the phone. "Hello?"

"Good. You're home. I'm on my way up." Bree disconnected before I said another word.

What was wrong with people?

I marched to the door and watched through the peephole. She emerged from the elevator with Gwen on one hip. Bree's hair was a mess, and her cheeks were flushed.

I opened the door before she knocked. "Everything okay? Get caught in a windstorm?"

"Can you watch Gwen for a few hours?" She set my niece on the rug at my feet and kissed her head. "Tom and I were working on the research grant, and she woke from her nap early. She won't go back down, so neither can I."

I blinked, unfollowing. "I thought you were working from home."

Bree smoothed her hair with one hand and lifted her chin. "We're watching adult films today as research, and we both feel the material is inappropriate for Guinevere. We thought you could keep an eye on her while we finish up."

I looked from Gwen to Bree. "You think adult movies are inappropriate for your one-year-old daughter?"

Bree nodded.

"And you drove all the way here before calling to see if I'll babysit so you can do things to your husband. For research."

"Yes. Strictly research. I'd never ask you to watch her without notice if it wasn't for work."

"How'd you know I'd be home?"

"You texted me before dawn." She waved her phone in my direction. "'Working from home. Break-in at my place last night. Available until five online or by text.' I didn't bother calling to check up because I didn't want to fight with you. I wanted to, though. Call, not fight."

I examined the cryptic text. "I think that text was meant for Randall at the clubhouse."

She pursed her lips and rolled her eyes. "Very professional. What did my intended text say then? Never mind, don't tell me. You usually don't."

"You're suggesting I'm unprofessional based on a text? Texts are supposed to be brief. If I wanted to detail the whole story, I'd have sent an email."

She shrugged. "It's only an opinion."

I popped a hip. "I'm sorry. Are you the pot or the kettle here?"

Was she seriously not seeing this? It was a ridiculous conversation. Wasn't it? I looked at Gwen. I needed someone to bounce the crazy off when Bree was the crazy. "I'm happy to watch Gwen anytime. You know that. If it helps you get your groove on, all the better. Be back by three. I have a thing tonight."

She hugged me and disappeared.

"Gross." I dusted my shirt and locked up again. "Your mom's not gross, sweetie." I grabbed Gwen off the floor and snuggled her. "But I can't be sure exactly what you interrupted." I kissed her forehead and twirled with her around my apartment. "What do you think? Do you want to try some hipster cake?"

She slapped drool-covered hands on my shoulder and squealed.

"Me, too."

FOURTEEN

I ADJUSTED MY knickers and corset. Corsets were a beautiful but evil invention. Anyone who argued with that was either into BDSM or male.

Comic Con was underway, and I'd promised to meet Nate. The last-minute costume change made me later and sweatier than I already was. Nate and I had themed our looks and spent days creating the pieces from scraps. We'd labored over perfect custom *Alice in Wonderland* and Mad Hatter costumes with a steampunk bent. Gears and buckles everywhere. Lots of gratuitous gadgetry. We were sure we'd win a prize in the big contest. I'd had one striped stocking outside the door when I realized Alice was a terrible choice now. Once Dan saw me as Alice, he'd cuff every Mad Hatter in the building looking for Nate. Assuming he understood her one true pairing.

There wasn't time to visit the costume shop or make something else, so I got creative. Fortunately, I did my best work under pressure.

I twisted at the waist in front of my mirror, examining the results. Black shoes, tights, skirt, hat…white blouse, big bag, red scarf. The corset cinched my waist nicely and added a bit of flair to the traditional Mary Poppins ensemble. I kept the steampunk twist. Added a pocket watch on a chain and gears to the daisy on my hat. The skirt was short and the heels were high. I loved it.

I tiptoed in a circle on pencil-thin stilettos. "Mary, you little trollop. Whatever would the chimney sweep say?" I winked at my reflection, tucked my essentials into the giant bag and hooked an umbrella over my arm. "Top-notch. Spot-on. Cheerio!"

The convention center was packed and the lot was full. Lines of superheroes and villains wrapped the building. Comic Con sold out in a few minutes every year. It was the best thing to happen to northeastern Ohio since the Ren Faire. I skipped the line and scanned my phone against the new digital ticket taker. Boom! Three hundred people outside wished they'd downloaded that app. Suckers.

Energy zinged through the electrified air inside the building. I hugged my phone to my chest, soaking in the most magical place on earth. Voices blended in a heated buzz of excitement. I nodded to passersby like a proper English lady and swung my hips the way I imagined Steampunk Mary would. Larger-than-life posters of my favorite characters and movie scenes lined unending aisles of vendor displays. My arms itched to swing open in reverence. My feet ached to twirl.

I held it together. I was on a mission. The temptations around me had to wait until I located Nate and learned his side of the story.

Harley Quinn and Joker, my two favorite Batman villains, headed my way. I raised my umbrella. "Excuse me." They exchanged a look but didn't respond. "Sir, Madame, would you be so kind as to point me in the direction of the *Serendipity*?"

Harley Quinn pointed to an enormous Heroes of the Universe sign.

I performed a small curtsy, working to maintain poise, despite my ill-chosen heels. Nate hadn't told me where to find him, but we always visited *Serendipity* first. If I was forced to bet, I'd put my spoonful of sugar on *Serendipity*. The short-lived television show set on the airship was the one that brought us together. He'd never met a girl who enjoyed sci-fi. I hadn't met a guy who earned the right to know that much about me. Most men were more interested in the size of my bra or bank account than what made me happy. Personal interests were second-date material, and my dates never made it to a sequel. Some hadn't made it to dessert.

The crowd grew denser as I approached the section of the building featuring space-themed fandoms. A group of Power Rangers performing in the main aisle slowed me further. I hooked the umbrella over my arm and sucked in a breath.

"Pardon me," I prattled in my best British accent. "I'm late for tea. The children need me. Be a dear and move your arses."

Several yards from the airship, a man in a gray suit caught my eye. He was scanning the crowd in a continuous sweeping motion.

Dan. I bit my lip. Now what?

I needed to get close enough to stake out the airship without being seen by the detective. I ducked through a line of Dorothys and hid behind Glinda the Good Witch's oversized skirt.

"Why, hello, Mary!" one of the Dorothys called.

I waved a gloved hand and whispered. "Lower your voice. I'm hiding."

"Oh, dear," the Dorothy murmured. "Is it the Wicked Witch? Do you see her? Does she have her flying mon-

keys? We'd better find Lion, Scarecrow and Tin Man."
They scattered, leaving me with Glinda.

"That was dumb. Why would Mary Poppins hide
from the Wicked Witch or her monkeys?" I straightened, adjusting my corset and fluffing my skirt. Dan
had disappeared into an open panel room.

I smiled at Glinda. "I'm dreadfully sorry about that."

Glinda nodded, magnanimously. "That's all right,
dear."

I turned my phone over in my hand, checking for a
message from Nate. Nothing. I scanned the thickening
crowd. A familiar velvet top hat floated above heads in
the distance. My heart skipped. *Nate.* I hustled to the
Serendipity airship and entered the cargo hold.

Nate sat on a wooden crate. He tipped his giant
bronze velvet hat.

Elation tore through me, and I tackled him. "Oh my
goodness, I can't believe you're here. You're okay?" I
patted his cheeks and looked him over. "You're okay!"
I hugged him again. "I've been scared to death every
night that you wouldn't come back." I wiped my nose
on my wrist and whacked him with my free hand. "You
could've called. Bought a burner phone or used a pay
phone or something."

He held my hand to his chest, probably so I wouldn't
hit him again. "Sorry. I've never been on the run before, and it's harder than you think. I'm following the
detective who's following me. He's actually here right
now. It's all very complicated."

I backed up a step to get a good look at his face. "His
name's Dan Archer. I saw him too. He's not that bad
for a guy trying to capture you. Are you sure you're
really okay?"

His bright smile lit my heart. "Better now, but yeah. I'm not hurt or in imminent danger at the moment."

I slouched, suddenly overcome with relief. "What happened that day? I can't figure it out. I visited Jillian. She said you were looking into Punisher for me. Is that what this is about?" It seemed impossible for the two to be related, but what else could I make of it?

Nate's eyelids drooped. He led me to a small alcove in the ship, away from rubberneckers and eavesdroppers. "I can't believe Baxter's gone. This has been a complete nightmare." He squeezed my hands in his. "I should've known he was up to something sooner and stopped him that night."

"Tell me everything."

He sniffled. "Baxter liked you. You know that, right?"

I nodded, wrangling emotion and doing my best to compartmentalize.

"Well, he wanted to impress you. He knew Punisher gave you a ton of crap on REIGN, and he thought if he could get him to quit the game, you'd reward him with your love."

"Ew."

"Not that kind of love. Like your *love* love."

"Oh." *Aww.* "Go on."

Nate wetted his lips and looked over each shoulder. "He made another account for REIGN and joined Punisher's kingdom under the fake name. He was in the chat room for the kingdom and saw Punisher ranting about someplace that sounded a lot more like Horseshoe Falls than anything in the game, or anywhere else he could think of. I said he was reading into it, but he insisted, so we checked it out to shut him up. Baxter traced his IP address, and it turned out to be one in town."

I gasped. "In our town. Like in real life?" I whispered the last sentence. Thoughts spun and collided in my mind. Punisher was part of my online life. Those people weren't real. They were abstract.

The argument failed. Nate and Baxter were real. I was real, but the lines were blurred.

Nate batted emotion-glossed eyes. "The IP belongs to a library in Akron. That's only twenty minutes from Horseshoe Falls, so we went there and posed as tech support. We reviewed the online activity for each terminal and found one with some interesting documents in the trash."

I smiled in approval. Combing through files that had been trashed and deleted was savvy work.

Nate's smile was gone in a flash. "That's when we saw the forms. Baxter was right. Whoever Punisher is, he's planning something at Horseshoe Falls. There were files with the community logo on the computer. Why would someone forge Horseshoe Falls documents? It's practically a retirement village."

My heart raced frantically. Punisher sent the emails to Horseshoe Falls. He'd killed my best friend. Tortured me online. I gripped Nate for balance. He'd been to my home.

Nate arranged his hold on me as I processed the unthinkable.

A few cleansing breaths later, I forced myself to make better use of my time with Nate before he disappeared again. "It's already happened. Someone spoofed the clubhouse email and sent residents bogus coupons and scheduling links. We found out about it when they tried to collect on the deals or appointments. Residents are outraged. The staff was in an uproar. The founder threatened to fire us all. Two homes were burglarized.

Stella was stabbed. It's been bad." I motioned between us. "Our apartments were both invaded." Something itched at the back of my mind. "You think Punisher's trying to ruin my real life? Is this about me? Wait a minute. What was Baxter going to do before he knew Punisher lived nearby?"

Nate looked as if I'd knocked the wind out of him. "I don't know what this is about. Baxter only wanted to make Punisher quit the game. He planned to drive him crazy the way he tortured you, until he finally left REIGN and gave you peace."

"That's sweet. Do you think he knew all the other stuff that was happening?"

He shook his head. A defeated expression crossed his brow. He lifted and dropped his shoulders. "Baxter copied everything we found at the library to show you, but the overgrown rent-a-cop kicked us out when we tried. After work Baxter was supposed to meet me at the pub for drinks. He never showed. I tried his place, your place and then Horseshoe Falls. You were working late, so I thought maybe he caught up with you there."

The knots in my stomach twisted into my backbone. "Were you there when he died?"

His eyebrows shot up. "No. Oh, no way. I was on my way there when an ambulance and two squad cars passed me. When I got to the guard gate, a couple of cops had blocked the entrance. I knew it was something bad, so I parked at the driving range down the street and cut through the forest. I thought whatever Punisher had planned must've happened and Baxter would want details. When I got to the clubhouse, I saw you outside with the big guy from earlier. I heard what you said. Baxter was dead and I knew I was in trouble. If not with the murderer, then with the police. I took off and stayed out of sight. I'm trying to figure this out from the periphery looking in. I knew you'd see the laptop and meet me here. Did you say my apartment was tossed?"

"Yeah. I cleaned it up after the police left." Another question jumped to mind. "Where's your car?"

"I swapped with my little brother's girlfriend. She got my new Navigator. I got her twelve-year-old Civic."

I cringed. "Can you even drive that? You can barely ride shotgun in Stella."

"I'm getting more flexible."

"Huh." I needed to visit the driving range and see if anyone else made a trip through the woods that night.

He swiped his big hat off and scrubbed twitchy hands over naturally red hair. "What'd they take?"

"The laptop. They tore the place up but, other than the laptop, everything seemed to be there when I cleaned it up. Someone did the same thing to my place last night. I bet they're looking for the information Baxter collected. Whatever Baxter found must be pretty incriminating."

Nate seemed to consider my words. "I thought all he had was the deleted logos. If there was more, he never told me."

"Maybe he found something before he went to see me at the clubhouse that night and the killer got him instead. I'm going back to his place. I want to see if he has any external hard drives or memory devices lying around. Something he might've kept the files on."

Nate took my hand. "He doesn't."

"How can you be sure? You don't know everything he had on Punisher, and you didn't know he went to my office that night."

Pain swept over his lightly freckled face. "I can't believe he's gone. If we work together, we can find Baxter's killer. If anyone can it's us."

I stepped into his arms and held him as he rocked with emotion. Maybe everyone needed an ugly cry sometimes. I buried my face into the curve of his neck and held tight. I wasn't ready to say goodbye again, but Dan was somewhere in the building and we needed to separate as soon as possible.

A long shadow covered us and stayed. "Figures." Jake's voice ricocheted off my heart.

I spun in front of Nate, blocking him with outstretched arms. "Stop."

Jake quirked a brow behind round glasses. The lightning bolt drawn on his forehead crinkled. "Is that a fugitive behind you?"

"No. He's not under arrest or in violation of any warrant. Nate's been on vacation and he had no idea the police were looking for him."

Nate gasped behind me. "What? The police are looking for me?" His faux sincerity fooled no one, but it didn't stop him. "This is brand new information."

Jake looked over my head. "I'm afraid you're going to have to come with me."

"No." I threw my hands in the air like a basketball player blocking a shot. "He's innocent." I turned to Nate. "Tell him what you told me. He can help us."

Nate reluctantly relayed the wiki version of what he'd told me.

I gave Jake my most pleading expression, hoping he'd accepted Nate's innocence. We needed someone on our side when we faced off with Dan. "Do you have to turn Nate over to Dan? I don't think he's safe. If you let him go, I'll stay in touch with him. We'll buy burner phones. Nate can help us."

Jake looked at Nate.

Nate moved to my side. "I haven't done anything. I'm not technically on the run because no one's asked me to come in, yet."

Jake adjusted his stance. "Because we can't find you."

I made my face as sincere as possible while trying not to kick him. "Please give us a chance to find this guy. I know we can. I'll tell you every move we make, and you can decide along the way whether or not to tell your brother."

Nate scoffed. "Your brother? Jeez."

Jake grabbed Nate's arm.

"Hey, you don't have to be rough." He snapped his arm free of Jake's monstrous grip. His voice rose an octave. "What is this? I haven't done anything. Tell me what you think I'm guilty of besides being dapper?" He smoothed the sleeve of his velvet jacket. "Or is being ginger a crime now?"

Jake rubbed his stubble-dusted cheeks. "I took your spreadsheet of the Horseshoe Falls residents and added to it."

Impressive. "What'd you add?"

"The residents with break-ins had the highest net worths. Of the top five wealthiest, two registered complaints about spam emails from the clubhouse, and one of those two is at least one hundred and probably never used a computer in her life."

"So, why complain?" I wondered.

Nate cleared his throat. "It was probably whoever's in charge of her caretaking, not actually her who complained."

Jake froze. "Get down." He forced the words between gritted teeth.

Nate hit the floor, and I looked for the danger.

Jake stuffed Nate into the crevice between the convention center wall and *Serendipity* cargo bay door. "Dan's here. Stay down and shut up." He turned anguished eyes on me. "What are you supposed to be?"

"I'm Mary Poppins."

His gaze raked over my corset, heels and skirt. "That's not what she wore."

"I have a steampunk twist."

"You sure like to show off your legs."

I made an obnoxious face. "What are you supposed to be?" His striped tie and glasses made it clear, but something in his swagger negated the costume attempt. "I don't get it," I lied.

He pulled a narrow brown wand from his back pocket. "I'm Harry Potter. I thought you'd know him. He's a little wizard guy. Here comes Dan. Don't make me regret this."

Before I could thank him for not ratting on Nate, he dropped his hands to my hips and pulled me to him.

"What?" I squeaked. My thoughts piled on one another as Jake's mouth grazed mine.

"Be still." His warm breath sent fever over my limbs. My brain, however, demanded he unhand me. The fever won.

He leaned into the corner, using me as a shield for as much of his too-tall frame as possible. His lips, all the while, floated just above mine. "He's passing now. Public displays of affection make people uncomfortable. He's unlikely to look directly at us. I think we're going to be okay."

I wasn't so sure about myself. My mind and body had detached sometime after the hip grabbing.

Jake extended his arms with me attached. I stumbled

to keep my balance. "He went toward the arcade. You need to get your buddy and keep him close. You don't want to lose him again. This crowd is good for hiding. Smart move."

My mouth hung open. I couldn't shut it. It had stopped listening to my brain, too.

"Go," he urged.

Nate poked his head through the hole where Jake had stuffed him. "Come on." He grabbed my hands and pulled my poofy skirt and giant bag through the space between walls. We landed near the rear exit and bathrooms.

I dusted my costume and adjusted my glasses. "What the hell just happened?"

"Where's Waldo let us go." Nate smiled. "Time to split up again." He kissed my head and darted into the men's bathroom.

A new round of nerves coiled in my tummy. We escaped Dan, but now I owed Jake a favor.

FIFTEEN

I PARKED THE Crown Vic in the lot outside Baxter's building and hustled up the steps. The process took longer than usual in stilettos. His Welcome mat was gone. Stolen? Or had his family come and gone already? I knocked and tried the doorknob. To my complete horror, the door opened.

I slid out of my heels, in case I needed to make a run for it, and brought 9-1-1 up on speed dial. I hovered my thumb over the screen. Help was one quick tap away.

I held my breath and listened. Silence roared through the room, accompanied only by the muffled sounds of neighbors' televisions and occasional honking from the busy streets. The rooms were void of personal touches and smelled faintly of lemon. "Hello?" I left the door open and crept inside.

A row of boxes marked *Donations* lined the wall near the door. His parents must've come like Jillian said. The ever-present knot in my tummy tightened. Baxter wouldn't be home again.

I shut the door and poked through the boxes. Old clothes, shoes, cracked dishes. No computer equipment or paraphernalia. Where would Baxter hide something he thought was valuable? I checked behind his vent grates, the backs of framed photographs and along the top of his kitchen cabinets. A coffee ring on the counter drew my attention. Odd. Someone had cleaned the place thoroughly and left a coffee puddle.

Regardless. No computers. No incriminating files.

I turned the button on the doorknob as I left and secured the door behind me. I shoved my feet back into my too-high heels and knocked on the neighbors' door.

The woman watching Baxter's cat answered. The cat purred softly in her arms. "Can I help you?" She wrinkled her nose at my outfit. Clearly she didn't recognize me. Of course, I wasn't normally dressed like an alternative Mary Poppins.

"Hi." I lifted a hand waist high. "I wondered if you knew who cleaned Baxter's apartment. I came to check on things and it looks like maybe his parents have already been here?"

She nodded. "That's right. His brother was here several times, getting his affairs in order, and his parents came yesterday."

"I didn't know Baxter had a brother. Do you remember what he looked like?"

She huffed. "You didn't know he had a brother, but you're here asking about him? Are you a reporter? Jealous girlfriend snooping around? If you didn't know he had a brother, maybe you weren't close enough to be asking questions. Talk with the landlord if you want to know anything else." She turned away.

"Wait." I slapped my palm against the closing door. "What about the cat? His parents didn't want it?"

She shrugged. "They never asked about the cat."

The fresh lemon scent from his apartment rushed to mind. "I didn't see any bowls or a litter box in his place. Do they know you have him?"

That got her attention. "You were inside his apartment? When?"

I shook my head, mentally backpedalling. "No. When I stopped by before."

She dropped the cat behind her. "We brought the cat's things here when we heard what happened to Baxter. It didn't make sense to go next door all the time to feed him in an empty apartment."

"Do you still have the key?"

Her mouth opened and closed. She shut the door on me and called through the wall. "Talk to the landlord. We're finished here."

"Gee. Thanks." I trudged down the steps to Dad's car. Another fruitless attempt at sleuthing.

Baxter never mentioned a brother, and if he had one, wouldn't the brother help at the same time as the parents? Why come separately? I stuffed the key into the Crown Vic's ignition and gunned the engine to life. Maybe the family had a scheduling conflict. Maybe the brother and parents were feuding. There were a million possible answers. I pinned that to the growing list of things I'd never know.

My phone rang. "Hello?"

"Where are you?" Jake's authoritative voice irked me most.

"I'm in the car. Where are you?"

"In my truck."

I turned onto the highway and waited for Jake to state his purpose.

He didn't.

Small talk was stupid. "Can I help you with something? I'm driving and I don't want a ticket for not going hands-free."

"I'm leaving the convention center and wondering where Nate's hiding."

I merged into the slow lane on the highway with ease.

Dad's car had more power than poor Stella. It was nice not to worry I wouldn't make it between moving cars.

What had Jake asked? Where was Nate? "I don't know."

He growled into the receiver.

"What? I'm not his keeper."

"Yes, you are his keeper. You promised to keep tabs on him. You promised, and I believed you."

I checked the mirrors and moved into the fast lane, enjoying my newfound horsepower. "I said I'd stay in touch with him, not keep tabs on him. When he went to the men's room, I left. What's the big deal? Besides, he's not hard to find. He's with Dan."

That earned an extended silence.

"Hello?" I shook the phone and examined the screen to be certain I hadn't dropped the call. I imagined him rubbing his hair into messy spikes.

"Why do you think he's with Dan?"

"Never mind."

My thoughts raced over details of the day. Jake's voice yammered in the background, making it difficult to drive and concentrate. Something stellar occurred to me as I passed the exit for my apartment and headed for work instead. "I know what happened."

He stopped talking.

"Meet me at the clubhouse. I have an idea about what happened during the break-ins."

An engine sprang to life on the other end of the line. "I'm on the way."

The clubhouse was creepy at night. I paced my office, trying not to think of the last time I stopped by after business hours. A chill crawled up my spine. Better to wait in the lobby. I pulled my office door open and screamed.

Jake's hand landed at his hip, as if to pull a nonexistent firearm. "What the hell?"

"I was on my way to the lobby." I panted and bent forward at the waist to catch my breath.

He motioned me to move ahead, and followed me to the lobby. I dropped onto the big couch near the concierge desk and willed my pulse to settle.

Jake's gaze climbed my legs. "Are you planning to change or is this new look permanent?"

I blinked. His Harry Potter garb was gone, replaced with his usual urban cowboy vibe. I'd love Harry forever, but I preferred this look on Jake. He stared. What was the question?

"Why did you tell me to meet you here?" Sharp blue eyes fastened me in place.

I shook my head, erasing cobwebs from my thoughts. "I went to Baxter's place after I left Comic Con." I pressed a palm to my heart. "I can't believe I missed all the panels and photo ops and games. I was supposed to win the costume contest."

His eyes raked over me, looking somewhat darker and more intense than I was prepared to handle. "Why were you at Baxter's?" His voice was thick with frustration.

"I wanted to find the files Nate told us about, but I was too late. The whole place has been packed up. There are a few boxes, but they're marked for charity. All his computer equipment is gone. The neighbor said his family came and cleaned the place."

Jake motioned to me. "You talked to the neighbor dressed like that?"

"Yeah. The neighbor was a little rude. I think she stole his cat."

His words registered a moment later.

"Hey, I'm Mary Poppins, not a serial killer, not that there's a costume for that. Most serial killers look like you."

"That's not a Mary Poppins costume. Maybe Mary's twin sister the strumpet, but not the nice babysitter who sang songs and flew around on an umbrella. You're more like a burlesque Poppins."

I beamed. "Thanks."

His face scrunched into a knot. He raised his palms. "Let's focus. You went to look for the files but didn't find anything. Why are we here?"

"I know what happened during the break-ins. I think the burglar broke in and manually installed the virus. He sent the virus in those bogus emails, but not everyone opened the link. I'll bet if we ask the residents with break-ins, they'll tell us they never opened the emails or clicked the links. Whoever created the email was forced to go to Plan B to install their malware."

He nodded. "Smart. Let's see if any of those residents are home and feel like a chat."

I jumped to my feet and kicked off my stilettos. "Give me five minutes to change. I keep a gym bag in the locker room. Obviously, you don't want to be seen with me dressed like this."

Jake didn't argue. He trailed behind me toward the gym locker room, dialing residents as we walked.

I stood a little straighter. *Mia Connors, the Burlesque Mary Poppins*. Cha cha cha.

Jake waited outside the locker room door while I slid into an old college T-shirt and jogging shorts. I unhinged the pins from my hair and unraveled it down my back, a total mess from the twisted updo I'd worn all day. I jammed thankful feet into flip-flops and left my gym shoes in the locker.

"Ready." I emerged relaxed, able to take my first deep breath in hours.

Jake glanced up from his phone, and a small smile curved his lips.

"What?" I arranged the costume pieces over my arm. "You preferred Burlesque Mary?" What a shocking surprise. A man who prefers short skirts and corsets to someone else's comfort.

"No." He shook his head. "Not at all."

I narrowed my eyes. "Yeah, right."

His small smile became serious. "I prefer real to make-believe."

The stilettos and corset in my hands grew heavier. My dumb heart grew lighter. "Who should we contact first?"

He slid his phone into his back pocket. "Bad news. No one answered my calls. I left voice mails with a vague explanation and a request that they bring their laptops to you tomorrow."

A round of excitement coursed through me. "That's brilliant. I know what to do." I jogged to my office and dropped the costume inside the door. "I'm sending an email offering to clean their computers. I'll apologize for the email issues earlier and offer the computer cleaning service for free. Warren and I can do it while they're at the clubhouse for another reason, or they can drop them off and I'll return them at the owner's convenience."

I opened a publishing program for creating flyers. "I'll post flyers on the clubhouse doors and put them in every resident's mailbox. After the whole debacle, I can't be sure anyone will open a clubhouse email. Once we have the laptops, we can run antivirus software, lock down the systems to protect them in the future and check for questionable files on their hard drives."

"You think that'll work? Some people didn't like the coupons."

My fingers danced over the keys. "But everyone likes apologies and free stuff."

He leaned his backside against my desk and watched me work. "You're good at this. When you first told me you planned to investigate, I took it as a joke."

I sniffed. "Well, I like a challenge, so this has been fun. Plus, it's keeping my mind off the bad things and making me feel useful."

He stretched long legs in front of him and crossed them at the ankle. "I think it's more than that. You've got heart, Connors."

I fought the heat racing over the bridge of my nose and across both cheeks. "So you're saying sometimes dogged hard-headedness is a virtue."

"Something like that."

I opened a browser window and searched for Veris, the company where Baxter's dad worked in Ecuador. He was a high-up and guaranteed to be listed. "Bingo."

Jake turned for a view of my screen. "What are you doing now?"

"Sending a quick email." My fingers hovered over the keys. How could I start something so sensitive to a man I'd never met? One who'd lost his only son, or at least I'd thought that until an hour ago. I did my best to get to the point, ask about the brother, and send my thoughts and prayers to their family. "The neighbor said Baxter's brother had been to the apartment, but I don't think Baxter had a brother."

"Who was the email to?"

"His dad's work email. He's important enough to be

listed and if he's anything like his son, he'll be checking email, even if he doesn't answer." Fingers crossed, he'd take the time to respond to this one.

"I can ask Dan to check the files. You didn't have to do that." He pulled his cell phone from his pocket and sent a text.

"Thanks. That helps, but this will clear it all up. Maybe he doesn't have a brother, but he has a close cousin or friend of the family who stopped by. I just need to know if they were aware of anyone else in Baxter's apartment this week."

"What'd the neighbors say he looked like?"

"They didn't. I told you, she was rude and sent me away."

"Maybe it was the outfit."

I hit Print, and the machine behind me purred to life. "You want to help me stuff a hundred mailboxes tonight?"

He levered himself off my desk and collected the flyers. "Can I drive the golf cart this time?"

"Nope."

I drove door to door, and Jake delivered flyers, pulling mailbox doors and tucking a paper inside each. Silver moonlight bathed the lake beside the falls in a shimmery glow. I stopped the cart and strained my eyes. "Do you see that?" Something moved in the distance.

The figure of a woman materialized from the shadows of the trees. She approached the cart with something in her hand. A camera. "Hi."

Jake climbed out of the cart and met her in the street outside my door. "Everything okay, miss?"

"Yeah." She looked at me and smiled. A cone of streetlight illuminated her familiar face as she arrived at Jake's side.

I smiled back. "Tennille, right?"

"Yeah." She shifted the camera into her left hand and offered Jake her right. "I'm Tennille King. I live on Oak Street." She pointed into the distance. "I'm a photographer. I have a studio, but I take promotional shots for the community."

Jake pressed a large palm against the hood of the cart and relaxed. "Are you taking promotional shots right now?"

She turned her eyes to the sky, dropping long blond hair over both shoulders. "No. I just love the night sky. Something about it is so ethereal. Enchanting."

Bullfrogs and whippoorwills sang in the distance, punctuated by a chorus of crickets. Fireflies danced in a beautiful reverse cascade above the field near the water. The view really was beautiful.

I sighed. "I love it here."

Her wide blue eyes twinkled in agreement. "So, what are you two doing out so late? Romantic evening ride?"

I clutched a handful of flyers to my chest. "No. Not at all. We're delivering flyers and not doing romance." I closed my eyes and counted back from three. What was wrong with my brain? *Not doing romance?* I longed to bounce my forehead on the steering wheel.

"It's kind of late for playing mailman, isn't it?"

I waved the crumpled flyers in one fist. "Busy, busy, busy. You know we techies never stop."

Jake looked like he thought I'd lost my mind. He freed a wrinkled flyer from my grip and passed it to Tennille. "Free computer cleanup at the clubhouse tomorrow. Give Mia a call if you'd like to schedule an appointment." He rounded the hood and climbed inside the cart at my side. "Have a nice night, Mrs. King."

I handed the flyers to Jake and angled away from the grass.

"What on earth was that about?"

I had no idea, so I changed the subject. "She was nice."

"Yeah." He watched as I drove.

I bit my lip and peeked at him as I steered down the next street. "Pretty, too, I think."

He turned his face away and smoothed the flyers on his lap. "Sure. I've always preferred brunettes, but she was cute."

I sat straighter, shoving brown bangs away from my glasses. "Me, too."

SIXTEEN

I ARRIVED AT work more than an hour early. As much as I wanted to start snooping for malware on residents' hard drives, other things weighed on my mind.

Bernie waved from the guard gate. "Aloha!"

I smiled and swiped my card, wondering absently if I could arrange for Jake to spend time at the guard gate. He could use exposure to Bernie's eternally sunny, highly contagious disposition.

I pulled through as the candy-striped lever rose. Bernie walked alongside the car until I stopped.

I dragged cat-eye sunglasses down the bridge of my nose. "What are you doing?"

She leaned near my open window. "Did you read my blog today?"

"No." I'd completely forgotten. "My brain's on overload." I fired a finger gun at my head. "What'd I miss?"

She donned her ornery Cheshire grin. "It was my favorite post this year. I'd planned to write about the beauty of summer nights in Ohio and how it feels to know my family on the big island and I see the same beautiful moon and sky, but while I was choosing a photo, I changed direction a bit."

I leaned against the door, eager for more information. Normally, she got to the point. Whatever she had must be good for all the lead-up. "Go on." Had she seen a crime underway? Caught sight of a UFO over the falls?

Every possibility from superheroes to talking ducks ran through my brain.

"Intrigue." She stretched her eyes wide.

A car honked behind me and pulled up to my bumper.

I waved an apology to the driver and goodbye to Bernie. Intrigue? "I'll check it out as soon as I get to my desk."

"Take the poll," she called as I drove away.

Dad's Crown Vic stuck out of my parking space by a foot. Only one other car shared the employee section of the parking lot at this hour. Randall's. Exactly the man I planned to check up on.

I hustled through the building with rejuvenated curiosity. At my desk, I pulled up Bernie's blog and logged into the clubhouse security software for a thorough investigation. Passcodes were listed alongside dates and times anyone set or unarmed the clubhouse alarm. I cross-referenced the codes with employee badges and found a pattern I didn't like. Coupled with personal observations, I wasn't sure if the dread in my tummy was mostly fear or hope.

Randall hadn't used his pin to close up before eleven for the better part of twenty days, but he opened every morning at five. Strange for a manager whose shift was eight to six. Until recently, he'd always been the one to set the alarm before leaving on time. The past three weeks something changed. Marcella's pin even showed up once or twice this month. Both times were after nine.

My phone buzzed with a new text message. Jake's name appeared on-screen. He'd gotten a return call from one resident with a break-in. I could stop by the residence and take a look after I got to work. *News for you, buddy, I'm already here.*

I grabbed a flyer and a blank sheet of notebook paper and headed to the concierge desk.

A guy dressed in black pants, a shirt and a tie filled coffee containers. He smiled as he worked, stuffing the condiment bowls with sweeteners, creamers and little wooden paddles. "Fresh coffee for a beautiful lady?"

"Please." I nodded in appreciation. I'd never seen the one responsible for my unending supply of gourmet coffee. Now I knew who he was, and I loved him.

He winked and turned a cup over. "Cream or sugar?"

"Both, please." It was just like in my dreams, a handsome young man making me coffee.

He hovered the cup between coffee containers. "Regular or decaf?"

The fantasy ended. If he didn't know which kind of coffee to serve a lady at 6:00 a.m., he could probably fill libraries with the other things he didn't know about them. "Regular."

He filled the cup and passed it to me.

I sighed over the end of the fantasy and stirred the little paddle through caramel-colored heaven.

My phone dinged with a fresh email and I tapped the screen to life. It was from the Veris Company. I swallowed, my heart suddenly pumping in my throat, and opened the message.

Jake strode through the lobby like he was leading an army to war. He held his cell phone to one ear. His tone and cadence reminded me of the soldier he'd once been. His gaze landed on me, and he froze. He changed direction, moving straight toward me as he disconnected the call. "You're here early."

I taped the flyer and blank paper on the desk beside the coffee. "I made a signup sheet." I lifted a pen and scratched, *Sign Up* across the top. "Plus, I can't sleep."

He gave me a long look. "Why? What'd you do?"

"Nothing." I pressed my lips together. "Fine. I was following a lead."

He worked his jaw, unspeaking.

I needed a new subject until I had time to explore my other suspicion. "Baxter's dad returned my email. He only had one son and the only people Baxter spoke of with any consistency were Nate and me. He had acquaintances at work and a new love interest, but nothing like a brother."

"And?"

"And I think the killer posed as Baxter's brother to gain access to his apartment and search for evidence against himself."

"We'll talk to the neighbor and the landlord, check the security videos outside the building. See if they can identify the brother."

"Great! When can we go?"

He made a crazy face. "Not you and I. Dan and I."

"Why would he take you? And if you can go, why can't I? I was the one who gave you the lead."

"Did you get my text?"

"Yeah. The call you were on sounded serious. What was that about?"

"Work." He clenched and unclenched his jaw. "What'd you mean yesterday when you said Nate wouldn't be hard to find because he was with Dan?"

I waved him off and blew across the top of my steaming coffee. "He's following Dan. So, Dan can relax. He doesn't have to try to find him anymore. He's never far away."

Jake stared. He tipped his head back and released the kind of belly laugh I made when someone tripped or fell.

I jumped. Since when did Jake laugh like that?

He smiled like he'd won the lottery. "Nate's following Dan around town while Dan's trying to find him?"

I shrugged. "Sure. Nate's just as interested as your brother in learning the truth, probably more. He figured following the detective would help him get answers faster."

The phone rang, and he tapped the screen, laughing silently. "Archer."

Humor drained from his face. "Okay." He disconnected with a grunt. "What do you know about the registers at the coffee shop?"

"Do you mean at the Dream Bean? I've worked on them before. What's going on?"

He scrolled through his phone, no longer looking my way. "Their point-of-sale terminals are acting up, and their customers are going next door for coffee."

"Uh-oh." I snapped a to-go lid on my coffee.

"Why'd I get that call? Should this call have gone to IT?"

I grimaced. The Lindseys owned Dream Bean and the Kubickas owned Sweet Retreat next door. They were competitors. "I'd better get over there. You should come in case it gets messy again."

He frowned. "Did you say again?"

I gathered my coffee and a napkin in one hand. "Have you ever seen crullers and jelly rolls stuck to a window?"

Jake crunched his nose. "Jeez."

I stuck the coffee paddle in my mouth before tossing it in the trash. Mmm.

Down the hallway to employee offices, Randall and Marcella parted ways outside the conference room.

I baby-stepped toward the hallway. "Hey. You know

what, give me ten minutes. Go ahead without me, and I'll be right there." I cradled the coffee to my chest and speed-walked to Randall's office. I hated to rush my talk with him, but this seemed like a week where anything could happen, and if I didn't talk to him before I left, he might be abducted by aliens before I got back.

"Knock, knock," I called through his open doorway.

Randall shuffled papers at his desk. He raised his eyes at the sound of my voice. "Mia? Come on in. Have a seat." He motioned to the chair across from him. "Please tell me you have good news. I could use some good news." His mask of misery told me how true the statement was.

"Well, not yet, but soon. I have a question, though." I checked over my shoulder to be certain Jake wasn't bogarting this lead too.

Randall slumped in his chair. "We need something to tell the founder. He was here before dawn talking to the golf pros and anyone else willing to complain. He's taking notes and making a plan to can us all. I can't lose this job." His voice cracked with desperation. Beads of sweat lined his brow.

I couldn't work any faster on the emails. The founder needed to put on his patient pants. I needed to get the conversation back on track before the Lindseys and Kubickas ruined all the good desserts. "Randall, are you living in your office?"

His eyes stretched wide. "What?"

I slid into the chair he'd offered and crossed my legs. "I'm working on the email situation. I'm close to finding out who sent them and why but, right now, I need to know if you're sleeping here at night."

He leaned away from me, shock opening his mouth and coloring his cheeks. "Of course not."

I lifted a finger toward his credenza. "I saw the blanket and pillow in there. There are food containers in the trash. Your minifridge is fully stocked, and you haven't been closing the clubhouse on time using your key code in nearly three weeks. I checked the security system log when I got here this morning. Your car was already in the lot with dew on the windows. You haven't set the alarm until after eleven most nights. You've even forgotten once or twice."

"Mia." Randall stood, and I jumped to my feet.

"Stop right there. I'm not done." I didn't know why he was there instead of at home, but the reason couldn't be good. "You were here when Baxter died, weren't you? Why didn't you tell anyone?"

"I can explain." He stepped around his desk, and I leaped toward the door.

Jake blocked my escape, lurking again. His specialty. "Randall?"

Randall stumbled to my side, facing off with the head of security. His glassy eyes and trembling lip screamed guilty. Of what, I almost hated to ask.

I turned my back on Jake, hoping he'd support me when I repeated my question. "Were you here when Baxter was murdered?"

Randall suddenly pulled it together. "I don't have to answer that."

"Why wouldn't you?" I locked my hands together so I wouldn't smack him. Who would keep such important information a secret? I didn't want to follow that thought through. "If you don't answer, it makes you look guilty. Tell us why you were here." My tummy flopped. Could Randall have killed Baxter to keep him from telling anyone he was living in his office? People had been fired for less, and he'd made it clear he needed this job.

Randall went back to his chair and typed on his keyboard. "I have work to do. I'd appreciate it if you both leave."

"No way." I checked over my shoulder. "You can't pretend we aren't here. You have to answer us."

Jake moved into the office and closed the door. He pulled his phone from his pocket.

I inched toward the desk. "Randall, just tell me what you know. Anything you heard or saw that night might help me figure out what happened to my friend. I need to know what you know. I need to know you didn't do this."

His grim expression softened. "Sorry, Mia. I'm not talking without a lawyer."

I slapped his desk. "Jeez. You're not under arrest. We're not the police, for goodness' sake."

Jake's voice rose. "No, but the police are on their way. Randall, I suggest you call that lawyer."

"Wow." I turned on Jake. "You stole two leads in ten minutes. That has to be a world record. Congratulations. I was handling this."

His indifferent expression deflected my wrath. "I've got this from here. I'll meet you at the coffee house when Dan gets here."

"What? Why do you get to stay and talk to him?"

He tapped a long tan finger on his name badge. "Head of Security." He pointed at me. "Computer girl."

I made my meanest face. "Nice to see you finally found a name badge, but this computer girl is the only reason you're standing here questioning him."

Jake opened the door and motioned me to leave. "The Lindseys and Kubickas need you. I've got this under control."

Randall groaned. "Oh, no. What's happening at the Sweet Retreat now?"

I shot Jake with eye missiles. "Ask the head of security. I'm just the computer girl."

I shut the door with attitude and paced the hall, testing my hearing. I couldn't leave Randall alone. If he wasn't the killer, then I'd ratted him out. This was my fault. I pressed my ear to the door. Jake had no business eavesdropping on us.

"What are you doing?" Marcella appeared behind me.

I clamped a hand over my mouth to stifle a scream. I released my fingers slowly as I remembered how to breathe. "What are you doing?" My stage whisper was raspy with fresh panic.

She smiled. "Besides trying to get your attention for the last two minutes? Not much. Who's in there with Randall? I need to go over a few things from the budget meeting. Are you in line to see him?"

I grabbed her elbow and towed her away from the door. "He's in there with Jake, and the police are coming. Maybe we should wait for them in the lot and make sure there's no scene. We can't let the residents freak out. Randall said the founder's here, and he's already mad about the emails damaging our image. Imagine if he saw the clubhouse manager getting arrested *at the clubhouse*."

She made the sign of the cross and murmured in Spanish. I made out the few words she said most often. All swears. She finished with a nod. "Okay. Let's go, *gorda*."

We jog-walked to the parking lot and attempted to act natural as residents came and left the building. No sign of Dan or a squad car.

I leaned near Marcella. "Did you know Randall was sleeping in his office?"

A light blush tinted her cheeks. "He was?" She stared ahead, avoiding eye contact.

"Did you know?"

She shook her head. "No."

"You used your code to set the alarm before leaving here a couple times this month. It was late. Nine at night."

Shock and an emotion I couldn't pinpoint raced over her features. "I had a lot of paperwork to finish up, and my son and his friends are too much of a distraction to take work home. With all the scheduling complaints lately, I've been busier than usual during the day and rarely at my desk."

I nodded. "That must be frustrating. I didn't mean to be rude."

"It's no problem." She smiled sweetly.

Why didn't I believe her?

I tilted my face skyward. Another perfect summer day masked a myriad of Horseshoe Falls secrets. The light breeze and gentle scent of lilacs gave no indication the Lindseys and Kubickas were probably ready for pistols at high noon or that Randall had spent last night on the office couch.

A rotund man in a black suit and hair plugs exited the clubhouse. "Mia Connors?"

I forced a smile and tried not to swallow my tongue. The founder had spoken to me on several occasions, but he never remembered me. He shook my hand every time as if it was the first.

"Yes?"

"I'm Sport Barrow. I own and operate the Horseshoe Falls community. Do you have a minute to talk?"

I glanced at Marcella, who pretended to text.

"Of course. Would you like to talk in my office?" *In other words, not here because the police are coming.*

"No. This is fine. I just need an answer." He dug one of my black business cards from his inside jacket pocket. "What do you know about this?"

"Huh. Hmm. What is this? I don't know what you mean."

He flipped my card in his fingertips. "You're head of IT. Correct?"

"Mmm-hmm." I sealed my lips, praying not to ramble, choke or confess until I heard the accusation.

"I've heard chatter in the community about an online investigator using my club as his personal hunting grounds. Have you heard anything like that?"

I shook my head. Nope. Nothing at all like that.

"Find out if it's true and see to it I don't find any more of these cards around the community. I don't want to hear my members' private lives were invaded by some hack for a dollar."

I pried my lips apart. "I'm not sure what can I do to stop them from hiring an investigator."

He glowered, all pretense of a good nature erased. "You're the frontline of technological defense in this community. If you can't stop some two-bit hack from invading my residents' privacy, I'll find a man who can."

My face scorched with emotion. A man? Was that a joke or an intentional jibe? My fingers curled into fists at my sides. Could the day get any worse before breakfast?

A police cruiser crept into view and pulled into the clubhouse lot.

Yep. Things could always get worse. How had I forgotten?

Mr. Barrow let out a string of slurs rough enough to make my dad blush.

Yep. Worse.

SEVENTEEN

Dan angled into the lot with his big truck, custom lights flashing beneath the grille. He climbed down and smirked at me before introducing himself to Mr. Barrow.

I chewed my nails and contemplated what to do. My options were awful. As much as I wanted to help, Dan wouldn't let me get involved. He still seemed to think I was hiding Nate from him. I scanned the area. Maybe Nate had followed him here.

Mr. Barrow stopped at the clubhouse door and called Marcella to join them inside.

A pebble of guilt formed in my tummy. No one would've known Randall was living in his office if I hadn't questioned him. No one would know, except me, if Jake wasn't a relentless stalker.

The Lindseys needed me, but their shop was too far from the clubhouse for me to know if Dan hauled Randall out in cuffs.

I grabbed my phone and scrolled through the REIGN updates. My knights were all over Punisher, which should have made me giddy but didn't.

I opened a search engine and navigated to Bernie's blog.

A pretty picture of the night sky was centered under Bernie's *Aloha from Ohio* logo. The newest headline:

Mysteries Abound. "Oh no." If Bernie reported on the murder and all the strange things happening in the community, she could incite a panic. It was one thing for residents to hear rumors and gossip, but a whole other thing to see those things online in print. As long as the email problems, burglaries and other crimes stayed as they were, whispers on cautious lips, Horseshoe Falls could survive this. If people started seeing it posted on the internet, we'd have a mass exodus. People chose gated communities for their safety.

I scrolled Bernie's page to get a full view of the article and turned my phone so more would fit on the screen. Her words swept through my mind as I scanned for the meat to her story.

...You know I'm no gumshoe, but I love a good intrigue. I normally cover events that have come and gone, but the mystery I've got for you today is as ripe as the strawberries in Macy Cramer's garden. (Thank you for those berries, Macy!)

I rolled my eyes and scrolled some more. All this buildup. Was Bernie taking a theater class?

It's no secret something strange is going on in our little community. A beloved employee (Mark, our head of security) stopped coming to work. A new face appeared the same day (Jake Archer— new head of security). There were break-ins leading up to the odd and sudden switch in security heads. A murder immediately after (prayers for the young man's family and friends). And the founder's been spotted here more than once in a week. What's happening, Horseshoe Falls? Comment below with your best guess or insight. When you're finished, take the poll for a pint of Macy's sweet berries!

I scrolled faster and with purpose.

The photograph of an owl on a limb sat above Bernie's poll. A smooth, velvet sky and millions of tiny stars framed the shot. A red circle, added by some photo software, circled the clubhouse golf cart, with me at the wheel and Jake climbing back into his seat after delivering a round of flyers. His head was conveniently blocked by a mass of oak leaves stretching from the owl's tree in the foreground.

Beside the owl photo was a blurry shot of the Falls Fountain. Moonlight glinted off the water and what appeared to be a couple stood in the shadows.

Sheer, morbid curiosity drew my eyes to the poll, a simple click-to-vote widget with three questions. 1. *Who are the people in these photos? 2. Are they lovers or conspirators?* And finally, 3. *Do you want to know more?*

Thirty out of thirty-three voters agreed it was me driving the cart. They were split on whether or not the drive was a date and if the mystery man lived in Horseshoe Falls. They also assumed I was the woman in the second photo. No one thought I was conspiring, but every voter wanted to know more. The only thing that could make me more spotlight-centered in the community now was if I turned green and shaved my head. It was only a matter of time before a clubhouse employee commented. Everyone was in the conference room when Dad asked Jake if we were dating.

Comments ranged from conspiracy theories involving the stock market to requests for Tennille King to

contact them. I was one of those. If she took the photos
for Bernie's blog, she might have captured something
useful to my investigation.

The commenter theory that niggled my mind most
was one about the couples in the pictures. Could a pair
of adulterers be behind the murder? What if they were
interrupted by Baxter that night and couldn't afford
to be caught? Cheaters had a lot to lose, especially in
Horseshoe Falls where prenuptial agreements were as
vital and ever-present in marriage as wedding rings.
Unfortunately for me, I was the only person recogniz-
able in the pictures.

"What are you doing here?" Jake's voice nearly
scared the coffee out of me.

I shoved my phone into my pocket. "Waiting. I want
to know if Randall's okay and if he told Dan anything.
What's going on in there?"

He squinted into the sun. "Have you been standing
here the whole time?"

"Yes."

He nodded into the distance. "Let's go check on the
coffee shop people. We can talk as we move."

I followed Jake through the parking lot and onto the
pathway leading to the shops. "Do you think Randall
did it? Killed Baxter, I mean."

Jake moved to my side, matching his pace to mine
when the path widened. "He was here that night. He
talked to Dan, but we don't know if he's telling the
truth. We've only got one side to the story."

"Right, but as far as we know, Randall didn't have
a motive to kill Baxter."

Jake shoved his fingers into his pockets. "Maybe he
didn't want Baxter ratting him out for living in his office. He would've lost his job if Mr. Barrow knew that.

Good eye by the way, for spotting the blanket and pillow."

"I wasn't trying to get him into trouble. I only hoped he'd been here that night so there was someone, besides the killer, who could shed some light on my investigation." I sighed. "He did say he couldn't afford to lose his job. I can't believe he'd kill to keep it, though."

"There's always the possibility he got spooked and hit Baxter in a panic. He was an intruder. Though, that's a lock I can't quite pick."

I looked both ways and crossed the street beside a line of geese. Why had Baxter been in my office after hours, and how had he gotten in?

I stepped onto the sidewalk outside Dream Bean. "I don't know. Baxter was hit twice. Once in the face with a tablet and again with something much heavier. I can't imagine someone who was spooked by an intruder sticking around for a second hit. I think I'd have called 9-1-1 and locked myself in another room after the first blow, wouldn't you?"

Jake chuckled. "No, and I'm not convinced you would've run either."

"Right. I forgot I was your original suspect. Every time you start to grow on me, you say something like that."

He opened the door to the Dream Bean and held it for me. "Angry ladies first."

Scents of fresh roasted coffee, melted caramels and sweet cream whipped up my nose and improved my mood.

Jake took a seat at the counter beside the register and eyeballed me. "Did you moan?"

"So what? It smells good in here. I like coffee." I dipped past him, managing not to stick my tongue out.

Darlene Lindsey, the shop owner, was clearing cups and saucers from a table near the wall.

She jumped when she saw me. "Oh!" The stack of dishes in her hand buckled.

I covered the toppling pieces with my palms to steady them against her apron. "Sorry, I didn't mean to sneak up on you. I thought you saw me come in."

"It's not your fault. I'm on edge. We lost two hundred dollars this morning. Dumb technology." She passed the new register with a glare and lowered her burden into the prep sink behind the counter.

I slid in beside her. "Care if I take a look at the terminal?"

She waved her approval. "I don't know what was wrong with receipts in ink and good old-fashioned cash."

Jake swiveled on a squeaky bar stool. "How'd you lose two hundred dollars? Your customers went next door?"

I stretched my eyes wide and shook my head. That wasn't a can of trouble he should open. She lost the money. No one needed an ambulance. Everything was good.

Darlene untied her apron and hung it on a hook beside the sink. Her white capris and navy striped top had a cute nautical theme. She clucked her tongue. "Of course not. That's ridiculous. I wasn't going to let my customers go to the competition." She tipped her chin high. "I gave away my coffee. Forty cups."

Jake leaned back. "You charge five bucks a cup for coffee? Good news. You didn't really lose two hundred dollars. You probably lost closer to fifty. Your mark-up's extraordinary, overhead and net cost considered."

I moved my eyes back to the register's display, hoping to disappear. I identified the problem with zero effort. "What do you think happened to the register?"

She exhaled long and hard. "It won't work. The screen's black, and the drawer won't open. Those Kubickas were in here talking about Bernie's blog while Stuart and I set up for the day." She focused on a loose thread at her shirt hem. "Anyway, they left, and the register was dead. I'm just glad they weren't here to see it happen. We took cash from the people who had it, but most needed to use a credit card. By seven the credit customers we'd turned away were telling people on the sidewalk, 'Don't go in there unless you have cash,' and those people were changing direction without even coming inside."

Jake nodded. "Did you consider closing up until Mia got here or putting a cash only sign in the window?"

She raised her hands overhead. "I just said people needed to use credit cards. How would a sign help?"

"How did giving your coffee away help you?" He emphasized the last word.

Darlene looked at me. She didn't have to say anything. She had the universal woman look of, "pft, men."

I nodded and smiled.

"What?" Jake asked. "What was that look?"

I shrugged. "She bonded with the people over free coffee. People like free stuff. The customers appreciate it, and they'll be back."

I pointed to her cute red flats. Delivering unpopular news was best served with a compliment. "I love your shoes."

She beamed. "Thanks. I found them at the outlet mall. Have you been there since they opened the Smarty Pants boutique?"

"They opened a Smarty Pants in Ohio?"

She nodded slowly. "Thought of you as soon as I walked in. Amazing retro patterns and cuts. The prices are high, but it's not like you can get their stuff anywhere."

I nodded. My thoughts were on Randall, despite the small talk, which, thankfully, she kept going after one compliment.

Darlene's face was open, expecting something. She'd definitely asked me a question.

I moved on to another topic. "Where were you the night the man was murdered at the clubhouse?" My heart clenched. Calling Baxter "the man" felt wrong and impersonal. I'd miss the funeral since the paper said his family was flying him back to Ecuador.

She deflated. "Oh, sweetie. I heard that man was your friend."

"Were you at home or out for a walk? Maybe you've heard something interesting from one of the residents and want to share? Dream Bean's a hotspot. You must hear things."

Darlene looked at the ceiling. "Well, there was one thing, but it's nothing, really. My husband says I let my imagination get away from me."

"What do you mean?"

"I watch a lot of television. Sometimes I fall asleep with it on, and Stew thinks the ideas get in subconsciously." She tapped her temple.

I shook my head. "No. I mean, what did you see that wasn't anything?"

She glanced at Jake.

"It's okay," I assured her. "He's with me."

She wet her lips and closed the small distance between us. "I was on my way home from spin class, and I thought I saw something between the trees near the stables. I thought it was a bicycle at first, because of the reflectors and speed, but it didn't matter, and I'd had a long day."

"Anything else? Did you get a look at the bicycle? The rider? Tall or short? White? Black? Anything else at all?"

"No. I'm not even sure it was a bike. Maybe Stew's right." Her eyes lit up. "I did see Bernie's blog this morning. If the residents are on the case, we'll have answers in no time."

I bit my lip, snapped the power button on the register to ON and turned to face her. "You're all set here." The register hummed to life and printed a test receipt.

I patted the register and rounded the counter near Jake. "I'm going to stop by the residence you texted me about earlier, and check out the computer. If you have a chance, Darlene, set up an appointment to have Warren or me scan your laptops."

I grabbed my phone and sent Warren a text with a heads-up. "I forgot to tell him."

Darlene's sharp brown eyes locked on mine. "What did you think of the poll?"

I scooted backward. "I think your register is up and running. I might make a quick trip up to Smarty Pants soon. You look pretty." I dusted my palms together. "Don't forget to bring your computer in for a scan."

Her forehead wrinkled. "Why?"

"We're offering a free service. Antivirus software and removal of malware."

"Our computers are protected under a plan I bought at the store."

Jake cleared his throat. "Did you receive emails from the clubhouse with coupons or links to schedule services online?"

"No."

Why not? The Lindseys were Horseshoe Falls residents. "Could the messages be in your spam folder?"

She shook her head. "No. I empty that every few days. I've never gotten anything from the clubhouse in my email. Do I need to sign up?"

She turned her gaze on the register as it finished the long printout. "Hooray! You fixed it. I knew you would. What did you say happened? You finished so quickly. I expected to make a call to the company for a replacement."

I never knew how to answer these questions. I stepped away as she approached with careful hands and suspicious eyes. "It was no big deal. Nothing serious or to worry about. There was a power-related issue, and your terminal wasn't getting the proper power to run…properly." Yikes.

"Stew!" Darlene wound through the empty tables and yelled into the storeroom with vengeance in her eyes. "Stewy! Stew!"

I nudged Jake's elbow. "Well, I'm going to go, but you should stay a few minutes."

Her husband arrived with a tray of steaming scones. "Why are you yelling? I could've burned my scones!"

"Toodles." I wiggled my fingers at Jake and moved toward the door.

Darlene's voice rose behind me. "Mia says we had a power problem. As in the register wasn't getting enough power. You know what that sounds like to me?"

He arched his eyebrows. "Sounds like you turned it off again while you were scrubbing counters and didn't know you did it."

"Or those sneaky Kubickas didn't come to talk about Bernie's blog. They came in here for sabotage."

Jake dropped his head to the counter.

I zipped through the door and headed back to the clubhouse by way of the guard gate. I had a question for Bernie.

EIGHTEEN

DAN'S TRUCK WAS still outside the clubhouse, so I used my swipe badge and slid in through the back door. Using the front door seemed the quickest way to run into him or Mr. Barrow, and I'd had enough of them both for the day. The halls were impossibly quiet as I tiptoed toward my office, careful not to let my kitten heels smack against the granite floor.

A quick visit to the guard gate gave me hope. Bernie confirmed the photos were taken by Tennille King, as implied by her blog commenters. I was willing to bet she'd let me take a look at any photos taken the night Baxter died. Especially after Bernie called the community to action.

Relief washed over me as my office came into view. I ducked inside and pressed my back against the door. Mr. Barrow and Warren looked up at me from Warren's computer.

"Hello." So much for not drawing the big guy's attention.

Mr. Barrow stood behind Warren's desk chair, leaning over his shoulder. He turned away as if I hadn't snuck inside and plastered myself to the door.

I walked casually to my desk and brought up Bernie's blog on my laptop to examine the photos. The couple near the fountain was mismatched. The man was tall. A shadow smudged his silhouette, distorting it beyond recognition. The woman was small, possibly pear-shaped with hair worn tight to her head. They could be anyone. Nothing against Bernie's flair for the dramatic, but a couple by a fountain and a couple in a golf cart weren't exactly evidence of anything more than the fact people went outside after dark.

No new blog comments.

Mr. Barrows straightened with a creak. "So, if you see anyone with this card, I want to know immediately. Find out who gave the card to them and what this little marking means." He flicked the card into the air, and it landed in Warren's coffee.

He scooped it up in an instant, swinging it carelessly to remove coffee drops. "Yes, sir."

Marcella opened the office door and smiled. "I have gifts for the brains of this operation."

Mr. Barrow's smile fell when she moved to my desk.

"You've gotten a great response to your flyer. These were dropped off by residents on their way to work. They received your flyer with the morning paper and were excited for the new service. They'll be back at five to pick them up, unless you text or email them otherwise. I asked each resident to put everything you need on a sticky note attached to their computers. Usernames, passwords."

She unloaded half a dozen laptop bags from her shoulder before giving the boss her attention. "Mr. Barrow? Detective Archer's ready to leave. He'd like to see you again before he goes."

The tight bun she wore took on a new appearance. I stood. "Marcella."

Her smile wavered. "Yes?" A blush rose up her bare neck to tint her cheeks. "Everything okay, Mia?"

"Sure. Um." I cleared my throat and smiled, unconvincingly, by the look on her face. "Your hair looks nice like that." What else could I say? Why was I standing?

She touched wisps of hair at the nape of her neck.

Warren and Mr. Barrow were too near to speak freely. Speculation was dangerous. I'd have to be careful this time or Jake might haul her off to jail, too.

I dropped my gaze to the laptop, imagining Marcella in the woman's place by the fountain. "Can we talk later? I'd love to get your flan recipe."

She pressed her lips tight and nodded.

We both knew I only ate salads and takeout because I didn't have to go near an oven for either.

Mr. Barrow shot me a weird look and followed Marcella through the doorway.

Could he be the man in the photo? Would an evening rendezvous explain why she'd set the alarm after nine a couple times this month?

I turned to Warren with an overdue question. "Any idea who those black cards belong to?"

"Nope."

So, my secret was safe for now. If Warren didn't know, the rest of the staff probably didn't either, and residents had no reason to rat me out to Barrow.

I patted the stack of bags. "You want to split these laptops? Divide and conquer?"

He rolled his chair across the small distance between us and collected half the bags. "You want me to run a virus scan and add malware protection software?"

"Yes." I scrolled through my texts for the address where I was supposed to go next. "How'd you know?"

He pointed to a stack of extra flyers on my desk.

"Right. Also, we're looking for any common suspicious files. I'm trying to rule out the possibility the computers were all infected with the same virus after receiving the bogus clubhouse emails and clicking the link. For some reason, I can't get a list of complaining residents from the staff or Randall, so we'll check them all. At the very least, we're improving relations with the free service."

He unzipped the first bag and shoved black framed glasses higher on his nose. "Gotcha. I'll see if I can figure out where the links from the emails went and why."

"I've been to the page. It was well crafted. I'd love to know why. If you get any ideas, let me know. We'll brainstorm when I get back. Jake's sending me to a residence now. Maybe I'll get some insight there."

On cue, Jake opened the office door and stared.

My neck and chest heated. "What?" I asked, horrified by the ridiculous response I had to him.

"Those coffee people are crazy."

I shrugged. "I like the Lindseys." Then again, I wasn't in my right mind lately.

He sucked his teeth. "How'd it go at Mr. Fritter's?"

"I'm looking for the address now."

Jake opened the door as wide as possible and secured it with his backside. "Come on. I'll go with you. I need to ask him some questions."

I grabbed my badge and swiveled in my chair to face Warren. "Are you okay working on those alone for a while?"

He sniffed and shook his head.

"No?" Was that a no?

He raised his eyes to me. "Yeah. Let me know what Fritter says." Emotion tainted the words. Hostility?

"Mmm-kay." Apparently Mr. Barrows put him in a mood. "Be back soon."

The moment Jake pulled the door shut behind me, I turned for Randall's office. The door was open, and he was gone, along with his blanket and pillow. "Was he fired?"

Jake shrugged. "He went with Dan."

Alarm shot through me. "With Dan where? To jail?"

"To the precinct." Jake touched the small of my back with his fingertips and steered me to the club's golf cart outside. "Get in. I'm driving to Fritter's."

I climbed in, weary of resident eyes, and arranged my skirt across goose-pimpled thighs. "The breeze is chilly."

"Looks like rain." Jake pulled onto the main road with a punch of the pedal, nearly dumping me on the asphalt.

"Jeez!" I grabbed the dash and seat. My bottom slid to the protective bar guarding the doorframe.

He grabbed my arm and towed me back in place. "Sorry. That looked like a rabbit's nest at the edge of the lot." He glanced at me. "Are you okay?"

"Fine." I watched his expression for signs of deceit. I needed to get some material on body language and interview techniques. "A rabbit's nest?"

"You should contact the gamekeeper here and let him know. The maintenance crew could hit it with the mower."

"Barf." I looked behind us. "That's awful. Why would you even think of that? What about predators or something?"

"All possible."

I searched my phone for the gamekeeper's extension. "Bunnies. Good grief. How do they live?"

Silence.

"I'm serious. How do bunnies survive? They have no defense. If something came to eat the babies, what could the mama do? Cute it to death?"

Jake frowned. "She'd carry them someplace safe. Haven't you seen a dog or cat carry their litter? They pick them up by the scruff and move them."

"How could she move a bunch of babies? Everyone else would be eaten while she moved the first one, and the predator would just watch where she took the other one and eat it too."

He shook his head and blinked long and slow. "Are those numbers on your dress? I thought they were polka dots."

I hooked hair behind my ear and dusted the crisp white material over both thighs. "No more talk about bunnies?"

"Did you call the gamekeeper?"

"I sent him a text."

He nodded.

I traced the itty bitty zeroes and ones on my dress. "It's binary."

His cheek twitched. "You are a geek."

"Like I said." I smiled. "Do you know what that means? Binary?"

The frown returned. "Binary is a system using only two numbers, zeroes and ones, to represent all decimal numbers."

"Correct." A trio of horses sauntered past. I waved at the family riding.

My phone buzzed with a new text. "It's the gamekeeper. They'll move the bunnies."

Jake turned right onto Maple and left on Sage. "This is the place." A black mailbox with *Fritter* painted on the side anchored the end of a short brick driveway. He shut down the cart and touched my arm with one finger. "Randall is separated from his wife and has been sleeping in his office. He's probably not guilty of anything more than drinking too much at the local pub and passing out at the clubhouse that night. Dan's letting him go, but he's still on our radar. I thought you should know."

I nodded, thankful for the trust involved in his reveal.

"Ready?"

"Yes." I climbed out and examined the dark brick home, trimmed in black and outlined in heavy bushes. "This place could be broken into in broad daylight. Look at all this shade."

Jake left me at the cart and rang the bell.

I nosed along the path wrapping the house. Maybe this home had been chosen for easy access?

"Mia," Jake called from the porch.

"Coming." I dashed back around front and climbed the steps to his side.

Mr. Fritter stood in the doorway. "Come in."

We followed him into a soaring two-story foyer with dark cherry stained floors and paneling. A chandelier in wrought iron dangled overhead and a number of unfortunate animal heads hung from plaques around the room. I covered my mouth so I wouldn't speak. Stuffed animals were on my list of *what-were-you-thinking*? And whatever he was thinking was none of my business.

Mr. Fritter crossed the foyer and beckoned us. "I use the computer in the library. It's new but stationary. If I had a laptop, I would've dropped it off."

"It's no problem," Jake answered. "I'd hoped to talk to you about the break-in anyway, so I tagged along with Mia."

Fritter opened a door nearly twice my height and gave Jake a thorough looking-over. "Who did you say you are?"

"Jake Archer. I'm the head of security here." He extended a hand.

"No uniform?"

Jake shot me a droll look, probably hearing my mental "I told you so."

"Maybe point out your badge," I whispered to Jake as I made my way to an oversized mahogany desk.

Mr. Fritter looked to me. "What happened to the other security fellow?"

I pulled the leather luxury chair away from the desk and relaxed onto the seat. "He's taking family leave, but he'll be back."

Mr. Fritter dithered in the doorway. Jake circled the room, paying gratuitous amounts of attention to the windows.

Fritter's computer screen was locked. I tried "Animal Murderer" for the password. No go. I scanned the room. A degree from Oxford hung from the wall behind his desk. "What year did you graduate from Oxford?"

"Seventy-two. Why do you ask?"

My fingers flew across the keys. Bingo. "Your screen was locked. I needed the password."

Jake snickered but kept his eyes on the window.

Mr. Fritter harrumphed. "I suppose it's time for a change then."

"Probably. I'll leave a list of things to avoid using this time. Is there paper in the drawer?" I pulled the center drawer open and snagged a pad of plain paper. "May I?"

He looked more irritated than necessary. He had to know that password stank.

I scratched a quick list: *birthdays, anniversaries, 1234, password.*

Jake turned to face Mr. Fritter. "She's going to be a

few minutes. Would you mind if I asked about the night your house was broken into?"

Fritter took a seat on the couch and Jake positioned himself on the edge of a chair.

I opened a search engine and got busy. Fritter had his email bookmarked and his password saved. *Dumb*. The inbox was full of junk, ploys for money, penis enhancements and weight loss offers. His trash and spam both contained the bogus clubhouse emails. "There are over a dozen emails from the clubhouse in his spam folder."

The guys stopped talking.

Jake came and looked over my shoulder.

I pointed to the screen. "Look at this. There are a dozen variations of the fake clubhouse emails here. Specials, coupons, requests for responses. The advertising gets steadily more aggressive until two days before the break-in."

"And then?" Jake asked.

"Then nothing. There hasn't been a single email from the clubhouse since the break-in." I lifted a finger. "And those emails weren't really from the clubhouse, Mr. Fritter."

He guffawed. "Then who were they from?"

Jake swiped the notepad off the desk and handed it to Mr. Fritter. A small black business card fluttered to the floor by his foot. "Take her advice on these password suggestions. She's good at this. If she can access your email, someone with ill intent can too. Are you wondering how she got into your email?"

Fritter's jaw dropped.

I slid my shoe toward the fallen card, but Jake stopped me. "I'll get that." He retrieved my business card and turned it over in his fingertips. "Mr. Barrow's on a headhunt for whoever this card belongs to."

Mr. Fritter collected it from Jake's fingers and slid it into the pocket of his trousers. "It's none of Mr. Barrow's business." The look on his face was somewhere between fear and indignation.

I smiled.

Jake turned his face away, but he might've smiled, too. "Mr. Fritter, where did the burglar gain entrance?"

Under cover of a million trees and bushes. I buttoned my lips.

"Through the basement. I have a walkout. There are glass patio doors in the backyard. Would you like to have a look?"

"Yes." I scurried to his side. My investigation was gaining momentum. Whoever sent the emails had tried everything to get Mr. Fritter to open them. When he didn't, they decided to take action, and Fritter's house was perfect for breaking and entering.

We walked to the basement door, through rooms filled with defenseless animals and some pretty scary ones, all stuffed and mounted to plaques. By the time we reached the doors, I swung one open for fresh air so I wouldn't throw up. "Are you kidding me?" As if the trees weren't enough, a stout brick retaining wall ran away from the doors on either side. People in the backyard probably couldn't see someone breaking in. "Nuts."

"Buckeye," Fritter explained. "It's the only producing buckeye tree in Horseshoe Falls."

Jake pointed overhead. "Your light's out."

Fritter didn't look. He scooped a buckeye off the ground. "They burn out all the time. My motion light's out, too."

Jake furrowed his brows. "Mr. Fritter. They haven't burned out. They're broken."

"Whoa." I arched my back and craned my neck for a good look inside the fixture twelve feet overhead. With all the stupid shade, it was easy to miss. "What about your alarm? Why didn't you set it that night?"

He huffed. "Is this what they mean by questioning the victim for their part in a crime?"

"No, sir." I backpedaled. "I didn't mean to say it was your fault. Of course it's not your fault."

Jake stepped between us, blocking Fritter from my view and allowing my brain an escape. "Do you normally use your house alarm?"

"Yes. When I travel."

"Not on a daily basis?"

"No." He crossed his arms, looking less than menacing in his Mr. Rogers sweater. "I live in a gated community. They're supposed to check people at the gate. You can't even come here without a guest pass." His brows rose to his hairline. "Do you think the intruder lives here?"

Jake lifted his palms. "I'm just gathering facts, Mr. Fritter."

He waved us back inside and locked the door. "The police have already taken my statement."

I pointed to the knobs. "Do you always lock the doors?"

He nodded. "Of course."

Jake wiggled the doors. "They're secure."

Mr. Fritter nodded. "I had the old ones replaced the next morning."

Confusion churned in my head. "You lock up but don't set the alarm? The community is too safe for an alarm but not safe enough to leave your doors unlocked?"

He looked from me to Jake. "Old habits."

"Where were you that night?" Jake tried again.

"I was at the Mastersons' for poker night."

Interesting. "Where do the Mastersons live?"

Jake tapped the screen of his phone. "Mr. Fritter, the Mastersons had a break-in too, didn't they?"

"Yes, the following week. We played cards at the Coopers'. While we were talking about what happened at my house, his was breached as well. Ironic, isn't it."

"More like well played. Someone knew your poker schedule." My mind raced. "Who has access to that information?"

Fritter frowned. "Now you're suggesting it was an inside job?"

"No." Jake interrupted. "Mia? Did you do everything you needed to do with Mr. Fritter's computer?" His eyebrows made strange jumpy motions.

I wrinkled my nose. "I need five more minutes." I dashed back to the den and copied a few suspicious files. The crystal dish on his desk held a bevy of coins. All from Alcoholics Anonymous.

Fritter's voice echoed across the room. "I've been clean for thirteen years if you're wondering."

I pressed a hand to my heart. "You scared me."

"Snooping tends to put people on edge."

Right. Jake arrived on Fritter's heels.

"I'm finished here. The antivirus software is scanning your files. Follow the prompts to finish up when you're ready. Call if you need anything or have questions. Sorry to have taken so much of your time."

We excused ourselves. Fritter seemed relieved to see us go.

I climbed into the golf cart and rocked my dress underneath both thighs, protecting my skin from the hot leather upholstery. My knees bobbed, frantic with new information.

"Well?" Jake slid behind the wheel. "Did you find anything on his computer?"

"Besides an unhealthy amount of two-for-one stuffed Bambi ads? Not really. They should outlaw taxidermy as a profession."

"Besides that."

"I'm not sure yet. There were a few questionable files, but I don't know what I'm looking for. I'll have to check them all. It would help if I had other computers to compare the files with. I need to talk to Warren and see what he found on the laptops." I wiggled a thumb drive between us. "If one of these files is on all the computers, we'll know which was downloaded by residents under false pretenses."

Jake reversed out of Fritter's drive and headed toward the clubhouse. "Back to the office then?"

The family on horseback trotted in the field across the lake.

"What if we swing by the stables first? Darlene said she saw someone in the trees the night Baxter died. Maybe the Valentines saw something or there's a clue in the woods."

Jake switched into Drive and zipped down the road to the stables. "As you wish."

I clutched my phone on my lap. "Did you just quote *Princess Bride*?"

He looked to me with curious eyes. "You know *Princess Bride*?"

"Inconceivable." I shook my head all the way to the stables.

NINETEEN

WE ARRIVED AT the stable as the family on horseback entered the pasture. The lights in the office were off; the curtains were drawn. A whiteboard with caricatures of a horse and rider surrounded by stars leaned against the window.

Jake read the accompanying words. "'We've hit the trails! Hope you will too. Be back in the morning.'"

I slumped. "I guess the Valentines are camping tonight."

Jake lifted his chin toward a set of cameras mounted overhead. "They might have something on their security feed. I'll come back in the morning."

I headed down one side of the building. "Let's check out the trees on either side while we're here. Maybe there's a clue?"

Jake took the other side without a word.

I tiptoed along a pseudo path, keeping my heels from sticking in the ground. Scents of earth and pine mixed with the faint aroma of hay and horses. Nostalgia overtook me. Bree and I spent hours in the forest as kids. Mom and Dad insisted. Hiking, biking, camping, anything to keep us in the sunshine. I always brought a book.

Jake appeared around the backside of the building and headed my way. "The storm's close. Let's get you and the cart back to the clubhouse."

"No signs of a bicycle over there?"

"No. Lots of footprints."

Branches overhead swung in the growing breeze. I rubbed my arms. "Residents spend most of their time outdoors. Hikers. Birdwatchers. Kids blowing off steam. It's probably why the Valentines put up security cameras. Horseshoe Falls isn't airtight. The woods are a good place to fool around or party quietly."

"Speaking from personal experience again?"

A few thin raindrops fell from the leaves overhead and burst on my shoulder. I turned on my toes and walked away. I hadn't done much in the way of teen angst, but I'd saved Bree's behind more times than I could count. Neither fact was any of his business.

The sky dimmed as we moved toward the cart. He didn't seem like a guy who'd found a clue to break the case, but I couldn't shake the sensation he might be keeping something from me.

"No new leads?"

He turned his hesitant gaze on me. "No. You?"

"Nope."

I waved as the family we'd seen earlier dismounted their rides and led them to the stables. The mother and daughter smiled awkwardly. Hopefully they hadn't read Bernie's blog and begun speculating about me and the cart.

Who was I kidding? Everyone at Horseshoe Falls read Bernie's blog. I couldn't be seen with Jake without sending the rumor mill into double overtime. I definitely couldn't get back in the golf cart with him.

I redirected my path, veering away from the cart. "Well, I'd better go talk with Warren."

Jake grabbed my arm. "What are you doing? We have the cart." He released me, looking away.

I stretched my arms across my chest and overhead. "It's a beautiful day. I should get some exercise. Enjoy summer while it lasts."

"It's eighty-four and humid with a ninety percent chance of a thunderstorm. Get in the cart."

"No thank you. I think I'll walk."

Jake glowered. "Is this about that blog post? You don't want to be seen in the cart with me again? Afraid someone might get the wrong idea about us?"

He was good. I feigned irritation. "Of course not. I decide who I ride in carts with." I took a step and halted. "How do you know about Bernie's blog?"

"It's my job." He dragged the final word for several beats as if I'd missed the obvious.

I turned back to the road.

"You can't walk a mile in those heels. What about your white dress? It'll be covered in road dust."

I spun on him. "These are kitten heels, and road dust isn't a thing." I glanced at my dress. Hopefully.

"Here." Jake handed me the key to the cart. "You take the cart. I'll walk."

Relief swept through me, but my cover was blown, and I couldn't let him know he was right. "What about my exercise?"

He shook his head and walked away.

I powered up the cart and drove alongside him. "What if it rains?"

Thunder clapped on cue and rolled across the sky in ominous warning. Sprinkles fell on Jake's head. He looked up but kept walking.

I pressed the little pedal under my foot. "Jake." Pride and an infuriating sense of courtesy warred within me. "The rain."

He kept moving. "I've been through worse. Following you around, for example." His cheek kicked up into a lazy half smile.

I stamped the pedal and angled past him, blocking his path. "That's it. Get in."

Rain fell harder with each passing second. Heavy drops traced paths down his cheeks and darkened his shirt. He climbed onboard with a strange look in his eyes. "Thanks."

I hurried back to the clubhouse, thankful for the rain. Residents weren't on the streets putting two and two together about me, the cart and Jake. "That wasn't me in the picture by the fountain."

"Does it bother you that much?" His gaze drifted over everything but me.

"What?"

"That someone might think you're dating. Aren't you exactly the type of girl who's supposed to date?"

I whipped the cart into its space at the clubhouse. Thunder boomed overhead. "What's that supposed to mean? Because I'm nearly thirty and single I'm supposed to scramble through life begging someone to love me? I have people who love me." They were blood related, but whatever.

"I meant…I don't know…young, happy. It was a compliment. And I changed my mind about happy. I take that one back."

"You suck at compliments." I yanked the key from the cart. "I've already told you. I dated, and it was awful. I don't need to be in love. I'm just fine on my own."

He climbed out and headed for the door, mumbling under his breath and shoving wet bangs off his forehead.

I gave chase. "What do you know about dating anyway? You push everyone away with your grouch face and rude comments." I wiped frantically at my rain-soaked glasses.

Jake stopped to open the door for me.

I bounced off him and stumbled back a step to gather my wits and adjust my glasses.

"This is my thinking face and you bring out the worst in me, so don't make assumptions about my life outside your view." He gave me a sharp look and went inside without me.

MY DAY STANK. I drove home like a zombie. Five nights of restless sleep had caught up to me with full force. Jake's attitude didn't help. He hated following me around so much, he stopped. Not a single word for the rest of the workday. Fine by me. I'd found Nate on my own, and I could find Baxter's killer and Punisher too. I was already one third of the way to my goal. I hadn't actually heard from Nate since Comic Con, but still. I'd found him. After he emailed me.

I slunk into my apartment and dropped everything on the floor. I face-planted onto the couch and dragged an afghan from the armrest over my head. "Good night, world."

Someone cleared their voice.

My heart crammed into my throat. I inched fingertips over the material and peeked out.

"Hey." Nate wiggled his fingers at me.

I ninja jumped off the couch and into his arms. "Where have you been? I'm so confused." My throat ached with a sharp wedge of emotion. "I'm trying to figure things out, but it's so complicated, and I have this mess going on at the office thanks to stupid Punisher."

Nate wrapped me in a tight embrace and rested his chin on top of my head. "I know. I can help you with that." He rolled his chin away, positioning his cheek on my head. "I need a favor."

I pulled back. "Anything. What is it?"

"I need to stay here until we figure things out. Detective Archer put a BOLO out on me. I heard him make the call."

"BOLO?"

He smiled. "Be On the Lookout. It's what they're calling an All-Points Bulletin these days. I'm learning new lingo."

Nice. I guessed following a detective was a learning experience. "Sure. Okay. Yeah. Of course. Do you need me to buy you anything? Clothes or bathroom stuff?"

"No. I brought some things with me." He released me to climb onto a stool at my kitchen counter and steal an apple from the bowl. "I hoped you'd let me stay. It's kind of your fault I had to use your emergency key and let myself in."

I started the Keurig. "I need coffee if we're going to stay awake." I grabbed an apple but lacked the energy to lift it to my mouth. "Wait. How is that my fault?"

"I got Baxter's neighbors to let me in when I realized I couldn't stay at my place. I stayed there at night until you came over and locked up on your way out."

"What?" I collected my coffee and climbed on the stool beside him. "You got the neighbor to let you in?" I slapped the counter. "You're the mystery brother. I emailed his dad to ask about you. I thought maybe the killer was after something."

"Nope. Just me."

"Smart. No one would look for you there."

"The cops were probably there the night he...you

know. I stayed out all night that night and walked around the next day trying to make sense of things. Then I needed to sleep, and I came to our building, but a squad car was out front. I overheard them asking the landlord where he thought I was. They said it was in conjunction with a murder. They thought I killed Baxter."

I rolled my eyes. "Get in line."

The doorbell rang, and Nate ran for my bedroom.

I used the peephole. "Daddy!" I opened the door and gave him a hug. "What are you doing here?"

"I came to invite you to dinner. It doesn't feel right, me having a full house and you eating here alone with some cop staked outside."

I ran to the window. "Jeez. He's out there again."

Nate approached Dad with a hearty handshake. "Hey, Mr. Connors. How are you?"

"Better than you, I gather." He looked Nate over. "Being on the lam is hard on a fellow. You hungry? We're having a big dinner. Whole family's coming. I'm trying to talk Mia into joining us. She's sure to say yes if you do."

Nate approached me at the window and peered out. "I don't think so. I'm currently a fugitive and possibly on a killer's hit list. Another time?"

Dad opened the door. "Whatever you say. Come on, Mia. Your mother made shortcakes."

I tapped the glass. "Do you see this? I thought he'd given up on stalking me or he'd set his brother up to do it."

"Uh-oh." Dad's voice was raspy. The door clunked shut.

Nate and I turned like spokes on a wheel, absorbing Dad's problem in unison.

I groaned.

Nate swore.

Jake stood behind Dad, hands on hips, scowl on lips. His heated stare stole my breath.

"I can explain," Nate began.

I jumped in front of him. "You don't have to tell him anything. What are you doing here, Jake? How'd you get inside?"

"Hello," Dad said coolly. "Nice to see you again, Mr. Archer."

Jake nodded a response, attention focused on Nate and me.

Nate nudged me with his elbow. "Why's the club-house security guy at your apartment?"

I had no idea.

Dad rubbed his palms together. "Well, I came to collect Mia for dinner, but it seems she has company and the only polite thing to do is to invite you all."

Jake rocked on his heels. "That's very generous. I accept. I'd hoped to talk to Nate a bit while I was here."

I marched toward him. "Nate isn't going. How did you know he'd be here? I didn't even know he'd be here."

His eyes twinkled. "You should have. You told me Nate was following Dan, and Dan's outside, so Nate had to be close. Checking your place made the most logical sense."

Nate grabbed his coat. "Dinner sounds great, Mr. C."

"Where are you going?" I wedged hands on my waist. "You just said you couldn't go. Killer's hit list, remember?"

He looked at Jake. "Well, you're not leaving me here with him."

"Wonderful." Dad motioned us to hurry. "Know what also sounds good? Shortcakes."

Nothing had ever sounded worse than shortcakes.

JAKE AMBLED ACROSS the street to Dan's truck and leaned on the driver's side window ledge, blocking Dan's view of Nate as we ran from the building. They spoke while I angled the Crown Vic away from the curb behind Dad in Mom's Prius. Nate hid on the floorboards behind me. Jake's truck showed up in my rearview mirror a few blocks later. Miraculously, Dan stayed behind. I couldn't help feeling relieved. At least my place was guaranteed to be safe. What kind of dummy would break into my apartment with a cop out front?

I turned onto the next street and swatted my hand over the backseat. "You can get up."

Nate popped upright with a laugh. "This is kind of cool, right? All the cloak and dagger."

I glared in the rearview. "The cops are looking for you, and Baxter's gone." *Gone* was as close to the D-word as I could manage. If I said it one more time, I might join him.

He caught my gaze in the mirror. His lids cast shadows of long pale lashes over his cheeks. "I meant the sleuthing and hiding, not the reasons for both. It's kind of like LARPing."

Live Action Role Play was done by willing participants with guidelines and sometimes a script. This was something else. Too real. "I thought the same thing about cracking the case. We're collecting clues like in a game, but this is scary." I checked my rearview. Jake was either talking to himself or using Bluetooth. "At least now that we're roomies, we can work together."

"What about your cowboy? You think he'll let me stay or narc to his brother?"

How could I know? "People are squirrelly. He helped us at Comic Con." I tugged the material of my dress away from my chest, remembering the way he hid himself, using me as a shield.

I followed Dad into the driveway, and Jake parked behind us on the street, completely blocking my exit. "We're trapped."

"Speak for yourself." Nate got out with his hands up. "Please don't shoot until after the shortcakes."

Dad barked a laugh and came to clap Nate on the back. "Are you getting taller? Those Irish bones keep growing, huh?" He patted Nate's gut. "Keeping in shape. That's good when you're on the run." Dad winked at me as he led Nate inside.

Jake sauntered to my side, watching Dad and Nate with clear skepticism. "A retired cop has no problem with his daughter hooking up with a man the cops are looking for?"

I swatted his arm. "My dad was a darn good cop. He's got instincts you don't understand, and he knows Nate like I do. Nate's wicked smart and one of the kindest men I know. He couldn't hurt anyone, and we're not hooking up. Don't be an ass."

He kept his gaze on the door where Dad and Nate had disappeared. "He could."

My jaw dropped. "Presume much?"

"Hurt someone. I meant he could hurt someone." Jake lifted his eyebrows. "I looked him up. Nate was a boxer. A junior light heavyweight. Have you seen a fighter leave the ring? He's hurt a few people."

I curled my fingers into fists at my sides. "If you grow up in the Green family, you fight. Even his sisters are boxers. The minute he graduated and got a real job, he stopped competing and focused on his career. He might've hurt people in the ring, but that doesn't make him a guy who hurts people."

"Why take boxing that far and drop it?"

"Because he's smart." Too smart. Socially awkward and confused by people. "His family's important to him, so he did what he could to fit in, even if they don't always understand one another."

"Sorry. Are we still talking about Nate?"

"Mia!" Grandma waved both hands overhead from the front porch. "Come inside. Bring your beau."

I turned on my tiptoes and walked away. "Come on." My face burned. This dinner was the official worst time of my life and it hadn't even started.

"Grandma, this is Jake Archer."

He extended a hand and Grandma lurched at him. "Come here, big boy. I'm a hugger."

Dad, Nate, Mom and Bree stood in the kitchen, sipping wine and observing.

Grandma clutched Jake's hand and towed him to the kitchen. "What can I get you to drink? We like wine, but we have rum, too, and I think some fancy-pants beer." She snapped her fingers at Dad. "You got any of that fancy beer?"

Nate rounded the island and handed Jake a small glass. Amber liquid sloshed inside. "How about scotch?"

Jake examined the drink before accepting. "Your girl defends your honor pretty fiercely."

Nate smiled.

"Nothing to say about that?"

"Nope."

I poured a glass of wine. My family stared.

Grandma split the guys up. "Nate, can you help set the table? Jake? Can you answer a question for me?"

He nodded.

"Were you the man in the photograph on Bernie's blog?"

He looked at me. "Yes, ma'am."

Oh, jeez. "Why did you say that?"

"Ha!" Bree did a stupid dance and made the universal sign for gimme gimme. Palms up, fingers opening and closing at super speed.

Mom, Dad and Grandma handed her cash.

"Do you see?" I lamented between sips. "Now you've given them ammunition." The cool white wine soothed the edges of my day. Maybe I shouldn't care if my family thought there was something going on between Jake and me. Let him deal with the crazy and the questions. I sipped again. He'd be gone soon, so who cared? What would it matter?

Tom entered a moment later, with Gwen on his hip. He handed Bree money too.

Jake chuckled. "I like it here."

I pointed my glass at him. "You don't know what you're saying."

Tom squeezed me against his side. "Hey, Mia."

Gwen pulled my hair.

He offered a hand to Jake. "I'm Tom, Bree's husband. This is our little princess, Gwen."

Jake accepted the hand. His gaze drifted to me. "Tom MacAngus?"

Tom stepped back. "That's right. Have we met? I'm sorry if we have. I have a bit of Daddy brain." He pointed to his head. "Bree and I are working long hours on the grant, and Gwen doesn't sleep much."

I interjected before Tom elaborated on what he and my sister were up to for long hours. "Jake saw the photo of you on my refrigerator."

Tom exchanged a look with Bree across the room.

She sashayed out of sight with a soft, "Mmm-hmm."

I pressed the glass to my lips before I said anything else.

Nate returned with a smile. "Table's set. Let's eat."

Mom and Dad took their places at either end of the table. I poured a fresh glass of wine. Bree and Tom made human bookends with Gwen in a high chair between them, filling one side of the table. Nate, Jake and I sat on the other. I took the seat between the men to defuse testosterone outbursts and minimize Jake's questions.

My plate weighed a ton, filled to capacity like it was my last meal. Every savory calorie made a direct trip to my hips, but I'd worry about that later. Meanwhile, it was delicious and kept my mouth busy so no one would ask me any questions.

Jake wasn't as smart. He spent more time watching than eating.

"So, Jake," Bree began. "You're the new head of security at Horseshoe Falls?"

"Yes."

"How do you like it?"

He swirled his scotch and made eye contact. "Well, I came at a rough time, but I enjoy what I do."

Eye contact meant telling the truth, right? So, why did his answer feel like a dodge?

He *had* come at a rough time. Bernie had made note of it on her blog. She pointed out the giant obvious thing I'd missed. Jake arrived the same day Randall held the staff meeting about the bogus emails. The day Mark began his leave. The same day I answered the alarm and found Baxter in my office. Was it the wine, or did that seem shady, like Jake was somehow involved in this?

"What exactly do you do?" Bree pushed. "You seem to spend an inordinate amount of time with my sister. The last guy didn't do that."

Nate hung an elbow over the back of his chair and looked around me to Jake. "Yeah. Why is that, Jake?"

Grandma leaned forward on both elbows. "This is getting good. Speak up so I don't miss anything."

I dropped my fork, forced to answer a question that wasn't even directed at me. "He thought I did it. He followed me around looking for evidence I killed Baxter."

My family froze. Their combined attention turned to Jake, and I practically saw the pitchforks being distributed.

"Not now." I jumped in, overwhelmed at myself for throwing him to the mob. "Not anymore. He doesn't think that anymore."

"Is that true?" Nate's voice was deeper than usual.

Jake nodded. "It's true. I've got a few questions for you, though."

"Shoot." Nate answered before I could stop the madness.

Wherever Jake's questions went wouldn't be good.

I lifted the nearest bowl. "More mashed potatoes? Anyone?"

Jake turned in his seat and looked around me to Nate. "You seem at home here. You two were closer than I thought."

Nate smiled.

Jake didn't. "Were the two of you ever close in another way? More than friends?"

Dad groaned. "You're going to ruin my shortcakes."

Mom bobbed up and grabbed her plate. "I'll get the shortcakes. Bree, would you help me clear the table?"

"Not a chance." She motioned to Tom. "Tom will help."

Tom followed Mom to the kitchen.

Bree butted in. "You two have been close for years. You mean to tell me you never…"

I shook my head, lips pressed tight.

"You've slept over at one another's apartments. You're both gorgeous. Are you kidding me? Never once? Not even a heated kiss?"

I continued wagging my head.

Tom scooted back into the room. "What was the answer? I missed it."

Nate tipped back in his chair. "Your wife thinks I'm gorgeous."

Tom moved behind Bree's chair and kissed her head. "He really is." He loaded his arm with dirty plates. "Will either of you admit to thinking about it? In the name of research. No judgment."

Jake wrinkled his forehead. "Research for your grant?"

"Human sexuality. What about you? Have you ever thought about Mia in a sexual way?'

Jake balked. "What?"

I covered my face with both hands. "I'm dreaming. This kind of thing doesn't happen in real life, so I'm dreaming."

Nate patted my shoulder. "Quiet, sweetie. I'm waiting for this answer too."

To my relief, Jake didn't answer.

Bree clucked her tongue. "You spend all your time tailing Mia, but you don't have to. How else do you explain that? Are you sexually attracted to my sister?"

He exhaled long and loud. "I believe we're still waiting for an answer from Nate on the subject."

Nate laughed. "No. By all means. Go ahead. You first."

I stood, and my chair tilted back.

Jake caught the chair.

Nate caught my arm. "Whoa." He steadied me while Jake righted the chair. "You don't normally have two glasses of anything stronger than diet soda. Maybe you should sit."

"I think I'm ready to go home."

Dad stood, tossing his napkin aside. "What about the shortcakes?"

Nate waved him off. "Let me talk to her." He walked me to the kitchen and poured me a glass of ice water. "You okay?"

"Yeah." I sipped the water and walked in a small circle, clearing my head. "It's been a terrible week."

Nate leaned against the counter. "You're not kidding. Did you know someone hacked all my online accounts? Anything I didn't seal watertight was infiltrated and erased or ruined. Everything in my REIGN kingdom was destroyed. My buildings were sieged. That can't be a coincidence. It had to be Punisher. Who else would go after my gaming life?"

A full-on digital assault. "Do you think he knows you tracked him to the library and found the clubhouse logos?" I gasped. "If he knows that, he must know you know he was giving viruses to our residents."

Nate pushed off the counter and refilled my water. "That's just a theory."

Jake stood in the doorway.

I braced my palms on the counter. "Punisher wanted to ruin me. He attacked my work life. Baxter tracked him down to confront him. What if they agreed to meet in person and he was at the clubhouse that night?" My voice softened. "What if my online nemesis killed my real-life friend?"

Nate rubbed my shoulders. "It's possible. He knew we'd found evidence against him. He might've thought we knew who he was."

I struggled to push my voice above a whisper. "It's such a small world."

A vein in Jake's neck pulsed. "Is it?"

I gulped the rest of my water. Wine churned in my tummy. I could've brought this on. I could have unintentionally caused Baxter's death. "I'm ready to go. Are you ready to go?"

A room full of gazes warmed my cheeks. My family had filtered in from the dining room, overhearing everything. Mom approached slowly, as if she might scare me. Dad carried a stack of plastic containers. He handed two to Nate and one to Jake. "You can't leave without taking some of Gwendolyn's shortcake."

Bree arrived on Dad's heels with a smile and a round of hugs. She stage-whispered against Nate's cheek. "Mia never has a second glass of wine."

Nate kissed her cheek. "That's why I'm driving."

Jake lifted the container of shortcake. "Thank you all very much for dinner. Mrs. Connors, it was delicious." He shook Dad's hand then reached for Mom's. "I will dig into this the minute I'm home."

He looked at my sister longer than was socially acceptable. "Bree. It was interesting."

She beamed.

Nate bumped the toe of his shoe against the floor. "Freaky, isn't it?"

"What?" Bree and I asked in unison.

"Yeah." Jake nodded, eyes focused on Bree. "They're identical. Even the hair. Who wears their hair that long anymore?"

Bree rocked in place, probably feeling as if her extra baby weight didn't show. "We wear it long for the Renaissance Faires. It's part of the look. Plus, Tom loves it."

Tom whistled in agreement.

Jake turned his eyes on me. "What about the glasses? Part of your look?"

"Bree wears contacts." I twitched under his scrutiny. "Our similarities stop at appearances."

Nate wrapped a protective arm around my shoulders. "They say that, but they're more alike than they think."

I blew a raspberry. "Whatever, fugitive."

Jake choked out a sound that almost passed for a laugh. "I'll see y'all later. It was truly nice being here. Thank you."

He sauntered through the door and removed his obnoxious truck from the path of Dad's Crown Vic.

A half dozen hugs and too many air kisses later, Nate and I climbed into the escape vehicle.

I collapsed into the passenger seat. "Thanks for driving."

Nate started the car. "Thanks for housing a fugitive."

"Sorry. I know you aren't a fugitive. Not really. You're exactly what you seem, a six-foot, two-hundred-pound teddy."

He gave me a lazy half laugh as we reversed out of the drive. "Well, that might be true where you're concerned, but I'm not always so cuddly. Some people are frightened by my aggressive nature and sizable guns." He flexed his arms, releasing the wheel one hand at a time.

"Right. Hey. How will you park the car without Dan seeing you?"

Nate winked and flashed his easy smile. "Don't worry about me, honey. This ain't my first rodeo." He reached behind the seat and yanked a pull string bag from the floor behind me. "I brought a disguise just in case." He tugged a gray-and-black beanie over his head and pointed to a button-down bowling shirt with giant pins on the back and *Jim* embroidered above one pocket.

"Hipster chic. Nice."

"Thank you."

The houses of suburbia sped past my window as we veered onto the highway. "What if I picked a fight with Punisher online and he found me in real life?"

"You can't think like that. Besides, he tore my virtual life to shreds, not yours. How do you explain that based on your theory?"

I smiled, glad he hadn't agreed with me. "My accounts are properly protected. I've told you before. You can't use Fighting Irish for every password."

He laughed.

We rode in silence for several blocks. Nate stole looks at me every few seconds.

"What? Say it." I picked at the flaking polish on my nails.

"I'm not convinced Jake Archer is who he seems to be."

"What do you mean?"

"I mean, I'm a big teddy bear, and he's not a temporary clubhouse security guard."

"He did show up the same day this all started for me." I pulled my phone into my lap. The warmth of wine thrust away. "One way to find out."

Several quick searches later, I had nothing. "No social media profiles. No arrests, bankruptcy or divorce."

"Try his service record."

I snapped my fingers. "Right. Maybe he was in
the paper somewhere. Small towns do big homecom-
ing parades for soldiers fresh from the war. No. Hang
on." Think. Think. Think. "I can find him through his
brother."

"Dan? That guy won't have any social media profiles
either. His record's clean, too. He's a cop."

"Not Dan. Eric." My fingers dashed across the
screen. "Eric's at least ten years younger. He's getting
married, and they have a website to keep guests updated
and get feedback on decisions like food, drinks, music,
location…you get it."

Bingo! The wedding site had a list of friends and
family. I raced through Eric's list and clicked on
groomsmen.

Nate slowed. "Did you squeak? What does that mean?
Tell me he has naked photos. Tell me he's dressed as
Batman for Halloween. Something to bring him down
a notch the next time he looks at me like a criminal or
you like he's got a secret."

I shoved my phone in his direction, ignoring the secret comment. "How's this?"

He swerved on the dark street. "You have to read it
to me. I'm driving."

I gritted my teeth and forced the words through.
"'Groomsman number two, FBI special agent Jacob
Archer, is another proud older brother of the lucky
groom.'"

I typed the new information into another round of
searches, starting with the FBI.

Nate didn't speak.

"Are you kidding?" I growled at a two-year-old article covering the growth and expansion of a local task force. Jake's picture filled the tiny screen of my phone. His more accurate title trimmed the bottom.

I shook the phone in Nate's direction. "Read it!"

He pulled the car onto the shoulder of a neighborhood street and removed the phone from my hand. "Special Agent Jacob Archer, Cyber Crimes Division."

The week suddenly made a lot more sense. "He's in so much trouble when I see him tomorrow."

TWENTY

I SPENT THE night fuming over how to confront Jake and dressed before dawn in my cutest, who-the-hell-cares-if-you-think-it's-short dress. My pedicure looked delightful in my new patent peep toes, and I was cover-shoot ready. When I faced off with Jake Archer, FBI, and announced his cover was blown, I'd do it looking amazing and nothing like I felt. No more agonizing over the fit or length of my skirts. My clothes were striking, retro-chic numbers, and if he knew about anything besides blue jeans and lies, he'd realize having my own style was something to admire about me, not something to condemn. Jerk.

I dashed outside and headed for the coffee shop drive-thru down the block. This was a triple espresso latte kind of morning. I bought a scone too. Maybe Jake would like to try his game on a caffeinated, sugared-up Mia. He'd lose.

I sucked liquid energy through an oversized straw all the way to Horseshoe Falls. To my dismay, the club-house lot was nearly empty and, according to Dad's dashboard display, it was only 7:05. The staff wouldn't arrive for almost an hour. My fingers twitched with the rush of breakfast. I sloshed the bucket-sized latte, mixing bonus espresso shots and caramel syrup with melting ice. Time to go inside and wait for Special Agent Archer.

I jumped out of the car. The clubhouse was still, save for the distant clang of cooks preparing breakfast for Derby's buffet. I bypassed my office, eager to confront the little liar. An ambush was a brilliant idea. I'd wait in his chair. Surprise him when he rolled in. I dashed through his office doorway and nearly swallowed my tongue.

Jake sat at his desk, sorting through a file two inches thick. "You're here early. How was your slumber party?"

I seethed. "You."

Surprise wrinkled his brow. He dropped his pen. "Me?"

I bobbed my head, no longer able to access the argument I'd practiced on my way to work. "I know who you are. How long did you think you could hide that from me?" A rush of disappointment replaced my anger. "Why would you hide that from me?"

Betrayal burned my belly. He'd lied to me. Why was I so awful at identifying actual friends and acts of kindness over ploys to keep me in sight and plays for my money? Men were the worst. People. People sucked. Hard.

Jake angled back in his chair, the file before him forgotten. "Shut the door, Mia."

I obeyed.

"Sit."

My brain screamed about the audacity of issuing me orders, but my legs obeyed. I shoved the giant green straw between my lips and gulped the remains of my coffee.

He laced his fingers behind his head and appraised me.

"What?" I deposited the empty cup onto his desk. "Why are you looking at me like I've done something wrong when you're the fake?" Jake the Fake. I raised my eyebrows in a challenge. It probably wasn't even a coincidence that rhymed.

"What'd you do when you got home last night?"

Nate and I had researched Jake for hours, digging up every newspaper article, military honor and report card he'd been issued since the nineties. I'd eaten both our take-home shortcakes. "Nothing."

Jake lurched forward in his seat, planting forearms on his desk with a whack. "Don't lie to me, Connors."

"Oh, I'm not the liar in this room, and you know it." Suddenly I wished the door was open.

Piercing blue eyes fastened me in place. "What do you know about Wilbur Donahue?"

The words smacked me in the face. "What?" *How'd he know about that?* Wilbur was the genuinely good guy I'd researched for Lacy last week.

"Wilbur. Donahue." He pronounced each word with menace. "His ID and credentials for National Bank were stolen last night. The cyber footprint on his life was yours."

Ice spread in my gut. "Wait a minute." I bounced to my feet. Nate's life had been hacked too.

"Sit down."

"No. I will not sit down. I'm not yours to control, and you have no authority over me." Granted, the words were more a reminder to myself than him. With what he accused me of, I might be his to boss around. Stuff had just got real. *Think.* I pulled in two long breaths through my nose, releasing the tension through my mouth. "Am I being charged with something?" Judging by the expression on his face, the dare in my voice surprised him.

He stood, marching slowly around his desk to intimidate me. "Should I charge you with something?

What did you do, Mia? Tell me and things can go a whole other way."

My mouth fell open. "Are you playing the good cop *and* the bad cop? You can't be both cops. That's not how it works."

He widened his stance and leaned against the corner of his desk, painstakingly rolling each sleeve on his dress shirt to his elbow. Letting me stew in my curiosity. He raised expressionless blue eyes to mine. "Let me tell you how this goes. First, we charge you with identity theft and haul you into custody, where you'll be remanded for bail, which we know you can afford, but before you leave, I'll interrogate you. I will get the answers I'm looking for. You might as well start talking now. Save yourself the embarrassment of being hauled out of here in cuffs."

I pulled my chin back. "You can't cuff me for nothing."

"I can if you try to hit me."

I did want to hit him. My face burned with humiliation. His smarmy face begged for a slap.

Opening up to him about what I did for Lacy was a breach of contract to every client. How could I be trusted if I cracked under the pressure of one jerky agent?

"What if we trade information?" I lowered my jittery frame into the chair before him.

He scoffed. "You want to cut a deal already? Good grief, Mia. What are you wrapped up in?"

I kicked him, and he jerked his leg back. "Sorry. I was crossing my legs."

Jake moved to a safe distance around the side of his desk. "What kind of trade are you asking for?" He set his phone on the desktop and tapped the screen.

"This is Special Agent Archer. I'm talking with Mia Connors." He recited the date, time and location of our meeting then pointed the phone in my direction. "Mia, you were saying?"

I cleared my throat. "Well, Special Agent Archer." I made a sour face as I stated his title. "I was saying that I need you to use discretion with any information I give you. There are things I don't want repeated. I understand I'm stuck, so I'm willing to tell you some things I'd rather not." I calculated the absolute minimum information I could spill and still leave without a trip in cuffs. He was right. That mortified me.

He waited impatiently as I composed my thoughts. "Go on."

I leaned forward, making sure my words were picked up by the device but not so loud that they carried through the closed door. "I researched Mr. Donahue for someone else."

"Your accomplice?"

I made a nasty face the recorder couldn't capture. "Give me a break. I researched him for someone he dates. Someone who didn't want to get emotionally involved with a man who might hurt her in any number of ways. I dug up public records only and shared the files with this woman. I also checked for accounts on social media as well but, aside from pictures taken at business events and fundraisers, he didn't have a web presence."

Jake snapped the recorder app off. "Is this the file you took to the leggy blonde?"

"Lacy." I dragged her name for two long syllables. "Are all women just a list of body parts to you? I'd hate to hear what you call me behind my back. My legs are a little on the stumpy side."

He circled his pointer finger in the air, in a universal hurry-the-hell up move. "What else?" He restarted the recorder.

"Nothing else, but I did notice I wasn't the first person to research him so thoroughly. I remember making a mental note. I figured if I dug deep enough, I'd see a legal battle. Lawyers are relentless detectives if winning a case will make them rich. I didn't see anything obvious to chase, so I let it go."

"And?"

"Nothing. There's nothing remotely evil about Mr. Donahue. He's a nice old man."

Jake stopped the recorder again. "The black business cards are yours. You do this for Falls residents? Look into people's business?"

"I research. That's it. Like I've told you before, I gather online information made public, sometimes for people like Lacy with a fortune to lose. Sometimes to parents who worry their children are going down a dark path. Sometimes for clients who want things scrubbed from the web. A wild trip to Vegas, that sort of thing. That's it." I lifted my palms. "I don't steal identities or hack into banks. You've got the wrong girl."

"What else?"

Jeez. Was he daft or could he earn prizes for most-dogged agent? I glared. "Nothing else, except you're the one who owes me answers, not the other way around. I had no idea someone was gunning for Mr. Donahue, but you lied to me every day."

He stared at my legs. "Your foot hasn't stopped bobbing since you sat down. Telltale sign of guilt or anxiety. Anxiety is usually a direct result of guilt."

"I drank a freaking vat of coffee this morning, and I came here to tell you how horrible you are. I didn't expect to be interrogated. I haven't done anything wrong.

Unlike you." I stuffed a fingernail in my mouth and gnawed around the edges.

Jake's shoulders relaxed. "Someone else researched him?"

I nodded, unwilling to release my poor finger.

He tapped his phone screen while my mind raced.

I uncrossed and recrossed my legs. "Can your guys dig deeper? Find out who was there before me? If they can't, I can help." My heart thundered in my chest. "I think I'm having a panic attack."

"I think you overdosed on caffeine." He shook the empty coffee cup and tossed it into his trash.

Maybe. "Hey. I remember seeing Mr. Donahue lived in Horseshoe Falls a few years ago." I pulled my gaze from the carpet to Jake's blue eyes. "That can't be a coincidence, right? The emails and break-ins with our current residents, and now the ID theft of a former resident." I bounced. "So, this obviously isn't me. Right? You see that? This is the work of whoever sent those emails and distributed that virus."

He shook his head. "Not so fast, Coffee. You're overlooking the obvious. Those emails were a visual match for the work correspondence you send. The break-ins happened in a closed environment where you have free rein, and you recently researched the man whose identity was stolen. You could easily be behind all these things. Maybe you sent the emails for a nefarious reason I haven't uncovered yet. You know what Sherlock Holmes says?"

I nodded. "Shut up so I can think." Sherlock Holmes said when we eliminate the impossible, whatever remained, however improbable, must be the truth. Jake wasn't clear on what he thought was impossible, but something else settled in. "You admit the idea of me as

the notorious cyber-criminal you're looking for is improbable? You see I have no motive. I don't need their
money, and I work here. Why ruin that?"

Jake nodded, tiny nearly imperceptible movements,
but he agreed. He didn't seem wholly convinced I was
the villain he sought.

Time to use that to my advantage. "Holmes also said
investigation is all about the data. You can't form a true
case on faulty data, and you can't do a proper job of
finding the criminal if you don't approach this with a
blank mind. You started your investigation with a theory, and now you spend all your time trying to prove
yourself right. That's why you're getting nowhere."

His tormented expression worried me.

I used his tactic against him and settled against the
back of my chair. I'd wait him out.

The silence killed me. I worked to focus my thoughts
while he watched me.

"How do you know so much about Sherlock
Holmes?"

"That's your question? You've got me pegged as a
felon and you want to know how I can quote Sherlock
Holmes? Are you kidding me? He's a classic and my
personal hero." Among many, but still a hero. "How do
you know so much about him?"

"He's history's greatest detective, Pink Panther
aside." An almost-smile tugged his cheek.

I pulled my laptop from my bag, done talking.

Alarm crossed Jake's face. "What are you doing?"

I focused on the screen. "Well, I can't sit here idle
while you do your best to form a case against me."
I opened window after window, following a hunch.
Five minutes later, I shut the computer and stowed it in
my bag.

I stood, tossed the strap over my head and secured it cross-body. "Come on."

He rounded the desk to my side without hesitation. "Where are we going?"

"We're going to visit the Valentines. They should be back from riding by now, unless you plan to cuff me, charge me or question me some more?"

He shifted his weight, foot to foot.

Well, that was good news. I opened the door and cast a look over my shoulder to be certain he followed. "I looked up all the break-in victims, and they all lived here at the same time as Mr. Donahue. You still think that's a coincidence?"

Jake followed me to the golf cart outside. "I never said that was a coincidence. I don't believe in coincidences. I said it *wasn't* a coincidence that you're at the center of every thread I pull."

I got behind the wheel and motioned him to the other side. "Get in."

He climbed in and shot me a weary look. "Are you over the fear of being seen with me? That was fast, unless you were up to something else yesterday."

I angled the cart onto the road. "Yesterday was a long time ago, back before you worked for the FBI Cyber Crimes Division and came here to charge me with something sinister. You came here for me, right? Cyber Crimes usually looks at tech support first."

He stared blank-faced at me.

Since he'd threatened to cuff me if I hit him, I kept talking. "We're most definitely not involved in anything beyond finding the truth. People will see that. You do want to find the actual criminal, right?" I peered at Jake, half-afraid he was one of those cops who'd rather be right than just.

"Of course," he snarled. "What kind of man do you think I am?"

I pressed the pedal harder. "Considering what you think of me, I don't see how that matters. Just tell me one thing. Were those people even your real family? Or did you stage the engagement with a bunch of FBI agents to try to lure me into letting my guard down and confessing my crimes over chicken and biscuits?"

He turned away from me. "You're ridiculous."

I nodded in mock agreement. "Oh, yeah, sure. I'm totally the ridiculous one, says Mr. Temporary Clubhouse Security Guard."

His fingers curled into fists on his lap. He didn't speak.

I took a few calming breaths. "It seems to me that whoever is after these guys might have also lived here at the same time as them. I can't think of another reason all the victims would have this community in common. There has to be a vendetta. We need a list of all the other residents in that time frame."

He narrowed a snooty look on me. "Fine, but tell me this. Are my men going to call me back and tell me you lived here during that time?"

I dropped my head forward and slowed the cart. "Yes, but that's a straight coincidence."

"Says the girl who doesn't believe in coincidences."

I jammed the pedal. "Since when do you pay attention to anything I say?" Only when it can be used against me, probably.

"Since it's my job."

I pulled into the lot near the stables and fought off a tirade. This wasn't the day I'd imagined. This was the kind of day that made a girl want to try out her passport.

Herman Valentine waved from outside the stables.

The brush in his hand made me smile. The quarter horse beside him had a luxurious brown coat and black mane. The Valentines loved their horses like they loved their children. My heart swelled with respect and admiration anytime I saw them with the animals.

I bounced out of the cart and headed for Herman. "Hi." I waved back, smiling, openmouthed to put him at ease. Putting last night's body language research to use seemed a good move. I'd spent hours reading on the subject after Nate and I exhausted links to Jake's true identity. "She's beautiful." I pointed to the horse.

He beamed. "Thanks. This one's Jennifer's. We call her Lady. Are you here to ride? I can get your horse ready in a jiff. Are you going together?" He eyeballed Jake, who arrived late to my side.

Jake raised his hand to shake. "Jake Archer, Head of Security."

I blew a quiet raspberry.

Jake glowered. He shook Herman's hand and motioned toward the office. "Can we talk inside, Mr. Valentine?"

"Sure. Let me get Lady into her stall, and I'll meet you there." Herman led the horse to the stable.

I stormed to the office door and opened it with a flourish.

Jennifer turned in her chair and squealed. "Mia!" She dove into me with an eager hug. "I haven't seen you in forever. How are you? How's Faire season going? Did you see your picture on Bernie's blog?" Her gaze lifted to Jake behind me. "Ah, the mystery man."

Jake made a strange face. "Why do you say that?"

Her easy smile turned cocky and confident. "Your watch. Your stance. Those boots. Plus, I'm blonde, not blind. Blonde isn't a reflection on my IQ, handsome, but I do like to have fun."

I laughed. Suck on that, smart guy.

The door swung wide, and Herman stepped into the small office, dusting his palms. "Can we get you guys anything to drink? Coffee? Iced tea? Water?" He dragged a pair of chairs near Jennifer's desk and motioned for us to sit.

Jake murmured something about me having had enough coffee.

I sat.

He stood.

Herman turned to his wife. "Jake's the new head of security."

Jennifer squinted at Jake. "Military?"

Jake gave one sharp nod and stood straighter.

Herman and Jennifer lit up. The couple had served together years ago. Jennifer had opened the stables when I was in high school, but Herman was recently retired from the Pentagon.

Jake took the seat beside me and kicked his long legs out in front of him. "Can we see the footage from your security cameras? Early last week, late in the day."

Jennifer brought the displays up on her monitor and typed in the date of Baxter's murder. "You're looking for the night the boy was killed at the clubhouse, right?"

I nodded.

Jake leaned forward, elbows on knees, absorbing the feed as it ran.

We watched as Jen located the footage closest to Baxter's death. My heartbeat slowed. Weight settled on my chest, stifling my breaths. "Go back." I raised a hand to the screen.

Jennifer rewound the video thirty seconds.

I scooted to the edge of my seat. "Do you see something flashing?"

The small crowd nodded.

"Reflectors," Herman said.

I turned to Jake. "Just like Darlene said she saw on her way home that night." I looked to the Valentines. "Did you guys notice any tire marks, like a bicycle might make?" I looked out the office windows, trying to acclimate myself with which direction the flashing had occurred. "Which way is this tape covering?" I stood for a better view.

Jen shook her head. A sad smile tugged her lips. She covered my hand with hers. "I'm afraid yesterday's storm would've washed away any prints left in the dirt."

Great. I sat down, defeated. Again. "We looked right before the storm, not well, but we looked. There were only footprints."

Herman turned to Jake, apparently working something over in his mind. He squeezed his chin between a thumb and forefinger. "You know, I knew an Archer when I was in the desert. Relation maybe?"

Jake rubbed his palms down along the seams of his pants. "Maybe." He never broke the straight-faced routine. "Mia says you get a lot of traffic through the woods. Can I get a copy of this tape?"

"Of course. Take this one."

Jake stood and extended his hand to Herman. "I'm going to get Mia back to work and touch base with you later, once I've reviewed the tape, if that's all right."

Jennifer stood and gathered me into her arms for a departing hug. "Let us know if you need anything else."

Herman winked. "Anything at all."

I climbed into the passenger side of the cart and turned to face Jake. "Did I cause all this?"

His gaze lingered on mine.

"What?" I demanded. "What are you thinking?"

My phone rang before Jake answered. He pulled onto the asphalt road ahead of us. Grandma's face filled the screen. If I rejected the call, she'd call back until I answered. I put the phone to my ear. "Hello?"

"Mia? It's your grandma."

"Hi, Grandma. Everything okay?" *I'm being investigated by Cyber Crimes at the FBI. How are you?*

"We're eating at my place tonight. I've got a finished shipment of eye cream that needs labeled, bagged and boxed. I'll get pizza, chips and whatever else you can eat while you work. No wine for you. Be here at five and bring your sweetheart."

If she meant Nate, I doubted I could peel him off Dan's tail two nights in a row. If she meant Jake, I wasn't sure I could dodge him if I wanted, but I definitely didn't want to eat with him again, the liar. "I think I'll come alone tonight."

Jake's hands tightened on the steering wheel.

"I'll call you after work." I slid the phone into my laptop bag on the floor. "We have packing parties when Grandma finishes a big order of eye cream. It's a recipe she won't hand off to her manufacturer. She thinks it's a delicate process and requires a personal touch. I think she's sentimental and likes putting us to work."

Jake turned into the clubhouse parking lot and parked. He twisted in his seat to face me. "I was sent here to investigate you on a series of identity thefts. As you discovered, the bulk of breaches crossing my desk in the past three months either happened here or to former residents of this community. In every scenario, you're the obvious connection. I can't deny that. I don't care what Holmes said."

I climbed out of the cart and headed for the clubhouse. "Then why not arrest me?"

He followed a half step behind. His truncated gait matched mine awkwardly. His head angled low near my ear. "Because a decent agent follows his gut. I don't think you're behind this, but I can't ignore the evidence to the contrary. Whatever plans you just made, you'd better count me in. There'll be no new identity thefts while I'm here. Got that?"

I yanked the door open and marched inside. Work today would officially suck and tonight's packing party would be one for the scrapbook.

TWENTY-ONE

I SLIPPED OUT for lunch and made a trip to the local driving range situated behind the Horseshoe Falls community. I parked the Crown Vic and said a prayer before stepping inside the small office.

A man in a white logoed shirt and khaki pants met me at the counter. "Can I help you?"

"Hi. I'm assisting in an investigation at Horseshoe Falls. There was a murder last week." My tongue thickened. "I noticed the community is only fenced as far as the woods there." I pointed out the window to his driving range. "We have reason to suspect the murderer parked here and cut through the woods at the edge of your range to commit the crime."

Blood drained from his face. "You're kidding."

"No. I'm sorry to say, I'm not. If you'd let me review the parking lot footage from your security cameras, it would be an incredible assist."

"If it leads to a capture, do I get a reward?"

I mulled that over. "Would you be unwilling to help if there was no reward?"

He tapped both thumbs on the counter before giving in to humanity. "Fine. Come on back."

I followed him to a closet-turned-camera room. He pulled out a folding chair and pointed to a collection of tapes. "I keep them a week at a time before I tape over. This is the first time I've ever needed them."

"Thanks. Do you mind if I look while I'm here? I won't be long."

"Knock yourself out."

I slid onto the chair and selected the tape from that night. I forwarded to the time of death and watched for the killer to make his getaway.

The edge of the woods were in the far corner of the screen. I forwarded the tape and watched bats zoom past the moon. Dark cars polka-dotted the dark lot. Several minutes later, a figure darted onto the screen and sprinted across the range toward the lot. I strained for a clearer image on the black-and-white pixilated monitor. Where was the super-zoom feature every sleuth used on TV? The figure closed the distance at a clip and disappeared off the camera's radar.

I slapped the table. My fingers itched to rewind and watch again. I forced myself to focus on the lot. Whoever ran off screen had to leave somehow. Hopefully, they left in view of the camera.

Minutes later, another figure appeared at the woods' edge and drifted across the range, bent forward and moving erratically. Were they partners? Was the second one injured? I watched with bated breath as the second figure drew near, climbing the small bank into the lot with effort. Free of the grass, the figure straightened and huffed for air. This figure was a woman. She swung a car door open and the interior light illuminated a too-familiar face.

Marcella closed the door and reversed the beat-up sedan out of sight.

I gripped the chair and weighed the implication.

Nate's car barreled into the lot seconds later, nearly meeting her at the parking lot entrance where she'd sailed onto the road and out of sight. He jumped out and ran full speed across the range and into the woods. I knew the rest.

What I didn't know was what Marcella was doing in the woods that night or why she was driving that junky car when she owned a high-end SUV. I also didn't know who'd run out a moment before her or where they went. I watched the tape in double time, waiting for another look at the mysterious figure. It never made a reappearance.

"Excuse me?" I stopped at the desk on my way out. "Is there more parking available nearby?" The farm behind the range meant Figure One couldn't have simply dashed to a car left on a nearby street. If he ran through farmland to make his getaway, I'd never find him. I doubted farmers kept security cameras.

"Miss?"

"I'm sorry." My cheeks burned. The possibility I'd never be any closer to finding Baxter's killer settled into my chest. "What was the answer?"

"About three years back we added overflow parking, but no one uses it. It was hopeful thinking."

I spun in a circle. "Where?"

"Out back. There's a set of steps to the lower lot."

"Do you have cameras there?"

"No. The cameras are for the office more than the cars. Why?"

"Thank you." I dashed outside and across the parking lot behind the building. A red metal handrail disappeared over a small hill. I stopped without descending. Baxter's car was in the lot.

I DIALED MARCELLA on my way back to work. She didn't answer.

"Bernie!" I waved from Dad's car as I swiped through the guard gate.

She met me with a skip in her step. "Have you seen the blog?"

"Not today. What did you post?"

"Free Randall. We're planning a rally tomorrow night if they haven't let him go. You know they only have seventy-two hours to charge him or set him free. Can I count on you to be there?"

"Maybe. Do you know if Marcella left for lunch?"

Bernie went into the booth and scrolled through her computer screen. "No. She hasn't swiped out since she got here this morning."

"Thanks." I waved goodbye and headed for the club-house.

Marcella's SUV was in the lot, but she wasn't in her office. I left a note on her desk and considered my options. I could page her. That would help if she was in the building, but she could be anywhere.

The image from Bernie's blog came to mind.

I left the way I came in and made my way across the lot toward the fountain.

Marcella sat on the stout but decorative stone wall. Her hair was pulled tight in a bun. "Mia." She jumped to her feet and dusted her backside. "What are you doing here?"

"I saw the photos on Bernie's blog yesterday. You were the woman by the fountain, weren't you?"

"No. Of course not." She lifted her palm to my cheek.

I backed away. "I spent my lunch hour reviewing security footage from the driving range."

Her hands fell to her tummy.

"You were here the night Baxter died and you didn't say anything."

"No, *gorda*."

I lowered my voice to a steady seethe. "I saw you."

"I can explain."

I tented my eyebrows.

Her crimson lips quivered. "I can't explain."

I turned to leave, half expecting to find Jake hidden in the flowers. I needed to tell Detective Archer about Baxter's car and the tape. Let him talk to Marcella.

"Wait." She grabbed my elbow. "Mia, I'm sorry. I left my purse in the office that night and I had a date. I couldn't swipe in at the guard gate without my badge, and I couldn't go out without my purse. I was forced to go the long route through the driving range."

"Where was your car?"

"I borrowed my son's car. My date was picking me up, so I let my son take the nice car on his date."

"You were getting picked up for a date after nine at night?"

She gave me a sad look. "We were going dancing. The band didn't even begin until ten. You're sometimes old for your age, *gorda*."

"Did you know what happened to Baxter? It happened while you were here. Please. I have to know." My voice softened to a whisper.

She shrugged and pulled me closer. "I am so sorry about your friend. I had no idea until morning. I heard the alarm and thought I'd somehow set it off when I went inside, so I ran." She swiped a tear with the pad of her thumb. "I'm so sorry I didn't tell you sooner."

"Did you see Randall there?"

"No."

I wiggled free of her grip and stumbled back to the clubhouse with too much information to process in one lifetime. Marcella had lied to me. Again. The guilt burdened her gentle features. I only wished I knew why, and if anything she'd said was true.

GRANDMA MET JAKE and me at the door, wearing her business face. "Pizza's in the kitchen. Product's in the dining room. I've got the table set up in an assembly line. You know the drill." She pulled us inside. "I don't want to make this an all-nighter, so get moving." She turned on her heels and headed for the dining room.

I closed the door and moved toward the kitchen, listening for Jake's footfalls behind me, inexplicably nervous about bringing him along. I stepped through the archway between Grandma's foyer and main hall. The click-clack of my heels on hard flooring rattled my nerves. "You know what? How about the two-cent tour? I want to change."

Jake followed dutifully, silently, up the curving mahogany staircase to the second floor.

I pointed to the doors as we passed, unnerved further by his inexplicable silence. "These are guest rooms. That's the upstairs office. No one uses it. Bathroom. Second floor laundry. Auxiliary library. Bree's room. Gwen's room." I dipped into the next open doorway and switched the light on. "My room."

Jake leaned against the doorjamb.

Old punk band and movie posters covered the walls. A head-and-shoulders shot of my favorite Batman actor was pinned on the ceiling over my bed. *Way to be creepy, Mia.*

"I'll only be a minute. You can sit if you want." I pointed to the gaming chair by the television.

My nerves were shot. The coffee must've stuck with me all day. I dug through my closet for something I didn't hate but also didn't like enough to care if it got a pizza stain. "Hang on." I ducked inside and closed the closet doors behind me. Sensor lights illuminated the space. I called through the slatted doors. "I need to change if I'm going to have room for pizza, chips and cookies." Was that too casual for us now? How did someone treat the attractive man who wanted to arrest her? Was there a benchmark? Some kind of industry standard for this?

I tugged on a pair of white capris and a well-worn V-neck fandom shirt. "Almost done."

When I reopened the closet doors, Jake was on the opposite side of my room, fingering my bookshelves, trophies and personal photos.

"Looking for clues?"

He gave me a thorough looking over. "Trying to get a feel for who you are under the fancy labels and four-inch heels."

"Girl next door?"

"Not mine."

I grabbed the teddy from my bed and flounced onto the comforter. "This is Teddy Roosevelt." I waved his fuzzy arm at Jake. "I got him as a toddler. I literally can't remember him not being in my life. Grandma never changes anything in here. Whenever I sleep here, it's like I never left."

Jake twisted at the waist to face me. "You have ribbons for track, swimming, tennis, archery, skeet and distance biking. I didn't even know that last one was a thing."

"And?" I dared him to finish the statement. What? Girls didn't do those things? No. He wasn't a misogynist. Maybe he'd complain rich people got ribbons for everything. Who knew? I braced myself for a fight.

"You don't strike me as the athletic type."

"Dad insisted Bree and I stay involved in sports. He said, statistically, girls involved in sports were more likely to graduate high school, get better grades and not get pregnant. I dodged team activities because I don't understand the strange camaraderie and my coordination is limited. I also trained in dressage, but more for Lancelot's entertainment than mine."

"Lancelot's your horse."

"Yep."

"What about dancing or baton twirling? Those are big for girls where I come from."

I snorted. "Bree was the dancer, the cheerleader, the one everyone adored." Wow. Where did that come from? I tossed Teddy against the pillows.

Jake returned his attention to my things. "Archery's a little impressive."

"You should see me shoot. It's all just math. Physics, really." I rolled onto my tummy and opened the dresser drawers within reach of my bed. Aha! Socks. I peeled them on while Jake nosed through my life. "Any other questions?"

He leaned against my desk. "This is the biggest house in Horseshoe Falls."

"It's more than a house. It's Grandma's office, sometimes warehouse and publicity campaign center." I bit my lip, suddenly self-conscious of my too-large bedroom away from home.

He didn't respond.

I swung my socked feet onto the floor. "You get weird when the conversation gets in the vicinity of my money. Is it because you think I stole it? I somehow acquired it illegally and the multi-million dollar company I help run is just a façade to cover my crimes?"

His expression darkened, a snapshot of me on my stallion wedged between his fingers.

"No? Is the fact I don't need to steal anything blowing your hopes and dreams of arresting me?"

"You think I want to arrest you?"

I balked. "Well, yeah. Why else do you follow me around? You're waiting for me to slip up. Now answer me. Why do you get extra weird when my money comes up?"

"You don't date."

I climbed off the bed and glared across the distance. "That wasn't an answer or a question. You're worse at conversation than I am."

He dropped the photo of Lancelot and me onto the desk. "You said you tried dating and it was awful, but who did you date? Who, in rural Ohio, is in your socio-economic dating bracket and not over fifty?"

I couldn't gauge his meaning. "Are you suggesting a jilted lover is at the center of this crime spree? You think I'm being framed?"

His brows pinched together. "Forget it. What happens next? You changed. Now what?"

"Now, we eat." I hustled to the door, thankful for the change in topic and location. If I stayed alone with him another minute I'd break out in stress hives.

I led him back to the hallway and down the staircase. Gwen met us on the bottom step, where she climbed up and down endlessly. She grabbed Jake's leg when we reached the bottom.

"Oh." I grabbed her. "Don't, sweetie."

Jake waved me off. "May I?" He lifted her to his chest.

"I guess."

He bounced her in his arms. "Your aunt Mia was just about to tell me where she went at lunch today."

"No, I wasn't."

He turned careful eyes on me. "Any particular reason

you don't want to share that information? Don't say it's none of my business. You know what's going on here."

I didn't actually have a clue what he meant by that statement. I'd assume he meant the investigation into my alleged criminal behavior. "I wasn't offering because you never asked."

"Why not just tell me?"

Gwen slapped his cheek and laughed.

I raised an eyebrow. "Can we talk after we finish this? My family needs me and this can wait."

"After dinner then."

"We'll talk on the way back to our cars."

"Fine."

"Fine." I headed toward the kitchen. They followed. Gwen babbled as we made our way around the corner. The warm buttery scent of mozzarella mingled with a zippy tang of tomato sauce in the air. My stomach growled.

My family crowded around Grandma's massive center island, laughing and hooting like they didn't see one another on a near daily basis. They quieted as we approached.

"Hi." I grabbed a plate and napkin. "What do you want?" I lifted my eyes to Jake. "Veggie delight. Meat lovers. Cheese or vegan?"

"Meat lovers." He pulled out a high-backed stool at the island.

Bree gagged. "Red meat will kill you. It's already taken the life of the poor animal slain to make your meal."

I loaded slices onto the plate. "Chips and dip, tortilla scoops and salsa or cheezy puffs?"

"Chips and dip. What kind of dip?"

Mom came to Jake's side and stroked Gwen's chubby

hand. "Sour cream and onion. My secret recipe." Mom reached for Gwen. "I'll take her so you can eat."

Gwen wrapped dimpled arms around Jake's neck.

He smiled. "She's fine. If it's okay with you, I don't mind holding her while I eat."

Mom stepped away with raised eyebrows.

Tom smiled. "Not at all, man. Let me know if she gives you any trouble. She's a wild one. I think it's in the Connors genes."

Jake caught my attention. "Is there something for Gwen?"

I sliced a banana and tossed a handful of soup crackers onto his plate with it. "Here you go. *Bon appétit.*"

Jake handed Gwen a cracker for each fist and turned her to sit on his lap. "You have a beautiful home, Mrs. Potter."

I'd never told him Grandma's last name, but I supposed he knew lots of things about me and my family. I pushed a slice of veggie delight between my lips.

Bree's voice rose over the other restarted conversations. "You're a natural with her. Do you want kids one day, Jake?"

He filled his mouth with chips. Ah, that was my trick.

Unfortunately, it never worked on Bree. "Do you plan to marry?"

Tom leaned forward. "What do you look for in a partner? Anything you want to share would be terrific."

Jake glanced down the hall toward the door. As much as I wanted to be uncomfortable for him, it served him right. He insisted on coming along.

I dragged a rippled chip through Mom's yummy dip, delighting shamelessly in his discomfort. "Yeah, Jake. What would she be like?" A waif, probably. A damsel in distress so he could swoop in and save her from everything every day and she could hero-worship him for it at night. I chomped a stack of chips mortared together with dip, not liking the image I'd created.

He chewed his pizza slowly and swallowed. "I'm not sure there's a woman out there willing to tolerate me and my work."

Mom swooned.

Lovely of him to choose now to be charming. "Is your work hard to tolerate?" They still knew him as the temporary security guy.

"Some of my cases are harder than others. Sometimes the job consumes my life."

"Anything else?" Bree asked.

Jake cracked open a soda from the ice bucket on the counter and swigged, tipping the can back and closing his eyes. "Nope."

Everyone looked to me. I had nothing. That was the most I'd heard him say about himself.

Bree pushed. "Have you had someone serious in your life?"

"I suppose."

"Why'd you let her go?"

He set the can aside and looked at me. "She died."

My family blushed collectively and began a round of "We're so sorry" and "We didn't know."

He shrugged it off. "It was a long time ago."

The strangest sensation crept over me. I ate another chip.

Tom cleared his throat. "Well, Gwen seems to love you."

He gave my niece a long look. "Yeah. I have the bananas."

Grandma poked her head through the dining room

door. "That's my trick, too. I ply them with free food. Now get off your behinds and get in here."

I cleared Jake's plate when he finished and explained our cockamamie system for filling orders. He was a quick study. Bree kept up the inquisition as we worked, asking everything from preferences in women—short or tall, blonde or brunette—to feelings on a woman's chest size and her adventure level in bed.

To my ludicrous dismay, he preferred women with small breasts and a moderate level of adventure in the sack. I had enough in my bra for three small-breasted women, and my level of bedroom adventure capped out at taking my clothes off in front of someone who wasn't my husband. That was a lot of pressure. What if they laughed or blabbed every pudgy detail or snapped secret pictures? Statistically speaking, it took a fair amount of adventure to have sex without a secrecy contract in place.

Bree snapped her fingers an inch from my face. "Were you thinking about sex?"

My face heated uncontrollably.

"You were!" She scribbled something in a tiny notebook and shoved it into her back pocket. "Don't be embarrassed. The average woman thinks about sex twenty times a day. That's almost once an hour. More than once an hour if you think about the number of hours most women are awake."

I gave her my best stink eye. "Well, that information is inaccurate."

Tom rubbed his palms together. "That's what we intend to find out. How often would you say you think about sex, Mia?"

Jake laughed. Outright *laughed*.

"I don't."

Bree hummed. "You were like five seconds ago."

"Was not." I finished smoothing labels around the tubs of face cream. "Done."

Jake packed a box of freshly labeled containers. "Me too."

I nudged him with my elbow and spoke in my stage voice. "Well, that's it for us. Looks like it's time for me to get home." I stopped in the kitchen and grabbed a mostly full box of pizza. "I'll take this to Nate and Dan."

Jake snorted. He lifted the box from my hands. "I'll carry it. You can drive back to the clubhouse."

I hugged everyone goodbye and planted a sweet kiss on Gwen's sleeping face. The clock over Grandma's stove said after eleven.

Bree mimed a phone with her hand, demanding I call her when I got home. I didn't have the emotional energy for that. I kind of wanted to sleep until Christmas.

It was a beautiful summer night. The moon was bright and full. I tried not to think about what that might mean or how it might influence my insanity. I slid behind the wheel of our golf cart and aggravation crept over me.

Jake climbed aboard, eyes on the sky.

The irritation expanded. I reversed out of the drive, growing unhappier by the second. "What were you doing in there?"

"What?" Jake turned. His gaze warmed my face, making me angrier.

"You sat in there chitchatting about your supposed life, sharing alleged personal information. Was any of it true or did I just subject my family to your cover personality?" I pressed my foot against the pedal. What was I thinking? "I know about you, and I still agreed to bring you along, knowing you'd interrogate us. Knowing you were only going so you could track me. Maybe nose around the house for something to use against me. I'm such a total sucker."

"Hey, I had a good time tonight. I wasn't faking in there."

I jerked the wheel, guiding the cart on a rocky path around the next corner. I mentally buttoned my lips.

"Easy." He gripped the seat to stabilize himself.

I swerved for no reason.

"I wasn't faking in there. I know how important family is to you, and I respect that. That was real."

"Oh, okay. I totally believe you now. I mean, you've done nothing but lie to me from the moment we met, but I'm sure this time you're being honest. I mean, why not open up to my family? They aren't on your suspect list." I barked an ugly laugh. "Heck. Maybe they are? You said it yourself, I'm the link to everything going wrong. Maybe we're a crime family."

"I don't care if you believe me. I like your family, and I had a nice time tonight."

"Whatever."

"Why are you so angry all of a sudden? Is it the full moon?" He smiled.

I frowned. "I brought you into my family. I don't do that. I never do that." I hacked a throaty noise and glared at the huge white moon. Maybe this was the moon's fault. I never had outbursts. "Forget it. This isn't about you, but next time, you're not invited."

The moon's silvery reflection on the lake was twice as bright as during our last evening drive. I jerked the wheel into a U-turn, careening through the grass and bringing the cart back onto the road in the opposite direction.

Jake bounced on the seat beside me. "What are you doing?"

"It's a full moon."

"I don't think that will hold up in court if you get us killed."

I tightened my grip on the wheel. "Shut up."

"Where are we going, Connors?"

"To the stables. The moon's bright, and I want to see the area around the building at night, the same way Mrs. Lindsey saw it that night. Maybe she saw something other than a bicycle." I shuddered, remembering Nate had come into the community the way Marcella and another figure, probably the killer, had left. I could've lost Nate and Baxter both that night. He could've crossed paths with the killer. "You asked where I went at lunch today. I want to show you."

He quieted.

My mouth sprang into action, filling the void. "You can get into Horseshoe Falls from the driving range down the street if you go through the woods."

"How do you know that?"

"I lived here when I was younger and spent plenty of weekends here before that."

He shook his head. "Easier to sneak out of an old lady's enormous mansion than your parents' three bedroom place."

"That's right. Wow. You're really good at your job." I layered on the sarcasm and fought the urge to say more.

The cart rocked to a stop outside the stables office. I jumped out, eager to show off. Jake followed. I used my cell phone's flashlight app for a better view in areas where tree cover snuffed out the moonlight. "I have a clear view of the road from here. This must be the path the killer took. If Mrs. Lindsey was on Oak or Pine, she could've seen someone here. The tree limbs and crescent moon would've made it tough, but the little light that filters through the branches must've illuminated reflectors or something that looked like them."

Jake toed the ground and ran his palms across tree trunks as we moved. "Listen. I know you're angry with me right now, but I've got to say it again. I think you should stay at your parents' house until this is over. You'll be safer there. Your dad's sharp. He's trained to defend you and has a license to carry a gun."

Pizza spoiled in my tummy. "If we're right and Punisher is behind all this, he knows where I work. He knows where I live. He'd find me there too if he wanted. My parents wouldn't be safe. Besides, I can protect myself. Dad didn't raise victims. Bree and I were hounded on vigilance and basic self-defense. I perfected some of the moves in college. I'm fine. I'll get through this, find the killer and clear my name."

I moved carefully along the path, avoiding fallen branches and half-buried stones. "I'm going to talk to Nate tonight. I've changed my mind, and I think he should talk to Dan. He's only making himself look guilty by avoiding him. I can see that now. I know why he's doing what he's doing, but everything's getting murky. He's better off talking to Dan."

An arm snaked around my waist and turned to iron. Confusion scrambled my thoughts. "Jake?" A massive hand clamped over my mouth and smashed my lips against my teeth.

His voice was hot against my ear and cheek. "Those self-defense courses are a good start, Mia, but there are other factors involved in an abduction, like fear and an inability to act when you need to. In emergencies, time is…"

I widened my stance and dropped my center of gravity on instinct. Whatever he was saying didn't matter. The words became droning noise. Adrenaline kicked in, and my arms wrapped over his, anchoring him in place. With one quick motion, I dove forward, reaching for the ground at the last second and rolling to safety. Jake flew over my back onto his.

Air whooshed from his lungs in a loud puff. He choked while I regained my footing and raised my hands to fight.

"Oof. Argh." He rolled off the ground. "You smashed me onto a root." He kicked the earth, straightening to his full height with a little trouble.

I walked ahead, shaking off the adrenaline and forcing myself not to see if he was okay. "I think we need to talk to Tennille about her moon photos. I meant to email her earlier. I forgot, but I did leave a comment on Bernie's blog. Depending on where she was shooting the night of Baxter's murder, she might have caught something in one of her stills."

We cleared the trees a minute later and the driving range came into view. I forced my voice to still and not warble. "See the building on top of that hill? That's the office for the driving range. There's a parking lot there. Someone who wanted to get here unnoticed could park there and avoid the security gate. Mr. Barrow didn't enclose the Falls on this side to preserve the integrity of nature. I think he wanted to save money and figured no one would bother parking so far away and walking half a mile across a driving range and through part of the forest to get in."

Jake peered into the distance. "You've done this?"

"No. Not personally." I settled my breath and looked at him with as much confidence as I could manage.

"You asked where I went at lunch. I went to the driving range and reviewed the security tapes."

He brushed dirt from his backside. "Why would you keep that from me?"

"I saw three figures during the half hour following Baxter's time of death. Two came from the woods and went to the driving range parking lot. One came from the lot and entered the woods. I couldn't identify the first figure to emerge from the woods. I knew the second person, and the third was Nate. He showed up after the first two disappeared. He ran into the woods."

I chewed my lip. "The other person I recognized was Marcella. I confronted her and she lied. I also found Baxter's car in the overflow parking. I planned to call Dan this afternoon, but every time I picked up the phone to do it, someone interrupted. I knew I'd see you tonight and we could talk privately."

Jake worked his jaw side to side. A little blue vein pulsed on his neck. "Anything else?"

"I have the tape."

TWENTY-TWO

THE NEXT DAY was slow and sad. Seven days had passed since Baxter's murder. His parents had flown him home to Ecuador, and we were no closer to finding out who stole him from our lives. I rubbed tired eyes and refocused on the work at hand. Horseshoe Falls residents had responded to our offer of free laptop security by dropping off every device they owned from e-readers to MP3 players. Someone even brought in their label maker for a new battery. Warren and I attached a half sheet of green paper to all non-approved devices. I wrote a blanket explanation stating our service unfortunately was limited to laptops or tablets and signed it with a smiley face then ran off a hundred copies.

Warren cracked his knuckles and arched back in his seat, the lazy gamer stretch. We'd worked in companionable silence for hours until the building had grown quiet around us.

"What do you think about a file labeled DPIC?" he asked.

We scanned every computer methodically, careful not to open anything that wasn't suspect and thereby unintentionally invade someone's privacy. Sometimes it was hard to tell by file names.

I swiveled to see the laptop. "I haven't come across a file with that name." Warren held the screen in my direction. I blew out a long gust of air. "I don't know. I guess open it, and if it's nothing, we won't pursue it."

Warren set the computer on his desk and clicked. He giggled and shoved glasses higher on his nose.

"Was it nothing?"

He coughed into one fist. "No. It was exactly what it said. *D* pics." He pointed to his lap.

"Oh? Oh! Yikes. Oh, yuck." I dropped my head against my desk and laughed. "Jeez. Why do guys do that?"

"Why do people do anything?"

I smiled. "Right?"

The office door opened a few inches, and Tennille King stuck her head inside. "Hey, is this an okay time?"

I stretched to my feet and yawned. "This is an amazing time because my coffee is cold and my butt's asleep. You want to walk with me? Get a snack from concierge?"

She wrinkled her nose. "They packed up and took off ages ago. It's late. I thought I'd missed you for sure. It's creepy in here with the lights out."

I checked my watch. Nearly nine. "No one locked up? You just walked in the front door?" Randall hadn't been back since Dan came for him the other day. Maybe I was supposed to lock up? "Marcella told me she was leaving a while ago, but I assumed she'd locked up."

Tennille walked into the lobby with me on her heels. She sat on the nice couch and smiled a contagious grin. Her wide blue eyes twinkled. "Where's your hunky sidekick?"

I slouched into the seat beside her. "He went to review a security tape with some specialists and check into a male model's alibi."

"Which model?"

"You know the guy on the underwear billboard?"

Her mouth fell open. "The Tuff Stuff ad on I-77 north? Right off the highway? What'd Jake find out?" She wiggled her eyebrows up and down. "Married? Single?"

"Dating someone and kind of dumb, in a sweet way."

"Figures. He's probably not guilty then. No brains for the operation." She tapped her temple.

"No. He was on location for a shoot in Poughkeepsie."

"Bummer."

"Some people get paid to question models, and I'm here with Warren, checking laptops for spyware and learning more about our residents than I wanted to know."

"Porn?" she guessed.

I let my head bob loosely. "Porn. Nude selfies. Cats in clothing. Bad poetry."

She slapped my arm. "No way. Nude selfies?" She covered a giant smile with one hand. "Half the residents here are so…"

"Old? Wrinkly? Pale? Yes. Yes. And yes." She was too polite to say it, but I wasn't. It was factual. I'd seen it with my own bleeding eyes.

She roared with laughter and stomped her feet. Her Ohio State T-shirt and jean shorts said so much about her. Did my clothes tell people about me?

She worked a manila folder free from her bag. "Well, I don't want to keep you from your super fun project, but I brought the photos you asked for. I blew them up so you could get a better look, but I don't see anything suspicious near the stables or the clubhouse. It took longer than I expected. That's why I'm late."

"Don't apologize. This is amazing. And these are everything you took that night?"

"Every last photo, even the crappy ones, so, no judging."

I held up a couple of fingers, hoping to nail the Girl Scout promise.

She laughed louder and stood to leave. The dusting of freckles across her nose gave her pretty face a youthful glow.

She headed for the door. "See you around? Maybe we can get lunch or something?"

"Sure, I'd like that." I locked the dead bolts behind her and leafed through the pictures on my way back to the office. I hadn't made an impromptu girl date since college. How sad was I? My only current girlfriend had once shared a womb with me, and I couldn't stand her half the time.

Inside the office, Warren zipped another completed computer into its bag. "We're almost done. What do you think? Finish tonight or go home and finish tomorrow?"

I teetered. My eyes were bleary. My tummy was empty. I wanted to go home, but I also hated to spend another workday on something I could finish tonight. It sounded like Warren was willing to stay a little longer.

My phone buzzed. I grabbed it, expecting Grandma, but Sherlock Holmes's face filled the screen. "Hello?"

"Mia?" Jake's voice sent a thrill down my spine strong enough to curl my toes. The roar of his truck's engine echoed in the background.

"Yep. It's me. Everything okay?"

"I'm just checking in. Did you remember to set the alarm?"

I sank into my chair, lifting a finger to Warren so

he'd know I planned to answer his question soon. "As soon as we leave, I will."

There was a long pause. "Where are you going? Is Nate with you?"

"Uh, no. I'm at work with Warren, looking through stacks of laptops. Where are you?"

He hesitated. "I'm heading back from the Bureau. I had paperwork to catch up on."

A prickle of pleasure electrified my skin. He was candid to me about his affiliation with the FBI, and I appreciated the effort, even if I was still a little ticked he lied for so long.

"Tennille stopped by with the pictures she took that night. I wanted to check the computer at Baxter's work today, but I didn't have a chance."

"Dan already did that. The work PC's downtown in the evidence lockup."

"Any news on the video from the range?"

"Nothing yet. Anything on the pictures?"

I spun my chair in a slow circle. "Just a couple illuminated lines. I'm not sure what would cause that in the moonlight, but I have a new theory if you're interested."

"Vendetta?"

"No." I'd already told him that idea. "I think all the targets were involved in something together."

"Like what?"

I checked on Warren. He seemed busy, but I turned my chair away from him for good measure and lowered my voice. "Anything. Like the rotating card game Mr. Fritter and the others play now. Something that connected them. Maybe someone from the old group is trying to scare or bankrupt them. Maybe they were once partners in something scandalous."

"Vendetta," he repeated. "I'll see if I can find a link

between the victims, other than their time in Horse-shoe Falls."

"Thanks. Just so you know, I've already reviewed their job histories. They never worked together or were linked by charity events or alma maters."

"Duly noted. Why don't you go home and get some sleep. Lock up when you get there and use the peep-hole. Dan's on stakeout duty tonight, so Nate should be there too. He'll be there by eleven."

I considered my theory. "I'll call if I come up with anything else."

We disconnected and I slipped into the hallway to be alone. My gaze traveled along the security lighting and darkened hallway, remembering the night I found Baxter in vivid detail. I hadn't allowed myself to dwell before, but what if dwelling was necessary? Had I really checked everything in my office when the officers asked? I hadn't been in a clear frame of mind. What if I'd missed something?

I turned on my heels, forcing the voice of reason from my mind, and tried the knob on Jake's office. Locked. I moved down two doors and tried Randall's door. It creaked open, and I slipped inside. Apparently, our fearless head of security hadn't thought to lock Ran-dall's office after they took him downtown. His pillow and blanket were gone, but pictures of his family re-mained. A good sign for him. I opened each desk drawer until I found what I'd come for. Keys.

Outside my old office door, I held my breath and forced the key into the lock. The knob turned easily, and I was inside in seconds, wondering if the room was smaller with less oxygen than before. I paced the room on silent feet, seeking something I'd missed. Something everyone missed. If there was such a thing.

I traced the area around my keyboard, stirring an idea into formation. My gaze jumped to the candy dish beside my monitor. Dozens of novelty thumb drives were piled on one another. I dragged the bowl closer, digging through them with my fingertips, wondering idly if maybe one was missing and I simply hadn't noticed. "Oh my goodness." Breath caught in my throat. Nothing was missing. Something was gained. There were two Mjölnirs. Drives shaped as Thor's hammer. Nate, Baxter and I had bought them together at Comic Con last summer. I'd only purchased one.

I held both in my palm. What if one of the hammers was Baxter's? He'd tried to take my hand that morning, and I'd slapped him away thinking it was a creepy advance. What if he tried to get the drive to me discreetly when I refused to be alone with him? I braced a sweat-slicked palm against my desk as the weight of the theory settled in my heart. He'd snuck back that night, for the same reason the killer had broken into residents' home, not to take something, but to leave something.

Randall was living in his office. If he hadn't locked up that night, like the handful of other nights he'd skipped, Baxter could've come inside unseen, run into the killer and been murdered before he could escape. Randall probably heard the commotion, found the body and set the alarm so he wouldn't get in trouble for forgetting or get caught sleeping in his office. Calling the cops would've raised questions about him being there, so he hadn't called them. Once the alarm was on, the killer probably set it off by leaving through doors which had been safe to use only a few minutes before. The alarm caused the security system to call my phone, and I responded.

I shoved the thumb drives into my pocket. I needed

to go through the drives and figure out which was mine and which was Baxter's. More important, I needed to see what Baxter had given his life to tell me.

I snuck out of our old office and locked up.

Light shone around the edges of the door to Randall's office. I crept closer, certain I'd closed the door and turned the light out after taking the keys. Murmurs vibrated the air. I held my breath and pressed my back against the wall, listening as if my life depended on it. Maybe it did.

The cadence of Marcella's familiar voice registered. Her words were a beautiful purr of Spanish and English. "I'm so glad you're okay. I knew you'd be back tonight."

I dared a peek through the small opening.

Marcella wrapped Randall in her arms and kissed him long and deep. His hands slid down her back and I shut my eyes.

I tiptoe-ran back to my office to collect my things for the night. Was Randall the other figure from the video? Was he the one with her by the fountain? Were they in this together? Would they cover a murder to conceal their affair?

Warren was standing behind his chair. "Everything okay?" He slung his jacket over both shoulders and threaded his arms into the sleeves. "Are we going home?"

I couldn't bring myself to look at the drives with Warren only a few feet away. This was something I needed to do privately. A measure of guilt weighted my heart.

"Yeah." I opened the office door and held it for Warren to pass through. I set the clubhouse alarm and followed him into the parking lot.

He had half a dozen laptop bags over each shoulder. "I'll finish these up tonight and call if I find anything."

"Oh, no, I didn't even notice you had those. Listen. Forget them. We'll finish tomorrow. I'm going home to eat. You should do the same."

I dialed the burner phone I'd bought Nate. He'd be thrilled to hear I had the thumb drive. No answer.

Warren didn't make a move for his car.

I dialed Jake. He needed to know about the thumb drive too, and possibly about Marcella and Randall. Voice mail. Where was everyone tonight?

I left a message. "Hey, it's me. I'm headed home now. Remember those novelty thumb drives? I found an extra in my dish here at work. I thought you'd want to know. You can stop over to get it if you want."

Warren cleared his throat. "I could order pizzas and meet you at your place." His smile fell. "If you want. I mean, I'd need your address, and we've never had that kind of relationship." His cheeks pinked. "Okay. No. I've overstepped. I have a hard time sometimes." He waved his hands in a gesture I knew well. "Forget I said anything. I'll see you tomorrow." He faked a wide smile and walked away, looking exactly as I felt more times than I could count.

"Warren, wait."

Warren's hopeful expression softened me. Why not? I could use the company until one of the guys managed to answer their freaking phone.

"Okay. Follow me to my place. I'll order pizza on the way. I promise we won't work more than an hour after we eat and you have to promise to take half the day off tomorrow. You've put in too many hours already today."

His smile grew cartoonishly wide. "Deal!"

I called the pizza place and texted Jake details on my

way home, utilizing every second I sat at stoplights or waited for traffic to move. Hope filled my heart and warmed my belly. I didn't want to get my hopes too high, but how could I not? Yes, maybe there was nothing on the extra thumb drive.

…but what if there was?

TWENTY-THREE

I OPENED MY door with care, giving Nate time to scram if he hadn't gotten my texts about bringing company home. The lights were all burning as bright as Christmas, but the room was empty. I held the door with my rump so Warren could pass. He stood awkwardly six inches past the threshold.

I stowed my bag and hefted the food and two liter from his hands so he could unload the laptop bags. I'd ordered two pizzas, so there would be plenty left over for Nate. I'd added my favorite salad to the order for the sake of my waistband.

"Well, this is my place. It's small, but it's mine. Make yourself at home. I'll get some paper plates and napkins."

I set everything we needed on the kitchen countertop, eager to get a look at the thumb drive. "Okay. Help yourself to pizza and soda. Ice is in the freezer. I'm going to put on some jeans and be right back."

I speed-walked down the hall to my room and dove inside. No sign of Nate.

I stuffed my legs into jeans from a pile on the floor and tugged an old archery camp T-shirt over my head. I closed my hand over the drives and pulled the bedroom door shut behind me.

"Okay. Sorry. I feel a lot better now."

Warren was in the living room with food and a laptop, already working.

"Find the ice okay?" That seemed like enough small talk. Moving right along to my holy grail of a clue.

He didn't look up as I grabbed my salad and cup of pop from the counter. Judging by the dozen or so ice cubes stuffed inside, he'd indeed found the ice.

I set my things on the coffee table and pulled my laptop onto my legs. I peeked at Warren. "How does that laptop look?"

"Same as the others. I don't see anything."

I shoved the first thumb drive into my laptop and opened the file. Nothing. I ejected it with nervous fingers and it clattered to the floor.

Warren appeared to notice me for the first time. "Everything okay?"

I leaned forward, searching for the fallen drive. I enabled the flashlight app on my phone and shone it under the couch. The light bounced off Warren's obnoxious shoes. Bright white and silver. Luminous. Images from the stables' security footage and Tennille's photos swept through my mind. The reflectors were horizontal and close to the ground, not like a bicycle. Bicycle reflectors were placed much higher so they could be easily seen. Ugly silver-and-white shoes, on the other hand... I swiped the fallen drive into my hand and raised my gaze to his face. "Oh no."

He leaned forward. "You look ill. Are you okay? Maybe you should have a drink. Eat something."

I nodded.

When he looked away, I shoved the second thumb drive in place and waited for the files to open. I sent a quick text to Jake. Nervous. May be nothing. May be in danger. Come now. Please.

Hopefully the *please* would be enough motivation to rush his arrival. Hopefully, my suspicions were paranoia and nothing more. Hopefully, I wasn't sharing dinner with a killer.

I sipped the drink, jabbing my lip with ice and concentrating on the files lining up on my screen. I set the cup aside and jammed a forkful of chopped veggies between my lips, mounting a mental case against Warren based on his shoes. Silly.

Except, Warren had the skills to create the replica clubhouse email and webpage. He could easily create and administer the virus. Covering his tracks with an anonymous server wouldn't be a problem either, and he was an insider with access to residents' email addresses.

I glanced at Warren busily checking laptops for a virus he might've executed. He'd practically invited himself and insisted he come.

He knew about REIGN, too. I'd ranted more than once about my defeats. About Punisher. About *him*.

No. No, no. I turned to the waiting screen on my lap, praying I was wrong. Real answers were right in front of me. The first few files looked like the evidence Nate described from the library computer. Details and re-creations of clubhouse logos and letterheads. The next file had copies of private message conversations between Baxter and Punisher.

Baxter: I don't know what you're up to, but I know who you are and I know you're gunning for Mia. She's important to me. I won't let you keep this up.

Punisher: You think telling your friend you've been stalking me for her will make her want you? You'll sound insane. You'll lose her.

Baxter: I have proof. Files. I know you're phishing in Horseshoe Falls and I think I know why, but I'm willing

308   A GEEK GIRL'S GUIDE TO MURDER

to trade my silence for your relenting. Leave Mia out of this. Quit REIGN.

The temperature rose twenty degrees in my body. I lifted the cup to my lips and emptied it.

Warren shut the laptop and pulled an empty bag onto his lap. "Are you feeling okay? You look flushed. You work a lot of hours. You're at high risk for exhaustion, sickness, stress-related episodes."

Warren's face went a little out of focus. I rubbed stinging eyes. I was tired. I hadn't slept in a week. My stress level was higher than during grad school finals. A sinking feeling came over me as I scanned the conversations on my screen.

My head swam. Baxter had confronted his killer. For me.

Punisher: You'll leave it alone?

Baxter: Yes. If you'll leave her alone. ALONE. That means you have to leave Horseshoe Falls, too, Warren.

Bile rose in my throat. I read the final entry.

Punisher: Meet me at the clubhouse in an hour. Bring your evidence. I'll write up my two-week notice. We'll leave together. No more trouble.

Baxter: Deal.

I set my food aside and lifted my phone to send a mayday text to Bree. If anyone could wrangle the cavalry, she could.

I warred mentally. Should I keep him busy working until Jake showed up? What if he didn't show up? The words, "gunning for Mia," helped with my decision. "You're right. I'm spent. I think these laptops can wait till morning, and I should take tonight off."

Warren zipped the laptop into its bag and looked at me with an odd level of expectancy. "I can still take them home like I offered at the clubhouse. I can finish tonight."

I opened file after file. Baxter had caught Warren stealing personal information, including passwords and account numbers from half a dozen people. Mr. Donahue's file was there. I ejected the thumb drive and wedged it into the frame of my couch, beyond the cushions, into the deep crevice where popcorn kernels and Gwen's cereal pieces went to hide from the vacuum.

Warren stacked the bags neatly at his feet. "You have a nice place. Mine's a studio about ten blocks from here. Over the tracks. They haven't tried revitalizing my neighborhood yet." He snickered.

I knew the place. *Across the tracks* was code for where crime quadrupled.

I blinked weary eyes. What was he talking about? I dragged my gaze to his blurry face. Something was wrong. I couldn't concentrate. "You know what? Leave the laptops here. I insist. I'll finish. You take some time for yourself."

I stood to walk Warren out and my head spun. I pressed a hot palm over one temple. My phone buzzed in my palm. Bree could save me, but she lived thirty minutes away. Would she know I needed the actual 9-1-1? Why hadn't I dialed that instead?

"Sorry to rush you off. I'm feeling really weird. Why don't you take the rest of the pizza? I won't eat tonight. I think I'm going to take your advice and lie down."

Warren steadied me by one arm and returned me to the couch. He crouched in front of me. "You don't look very good."

My phone buzzed again and he removed it from my hand. "Here." He handed me another drink.

I sucked the pop like someone lost at sea. Thirst had

taken over, like some kind of transforming vampire. I opened my hand for Warren to give me my phone before he read my last text, but he slapped my fingers away.

"Hey." I jerked my arm back and marveled at the slur in my speech.

"You've got a new text. They want to know what to do. Who is that? No contact information."

Nate. I'd never stored his burner number.

He twisted my phone in the air between us. "Who is this?" He examined the screen. "What does that even mean? Why didn't you store their contact information? I'm going to respond for you." Warren tapped the screen, speaking as he typed. "False alarm. Going to bed."

Fear seemed to paralyze me. "Warren, something is really wrong with me. I think I need 9-1-1." My limbs weighed a thousand pounds each.

He moved in close, hovering in my personal space. "You're fine. Just feeling the roofie in your drink."

"Wah?" My tongue was fat and hairy.

He stood with a little hop and dusted his pants. "Yeah. I bought it from the guy on my block who stands there all day selling to crackheads and children. It's his special blend, so side effects may vary. You know, I live there because of people like you."

"Smart?"

"Rich." He opened his arms in a victory move then dropped them to his sides. "It's too bad you turned out to be so nosy." His English changed and slid into a heavy Latino accent like Marcella's, but with menace.

I closed my eyes and reopened them. Hoping for clarity.

He stroked my hair. "I like you, Mia, but you're one of them."

I tipped over on the couch and pressed one cheek against the cool upholstery, hoping to snap out of it. Mind over matter. Brains over street drugs.

Warren sat on my coffee table and crossed his legs. "You've forced my hand. I had more to do before I got to you, but you screwed that up." He launched from the table and circled the room. "You told someone we were together, so I need an alibi." He eyeballed me. "I could say you got a weird call and ditched me, presumably for a rendezvous with that redhead on the run. That might work."

My phone buzzed again, on the coffee table where he'd left it. Warren cursed in Spanish.

He rubbed his eyes beneath his glasses. "Have you ever been raped, Mia? It's awful. A really terrible thing. It's not sexual at all. You'd think that, but it's not true. Rape is a hate crime. All dominance and aggression."

I swallowed bullets of fear and focused every ounce of bodily control on the phone sitting two feet away. If I could lift my arm, I could knock it off the table and dial for help.

Warren paced. "I need to think."

I swatted the coffee table, missing the phone.

A slew of swears burst from Warren and I froze. Had he seen me?

He picked up a stack of magazines and threw them. "Maybe you were robbed." He tipped over a stand of movies.

When he hoisted his foot to kick a stack of laptops, I swung again, this time connecting with the phone. It bounced on the floor and lit up at my touch.

Warren looked outside. "I didn't want to kill you." He pressed his head to the wall beside the window.

I begged my pointer finger to cooperate and missed

the phone icon twice. A hot tear slid over my cheek. If I survived until eleven, Dan would be right outside.

I'd still die alone with a psychopath.

The colorful screen of apps confused me. My mind was slipping and it was all I had. *Come on, Mia. You're tougher than this. Fight it.*

Dad's voice echoed the sentiment in my head. *You weren't raised to be a victim.*

Clarity hit in an adrenaline-fueled burst. Notetaker! I tapped the tiny microphone and shut my eyes. Sound would activate the recorder. If he didn't take the phone with him, there would at least be a recording of my murder.

Warren knocked some more things around and collapsed onto the couch with me. He scooted me against the back to make room for himself on the edge. He put a hand on my hip. "What were we talking about? Right. Rape."

My tummy coiled against my backbone.

"My mother worked as a maid for fifteen years, at a home in Horseshoe Falls. Did you know that?" He lifted his brows as if this were an actual conversation. "It's true. She did. She wasn't ashamed either. Cleaning houses was honest work, and it kept me in Catholic school. That's important when you live in the hood. City schools—" He made a twisted face. "City schools are bad. Rough. Drugs. Gangs."

Warren finished his drink and turned on the couch to face me more directly. He patted my side, resting his palm in the curve of my waist. "Mama worked nights, weekends, any time the rich family wanted because she knew what that job meant for us. She hated leaving me alone, so after school, she picked me up and brought me with her if she needed to work late. It took her entire lunch hour to drive into the ghetto and get me, but she did. Every time. She protected me that way. Children don't stay home alone in our neighborhood. Not unless you want to hand them over to the gangsters and pushers. I'm getting off topic." He looked at the ceiling.

My mind raced through options for salvation. The recording would be great evidence, but surviving sounded really good too. I couldn't defend myself like this. I couldn't even speak. Dan and Jake might as well have been on the moon for all my inability to reach them.

Warren flicked my ear. "Pay attention. You're sleeping again."

I wiggled my head, willing both eyes open.

"After everything Mama did for me, she got to be violated, raped, during a fancy Horseshoe Falls Christmas party. I know. I was there. So were you and your sister, not that you remember me or recognized me when I applied for the job. I hid in the coat room that night to do homework while Mama worked because her boss said his home wasn't a daycare center. Mama always snuck me in when she brought me to work. Normally, I stayed in the kitchen, but there were caterers at the party, so I went to the coatroom. A couple hours later, a man tumbled into the room with Mama and shut the door. She was saying, 'No, not here, not now,' but he persisted, begging, groping, insisting. When she saw me there, hidden in the coats, she just went limp. Perfectly still. While he pressed his face against her body, she mouthed to me, 'Turn around.'"

Vomit rose in my throat.

Warren's voice shook with rage. "I obeyed Mama, but I could hear him. His drunk, slurred speech cooing disgusting things at her. Professing his love. I pressed my hands to my ears, but I could hear. I listened as he grunted his way through the despicable act. As he hurt her. I listened. That's not love."

Silence echoed off the walls and rang in my ears.

"She told me she quit a few days later, but I think she was fired. Mr. Donahue, the man who owned the home, probably couldn't stand to have his name sullied. I bet he told her to get lost and keep her mouth shut. So, she waits tables now, afraid to approach the wealthy again. Afraid to try. I had to go to public school when she couldn't pay my tuition anymore. I was beat up. A lot." He sniffed and wiped his nose on one wrist. "So, I learned to be tough. I learned there's no honor in fighting, and sometimes using your brain does a lot more damage than using your fists. No rules. Only survival. I vowed one day I'd punish the ones who ruined our lives. I made a list of every face I remembered from that party. Do you remember Mr. Donahue's rape party?"

I opened my mouth to protest, but a rivulet of drool slipped out instead.

"You and your sister, all dressed in your rich-girl best. We were the only ones under fifty, but I wasn't supposed to be there. You two followed me around, staring and giggling. You're half the reason I hid in the closet. I thought you'd point me out, ruin things for Mama if I dared be seen or say a word." He tapped a finger to his head. "I'm all grown up now. I'm not scared of you anymore. I even got a job as your sidekick. I put together a site and sent emails to the unsuspecting residents. They downloaded my malware and I watched. I documented their every keystroke after that. I have passwords, account numbers, everything I need to put them on my side of the tracks. Not that they'd survive there. Not that I'd care they didn't. You, on the other hand. I'd hoped to woo you and break your heart. That was before I got to know you. It didn't take long to see what you care about. Your online game. Your friends. I taunted you and I let them find me. They weren't that clever. Don't let them tell you otherwise. I sought them to hurt them, the way you sought me at that party and the way your people hurt my mother."

My buzzer rang.

Warren jumped. His gaze swept over the room. He pressed a finger to his lips.

"Mia?" Dad's voice carried through the door. "Mom and I brought shortcakes."

My phone rang.

"Mia?" Dad pounded louder. "Was that your phone? Mia? Open up."

Warren grabbed the phone off the floor and glowered at me. He drew a finger across his neck, indicating my punishment for recording him. He tapped the screen and shoved the phone into his pocket and crept toward the door.

A tidal wave of fear for my parents slapped against me. Thanks to my suffocating family and their love of shortcake, I'd live another few minutes. Dad might even call Jake if he was worried about me.

The knocking stopped. So did my heart.

Warren smiled and pressed his cheek against the door, peering through the peephole. "It's too bad your daddy's ex-police or we could've invited him in. I'm guessing he carries concealed."

He moseyed back to my side with a creepy come-hither look. "They're gone. Now, it's just you and me." He leaned over me, dragging hot fingers against my cheek, clearing the way for his lips. "I learned a lot that night in the closet." He traced the curve of my neck, dragging his open palm over my chest.

"Don't," I whimpered. Tot tears burned trails over my temples to my ears.

"Shh." He lifted the hem of my shirt and grazed the skin beneath. "Do you wear all those *I Love Lucy* outfits to scare men off or to invite them in? I can never decide. High necklines. Short skirts. It's confusing."

A sob blocked my throat and the world shimmied. I wiggled my head side to side.

He removed his hand from my waist and slid it between my knees.

"Mia!" Bree's frantic voice echoed through the doorway. Pounding began anew, either in my head or at my door, I wasn't sure.

I prayed with all my soul she was right about our psychic twin connection, and sent her a heartfelt mental message.

RUN! GET HELP! Call 9-1-1!! Break the effing door down!

If anyone in my family could bust me out of here it was Bree. Dad had a gun and police training, but Bree had blind overprotective sibling rage.

Warren smiled and spun to face the door. "Twins." He squeezed my knee. "Every man's dream." He flew across the room in wide eager strides and pressed his face to the door once more, peering through the peephole.

Boom! My front door burst open, whacking Warren hard enough to send him ass over teakettle through my entryway. Jake Archer, Dan Archer and half my family stormed the castle. Jake and Dan had Warren in cuffs before Mom and Dad could hoist me off the couch.

I wobbled on missing feet as a stretcher rolled into view, guided by two EMTs.

Mom kissed my head, tears streaming. "Oh, my baby." She stroked my hair and curled me into her.

Dad led us to the door. "Let's get you to the hospital."

Jake blocked our path. His FBI badge hung on a shiny beaded chain around his neck. "The stretcher's for her. There's an ambulance outside. They'll take Mia to the hospital. You can ride with her."

I forced my mind and mouth to form one precious word. "Bree?"

Jake chuckled and swung a thumb toward the hallway.

I blinked, adjusting my eyes and shifting my weight against Dad before I flattened Mom to the floor with me.

Bree's voice warbled and lifted through the drugs and confusion. Most of her words were curses. They wound through Warren's angry Spanish.

Dan had Warren in the hallway, hands cuffed behind his back, waiting for the elevator to open. While they waited, Bree did her best to beat the stuffing out of Warren. Dan pretended not to notice.

My eyes blinked shut against my will, and Dad's strong arms anchored me to him.

Mom cooed nonsense into my ear.

The elevator doors never opened.

TWENTY-FOUR

THE STEADY RHYTHM of *whoosh-whoosh-beep* worked into my dreams of foot races from childhood and beating Bree at video games. The predictable pattern of sound both teased and lulled my addled mind.

"She's fine." A strange voice pricked my contented state. "She's resting. From what I understand, she's had a rough week."

"But she wasn't injured?"

My eyes peeled open. The image was blurry, but my heart knew that voice. *Jake.* He and a man in blue scrubs stood at the end of my bed, heads pointed in on one another. The concern on Jake's face stirred my heart. I lifted my fingers, unsure if my mouth would work, and discovered an IV attached to that hand.

"She's been given fluids, and the drug's effects will wear off soon." Scrubs guy flipped through a couple of white papers on a clipboard.

Jake shifted his stance, twisting at the waist. "Thank you. I'd like to talk with her privately now. Is that okay?"

"She may be fuzzy on details, but you won't cause any harm, if that's what you mean. I'll send her family in."

"Give us five minutes?" Jake moved to my side and edged his hip onto the mattress. "Looks like you solved your case."

A broken laugh escaped my lips.

"How do you feel?"

I gripped the scratchy, over-starched sheet to my chest. "Violated."

Jake's eyes widened. Color rushed across his cheeks until they seemed purple beneath the stubble. He tightened and released his jaw in a slow and calculated pattern. "Did he touch you?"

"No. He slipped something in my drink." I puzzled. Jake's strange expression wound through my achy head until recognition of his suggestion dawned. "Wait. No." I pressed an open palm against my collarbone. "He didn't touch me. Not like that. Nothing like that. His mom..." The story flooded back. "Oh my goodness. His mother."

Jake pressed a callused palm over my hand. His strong fingers curled around mine. "We know. We recovered your phone. After a replay of that, Warren's going away for a long time. Maybe the rest of his life. I doubt his mother would want that."

I swallowed hard. "What he said about Bree and me wasn't true."

Jake pressed my hand in his. "Doesn't matter now. You were kids and my guess is Warren had some problems long before his mother's tragedy."

Emotion stung my eyes. Jake believed him. "I mean it. He was wrong. Bree and I followed him around that night because he was the only other kid at the party. He was young and Bree wanted to talk to him, play babysitter or something. She's always been that way with kids. She'd tried to engage him with smiles and laughter, but he kept running away and we were too stupid to come out and ask who he belonged to or if he wanted to play."

Jake groaned. His head fell back. "And he's harbored that against you all his life. People like that assume the worst in every scenario. They don't think. He was young then, but he's let the lies he told himself grow until they consumed him."

I scooted up in bed, eager to help bring the rapist to justice. "What about the man who attacked her when Warren was a child? Can he identify him? He said it was Mr. Donahue's party."

Jake stroked his jaw. "He fingered Mr. Fritter. Fritter and his attorney are with Dan downtown, but Fritter's claiming a drunken mistake. Says he and the woman had an ongoing relationship at the time and it wasn't what Warren thought. Either way, there's a statute of limitations on rape. He's been a dedicated member of his local AA since that year. Warren's mother confirmed her relationship with Mr. Fritter, but won't talk about what happened. It's complicated."

I redirected tear-filled eyes to Jake's stern but sullen face. "The whole thing is so awful. Every single thing about this week is wrong. None of it should've happened."

He dusted his thumb over my cheek. "The doctor says you're going to be all right. That little hammer thing had all the evidence we need to arrest Warren for the email tampering and the break-ins. It wasn't easy to find. I'm glad you left me a voice mail before you did drugs." He smiled. "We found the phone on Warren. I figured you couldn't have many hiding options in your condition, and you were on the couch when we got there. The recording and confession did the rest. You don't have to be afraid anymore."

I nodded, but my heart didn't agree. I'd be afraid for a long time after what I'd been through. If someone like Warren, someone I'd overlooked for a year, could be a calculating killer, then anyone could. "I think it might be time I bought a condo in Horseshoe Falls. Living downtown has lost its appeal, and I'm not sure I want to go back there. Ever."

He smiled. "I don't know about you, but a condo in Horseshoe Falls would make me feel a lot better."

I inhaled long and slow, adjusting to the scene around me. The itchy blanket irritated my arms. "Why do hospitals always smell like dry erase markers and Band-Aids?"

He tipped his head. "Really?" He inhaled. "I think they smell like bleach and stale coffee."

"Is there coffee?" I scanned the immediate area and found none.

A ruckus in the hall told me our alone time was coming to an end. "How'd I do on my first case, Special Agent Archer? On a scale of one to ten. Pink Panther worthy or is there a spot for me in the Cyber Crimes Division?"

He pushed off the bed, releasing my hand. "I think you should stick to making beauty products. Maybe get your conceal-and-carry license. You're good with a bow, but you can't carry that in your purse."

"I could if I was Link." Gaming images turned my thoughts in a new direction. "You were the new knight in my kingdom on REIGN. The ones you brought with you were from your team."

He feigned innocence.

I gaped. "You were onto Punisher days ago, and you never told me."

"How could I? I was the temporary clubhouse head of security, not Special Agent Archer to you then. We had Warren on the short list with no concrete evidence. When you said you'd invited him for pizza I dropped Nate at his brother's and headed over."

"Nate?"

His blue eyes twinkled. "Nate turned himself in for questioning. I took Nate to the Bureau to talk privately. We picked a bad time to ignore our phones."

"He turned himself in." I bounced my head against the pillow. "Told you he was a good guy."

Jake's smile wavered. "He really cares about you. I'd advise keeping him around."

"I don't know how you do it. This week was my worst nightmare come true. I plan to avoid all investigations from now on. If I lose a shoe, I won't even look for it."

"Atta girl." He pushed a loose fist against my shoulder.

Mom and Dad turned the corner to my room, arguing over the ingredients in hospital shortcakes.

"Mia!" Mom dropped the discussion in favor of crushing my cheeks between her palms.

She took Jake's place on my bed and Dad hovered behind her. Their voices blended with Bree's and Tom's as they entered the room. Too loud. Too fast. My attention focused on the man inching his way out of my life.

Bree set a disposable cup on the sideboard. "I brought coffee. I didn't figure you'd want to sleep again for a while."

"Thanks."

Dad broke away from us and stopped Jake at the door. I strained to hear what they might say.

Mom leaned into view, blocking Dad and Jake. "Bree's the real hero here. She called us asking for Jake's number or Nate's. She didn't care which, but I had both. That was the scariest conversation I've ever had. Your father had Jake's card, so he agreed to call Jake."

Bree beamed, soaking in the spotlight. "I knew

something was wrong before your text came, didn't I, Tom?"

"Thank you."

"What are big sisters for?"

Mom squeezed my hand in hers. "Nate's in the cafeteria. I'm sure he'll be here in a minute."

I squinted at Mom. "So you drove downtown to save me?"

She nodded quickly, dashing poker-straight hair against tan cheeks. "We live closer than Bree. We had no idea what had happened when we got there. Dan was outside and Jake nearly ran us all over on the sidewalk."

I winced. I'd seen the man park.

"Warren was faking a robbery. I hope my rental insurance covers about ten busted laptops. I'll probably lose my job."

"Nonsense. They love you at the Falls. Also, who cares?"

I did. I liked my job. I shook it off. I'd worry about my employment later. Right now, I had more questions. "So you came over not knowing if Dan or Jake would be there to back you up?"

She gave me a patient smile. "Sweetie, you're our little girl. Your father had his gun and holster on before I could finish the phone tree. You were in trouble. There was no decision to make."

The family phone tree was more like the tree Charlie Brown got for Christmas than a tree-tree. Grandma, my parents, Bree and I were the only names on it. Tom's phone was fair game if Bree didn't pick up, but that was it. *Wait.* "So, Dad had his gun with him when he came over? What was he going to do? Shoot Warren?"

She nodded casually, as if I'd asked to get coffee on the way home. "It's a good thing the Archers were there.

Who knows what your father would would've done to that boy if we'd walked in and found you like you were."

Dad and Jake approached Mom. Jake extended his hand, but she wrapped him in her arms instead. "Thank you," she whispered against his shirt, no longer stifling tears.

"It's no problem, Mrs. Connors. That's my job."

"Not for long," Dad said.

I blinked through a wave of frustration at being called *his job* and looked to Dad for elaboration. "What?"

Jake pressed his lips together a long moment before speaking. "I'm leaving Cyber Crimes for a position with the US Marshals Service. I've been on a list for months, and I got the offer last week. Now that this case is finished, I'll turn in my Bureau badge for the star I've always wanted."

I puffed air into my bangs. "Sure, because anyone can lead the FBI Cyber Crimes Division. Sometimes a guy needs a challenge." I bit the inside of my cheeks before I said more.

His deep blue eyes sparkled. "Don't underestimate the star. I grew up on Westerns, and you've met my family. Marshals are the ultimate lawmen."

"Will I ever see you again?" The words were out before I realized how much I wanted to know. Whatever small talk we made didn't matter. This mattered.

The room quieted. My family exchanged looks and waited with me for an answer that meant more than it should have.

A familiar round of booming laughter broke through my wall. In the hallway, Nate and Grandma waved through my window.

I lifted a weary hand, still waiting on Jake's answer. Jake tipped his head toward Nate and dragged his gaze over the family at my bedside. He leaned his face close to my cheek. "I think you've got everything you could ever need right here." He gave my hand a squeeze and stood too quickly. "Maybe I'll see you around the kingdom." He winked one blue eye and cast a sad smile to our spectators.

In another breath, Jake was gone, through the crowd and past the Irishman in my doorway. Out of my life without a goodbye.

No one spoke. They filtered out single file as Nate made his way upstream to my side. He motioned to the doorway. "Ouch, huh?" His expression said he'd heard what Jake said.

I swiped a reckless tear. A dumb tear that dared to wonder *what-if.* "That's life, right? Sometimes an almost-thirty-year-old girl who's sworn off dating falls for a guy who doesn't care or even notice." I bobbed my head. "It happens."

Nate climbed onto the bed beside me, smashing me into the guardrail at my other side. He stole the remote and changed the channel to race cars. "Well, the good news is you survived one feisty little psychopath, avenged Baxter's death and earned some serious bragging rights. You solved about fifty cases tonight. I'd say you're pretty badass, and I made it to Comic Con while on the lam. Righteous, right?"

I tamped my sadness. That could wait. "For sure." My traitorous eyes searched the doorway for Jake as my brain screamed for me to take a hint and let him go. "Thanks for saving my life."

He snickered. "You made the calls. Sorry I missed your earlier texts." He rubbed my shoulders. "I was taking your advice and making a recorded statement for Jake and his team. Baxter was more into you than I thought. Jake said that thumb drive had weeks of documented stalking. I don't think Baxter knew how much deeper this all went. He only knew he was going to impress the pants off you. No inference intended."

I swallowed a sob and batted away tears. "Warren said he baited you. He did it to punish me because he thought I was mean to him thirteen years ago. I should've been nicer to Baxter."

Nate slung a heavy arm around my shoulders and snuggled into the bed beside me. He adjusted the bed's angle with little buttons on the guardrail. "Nah. That's how you two were. Feisty. Sassy. Silly. You were friends, and he knew that, no matter what else he'd hoped for. Jake was right, though. You have everything you need right here." He gave my shoulders a little squeeze, and I leaned into his strong, protective frame. "Forget about Mr. Broody Pants. I can make you smile."

I wiggled my IV hand and made a face. I couldn't promise I'd forget about Jake Archer anytime soon, but I could definitely let Nate make me smile. "Okay. Deal. So, can I go home soon, or should we order takeout?"

Nate barked a loud belly laugh. "I say, let's go home."

* * * * *

ABOUT THE AUTHOR

JULIE ANNE LINDSEY is a multi-genre author who writes the stories that keep her up at night. She's a self-proclaimed nerd with a penchant for words and proclivity for fun. Julie lives in rural Ohio with her husband and three small children. Today, she hopes to make someone smile. One day she plans to change the world. Julie is a member of the International Thriller Writers (ITW) and Sisters in Crime (SinC). She is represented by Jill Marsal of Marsal Lyons Literary Agency. Julie sometimes writes as Julie Chase. Learn more about Julie Anne Lindsey at julieannelindsey.com.

To learn more about
THE GEEK GIRL MYSTERIES
and Julie Anne Lindsey,
please visit her website here:
http://julieannelindsey.com/

Also available from Julie Anne Lindsey
and Carina Press:

THE PATIENCE PRICE MYSTERIES:
MURDER BY THE SEASIDE
MURDER COMES ASHORE
MURDER IN REAL TIME

Read on for an excerpt from
MURDER BY THE SEASIDE:

"TELL ME THERE weren't any first floor apartments avail-able on this island." Claire leaned against the gray sid-ing of my new home, her cheeks pink from exertion and the hot summer sun. She reached out to test the weathered wooden stair railing leading to my door. It wiggled, and she inhaled deeply.

"None I could afford." I squinted up the steps to the landing. A stray lock of hair teased my cheek, and I jumped. Islands and bugs went hand in hand. I giggled at the mistake and shrugged. Time to get serious. There was plenty left to do.

"Besides, upstairs apartments are safer," I reminded Claire. "Didn't you pay attention to anything the FBI taught you?"

"Not really. I still can't believe they let you go."

"Hey, I was downsized, not let go."

Claire shifted a box marked Kitchen against her hip, trying to see the steps. Her petite five-foot-two frame was deceptive. She easily maneuvered boxes I struggled with. The fact she did it in four-inch heels said it all. She was small and mighty despite the southern belle upbringing, of which her smooth southern drawl served as a reminder. While Virginia was considered a south-ern state, Claire was a few borders north of her home state of Georgia. She called it Jawja. I called her cute.

"How will I get through those horrendous meetings without you?" she asked.

"Chincoteague is only a couple hours from you. We can meet on the mainland for lunch." My first trip up the steps and I already wished it was my last. "Or shopping," I huffed. I'd gained a pound a year since I left the island ten years ago. Three of those I didn't mind keeping, if they stayed in the right places. The other seven should be gone by the time I finished carrying everything up these steps.

See? Moving home had bonuses. Never underestimate the power of positive thinking.

Claire puffed air into long, side-swept bangs and waited while I opened the door. She gazed admiringly at the historic two-story next door. Pale blue with cream trim and plenty of detail, it reminded me of a gingerbread house. My new place reminded me of the dough, the kind that had been kneaded thoroughly and hit with a roller. Victorian was a local theme, especially among the homes in the center of the island, away from the pounding waves during storm season. On Main Street, the shops blended easily with the houses. Chincoteague was the picture of peaceful living.

Homes were in demand this time of year. Tourists rented every available space between June and August. I thanked my lucky stars to have been able to get this place—the one house I knew would be available on zero notice. A decade-old rumor labeled the house haunted. On an island rooted in superstition and watered with ghost stories, my new place was the equivalent of swearing in church—i.e., to-be-avoided. Luckily, I didn't believe in ghosts. I did, however, believe in low-cost rent and proving a point. Moving home was a real kick in the teeth after the big show I made of landing an FBI job on the mainland. Sure, I was working in human resources, but still…making a life for myself on the mainland had been a big deal. While it lasted.

"Wow. This place better come at a discount." Claire's nose scrunched up as she turned in a small circle.

The interior was layered in dust and dead bugs. I sighed in defeat. This was what came with the too-good-to-be-true price they charged me. Linoleum, paneling and shag. But it was nothing some Comet, a few throw rugs and framed pictures couldn't help. I could afford those things, although not much more. My dwindling savings had bigger purposes. Where I slept had to be secondary for a while. Besides, any place could be homey with enough TLC. I hoped.

Wiping a circle onto the window with my fist, I remembered why I loved the island. Water everywhere. I smiled at Claire. "Can you see the ocean from *your* apartment?"

She joined me at the window. Her latte-colored skin lit up with the twinkling of sunlight through very dirty glass. My new porthole-style window boasted a tiny stained-glass schooner in shades of green and blue. Stained glass was a staple on the island, right beside clapboard, shutters and anything in keeping with a marina theme.

"Alright. I'll give you that." She blew against the window and a storm of dust kicked up.

I coughed against my forearm and ran for the door. "Lunch."

Claire sneezed her way through the dust cloud behind me.

"Gah!" Sunlight blinded me the moment my eyes

were free of the dark wood-paneled walls. I shaded my eyes with one hand and stumbled down the steps toward my car. "Let me grab my purse."

"I think I had lunch upstairs. I ate a pound of dirt getting out of there."

"I'll borrow a hand vac from my mom."

"What about the rest of these?"

I looked at the pile of boxes sitting near the stairs. Carrying them up the steps one-by-one in the afternoon heat was like asking for a stroke.

A whistle slipped through Claire's glossy red lips, and I followed her gaze. A man made of abs and handsomeness jogged across the street. Hoodie up, he looked our way. I smiled. He didn't. Despite the short distance and a decade between us, I knew him. There would never be another set of eyes that shade of gray. None that made me drop my keys at the sight of them.

"Oops." I dipped down to scoop the keys into my palm. When I stood, he was gone, but the strange look he'd given me seared into my brain. Not how I'd imagined our reunion. In my version, the ten years since high school would melt away and he'd be mine.

If I wasn't still mad. Which I was.

"I'd move here just for that," Claire said. "Do you think he jogs by at this time every day?"

"I hope not. That was Adrian."

Eyes wide, Claire turned her head in the direction where Adrian had jogged away. "Well, he can't go far around here. According to the brochure, this island is smaller than my closet."

"Your closet is ridiculous. It's the second bedroom at your apartment. For your information, Chincoteague is a full seven miles long and three miles wide."

"Excellent."

Across the street, laughter bubbled out of the Tasty Cream. A group of teens stumbled from the crowded ice cream parlor. Smiles on lips. Not a care in the world. Couples moving hand-in-hand. Nostalgia hit me like a sack of bricks. The giant neon twisty cone sign transported me back to track meets and prom scandals.

"No one will bother the boxes," I told Claire. "How about I buy you some ice cream for being wonderful?"

"Honey, if that was Adrian, I'm thinking you could use the ice cream more than me." Claire raised an eyebrow. "Show me the way."

Wide brown eyes followed my finger toward the Tasty Cream, their curved lashes nearly brushing her brows. Before we met, Claire had a stint playing a princess at Disneyland. She didn't like to talk about it, but I bet she fooled her share of kids. I enjoyed reminding her she was immortalized in ten thousand family scrapbooks around the world.

"Adrian didn't look happy to see me," I said as we walked. Of course he wouldn't be. "The last time we talked, I smashed a giant twist cone into his face. And shirt. And car." I used to have a temper. Plus Adrian made me crazy.

The fact that he didn't seem glad to see me bothered me and it shouldn't have. My jaw tightened. He shouldn't get under my skin anymore—I'd had a decade to detox.

Claire pushed huge, white sunglasses over her eyes and stepped off the curb. "He deserved—"

The bark of a siren cut her off. She jumped back into me and we toppled, knocking heads and dropping purses. *What on earth?* The sheriff's cruiser tore past, lights blazing, siren screaming. Two dozen locals appeared from thin air before the car was out of sight.

"What the hell?" Claire hoisted herself up, dusting her backside and gawking at the flash mob gathered on the corner. "I thought you said nothing ever happens around here." She collected her shiny yellow clutch and offered me a hand.

"Nothing does. Why do you think everyone's outside staring?" I picked stray hairs out of my lip gloss. The wind blew dust over the pavement. A storm was coming. On an island the size of Chincoteague, even the small storms could be dangerous. I blinked into the sky. Still blue. A few lazy white puffballs lingered overhead, refusing to leave their post.

"I almost got mowed down by a sheriff." Claire examined her manicure. "There's grass under my nails. I'm going to need some fries to go with that ice cream."

"Deal."

We hobbled across the street and pressed our bodies through the crowd on the sidewalk.

The Tasty Cream was empty, but familiar red-and-white checkers smiled back at me from curtains and tablecloths. Black-and-white speckled flooring led me to the counter, past white iron chairs, their backs twisted into hearts, their tiny red cushions empty. The old soda fountain sparkled behind the glass counter, edged in shiny metal. Abandoned tables carried half-eaten burgers and melting ice cream. Purses lay on the floor under chairs. Everyone had relocated, pacing out front on cell phones, no doubt hoping they'd be first to score the daily scoop. For Claire and me, it was a winning situation.

"Patience Price!" Mrs. Tucker rolled around the glass

showcase and caught me in a hug. "Your mother said you were coming home. If she wasn't psychic, I never would've believed it." She stretched my arms out at my sides like an airplane and looked me over. "You're too thin. Let me get you something." Mrs. Tucker had run the Tasty Cream for as long as I could remember, and witnessed things I wish she hadn't—dates, soda sharing, teenage flirting, cone smashing...to name a few.

Claire's brows arched, crowding into her hairline. I ignored them. This was the first she'd heard of my mom's amazing psychic abilities. My parents were a package one had to experience for oneself.

"I'm renting the apartment across the street," I told Mrs. Tucker. "Above the old art studio. You'll be seeing plenty of me."

"Oh, sweetie. You've got your work cut out for you. They haven't rented that place in years."

Claire snorted. "When was the last time anyone lived there?"

"Decades." Mrs. Tucker shook her head. "This is on the house." She pushed a paper basket of fries and two milkshakes our way. "Come by for breakfast. I make a mean cappuccino now." Her round cheeks kicked up in a smile. Sweet as ever, she wiped her hands onto her apron and gave me an approving nod. "Welcome home."

"It's good to be here." Clouds of fresh baked waffle cones rimmed in chocolate and the scent of greasy burgers loomed over me. The perfect mixture of sweet and salty. A taffy machine twisted and pulled pink strips of heaven nearby. I was ten years younger standing there. All good things came from the Tasty Cream. I took a long pull on the best milkshake ever made. It took effort to get Tasty Cream shakes up the straw, but they never disappointed. "What was Sheriff Murray in such a hurry for?"

"Hard to say. He's been something lately." She leaned across the counter conspiratorially. "Being sheriff isn't easy when your deputy's a doofus."

I snickered. Deputy Doofus. Not long ago, Sheriff Murray owned that title.

Mrs. Tucker lifted a rag onto the countertop and made large wet circles over the glass countertop. Her heavily freckled skin reflected in the glass. The freckles almost made her seem tan, though the woman never made it outside before sunset. She always said she preferred people to nature anyway. "I imagine we'll all know as soon as someone figures it out." She tilted her head toward the knots of patrons outside.

Claire anchored her clutch under one folded arm and hefted the fries into her hand. She never let go of her shake.

I snagged a fry from Claire's basket and groaned. Mrs. Tucker's fries were delicious. The seasoning made my mouth water. I thanked Mrs. Tucker, and then Claire and I moved through the door onto the sidewalk as the crowd shoved its way back inside. From the looks on their faces, no one knew anything. Yet.

"I can't believe I'm home again. Trapped on an island with my parents." I started down Main Street on autopilot. "We should say hi."

"Listen, you got your master's degree for a reason. You've got a plan. Put that plan to work for you. *Patience Price, Family Counselor.* The only counselor on this little piece of heaven. You can't beat that for cornering a market." She shoved a fry into her mouth and moaned. Mrs. Tucker could season a fry with the best of them.

"I made flyers."

"I know. What I don't know is how you're going to make up with that hunky ex of yours. Excuse me, but you never mentioned that Adrian was smoking hot. My high school heartbreak was lanky with braces, some serious acne issues and Bobby Brown hair."

"I have no intention of making up with Adrian. Besides, this island is big enough for the both of us. No need to complicate things. I told you he abandoned me to play football, right? He can't be trusted. Adrian Davis has always looked like that, and he knows it."

By the harbor, we passed the bronze pony statue. A tiny picket fence kept tourists at bay these days. Island kids had hundreds of pictures of the pony, near the pony, on the pony, under the pony. My friends and I spent senior year coming up with the most ridiculous pony possibilities. The varsity volleyball team got a hundred thousand hits on YouTube after an interview with the pony. They dressed it in a photo-shopped gown and a few of the dimmer light bulbs performed some raunchy dance moves in the background.

Claire looked at the statue without comment. She was too focused on Adrian. "Mmm-mmm-mmm." She sucked on her milkshake. "At least tell me you left an opening to slide back in with him."

Let's see…what did I remember from the incident? Vanilla ice cream melting against his face and slipping across his lips as a crowd of catty high schoolers laughed and pointed. A combination of humiliation and fire had prompted me to jam the cone into his chest after I pried it from his face. After that, my broken heart caused me to crush it against the new leather seats of his convertible. Not my proudest memory.

"No. No room for sliding."

We continued walking. Tugboats bleated on the shimmery blue water that reflected a perfect sky. Seagulls squawked at fisherman, demanding their share of the day's haul, and a comforting layer of brine tinged the otherwise clean and flower-scented air. All these things spelled h-o-m-e. Houses on the harbor and along the causeway were newer than the rest. The few original homes were weathered to almost black. Along the inner roads, most homes dated back to the eighteen hundreds. Bed-and-breakfasts spilled purple flowers from barrels onto sidewalks. Signs on every corner boasted the home's age and owner's surname. History mattered on Chincoteague.

The town slogan was Relax, You're on Island Time Now. Growing up we joked the island *was* its own time, stuck somewhere that other places never were. Kids dreamed of leaving home to see the big world. I made it as far as Norfolk. Frankly, Chincoteague was better.

"I can't believe you kept this place from me until now. This island has everything. Hot guys. Good food. What's not to like?" Claire slowed her pace. "Except your apartment. Did the ice cream lady say your apartment hasn't been rented in decades? Ever ask yourself why that is?"

"Islanders think it's haunted." I shook my shake cup, shifting the ultra-thick ice cream inside.

"Haunted." Claire stopped short, looking as if she might not accept any future invitations from me.

"Island stories."

"I'd like to hear that one."

"We have lots of stories here. Small town, long histories, creative minds." I nudged her forward.

"Alright then, Miss Secret Pants. Tell me about how your mom's a psychic."

I stopped to wave my arms overhead. "Ta-da." The silhouette of a hand-painted pony stared back from the plate-glass window before us. Wind whipped off the water, swinging the store sign on its hinges above me as I struck my best here-we-are pose.

"The Purple Pony." She pulled her glasses to the tip of her nose, read the sign and looked me over. "What on earth is a purple pony?"

"My parents' shop, of course."

"It sounds a little like a strip club."

"If only." I wrenched the door open and waved Claire inside.

"Holy sh—"

"—ut up." I bumped her with a hip and smiled. A million candles and patchouli scented the air. Flower garlands roped through the wooden rafters. Twinkle lights stretched down to greet us. The little bell over the door brought my mom floating to the counter.

"Patience Peace Price. I thought you'd never arrive."

Claire coughed and choked. I made a point of never mentioning my middle name. This was why.

I gave my mom the stink eye and moved to the counter. "We got a late start. This is my friend Claire." I pulled in a lungful of air. The counter smelled of herbs and incense. The calming twang of Indian sitar music drifted from hidden speakers. Home sweet home.

"Nice to meet you, Claire." Mom bowed in Claire's direction. "We're so proud of our Patience. Embracing a new beginning. Forging her own path." She folded her hands in prayer at her chest and closed her eyes. We looked alike. Sort of. I'd never stand in prayer for no reason, but we shared the same round face, sandy hair and giant brown eyes. The similarities ended there.

"Peepee!" Dad's deep voice sounded nearby.

Claire jumped.

I cringed. As if a name like Patience Peace Price wasn't enough to saddle a girl with. The nickname killed me. Why not Pat?

Dad sat up from a bench not six feet away.

"Daddy." My heart leapt at the sight of him.

"Is that a candle in your ear?" Claire pointed her cup in his direction.

"I'm candling." Dad popped the candle out and dug in his ear with a white cloth. "It removes toxins."

"The Hopi Indians did it," Mom offered.

"Uh-huh." Claire looked at me for help.

I shook my head. They had their own drummer. I'd never heard the tune.

This was why I didn't go into detail about my family. I might've been born with the only sane genes in the pool. My folks were sweet and harmless but a lot to take in all at once. Mom wore her sun-streaked hair in a long, loose braid. It reached past her waist. Sometimes she put flowers in it, sometimes a pencil. Her long, flowing skirts were handmade. By her. Her peasant tops were older than me.

"We missed you." Mom ran a soft palm over my cheek.

"I missed you too." I dug in my oversized hobo for the envelope I'd stashed there. Thanks to an efficient last day of work, I managed to print a couple dozen flyers for my new counseling business. "Care if I leave these here?" I stacked them on the counter next to Dad's handmade soaps and a henna bracelet display.

"What's this?" She examined the flyer. A small, sympathetic smile appeared on her lips. "Honey, you're never going to get islanders to go to a counseling practice. Everyone would know, and no one wants to be known as the one who needs therapy. Maybe you could work here. You can read cards for us."

"Tourists love that." Dad looped an arm around my waist. "Did you lose weight?"

"No thank you. I have a master's degree. In counseling. It's my dream job. I refuse to believe no one will come. There aren't any other counselors on the island." I reached up to knock a bead of wax from my dad's jawbone.

"Why do you think that is?" Mom tilted her head.

"I can't read cards for a living. I'd have to sell my organs to pay off my student loans." Images of me in Birkenstocks and handmade dresses flashed through my mind. A line of tourists waiting to know their futures as told by me, a self-proclaimed, type-A personality who didn't believe in Tarot any more than she believed in Santa Claus.

"People do that," Dad confirmed. "On eBay."

"What? Sell their organs?" The possibility he could be right sent a shiver down my spine. "Ew."

"You can leave anything you like on our counter," he said. "Chase your dream, Peepee."

"Thank you." I turned.

Claire seemed to be enjoying the show. Like a spectator at a live performance of an insanity circus. She fingered through a display of Purple Pony T-shirts, but her eyes focused on us.

"Alright, guys, I'm going to finish moving in. Then I'll take a walk and look for some office space after dinner."

Claire turned in a slow circle. Crystals reflected rainbows over the shiny hardwood floors. A waterfall of beads separated the retail area of the store from the back room and more private reading rooms. The look on her face was priceless. Her lips parted. Her neatly arched brows pinched. Probably meeting my parents raised as many new questions about my personality as it provided answers.

"Be careful," Dad warned.

Muffled sirens complained in the distance. "There's something going on around here." Mom moved her eyes around the store ceiling slowly.

"Like what?" I looked back and forth between my parents. The sheriff had been in quite a hurry to get somewhere.

"We're not sure. The Pony's been dead today."

Sure enough, the store was empty for the first time that I could recall. People loved The Pony. My parents' shop was a hot spot. Locals came for advice on chakras and star alignment, love and gambling. My desire to help people started at The Pony—I just hoped to help in a different way. No patchouli required.

The front door swung open. We all jumped.

"What are you all doing standing around in here?" Maple Shuster, the local scuttlebutt personified, blocked the doorway, holding the door wide with one hip. "Brady McGee is dead. Someone bashed him on the head and left him at the marina."

"Oh dear. That's awful." My mother shuffled around the counter. She eased Maple onto a bench where people normally tried on moccasins or shoes made from cork and bamboo. "Can I get you something?"

My father appeared with a glass of water before Maple could answer.

She sipped and came around to a more coherent, less frenzied state. "That's delicious. It's helping already. Thank you."

It was sugar in tap water. Something my dad passed off as mystical and medicinal. I couldn't fault him. I'd seen sugar water cure everything from nerves to nightmares. People were strange.

"What else did you hear?" The words tumbled out of me. I couldn't believe someone had been murdered. Jaywalking was the worst thing I'd ever heard of happening on the island. Once in a while a couple of tourists got into a fight, but nothing like murder. I knew Brady McGee—not well, but well enough. He had a reputation for being hard, sharp-tongued and crude. His family moved to the island my sophomore year of high school. He was a senior and usually in trouble for fighting. Adrian had warned me to steer clear of him, saying Brady wanted to make a place for himself in our little town by showing people he was tough. I'd felt sorry for him after that. Worst logic ever. People crossed the street to avoid him. If he hadn't changed his attitude in the past ten years, the list of locals with an ax to grind was probably lengthy.

Maple's eyes widened with dramatic flair. She leaned forward on the bench and lowered her voice, as if she was about to tell the best campfire story of her life.

I held my breath in anticipation.

"I heard Adrian Davis killed him. The sheriff questioned him this morning. When he went back to bring him in on charges, Adrian ran."

"Ran?" My folks and I spoke in unison.

"Ran. Adrian is on the lam."

The words twisted and whirled in my mind.

He hadn't been out jogging. He was *on the lam*.

For murder.

Available wherever Carina Press ebooks are sold.

www.CarinaPress.com

Get 2 Free Books,
Plus 2 Free Gifts—
just for trying the Reader Service!

✦ HARLEQUIN

INTRIGUE

HI17

Get 2 Free Books,
Plus 2 Free Gifts—
just for trying the Reader Service!

HARLEQUIN
ROMANTIC suspense

HRS17R